EQUESTRA

E. D. Basso

Glens Falls, NY

ISBN 978-0-6151-5278-3

Published by E. D. Basso, Glens Falls, N. Y.

For all of us who dream of a place

Where troubles are fleeting;

Where poverty and hunger do not exist;

And everyone cares about their neighbors.

Good deeds done all the time,

And friendship is everlasting.

Dedicated to the memory of my father.
This book would not have been possible
without his blessing.

DEATH OF A KING

He bolted up, jolted awake. Gasping, his heart was pounding. Frightened, trembling, and perspiring, he struggled to catch his breath. As he gathered his wits, Zayo told himself it was only a dream, but it had seemed so real—almost <u>too</u> real for a dream.

Seconds later, his mother came running into his room, because she had heard the colt shouting in his sleep. Tarahnaha had never before seen her son so frightened. "Zayo?"

Her presence confused him. "Mother, what is the problem?" He pulled himself towards full consciousness and looked at her quite blankly.

From what she had heard from him, she hardly thought he was showing enough seriousness about what had happened. Her large brown eyes were full of questions. "Zayo, what has caused you to cry out?"

He shook himself awake. "Oh, it was only a dream."

Tarahnaha could not hold any confidence in what he was telling her. "Zayo, please; you have never screamed like that before. You are frightened. Please tell me what the dream was about." She knew that this was no ordinary dream which the crown prince had had. His sleep had always been quiet and restful, until now.

Zayo felt as if he had not slept at all, though it was nearly dawn. He knew that this dream was different from the many others he had had in the past, but he was not quite sure how. "In my dream, I saw one of our people. He was very different, but very beautiful. He had a long shiny, golden horn on his head at the front of his mane, which was white. His fur on his lower torso was a silvery gray. His eyes were golden. And he had the most beautiful indigo wings on his mid-back."

1

EQUESTRA

Tarahnaha was shocked, yet she could not make sense of what her son was telling her. She knew that no Caballian had ever had either wings or a horn, but both? Zayo, though, was not one for making up wild stories with such vivid details; like his father (and all other Caballians) his words were always of absolute truth. The details of the dream frightened him as much as they frightened her. But why now? What had caused it? And what did it all mean? He was considered far too young to have a prophetic dream.

Zayo took comfort in the beauty of what he had seen. His mother was somewhat worried about his placidness, but what could she expect from a twenty-four-year-old colt? He was only a youth, but he was her only foal, and he was the crown prince. She decided then and there that she would take her son to a shaman for counseling that morning, but she would not mention anything to Kayloor unless it was important. She did not want to hide anything from her husband about their son, but she also did not want to bother Kayloor with absolute nonsense. Tarahnaha knew that Kayloor trusted her to take correct action, and that she would do what she felt was best for Zayo. Her hunch was that her son was entering the pubescent stage, and that his hormones were affecting his concentration on his spiritual focus.

Tarahnaha, like all other Caballians, believed in learning everything about a given situation before acting too hastily, although she was a rather impetuous individual as far as Caballians go: she bore an unrelenting fervor to do everything that needed to be done at the first available chance. Zayo was also this way. And, he was like his father in that he was very eager to help others through their personal struggles, and he never thought twice about whether or not to help someone else who needed help. Many times, Kayloor would act with his heart leading the way; Zayo was very much like that.

Tarahnaha returned to bed after telling Zayo what they would do, and she found Kayloor awake. He had obviously heard the commotion through his deep slumber, not at all unusual for the equine abilities of a Caballian. "Tarahnaha, tell me, how is Zayo?"

She walked up to where he stood on their bed. Kayloor was one of the most handsome Caballians alive, and he was one of the most beloved. "He is fine now. He was disturbed by a dream; I believe he is in puberty. I will bring him to a shaman for spiritual channeling to teach him how to control his hormones." She embraced his ruggedly beautiful face and kissed his blaze, a beautiful diamond shape set on the olive skin of his forehead. The blaze is the mark of leadership among the Caballians; every

2

ruler was born with it. Since Zayo also has a blaze, he will become the king when his father dies.

Zayo was a very handsome colt, and he was near enough in age when he would be considered a young stallion (usually twenty-five). His humanoid face very much resembled his father's face, as far as its structure was concerned. He had the same olive skin on his upper torso as all other Caballians. But where his father had chestnut fur on his lower torso and his legs, Zayo had golden sand-colored fur, just like his mother, his mane and tail were dark brown, also like Tarahnaha's hair, whereas Kayloor had chestnut hair. Zayo had his father's curly hair, black eyes, and the blaze.

After breakfast, the crown prince and the queen went to visit a shaman. On Equestra, there were three shamans, but the wisest and eldest, whose name was Booralta, was the most important historian on all of Equestra; it was Booralta whom they visited. He had nothing to do with medicine (he was not a doctor), but he was specially trained to deal with psychology and spiritual influxes. He lived alone—he was a widower—but he did have frequent visitors, and now was the time for more company.

When Zayo and Tarahnaha arrived, he was alone, but he had been expecting them. Zayo had never before met Booralta, having only heard marvelous repasts of the shaman from his parents. Kayloor and Tarahnaha spoke with the shamans often, and valued their wisdom: though Zayo was their son, he had spent his four years out of school learning more of how to be the crown prince.

Zayo was not at all surprised by his surroundings at Booralta's small dwelling, nor was he surprised when Booralta greeted them at the door. But he was taken aback by the old stallion's beauty, for he had never been very close to him before: dark gray fur, wavy black hair, and slate-colored eyes; long cheeks filled with age; a smart nose with a slight flare at the bottom; his pointed olive ears were black-tipped and black-tufted; a long black beard; a mark of black fur covering his spine; and black ringlets around his legs below the knees. His skin showed no signs of aging, yet he was four hundred and thirty-seven years old; the average lifespan of a Caballian is four hundred and fifty years.

Tarahnaha and Zayo were immediately let into the humble abode. It felt very homely, yet there was a chill in the air—a chill which arose from just about everything. The mainstay of the house was the gathering room. Like the rest of the house, it had walls made of a dark red stone, numerous candles set into the mortar between the stones of the walls at eye level, a fireplace which was used for warmth as well as for cooking, and a deep, rich smell from the earthen floor. There were three expertly carved wood chairs around a round low-lying stone table, which almost seemed to beckon Booralta's guests.

The candles are made from a waxy substance which is very slow burning. It is found in much greater quantities than oil is found on Earth, but likewise, it is retrieved from under the ground, albeit by mining. The candles have a natural scent of reincarnated flowers, because the wax developed over millions of years by fossils. The wax is cut using various tools (which are made by shoemakers), and the candles were formed around stringy straw wicks (obtained from farmers) by softening the wax in warm water and pressing it into molds (molds are also crafted by shoemakers).

Before anything was said, Booralta set out some water for his visitors to drink, as was the custom everywhere; the pewter pitcher was filled with cold water piped into the house from a nearby stream. He also put out three crystal glasses on the table by the water. Both the pewter and the crystal are in abundance on Equestra; glasses and pitchers are made by artisans. The various crystals used to make the glasses come in a dazzling array of colors.

Zayo was eager to find out what Booralta was like, so he asked him, "You are a shaman?"

Booralta looked through the colt's steady, unfaltering gaze, and he saw a prince whose pensiveness was so deep that it disturbed the shaman. To test this he decided to play a psychological game with Zayo. "You are a prince?" he returned.

Zayo did not give any answer within a reasonable amount of time, so Tarahnaha said to her son, "You will not answer his question, Zayo?"

"Mother, he answered my question," Zayo replied.

Tarahnaha was disturbed by this rare talent which Zayo had just displayed, so Booralta said to her, "Most kings never were able to learn such judgment of character, Tarahnaha. But Zayo has a superlative edge; he understands psychology."

Tarahnaha looked at her son and she asked him, "What was the answer?"

Zayo replied, "Booralta is an honorable stallion. The obvious answer would be for me to tell you that he is a historian, or a shaman, or a psychologist, but no. My answer is that he has another talent which he is withholding until he finds out why we came here."

"Why?" she asked Booralta.

4

Booralta looked at her for perhaps ten minutes, and during that time he grew more despondent and more upset. Finally, all he said to her was, "You are pregnant."

But she hardly had time to feel happy over this news as he started sobbing, an emotion which Caballians do not readily show unless they are deeply disturbed by something (which is extremely rare). Tarahnaha grew upset by his actions, so she said to him, "What is wrong with my foal?"

He had the utmost difficulty composing himself to be able to speak, something Booralta had never had a problem with before. "I will call Pleeyedraha," Zayo offered; Pleeyedraha was a doctor.

In speech broken by sobs, and barely coherent, Booralta finally said, "Tarahnaha, there is...nothing...wrong ...with your foal. Kayloor...was just ...killed."

Tarahnaha was too shocked to be upset. "Kayloor is still young," she said. "We will have over three hundred more years under his leadership." She was deathly afraid of losing her husband: he was only one hundred and thirty years old, and Tarahnaha was one hundred and fourteen. She could not even accept the idea that her husband was killed. It seemed impossible that any Caballian would commit murder, or that he would be killed in an accident.

Booralta saw her reaction, so he said to Zayo, "Tell me about your dream."

Zayo suddenly felt a rush of mixed emotions. Anger, sadness, fright, happiness...they all blended together. He pulled himself together with remarkable composure. He studied Booralta for a long moment before responding. "Booralta, are you testing me?"

"No, your majesty," he replied. "Kuhoor had a dream the night before Mehntoor died, and Kayloor had a dream the night before Kuhoor died. Your family has been this way for many, many generations." Some more tears fell, but the shaman stopped them so he could continue. He knew he now had a desperate purpose—to educate a colt into becoming a king overnight. "I can only help you if I know what your dream was about."

Tarahnaha, through her grief, mumbled, "If I had only known what his dream meant last night, I would have sent for guards to protect Kayloor."

Zayo replied, "I saw a Caballian with indigo wings and a golden horn. He had silver-gray fur, gold eyes, and white hair. He could fly anywhere he so desired, and was...more famous than any other citizen.

5

What frightened me is that during a war he lost his wings, but they grew back."

Tarahnaha became delirious when she heard the word "war." "Zayo," she said, "do you know what you are proposing?"

"Mother," he replied confidently, "I know my history."

Booralta said to Tarahnaha, "Kayloor's murder will not start a war among our people. There will be a war, and it will be with others, not amongst ourselves. Every single Caballian will be a victim. Zayo will lead us to victory, and to find our freedom."

Zayo was starting to like Booralta very much, as he felt the old shaman giving him a nudge of confidence. "What about the winged Caballian?" the young king asked him.

Booralta, unfaltering, said, "In our folklore, such a symbol means great freedom for our people, and a great victory. But since you saw him with such great detail as to his appearances, I believe he will shortly become a living symbol; he will be born soon."

Tarahnaha could hardly fathom what she was hearing. "Of what parentage?"

"Caballian is all I know. The same factors that planted the seeds for Kayloor's murder also caused a developing foal to become a pegasus."

"Why?"

"Spiritual influxes are not allowed to destroy our people; we must always be left with some semblance of hope that will enable us to continue to live, for we live to protect the spiritual realms."

"Booralta, why must you speak in riddles?"

He shook his head at her. "This is no riddle, Tarahnaha. When you look at everything after it has happened, you will understand these things. Fortunately, young Zayo understands. He will become an excellent king."

"He is a unicorn," Zayo suddenly said to Booralta.

"The horn is merely a symbol," Booralta said. "He will work with you as if he were a part of your family. This is very important, because you will be more affected by the war than any other Caballian, even Pleeyedraha."

"That is ridiculous," Tarahnaha said, not wanting her family, especially her son, to be hurt any more.

"In order for a king to become successful during his reign, he must be self-sacrificing. All of the greater kings sacrificed the most to become great kings, and our people have always loved them for that. Zayo will be no different."

6

The trip back to the palace would take them an hour if they drove the transport straight through at the speed limit of two hundred and fifty miles per hour. But they were driving at half that speed, and would have to stop for a philinium recharge. "When we stop in Tokanar," Zayo said to his mother, "I must stretch my legs and walk." He did not realize it, but his edginess was a direct result of being told his father was killed, rather than dying in an accident or of natural causes.

"Whatever you do," she recommended, "use extreme caution."

The transport streaked across the grass road; paving was unnecessary since transports ride on air. As it approached lunchtime, they neared the town called Tokanar by the Caballians. Tokanar stood out as an overabundance of golden plant life on the horizon underneath a beautiful sparkling jade green sky. With Tokanar standing behind the fields, it seemed to Zayo that it would take forever to reach the city.

All of a sudden, with a bang and a thud, the transport stalled and landed flat on the ground. Tarahnaha checked it, only to find out that it had run out of philinium sooner than expected. She and Zayo got out, and started walking down the bluegrass road, leaving the transport where it had stalled; it would eventually be brought into town by a guard. There were still three miles between them and Tokanar, so they had to press to eat lunch at a decent time. Their appetites, though, were just about non-existent since hearing of Kayloor's untimely death.

Zayo was confused by everything that had happened since he had that strange dream where he saw the beautiful pegasus. He was very young by Caballian standards, having only lived one-eighteenth of his expected lifespan, yet he was now the king. Kayloor had been in the strongest years of his life (physically), and had adored his zealous son; he knew that Zayo would become a most excellent king in his time.

Tarahnaha contemplated how strange life had become since breakfast that morning. What would have happened if guards had been summoned? What would have happened if she and Zayo had remained home that morning? What would have happened if Kayloor went with them? What will happen to the murderer or murderers? How will their people react to Zayo's coronation, which must take place the day after Kayloor's death? How will Zayo's sibling react to being a bastard?

Zayo will soon learn to accommodate such feelings of grief, but only time will tell how fast he matures.

It was a very hot day; walking in the sunlight was very exhausting. They continued down the bluegrass road, which was lined on either side by everyellow trees, until Zayo suddenly ran from his mother past the everyellows on the right side into the moonsflower field. Moonsflowers are very special on Equestra. They bloom only once every five years, during the conjunction known as the great circle of the three moons. The beautiful indigo blossoms, which last for three full weeks, cover the entire planet with a wonderful odor which is almost a cross between roses and lilies. They had not bloomed in well over four years; they will bloom again in several months.

Zayo had heard a cry for help, and had gone to see who it was. He found a pregnant mare, about one-quarter of a mile back, laying on the ground in labor, and was having extreme difficulty dropping her foal, a task which a mare can usually handle alone. Zayo was not sure of what to do, but he thought it best to stop her from the panic which had overtaken her. "Hello," he said as he walked up beside where she lay.

"Thank the moons," she replied when she heard his voice, although she was still delirious.

Zayo did not know much about the birth of foals, but he knew enough to keep her talking. "What is your name?" he asked her.

"Lahrohnaha," she replied, "Lahrohnaha." The second time she said her name with more authority.

Tarahnaha arrived on the scene, but decided to stay back until the foal was born. She knew she could not do more than what Zayo could do; she was not a doctor or a nurse. Lahrohnaha did not know that Tarahnaha was there. "Lahrohnaha," he offered, "I will try to help you."

"Something is very wrong with my foal," Lahrohnaha said, struggling. "Its passage is creating excessive pain for me."

"I will send for a doctor."

"There is no time," she said. "The water was dispelled an hour ago, and—and I know it will be born any minute."

Lahrohnaha was right. She pushed hard, and it crowned. She pushed one more time, and it dropped into Zayo's hands. It was a big mess, but Zayo hardly knew what he was supposed to see. A feeble whinny came from the new colt as he took his first breaths. Zayo saw that his mouth was full of goop, so he cleaned it out with his fingers. The colt then made a much stronger whinny. Tarahnaha walked up, used her hands to tie the umbilical cord with some grass, and cut it against the shoe on her left forehoof. Zayo did not know what else to do with the new foal; as he pondered this, Lahrohnaha passed the afterbirth. Zayo then felt an abnormal formation on the colt's back, and wondered to himself, What is wrong with it? But before he could come up with any possible answers, the colt opened his eyes: they were a deep burnished gold. Zayo knew then that this was the pegasus from his dream; he started to shake a bit. He set the colt down on the ground, and observed him.

Lahrohnaha soon came to her senses, and she then recognized who had helped her. "My prince, I thank you for helping me. My son will be fine."

"Once he bonds and stands," Tarahnaha added.

"He is different," Zayo told her. "A life born in the shadow of death."

"He is no different from any other Caballian," Lahrohnaha said, trying to maintain the thought that her son was normal.

"It is good that you think that, but I know that he will be more important to our people than any other person who ever lived."

"High aspirations are good to have," Lahrohnaha said, "if you do not let yourself become blinded by them."

"That is true," Tarahnaha replied, "but Zayo is merely repeating what Booralta told him a short while ago."

"Dear queen," she said, "why would Booralta have told the prince about my son, and not Kayloor?"

Tarahnaha looked at her, her eyes quavering, and she finally broke down in deep sobs. Lahrohnaha knew nothing of Kayloor's death, so Tarahnaha's actions were a deep mystery to her. She had never before seen Tarahnaha cry, nor had any other Caballian ever seen the queen cry. Zayo held his mother in his arms, consoling her as best as any son possibly could. "My mother is pregnant," Zayo finally said to Lahrohnaha because he saw how puzzled she was.

This comment did not help any, because Lahrohnaha was even more confused than she was before. "I do not understand," Lahrohnaha said as politely as possible, trying not to hurt their feelings.

Tarahnaha pulled herself away from her son, and she walked away from them so that she could weep by herself. Lahrohnaha, though she was weak, saw that Zayo did not know what to say to her at all, so she said to him, "You mentioned that my son was born in the shadow of death. Who has died that grieves your mother so deeply? Is it Booralta? Or even Pleeyedraha? Dear prince, if it does not trouble you too much, I only ask that you tell me so I will know how to speak to her."

Zayo was feeling empty, and he could not put any emphasis behind his words to her, but he tried. "Lahrohnaha, my father was killed this morning."

"Forgive me," she said to him, "forgive me for calling you a prince

9

not once, but twice. I did not realize...I had been struggling all morning with my son. My body is weak and tired, but at least, alive. I am indebted to you for taking the time on this tragic day to assist me. I ask of you, though, to tell me why you said my son is different. Is there a reason why I had so much difficulty this morning?"

Lahrohnaha had a way of talking which seemed to warm a person's heart...Zayo could not refuse her request. "He is gifted," he began. "Gifted to be a living emblem of freedom. He was born with wings on his back, and will learn to fly as easily as we learn to run. I will need him more than anyone else to become a successful king when I am grown, and when he grows."

He left her for a moment to fetch his mother who came back with him as soon as she saw him; he did not have to say anything to her. Tarahnaha watched as the colt feebly stood up, and she breathed a sigh of relief. Lahrohnaha looked at Zayo and repeated, "'A living emblem of freedom'?"

"He will be the hope of our future," Tarahnaha answered, knowing what Lahrohnaha meant. "Here to atone for the wrongful...wrongful..." she could not continue; she started to weep again.

"The wrongful death of Kayloor?" Lahrohnaha asked.

Zayo nodded while his mother continued to weep. Tarahnaha soon stopped her weeping, and she said, "We must look to the future, and find the hope that your son represents, Lahrohnaha. He will be more important to Zayo than an adjutant will be, so it will suit them better if your family moved into the palace."

"If you agree," Zayo added.

Lahrohnaha saw how the idea sparked the fire in their eyes, and she knew she could not refuse. But she said, "I must speak with Toorahgo about this, though I believe he will agree to it."

"Is it just the three of you?" Tarahnaha asked her.

"No. We have a daughter, Ehspreeyetaha, who is eighteen."

Zayo looked down at his lavender vest, which was wet and covered with blood, so he removed it; Tarahnaha took it from her son. Lahrohnaha still could not stand up, so he said, "Mother, you should stay here with them while I go to Tokanar to fetch transportation."

Tarahnaha hugged her son and said, "Be careful."

Taking careful note of their location, Zayo took off in a full gallop.

MEHLANAHR

Tokanar was two and a half miles off; Zayo ran there in five minutes, and he reached the gate soon enough. Two guards were there, whose purpose was to keep track of the whereabouts of all of the Caballians, and to maintain that there were no truant students from school (although that rarely happened). Zayo did not realize Booralta had already spread the news that Kayloor had been killed, so when they knelt before him, he was rather surprised. "Your majesty," one of them said, addressing Zayo by the proper title for a king and only a king (a prince or spouse of the ruler is called "your highness.")

The other guard then said, "Our grief is deep."

Zayo eyed them sadly, and could see the grief on their faces. He collected himself and said, "I require a transport." They arose from where they were kneeling, and one of them radioed for a nearby transport to stop at the gate to assist someone.

Moments later, a transport arrived. A young stallion, who was thirty-four years old—not quite of age—was operating it, yet he seemed to be one of the strangest Caballians alive on Equestra. Zayo noticed that something was different about him, but he would not study him unless he could use his transport.

Since the stranger was not yet of age, he wore a pastel-colored vest; his was a powdery blue, that of an engineering intern. He stepped out of his transport and walked up to the guards; he gave no indication of being busy, nor did he recognize Zayo's back. "A transport is here as requested," he said to the guards.

11

"It is for the king," one of the guards replied.

"Kayloor?! Surely someone else is better suited to tending to his...corpse."

"Zayo," the other guard stated. "He is now the king."

Zayo turned around at the sound of his name; he had been lost in a daydream about his father. He looked at the stranger just as the young stallion said, "Zayo is a colt. A king has duties which only a citizen can perform." The stranger then recognized Zayo, but he did not regret his words.

"I do not think you should have said that," the first guard remarked.

"Why do you question my birthright?" Zayo asked the stranger.

"A birthright, perhaps, but your education is not yet complete; you are not fully capable of assuming all duties associated with being a king."

"Why do you assume that I cannot do what I was born to do?" Zayo asked, rephrasing his question so that the stranger would not be able to deviate from giving Zayo an answer.

"You are twenty-four, not thirty-five. Eleven years of your education are not yet finished. What do you truly know about passages and the placement of new citizens where they will be needed most, and what could you possibly know about questioning a couple to find out if they are fully compatible?"

"I set with my father on questionings, which is more to say than what you have ever seen. You have not reached your own passage yet, and because of that, you are also not married. I may be only twenty-four, but I know much more than most people give me credit for."

"Sitting through questionings does not teach you the philosophical basis for passages and marriages. A crown prince is taught these things through experiencing public exhorting at his own passage and marriage. Without our people fully teaching you everything they know, how will you be able to serve them in their best interests, and to understand their hearts? Your mind may be bent on serving them, but you must mold your heart and soul to fit the form required by our people. Otherwise, you will never be a good king."

"What makes you so sure that you know more about such things than I do? Answer me that."

"What makes you so overconfident? You do not know everything. You have so much to learn, actually, that you must be humbled before you can progress to higher learning."

The stranger was succeeding in provoking Zayo where he wanted to, but Zayo did not like it at all. "Why do you talk to me as if I have not learned anything at all?"

"Why do you talk as if you know everything? One thing I have learned from studying engineering with Oorahno: you can never be too sure of yourself. No one can. And no one ever knows enough. There is always more to learn."

"How do you mean this?"

"For more than fourteen million years, no king has ever been killed by anything before his life was biologically over. What killed your father?"

Zayo's eyes became downcast as he replied, "Caballians did it."

"Who are they?"

"I do not know."

"Where are they? What are they doing?"

"I do not know."

"What is the punishment for murder and treason?"

"Excommunication."

"How come the criminals are not incarcerated, and how come no guards are yet preparing for their excommunication?"

"Guards are not allowed to excommunicate anyone. I must do it."

"They must make things ready; the excommunication must be as much of a public spectacle as a passage or marriage is. The guards must also make preparations for your coronation. And the master shoemaker must make a crown for you."

"I do not want a coronation. It is a pointless event."

"Pointless to signify the end of one era and the beginning of another? Your majesty, you have much to learn."

Zayo quickly gave up on arguing with the stranger; he was becoming more depressed over his father's murder. He collected his wits, and got back to business. "A mare, Lahrohnaha, is in the moonsflower field, and needs to be brought to the hospital."

The stranger looked at Zayo in utter disbelief. "Why did you allow me to make conversation if someone needs to go to the hospital and needs transportation? Especially something that can wait until she is in the hospital?"

Zayo did not feel the urgency which the stranger felt; he knew Lahrohnaha would be fine. So he stood there, and deliberately studied the stranger for a long moment. And he noticed what was so different about him. All of the Caballians whom Zayo had ever seen wore their manes loose down their upper backs, only putting ribbons in them when they

13

braid their hair for special occasions. But the stranger wore his deep brown mane not braided, yet tied with a black ribbon at the base of his neck, and brought across his upper left shoulder so that the ends of it hung just above his naval. The color of his fur seemed to be a beautiful rich brown, yet it glistened like gold in the sunlight. Chiseled cheekbones and long, narrow cheeks, signs of his youth, were offset by big, beautiful, soulful chestnut eyes with long eyelashes, which were very striking against his olive skin. His nose was long and trim, with a very faint flare at the end of it. His lips were thin and taught shut. His chin bore the beginnings of a dark brown beard (such facial hair traits were common only to stallions his age or older). Finally, Zayo said to him, "A new life is not pointless, but neither is my father's death. I respect you for taking time to speak with me; listening to you reminds me that my mother is pregnant."

"By the three moons!" he suddenly exclaimed.

"In the moonsflower field, Lahrohnaha bore a colt about an hour after my father was killed. It was a very strenuous birth for her, and she cannot walk. She needs to be brought to the hospital. That is what I need you for."

The stranger looked at the young king and wondered to himself, How can he deal with all this stress? He is so overburdened that he seems confused. He needs much more help than just a transport today. I must help him; he needs proper encouragement, and I doubt if anyone is hardly in a position of no distraught over Kayloor's death to be able to help his son. I can mourn later. But for Zayo the crown prince, the one everyone says held the greatest source of pride for Kayloor, to become the king at the age of twenty-four? No matter what people think, he is not ready to take his father's place. The stranger signaled Zayo to follow him, and they climbed into his transport. As soon as they left the gate, the two guards who had been there were relieved by two others so that they could eat some lunch. The lunch hour was beginning, though Zayo and his escort were so busy that they did not notice the changing of the guard.

Only when Zayo was directing the stranger to where Lahrohnaha and his mother were waiting did he realize that he did not know this stranger's name. When the transport stopped, Zayo asked him, "Who are you?"

"I am the son of Hohnoor and Bailaha," he said, because he was not yet thirty-five years old.

He got out of the transport, and Zayo followed in close pursuit. "What is your name?" Zayo asked again.

14

"Mehlanahr," he replied, walking directly over to the mares. "Your highness," he said to Tarahnaha, "all Caballians will remember today, because all of Equestra burns under the unusually intense heat of Omistu when a great stallion was taken from us. Accept my assistance until you and Zayo are able to continue on your own."

"Such generosity," Tarahnaha replied, some tears escaping her eyes. "How will such a deed ever be repaid? No, it is best you stay with your family today."

Zayo and Tarahnaha were expecting Mehlanahr to say, "as you wish," but instead, he told her, "How long will your strength hold out, and will your son be able to do everything which needs to be done without your assistance if he needs to? And if you push yourself through too much stress, it will seriously affect your unborn foal. I am willing and able to help...would you actually refuse my help if you were not so grief-stricken? Please, good queen...be good to yourself when you must."

"How will I be able to do the same for you?" she asked him.

Mehlanahr saw how both she and Zayo were rather stubborn. "When the king of the Caballians needs help, no one ever questions him, because everyone knows that he will turn around and sacrifice himself for the needs of his people many times over."

Tarahnaha succumbed to his offer, because she knew that she would be a fool to refuse it. She could be stubborn, yes, but she had never proven herself to be obtuse. It was not long before they had Lahrohnaha in the back of Mehlanahr's transport. Zayo and Tarahnaha set with her in the enclosed back (Lahrohnaha held onto her suckling son), and Mehlanahr drove it away, back towards Tokanar. When Mehlanahr reached the gate leading back into Tokanar, he was stopped by the two guards who had relieved the two that had called him to help Zayo. They had to check his identification to determine if he was truant from his studies (which was a punishable crime, although it happened to be Mehlanahr's day off), and also let him know if he was being sought out by anyone else. Mehlanahr did not even think to look for his identification until one of the guards said to him, "May I see your identification?"

Mehlanahr looked for it for a few minutes until he realized that he did not have it with him, because he had intended on staying in Tokanar; he had been on a very short errand for his parents, an errand which was all but forgotten when he received the call that a transport was needed, and his was the closest to the gate at the time. Mehlanahr gulped as he realized the seriousness of the situation, knowing that the punishment for not having his identification was to have his tail disfiguringly clipped as high as possible so that it would take years to grow back fully. He could not help but shudder at the thought, yet he replied truthfully, "I do not have it with me, because the king sent for me."

They laughed at Mehlanahr, thinking that he was deliriously upset over Kayloor's death. The second guard then said to him, "Where were you when Kayloor was killed?"

"I was with my parents. I study with Oorahno every day except ninthday."

The first guard then said to him, "Did you say the king sent for you?"

"Yes," he replied.

"This is the south gate," the guard continued. "The palace is north of Tokanar. Are you so upset by Kayloor's death?"

Mehlanahr looked at him and replied, "What do you know of Kayloor's death?"

"What the master historian has told our people. You know what the punishment for forgotten identification is…?"

"Please, you must believe me. I would not have left Tokanar before had I not been summoned by the king. I must be allowed to get to the hospital immediately."

"Kayloor is dead," the second guard reiterated. "You are delirious. Go back the way you came, and we will forget to clip your tail."

"I am not delirious," he replied. "You do not understand what I am trying to tell you." He proceeded to climb out of his transport, and the first guard grabbed a sabre so he could fulfill his duty and clip Mehlanahr's tail. Mehlanahr saw the sabre right in front of him, but he said, "I will show you what I am trying to tell you." He wheeled around and started to walk to the back of the transport. As he did, the guard attempted to grab his tail, but Mehlanahr quickened his step. He walked around the back and pushed the button to open the hatch, whence the guard grabbed a solid hold of Mehlanahr's tail.

As the hatch opened, Zayo saw Mehlanahr, and began to say, "Are we at-"; he quickly fell silent when he saw the punishment Mehlanahr was about to suffer. "Stop!" Zayo whinnied at the guard, but the guard paid no attention to him, allowing the blade to catch momentum as it fell. Zayo saw this, and leaped out and grabbed the sabre in his hands just before it would have cut through Mehlanahr's tail. Zayo fell to the ground, facedown, and he let go of the sabre blade and clenched his cut hands into fists.

The guard let go of Mehlanahr's tail as soon as the sabre was taken from him, and he said to Mehlanahr, "What are you trying to do?" And to Zayo he said, "You ornery colt! Mind your own business!"

The other guard pulled out a whip, and struck Zayo across the back for interfering with what appeared to be a necessary punishment.

"Let my son be!" Tarahnaha cried out. "He is your king! It is bad enough Kayloor was taken from us today! Is this a conspiracy by our people against our family, and do you also wish my son dead?! Let me know, so I can also die a quick death, instead of living through such great torture!" She climbed out of the transport and left Lahrohnaha, who was asleep.

"Your majesty," the guard who had called Zayo "ornery" said, "please forgive me, but he does not have his identification."

Zayo slowly got up from where he was laying, and he turned to face them. "Mother," he said, "I will be fine. I only need Pleeyedraha to tend to my hands." Tarahnaha was not overly thrilled at her son's attitude, but again, she was becoming overprotective because of her husband's murder. "Do you know why Mehlanahr is here?" Zayo asked the guards.

"He said he was called by the king. We assumed he was delirious over your father's death."

"Did you kill my father?" Zayo deliberately asked them.

"Zayo!" Tarahnaha exclaimed, surprised at his tactics.

"Answer my question," the young king told them in a commanding voice.

"No," they both answered.

"From the way you were so eager to strike me down, I do not know whether or not to believe you. It is bad enough that Booralta told us that Father was killed by Caballians, but for you to strike me in such a way on the same day...where are your hearts, Caballians? You will ask Mehlanahr his purpose here, and you will find out why he had no identification."

The guard that had struck Zayo with the whip said to Mehlanahr, "What were you doing before you were called?"

"I was on an errand in Tokanar for my parents, Hohnoor and Bailaha. I was on my way to the bakery from my house to fetch some bread, because my grandparents spend time with us on ninthday. My twin sisters are too young, only ten years old, and my parents were busy with other tasks, so I was asked to go. The bakery is not far from our house, and I did not think that I would be leaving Tokanar being on an errand for bread, so I did not stop for my identification. I heard the other guards call for a transport when I was on my way from my house to the bakery, both of which are very close to this gate, so I came, figuring that the guards would recognize me when I returned; I did not know that the guard changed at lunchtime. When I arrived here, and found out that it was Zayo who had sent for a transport, I could not refuse his request."

The guards knew Hohnoor, and they realized who they were dealing with, for they knew that Hohnoor had twin daughters ten years old, and an older son near his passage.

"We must get to the hospital," Tarahnaha said to them. "Lahrohnaha may be asleep, but Zayo must also be tended to."

"Toorahgo's wife?" the first guard asked her.

"Yes," the queen mother replied. "Her foal was born today."

They saw Lahrohnaha, and nodded. "Not quite yet," Zayo remarked. "There exists an unsolved problem."

"What other problem can there possibly be?" she asked her son.

"If I were not the king, or even a crown prince, then the guards' actions would have been right for the situation. But my authority supersedes theirs when it comes to punishments. They are not allowed to question my stopping their execution of a clipping, nor are they allowed to strike me for stopping them; I can question them all I wish, because his striking me with the whip is a crime punishable only by excommunication."

"Your majesty," the guilty guard replied, "I did not know it was you. You are not wearing your internship vest."

He took his vest from his mother, and showed the blood on it to them. "Too impetuous to listen and learn that Mehlanahr was following my request (which he knew was vastly more important than any request for identification), and too impetuous to look upon my face to see my obvious birthright? You have no excuse for not realizing I am Kayloor's heir, acquiring the throne of our people today. You have seen me at all social functions before, and you knew that I resemble my mother. My father was killed, so you forgot what she looks like? How can a guard serve his king if he refuses to accept who his king is?"

"Your majesty," the other guard said, "I beg of you to forgive me for calling you an 'ornery colt.' I am as much on edge because of the great grief caused by your father's death."

"Twice you have asked me for forgiveness. I commanded you to stop what you were doing, but you did not listen. How can I forgive you of such treason?"

"Your majesty, it was a gross misunderstanding."

"I am your king, and I told you not to clip Mehlanahr, but you proceeded to attempt to clip him anyway." He held out his blood-covered fists. "My father was killed today, and my blood had to be spilled to stop an unrequited clipping because you would not listen to my command. Let there be no misunderstanding any further...the only punishment you will suffer for your treason is the only punishment acceptable by our laws, which is excommunication."

"Zayo," Tarahnaha said, "Are you Kayloor's son? He would have forgiven such a thing."

"Mother, I think it was Father's leniency that led to his murder today. Lenience allows the spirits of our people to become weak. I believe weak spirits are the cause of what has been happening today. No more leniency, and we will become strong again. Healing must be instigated."

PLEEYEDRAHA

Zayo called for six other guards. Two of them were to take the place of the guards at the gate, and the other four were needed to escort the two criminals to the refinery in Tokanar, where they would be held until their punishments would be administered the next morning. Those two guards were not responsible for Kayloor's death, though they had committed crimes against Zayo. There would be others excommunicated with them—those directly responsible for Kayloor's death.

Lahrohnaha was admitted to the hospital for observation, and was immediately seen by one doctor. Her husband Toorahgo was sent for.

Even faster than Lahrohnaha was tended to, another doctor quickly went about seeing to the young king—this was Pleeyedraha. Pleeyedraha was very old, but all of the Caballians recognized her more than any other doctor. She had dappled gray fur, shoulder-length gray hair, and beautiful blue eyes. Her stride was always confident and quick, yet unhurried; her steps were so light that it seemed as if she could walk on air. From just looking at her, it was impossible to determine her great age; at least one hundred years were easily hid under her beautiful demeanor. Her body was strong, and her hands were extremely nimble and adept.

Great age holds high grace among the Caballians, and there are good reasons for it: mostly because Caballians who are over four hundred years old are truly the most physically beautiful, and also because they possess the greatest knowledge, amassed from all their years of existence. Pleeyedraha was four hundred and forty-five years old at the time Kayloor was killed. She did not belong to the hospital; rather, the hospital belonged to her spirit, representing all of her work and accomplishments among her people. She was to doctors what Booralta was to shamans and historians—the master. That earned her the privilege to wear the black vest with green decorations as the master healer; all other doctors wore green vests. She had a student, an intern, who was several years older than Zayo, whom she had dismissed for the day when news of Kayloor's death was spread.

Pleeyedraha had to submit Zayo to heptalaser microsurgery to fix his injured hands. Heptalaser is how the Caballians refer to philinium heptaferriliate/laser-induced regeneration. After the patient undergoes microsurgery to reconnect all severed nerves, veins, and other tissues, he is locally injected with philinium heptaferriliate, after which the sutured area is very briefly touched by a laser, which caused the philinium heptaferriliate to speed up the healing process to a phenomenal rate—usually within an hour. There is no scarring left.

If Pleeyedraha had not become involved in the strenuous microsurgery, surely she would have had a nervous breakdown from Kayloor's murder. Kayloor had been like a son to her for she had known him since the day he was born. For the time, however, Pleeyedraha would remain the consummate professional—that is, until she finished her work for the day. Then her grief would certainly be as great as Tarahnaha's grief was.

The surgery on Zayo was going to take some time, so Mehlanahr stayed in the hospital for a while to speak with Tarahnaha, who otherwise would have set there alone and waited. When Tarahnaha saw him set across from her and not leave, she said, "Please, Mehlanahr, go home to your parents. They are probably wondering about what is taking you so long to get some bread."

"Your highness," he replied, "it is hard enough for me to even think about what Zayo did before. I fully deserved having my tail clipped for showing such a lack of responsibility and not having my identification with me."

"My son may be young, but he has never shown himself to be stupid. I know that he was sure of what he was doing when he did it. Why else would he have submitted the guards for excommunication? My son may not yet understand more mature feelings, but he knows so much about psychology and motivation, more than Kayloor would ever admit to knowing. I am sure my husband also knew those things, but he did not feel they were as important. In such respects, Zayo is the opposite of what Kayloor was."

21

"Surely Kayloor also had quick judgment."

"Kayloor was always deliberate. He always took his time to completely understand everything...Booralta sometimes felt he took too much time. Zayo understands things differently from his father. I will only question his judgment if I feel it is not proper, but I have never found my son's judgment to be wrong. I am quite accustomed to Kayloor and Zayo conflicting and pushing each other around because of their differing strengths. I would never intervene, but I enjoyed listening to their debates."

Mehlanahr thought about this for a moment, and almost laughed. What Tarahnaha was saying was so true, from what he had seen so far. He then changed the subject. "Surely you are not going to set here and idle your time waiting for him while Pleeyedraha works on him?"

"What else am I to do? Who can I turn to for help now? And how can anything be done about the criminals while Zayo sleeps? Only he has the authority to indict the criminals and put them in holding until their punishments are due."

"Zayo will be here until well after dinner. If you set here by yourself, you may surely have a nervous breakdown and lose your foal. You should be spending time with our people now, talking and thinking about anything but Zayo until he is ready."

"Where will I go? Most people are working now."

"If I may be so bold, my parents do not work on ninthday, and neither do my grandparents; they spend the day together with my sisters and myself. I was on my way to get bread for all when I was called by Zayo. Come with me to fetch the bread, then we will go to my house. You may interrogate me then all you wish, and I will answer all questions. And you will stay for supper."

The way he said it to her, she could not refuse; he was quite right. After alerting a nurse as to where she would be in case there was any change in Zayo's condition before she returned, they left.

It took Mehlanahr almost ten minutes to drive from the hospital to his house, but he had forgotten how much time had elapsed since he had left. Tarahnaha followed him through the front door; she remained standing in the shadowy corner of the doorway that led from the gathering room where she was to the kitchen where Mehlanahr went. She could be seen where she was, but she could not be recognized without proper light.

Bailaha, a beautiful mare with golden fur just a shade darker than Tarahnaha's fur, hair the same golden color, and chestnut eyes, was a baker in her own right, but when it came to ninthday, she did not keep any day-old bread for her family; theirs was always eaten fresh. She heard her son's footsteps, so she said, "Mehlanahr, which one of your friends has detained you this time?" She finished cleaning up their lunch (which Mehlanahr had missed), and she turned around to see him carrying enough bread for their supper.

He put the three loaves down, and said, "Mother, I was not detained by a friend."

Bailaha saw Tarahnaha's shadowy form, though she did not recognize the queen, and she smiled. "Not a friend?" she wondered aloud. "Who is she?"

He saw a rather approving look on his mother's face, so he replied, "It is not what you think, Mother."

She frowned a bit. "Mehlanahr, I wish you would have told me before; we do not have enough chairs for everyone. Even your sisters must set on the floor."

"I know. Any other day it would be fine to bring someone here. But any other day is not like today. Our king was murdered."

"He was killed," she replied. "How-" she began, but her voice was quickly choked as the front door opened, and light was cast upon Tarahnaha, enabling Bailaha to recognize the queen. She heard her husband's footsteps, and she walked into the gathering room, with Mehlanahr right behind her. Her parents and Hohnoor's parents followed Hohnoor through the front door into the den, and the twins were on their tails. Tarahnaha set down, and they all made themselves as comfortable as possible on the floor without a word. Things were a bit cramped, to say the least.

"Like I was saying, Mother, Kayloor was murdered. There is something mysteriously wrong, because an attack was also held upon young Zayo."

"Where is your son?" Hohnoor asked Tarahnaha. "I trust he is safe."

"He is with Pleeyedraha," the queen mother replied: she could not hold back her tears any more, and she began to sob again.

The fillies were frightened. They made their way over to Tarahnaha, one on either side, and they tried to wipe her tears away, but they kept coming. Seeing that their efforts were not working, they each grabbed one of her arms, and hugged them; Tarahnaha soon stopped her crying.

"By the three moons!" Bailaha exclaimed. "Fahleedraha and

Fehdooreeya have touched you today!"

"I need something to retain my sanity," Tarahnaha remarked. "I was told today that I am pregnant."

"Then Kayloor still lives," Hohnoor's father said.

Hohnoor's mother gasped, so Tarahnaha said, "It is quite all right. I am honored at my age to be carrying my husband's second foal. Many mares do not bear their first until they are three hundred years old. And I thank the moons that I was spared Ahmehlaha's fate. A foal needs it mother more than it needs its father."

"That is not quite true," Bailaha's mother remarked. "Who will teach Zayo before his passage?"

"Booralta knows best. When my foal is born, it will have an older brother to look up to. I am grateful that my son still lives. My sorrow and emptiness over my husband's murder will always be bitter, but when I think of how much Pleeyedraha is suffering, I wish I could do something for her."

"Why are you here and not with your son and Pleeyedraha?" Hohnoor asked.

"Pleeyedraha is operating on Zayo," Mehlanahr told his father.

"How was he attacked?"

None of them could believe the story that Mehlanahr related to them, especially since they knew that Kayloor had been killed that same morning. "Like I said before, something is mysteriously wrong. Those two guards were not involved in Kayloor's murder."

"Where are the guards now?" Bailaha asked.

"Zayo incarcerated them before going to the hospital, and he will excommunicate them in the morning."

"Excommunication?" they all wondered, except Tarahnaha.

"Yes. One for striking the king with a weapon, and the other for his act of treason in not heeding Zayo's command to stop what he was doing."

"What of those who committed the treachery against Kayloor?" Bailaha's father asked.

"When my son is finished in the hospital, and he feels up to walking around, he must locate them and incarcerate them, all of which must be done by breakfast tomorrow," Tarahnaha said.

Mehlanahr added, "After the criminals are all attended to by Zayo, he will be properly presented with his crown. Surely the end of Kayloor's era must be marked before Zayo's era can properly begin."

Equestra is a very temperate planet, when compared with others. Planet wide temperatures are moderate all year round: the warm season split is 90F/75F, and the cool season split is 70F/55F. It never snows. There are no thunderstorms, no earthquakes, no volcanoes, no tsunamis, no typhoons, no hurricanes, no cyclones. There are occasional light breezes, however. There is at least a sprinkle of a rain shower amidst the sunshine almost every day, which provides a bounteous habitat for an ever-abundant food supply for the vegetarian Caballians. The morning that Kayloor was killed presented some very strange weather: cloudlessly clear jade green skies, and pouring hot sunshine from the star they call Omistu; the temperature was well over 95F.

The circumference of Equestra around the equator is 9,720 miles, miles which are only inches off in measurement from their Earth counterparts. The Caballians, who found that the number 3 was the easiest for them to work with in their sciences, have made the best use of Equestra for all practical scientific purposes. The cube of 3 equals how many hours there are in an Equestran day—27. The length of an Equestran hour is less than a second longer than its Earth counterpart.

More simply put, as Equestra rotates on its axis each day, it rotates exactly 360 miles each hour; it also has 27 miles in each degree of a 360 degree sphere. Size wise, Earth is approximately 2.5 times larger than Equestra.

The water in Equestra's two seas, the Sea of Serenity and the Unknown Sea, is a beautiful yellow-green, and is very calm. There are a number of rivers, many of which have short waterfalls over rock formations which represent the strongest natural form of water power available. There are also a countless number of lakes, streams, and ponds.

What is a Caballian? That is what they call themselves, but they would be shocked at what we know them as: <u>Centaurs</u>. Their upper torso is human-like; their heads are somewhat larger than human heads. They have large eyes with pupils that become horizontal slits in bright light. Most of them have curly or wavy hair. Their voices are not exactly what you would call clear, because they always speak with a slight hint of a whinny (which is why their names are as they are). They do, however, have three distinct dialects of speaking, depending on which city they come from. Residents of Tokanar and its localities tend to speak pretty clear but a little fast; residents of Wateloqua and its localities speak with a slight drawl on the letters R, N, and D; residents of Laerion and its localities do not speak too slow or too fast, but they like to chew their words.

Many of them wear their manes (what we call hair) long; some of them trim them shorter, depending on vocational necessity. Their horse torsos and legs look very much like Arabian bodies, with a very noble appearance, and medium-sized strong hooves. Their hands are similar to human hands; there are a total of six digits on each hand. The outside and inside digits of each hand are opposers (thumbs). Of the four fingers between the two opposers, the outer two are approximately an inch shorter than the inside two. Their fingernails are flat and thick, and can often be troublesome to manicure, comparable only to their hooves. The two longer inside fingers are cleft between their respective metacarpals, down to approximately the same level where the opposers are attached. The palms are U-shaped; they include the fleshy areas between the metacarpals on either side of the cleft, and the muscular, fleshy area between the opposers. The portion of the palms which were injured on Zayo's hands were the areas above the opposers on either side of the cleft.

The Caballian government and education system are relatively simple. There is a king, though he is not considered to be a monarch; rather, his main job is to serve as a mediator to keep the peace among the Caballians. When agreed to by his adjutant, he can request to change an existing law or to enact a new law, but he can only do so if his adjutant agrees that it will be beneficial; all of their people must agree with it for it to be enacted. With the help of his adjutant and the three shamans, he has to carry out all punishments at public gatherings, but his job is not to police the people. His is a position of utmost respect, because he requires a specialized education which takes many years to obtain, often hundreds of years.

The education system provides the means for students to strengthen their weak fields, and also to expand their strengths so that they will properly be able to serve others. All foals attend school from their seventh birthday until their twentieth birthday; at that time, they are placed with personal vocational mentors to teach them individual trades. This one-on-one work relationship continues until the student reaches his passage at his thirty-fifth birthday, at which time he is tested for placement in the Caballian society according to the person's skills and the current need for such skills.

About an hour before they were to eat supper, Tarahnaha finally dared to ask Mehlanahr about his studies. "It pleases me to know that my son did what he did today for someone like you, Mehlanahr. He is a much better judge of people than I had ever presumed. I wish to know, though, who you are studying with."

"Oorahno," he replied.

"The master engineer?"

"Yes. Four months ago, I returned from a five-month-long field trip with several other interns and many engineers."

"Kayloor valued that mission highly, yet I had forgotten which interns went. How did you manage to keep atop of our culture and learn so much about our family?"

"Since we were not here, we were required to study the many different aspects of our culture. We had to study it as much as we studied the sciences."

"How did your parents react to your absence?"

"When I returned, they felt as if I had completed the greatest part of my career, though they had absolutely no idea of how my work had progressed."

"This being your day off from your studies, I am quite surprised that you even answered Zayo's call earlier. Why did you do it?"

"Sometimes, you must forsake yourself if someone else needs help. My family is here, and they are healthy, but how often is the king killed? You do understand..."

"Yes. You mean to do well, and to support Zayo as our king; will you rest before he is better? He still must excommunicate those who killed Kayloor before his coronation ceremony can begin; otherwise it will all be senseless." She still could not hold back her tears. As soon as she did come back to her senses, she said, "Please forgive me. I wish to hear more about what you are studying. What interests you the most about engineering? There are endless possibilities."

"Oorahno encouraged me to dissect everything that came to my attention. The most interesting aspect was that, when traveling faster than the speed of light, other dimensional facets are created which are completely different from the dimension we live in as we know it."

"A scientific shaman?" Tarahnaha mused, almost laughing.

He saw the expression on her face, and laughed himself. "In my mathematical and physical research, I have discovered that physical constants can move between those dimensions when traveling at those speeds."

Tarahnaha was now becoming more curious. "What exactly do you mean by that?"

"I have been designing engines for a new ship, one that will be able to travel faster than the speed of light. To use the ship as the physical constant, we should be able to move it from one point in the universe to another with only seconds elapsing."

The queen was shocked, mostly because she was hearing this from a thirty-four year old stallion. She knew that if he was successful with this type of work, he would become the master engineer, entitled to wear the black vest instead of the usual deep blue vest as an engineer. But she still had her doubts, especially since she did not know very much about either engineering or shamanism. "The challenge of an unequaled achievement is very intriguing, but do you think that other planets and stars would become obstacles when traveling great distances? I can hardly fathom what that would mean: perhaps the deaths of yourself and those you are working with, perhaps a permanent distortion in the realms which the shamans watch over, or even perhaps the end of our people?"

"Planets and stars exist in this dimension, not in the others which I believe we can travel through. It will act as a form of a bypass. I have spoken with Booralta many times, and he has concurred that it is a theoretically safe mode of transportation."

Tarahnaha thought to herself, Will Mehlanahr's discovery lead our people to the war Booralta told Zayo of this morning? Or will Mehlanahr do just the opposite, and help our people win the war? What else does Booralta know that he did not tell us yet? She tried to dismiss these thoughts, but she could not. But she did not mention them to Mehlanahr.

As soon as she finished her supper, Tarahnaha had Mehlanahr bring her back to the hospital. And what a relief it was to the queen when she saw Pleeyedraha approaching soon after she had set down in the waiting area with Mehlanahr. When Pleeyedraha saw the queen, she hastened her step. Tarahnaha arose from her seat, whence they embraced and began sobbing and wailing simultaneously. They continued like this for fifteen minutes, until they stopped as suddenly as they had started, and they set down.

"Who would have ever dreamt of such a conspiracy?" Pleeyedraha asked, though not expecting an answer.

Tarahnaha knew that Pleeyedraha had no other way of expressing her grief and anger at the situation; she asked the doctor, "How is my son?"

Pleeyedraha straightened herself up as best as possible despite her cramped muscles, and she said, "Tarahnaha, I have never seen a patient respond so well to heptalaser as young Zayo has. He has some remarkable strength and resiliency in his physiology. The only factor I can attribute it to is his lineage. I never performed surgery on Kayloor, but for your husband who survived his own doom that was written when he was born, he was just as resilient."

"Pleeyedraha," the queen said, trying to stay off of the subject of Kayloor's death, "I am pregnant."

This statement caught Pleeyedraha by surprise. She was so surprised, disbelieving, that she examined Tarahnaha with a scanner, only to find out that the queen was right. "Six months old," she finally said. "Nine more months."

Tarahnaha saw the somewhat relieved look on Pleeyedraha's face, and she said, "Thank you, Pleeyedraha. How long before my son is able to leave?"

"As soon as he awakes, and can walk on his own."

"Then it should be soon."

"I believe it will be quite soon."

TRAITORS

Kayloor's father, Kuhoor, was the king before his son. And he was equally as handsome in his own right. Kuhoor had been a very particular stallion, very finicky in everything that touched his life. While he was still the crown prince, and two weeks before her passage, they met; he was one hundred and thirty years old. It was no wonder to all other Caballians that Kuhoor found Ahmehlaha to be the only mare good enough to become his princess and future queen. To say the least, Ahmehlaha was very beautiful. No other mare could shine a light on her grace, nor could they match her charisma: she could almost be called a storybook princess. She was a nurse, and even though it was her manners that won Kuhoor's favor, she was exceptionally beautiful.

To say that Kuhoor was a difficult king to serve was not quite appropriate. He was extremely determined to have everything just as he thought would be best for his people. This determination did not escape his heir, but neither did Ahmehlaha's grace and charisma. Kayloor was her first and only foal; when he was born, Kuhoor was four hundred and ten years old, and Ahmehlaha was three hundred and fifteen. Ahmehlaha had a lot of difficulty with the parting, and died soon after her son was born; he never nursed from her to receive her colostrum that contained the bonding chemicals. The bonding chemicals stay in a mare's milk for one, maybe two days at the most, and they are imperative for a foal's body to begin to function correctly, especially standing up. Without receiving the bonding chemicals, a Caballian foal dies. The afternoon before Kayloor was born, Pleeyedraha had given birth to her first and only foal, a foal that was stillborn. When Ahmehlaha died, and Kuhoor's newborn heir needed a wetnurse, Pleeyedraha was the only mare alive with the bonding chemicals still in her milk, and by such was able to save the crown prince's life, taking him in as her own foal until he was weaned.

Pleeyedraha brought Tarahnaha to Zayo's bedside, and the two mares set there, silently, until the young king opened his eyes. Pleeyedraha picked up her scanner, and started to examine him. "How do you feel?" she asked while she worked.

He wiggled his fingers, moving his hands around as much as he possibly could, then he smiled at her and said, "Pleeyedraha, I knew you would fix my hands." He saw his mother and asked her, "Did you send Mehlanahr home?"

"I tried," Tarahnaha told him, "but I ended up going with him to his house, and spending the afternoon with his family. I ate dinner with them an hour ago, and he brought me back here. He is probably waiting for us; he knows we cannot obtain a transport at this hour."

Pleeyedraha finished her examination and told Zayo, "I have no reason to keep a healthy person in the hospital overnight."

When Zayo saw Mehlanahr in the waiting room, he said, "Thanks in excess, my friend."

Mehlanahr was glad to see that the new king was healed of his injuries, but he was rather surprised at how Zayo addressed him. "What do you mean by calling me your friend when we only just met today, your majesty?"

"A friend is someone who dares to risk himself in helping others. I am quite sure you take pride in yourself and the fact that you are a very well-to-do stallion. Despite this, you risked losing your tail to help Lahrohnaha."

"You can stand there and call me your friend despite the fact that I argued with you when we first met?"

"You were right—I do have many things to learn. I will learn those things from friends like you who take the time to point out my errors to me, more than what I could have possibly learned from spelling with my father."

"Enough," Mehlanahr finally said. "Do you know how late it is?"

"I am hungry."

Tarahnaha knew that something important was happening between her son and Mehlanahr, though she was not exactly sure what it was, so she

EQUESTRA

said, "Zayo, I will obtain some food from the kitchen here so that you can eat it in the transport." She walked away from them.

"What?" he wondered, although she did not answer him.

"You have many things to do," Mehlanahr told Zayo. "You will not sleep very much tonight."

"How difficult can it be to catch a couple of criminals?"

"How many of them were involved in your father's murder?"

"I do not know."

"Every one of them is surely guilty of one crime or another against your father. You must find all of them and incarcerate them by morning."

"I am sure that with your help tonight, it will not take very long."

"That is not all," Mehlanahr said rather coldly.

"What else is there?"

"You must retrieve your father's body so it can be burned."

"It does not get imploded?" Zayo wondered, unsure of what was done.

"Anyone else, yes. A king, never. His corpse must be burned in a bonfire in front of all of our people to signify his end before you can be properly crowned."

"My father never told me this."

"How would he have known that he would die at the age of one hundred and thirty? He felt he would have lived at least three hundred more years, as did nearly all of our people."

"'Nearly all of our people'?" Zayo repeated. "Why not all?"

"Can you truly count those who killed him?"

"No."

"Because you know, deep in your heart, that they must be punished. If you miss even one of them and do not punish him or her within twenty-seven hours of the occurrence of the crime, I am quite sure that you will live the rest of your life in misery, allowing him or her to live in our society when he or she denied your father of the right to live."

Tarahnaha came back with some food at that point. She had heard all of Mehlanahr's last remark to her son, and she knew that it was exactly the type of prodding Zayo needed to be his absolute best. Watching the two of them reminded her of her uncle Neeyahr, her father's brother, who had raised her. She remembered Neeyahr because he had been able to provoke Kayloor in a way very similar to how Mehlanahr was provoking Zayo, but she said nothing about it to them. And she now realized that Mehlanahr would indeed help Zayo and the Caballians win the war predicted for their future.

32

Tarahnaha handed the food to Zayo, and they left the hospital.

Tarahnaha's father was a stallion by the name of Hoor. Because Hoor was a carpenter, he wore a brown vest, the same color vest all artisans wore. He was the son of a farmer, and grew up a hundred miles south of Laerion. Not only was his vest brown, but his fur was brown, and his hair was brown. His eyes were the same dark brown as Tarahnaha's eyes were.

Hoor had a wife who was two months younger than he was; her name was Kehsahwaha. Hoor and Kehsahwaha were married at her passage, and Tarahnaha was born two years later. Tarahnaha was as pretty as her mother was, with the same dark brown hair, the same facial features, and the same body build. Kehsahwaha's fur was off-white, and her eyes were slate-colored. Kehsahwaha had a much older sister named Dehnohraha who resembled Kehsahwaha in very many respects, including her coloring. The main difference was that Dehnohraha had black hair, and dark eyes which were blind since birth. Dehnohraha is one of three shamans (like Booralta), and she lives and works in Laerion.

When Tarahnaha was three years old, her parents left her with her paternal grandparents for the day, and they set out to see Kuhoor, who had summoned them for some reason or another. Hoor and Kehsahwaha never made it to the palace, and their daughter never saw them again. A portion of the road which they were traveling on, which connected the cities of Laerion and Tokanar, was at that time just barely wide enough for a single transport to traverse safely at one time. This narrow portion was only a mile long, but the slightest error in navigating it was highly dangerous. Hoor forgot to check this portion of the road before setting out on it, as did another transport which was traveling north to Laerion (carrying four Caballians), and they collided, killing all six Caballians immediately. As soon as Kuhoor heard of this devastating accident, he demanded that the road be widened immediately; work began on it the next day.

Because Hoor's parents were very elderly, both being near four hundred, it was not very wise for them to constantly look after their granddaughter Tarahnaha (who was very precocious). Hoor had an older brother named Neeyahr, who was a farmer just like their father was. Neeyahr and his wife took in their niece, and raised her as if she were their own daughter. They had their own son, who had already made his passage.

When the crown prince (Kayloor) turned twenty-eight years old, he was placed with Neeyahr by Kuhoor. Neeyahr raised all types of fruit trees on his farm, which was several miles away from where his brother had lived before he was killed. What Neeyahr was instructed to teach Kayloor was not just farming, and not just about different types of fruits, but the type of philosophy which farmers by. They fast became the best of friends, although Kayloor did not pay much attention to Tarahnaha because she was sixteen years younger than he was. Kayloor continued to pay no mind to Tarahnaha when she turned twenty, and was designated to serve as an agricultural intern with her uncle.

Kayloor was forty-seven years old when Kuhoor died and left him the throne; Neeyahr was one hundred and twenty-four years old. Since all of Kayloor's predecessors had each chosen an adjutant to help them rule fairly, he also followed suit by selecting his friend Neeyahr, who knew how to make Kayloor think and act most honorably. Because of his new position, Neeyahr was required to move into the palace with his wife and Tarahnaha, who was now thirty-one years old. Within a week of their taking up residence in the palace, Kayloor was becoming extremely fond of Tarahnaha, who was easily his match on many philosophical matters. What secured Kayloor in the fact that Tarahnaha should become his queen after her passage was that Pleeyedraha (who was known for her persuasiveness) could not alter Tarahnaha's startling opinions of Kayloor's true intent in the least, because Tarahnaha saw Kayloor for what he was, and not for what Pleeyedraha made him to be like. Most Caballians usually allowed Pleeyedraha's relationship with Kayloor and her ideas to dictate how they treated him, which usually ended up better for him, although they were not always best for him and the rest of the Caballians.

Tarahnaha had the nerve to tell Pleeyedraha that the doctor's opinions of Kayloor, though they suited Pleeyedraha, were "Not quite what the rest of their people needed to view the king as," that he "should be treated with far more respect as the king, and not just the crown prince," and that he should, most of all, "be treated as a fully capable highly philosophical adult instead of a foal who had no other hope for life or success except through (Pleeyedraha)." Pleeyedraha meant well by her intentions for Kayloor, but she could not help but be overprotective. She knew that Tarahnaha was right, and she told the young mare just as much.

Kayloor and Neeyahr worked together for many years. One of the greatest moments for them during Kayloor's reign was the day that Zayo was born. What hurt Kayloor the greatest was the day that Neeyahr was killed in a farming accident. Neeyahr was one hundred and eighty-nine years old at the time, and the crown prince was six years old. Neeyahr's widow returned to Laerion. Zayo still has some vague memories of Neeyahr, although he does not remember very much.

Upon their arrival at the palace, they embarked on a full search. Neither Tarahnaha nor Zayo could handle searching on their own, and being the one who found Kayloor's body, so the three of them searched together. Their search was to no avail, however, as they could not even find a trace of any spilt blood staining any portion of the ground. The fruitlessness of their search upset all of them, but it did not take them very long to decide to go back to Booralta's house. It was not just that they needed to find out what happened to Kayloor, but they needed to find out who the criminals were so Zayo could apprehend them before the night was over. Just before they left, Zayo put on a clean lavender vest, gave Mehlanahr an imploder, and he placed his father's sabre in his vest.

The trip to Booralta's house took an hour and a half because of the darkness of the still clear night, but time passed quickly for them. As Tarahnaha reached her hand up to knock on the door, it opened. Booralta was there, and he had been expecting them to return to his house. "Please come in," he told them, whereas they heeded his request, and he closed the door behind them. "I was going to put out a call if you had not arrived within ten minutes from now."

Zayo now saw that there were four chairs around the table. He was beginning to realize just what the shaman's abilities were, but he said nothing to Booralta about it.

They set down at the table, and had some water. The shaman said, "Your majesty and your highness, I knew when you were here before what had happened to Kayloor, and who the guilty people are. But it was even more imperative that you find the pegasus and meet Mehlanahr."

"Meet me?" Mehlanahr asked. "Why? Because I agreed to help them when no one else would?"

Booralta could not help but laugh at Mehlanahr's questions; he was a very likeable young stallion. "There is much more to your friendship with Zayo," the shaman returned. "Yes, he needed your help today, but he will also need your help for the rest of your life."

"I am not helpless," Zayo retorted; he was growing tired. "I am fully capable of doing my job."

"Then what will you do tomorrow?" Tarahnaha asked her son. "At your coronation, you will be required to select one person to help you."

"I get to select someone to act as my stepfather?" Zayo asked her. "Or must I now travel around with a bodyguard?"

"Why must you be so stubborn and fiery?" Booralta asked him. "You need someone to step on your heels, and keep you at the peak of your honor and abilities. Otherwise, you will not be a good king."

"Then it is true that Mehlanahr will help us to win the war?" Tarahnaha asked.

"Yes."

"What war?" Mehlanahr asked.

"The war that will break out within the next year. Zayo will need your technology and insight to be a successful leader and king. Without your help, our future is very bleak."

"You are joking," Mehlanahr stated. "I do not wish any limelight or glory for myself. I am only serving my king because he needs my help."

"You just said it yourself," Booralta told him. "You will become the most successful engineer in our history. Prepare yourself for tomorrow, because your life is about to change."

"I may be stubborn and driven towards success by some very good teachers, but I am not Kayloor's heir."

"If our people and our young king cannot take advantage of what you are capable of doing, then what will be the purpose of your work? Each and every Caballian must use his talents to the fullest in order to serve our people and our king in the best way possible. If you work for yourself and yourself alone, what will the purpose of your work be? If that is the case, then you might as well be as dead as Kayloor is. Your modesty can certainly be appreciated, but you must not abuse it. Share your pride in your work with our people, and we will all benefit from it. And just as Zayo will benefit from you, you will benefit from him. The two of you need each other to be your absolute best. That is the way it must be for us to have a future."

"Our people will truly depend on my success?"

"Not just your success, but your innate ability to make Zayo think and learn everything he will need to learn as our king."

Mehlanahr was ashamed of himself for daring to argue with Booralta when he knew the shaman was right. "Booralta, I do not mean to cross you in this manner, but it has been a long day, and the grief of Kayloor's murder is creeping over me, catching up to me now when I was able to hold it off before."

"You know you must help Kayloor's son and heir. And you know you must help Kayloor's widow. Not only that, but you will be instrumental in teaching Zayo's sibling about its father, almost being a stepfather to it."

"You know what a high honor it is to accept such a position."

"It will bring even greater honor to young Zayo, who will become the greatest king our people have ever known."

"Then I have no choice in the matter."

"Good," Zayo replied. "I will give you Neeyahr's collar, and you will crown me tomorrow."

Mehlanahr nearly jumped out of his skin when he heard Zayo mention Neeyahr, and the collar which Tarahnaha's uncle had worn as Kayloor's adjutant, the collar which every single adjutant had worn in the service of his king. "Who said anything about being an adjutant?" he asked Zayo and Booralta. "I thought you only meant being his friend, Booralta."

Zayo laughed at him. "So you really do dislike it as much as I dislike the idea of a coronation! You, who told me earlier today that I had much to learn about a coronation not being a pointless event!"

"I meant that it is not pointless to our people, even though it may be pointless to you. How else will they celebrate your beginning as our king?"

"How else will they learn about the importance of my friend Mehlanahr, who has shown me much patience and has helped my mother? Perhaps we can laugh at it all together tomorrow. But you are right about one thing: why should we be so concerned about tomorrow when I still have so much work to do before I sleep? I really need your help tonight in finding the criminals and my father's corpse."

"Kayloor was threatened with, and struck by, a shot from an imploder," Booralta told them, talking about an instrument which was used for removing corpses. Because of these circumstances surrounding Kayloor's death, they will never find his body.

"Who are the miserable parties involved?" Zayo asked, furious that his beloved father was treated like a dead body by Caballians; he felt a rush of anger to want to rush their excommunications, but he knew it must be done in front of all Caballians.

Booralta continued on to tell him about the three guilty citizens, all of whom were stallions. He also told Zayo where the criminals could be found; they were all in or near Tokanar.

"I cannot properly burn my father's body tomorrow," Zayo replied, "but I will excommunicate his murderers first before the bonfire of the platform. My heart burns, wanting to burn them in his stead, but that is not in accordance with our laws."

Tarahnaha was shocked by her son's words, but she said nothing.

"That is the wisest course of action to take," Booralta told the young king. "It will bring you the greatest successes in your own reign."

As much as it tore at the royal family's hearts because of their closeness to Pleeyedraha, one of the criminals was a doctor Pleeyedraha worked with in the hospital in Tokanar, who was currently assigned to working the later shift in Tokanar; his name was Maroola. Maroola had also been Pleeyedraha's husband, but she had disowned him years ago when he could not accept the fact that she brought the new crown prince, Kayloor, home to nurse immediately after the death of their own son. Maroola had been miserable over losing their first (and only) foal, and was especially bitter over a tyrant king like Kuhoor creeping into his personal life. He knew it was best for their people, especially when she was given the black vest after she took charge of Kayloor's care, but he could not accept it.

Maroola had been off duty when Kayloor was killed; he did not start working that day until mid-afternoon. Now, he was in charge of keeping an eye on Lahrohnaha and Andrux.

The three of them left the transport; Zayo carried his father's sabre, and Mehlanahr carried an imploder. They entered the hospital and walked to Maroola's own office. The door was open, so they entered, Zayo leading the way. Maroola saw the young king, and was rather shocked; he did not think Zayo would be able to get around to arresting him because of his injuries earlier, but he now saw that he was wrong.

Maroola eyed Kayloor's sabre in Zayo's vest, but he decided to play coy for the moment. "Your majesty, and your highness, how may I be of service?"

"Step away from the computer," Zayo told him, "and walk into the center of the room, with your hands reaching towards the ceiling."

"I have patients here that must be tended to," he retorted.

"The same way you tended to Father?"

Maroola walked into the center of the room as he was told. "Lahrohnaha needs medical attention."

Zayo took the sabre and used its sharp tip to slice through Maroola's green vest, which fell to the floor. "First," the young king said, "I discharge you of your citizenship. You are not fit to provide medical assistance to Lahrohnaha, nor any other Caballian ever again."

"Your majesty, I do not understand."

"You were in such a hurry for me to be your king that you will die with that decision." Zayo used the tip of the sabre to scratch an "X" into

Maroola's chest, which marked him as a criminal requiring excommunication. It was not a deep scratch, but enough to guarantee that blood would fill in the lines of the "X" without it running down him. It was the most disgraceful mark that could be placed on any Caballian. "Now, you are ready for your excommunication before my father's bonfire tomorrow morning."

"What are you saying?"

"These will be the last words from my lips to your ears: Because you were involved in the treason behind my father's implosion while he still lived, you will be excommunicated while you are still alive."

Two guards soon came into the hospital with Pakoor, a doctor who was to replace Maroola for the night. The guards tied up Maroola, and took him away to the refinery.

The second criminal was not so difficult; it was an artisan named Wehrahn, who was at home. It surprised Wehrahn somewhat when he heard a knocking on his door, but it surprised him even more when he saw Zayo standing there with a sabre in his hand when he opened the door. "Your majesty," he said, showing his surprise, "how may I help you?"

"Step into your den," Zayo told him, and he did so; Mehlanahr and Tarahnaha followed Zayo in. "Reach for the ceiling with your hands," and Wehrahn did so. He cut Wehrahn's vest off in the same manner as he had removed Maroola's vest. Wehrahn did not question it, but faced his torture with more bravery than Maroola had. Zayo made an "X" on his chest also, and he said, "The only carpentry you will ever make again will be the sight of your sinews shrieking as your body and spirit are excommunicated, as you will be so punished because my father was imploded alive as a result of your treason."

"I deserve to be excommunicated," Wehrahn remarked. "I should not have been involved with Dahrohd's scheme to undermine Kayloor's wishes, nor of Maroola's angst over Pleeyedraha."

"I will not change my mind," Zayo told him.

Moments later, two guards arrived to remove Wehrahn.

The last criminal that Booralta had told Zayo about was a shoemaker by the name of Dahrohd, the same person that Wehrahn had mentioned as being the mastermind of the whole scheme against Kayloor. Dahrohd lived well within the city of Tokanar, so it did not take them long to travel to his house.

Dahrohd was not too surprised when he opened the door for Zayo; actually, he was rather mad at the young king for bothering to show up at all. Zayo pointed the sabre at him and said, "Move into the center of the den with your arms above your head so I can see your hands, and wiggle your fingers."

"Your majesty, what is the meaning of this?" he asked as he complied with the young king's wishes.

"You murdered my father, and now you act as if you do not know why I must arrest you for your crime?"

"How can you accuse me of such a thing?"

Mehlanahr got ready to use the imploder, for if Dahrohd suddenly attacked Zayo, the young king would be required by law to behead him right away in self defense. "Why do you fight my words," Zayo shot back, Ayou asinine fool?! My mother is pregnant, and my sibling will grow up without a father! You have dishonored my family, and you have dishonored our people! And your eyes reflect the demon of having drawn my father's blood! Dare to say one more word to me, and I shall cut you apart now, piece by little piece! Push me enough, and I will feed you to Ahrkoor's forgefire!"

Dahrohd saw the look in Zayo's eyes, and actually trembled. Zayo removed his vest, and marked his chest with an "X." Zayo then continued, "How dare you lie to me when I know it was you who fired the fatal shot of the imploder this morning, treating my beloved father like a corpse? I will not give you the pleasure of excommunicating you tonight. Rather, I will wait until the morning, and make a public spectacle of your sinning ways before my father's bonfire."

After Dahrohd was removed by two guards, Mehlanahr brought Tarahnaha and Zayo back to the palace. Being the middle of the night, Mehlanahr spent the rest of the night in the palace.

CORONATION

Zayo, Mehlanahr, and Tarahnaha were up early the next morning, and they had plenty of time to eat breakfast, groom, and braid their hair for the day's ceremonies, which were to take place on the palace grounds. Many Caballians were already there, arriving shortly after the palace residents got home, and then going to sleep until dawn so that they would be more refreshed than they would have been if they had arrived there just before the festivities began without a chance to rest.

A number of guards arrived early, and prepared the center of the platform for the bonfire; they all believed that Kayloor's corpse was going to be burned with the platform, but they did not know of how the king had died.

The last people to arrive for the bonfire were the remainder of the guards, who escorted the five criminals with them, all the criminals who were going to be excommunicated that morning.

Mehlanahr returned to his family as soon as he noticed their arrival. Everyone thereafter set down on the great lawn, and fell silent when Zayo called for their attention by raising his hands over his head. "My people," the young king began, "my beloved people, yesterday, my father was murdered by three Caballians; within the same hour, two other Caballians attacked me. Yesterday will be remembered as the most terrifying day in our history since the wars ended; today is the day that I put an end to the hatred. Let it be known that I will not withstand any grievous sin not in

41

accordance with our laws." Zayo summoned the guards to bring the five criminals onto the platform.

He then continued. "The three criminals are those who plotted treason against my father, and imploded him while he still lived. Because of this, they will be excommunicated. If that is not enough to banish them, then I will implode them, as they imploded Father. The other two criminals I now mark for excommunication." Zayo cut off their orange vests and sliced "X"s into their chests, just as he had done to the other three. "One of these two ignored my command to him; the other one struck me with a whip across my back. If it were not for Pleeyedraha, I would not be standing here now. Because those two criminals refused to think before they acted, instead of heeding my words, they will also be excommunicated."

The Caballians could not believe that they were going to be witnessing five excommunications. It was a remarkable thing for a Caballian to see five excommunications in a lifetime, but in one day...it said more than enough for what was happening to their spirits. Zayo's zeal was what they needed to put them back in the right way of life for their society.

The guards stepped back, and before the young king had any idea of how to proceed, Oorahno walked up to him, carrying what seemed to be an imploder, though it looked nothing like any imploder Zayo had ever seen before in his life—it was bulkier, and seemed to be made of pure gold. The master engineer then said to him, "Your majesty, this shifter belonged to your father, although he refused to keep possession of it. It was given to your father when he was crowned the king, and it had belonged to Kuhoor before him." He saw Zayo's eyes open a bit, so he continued. "It is many eons old; all of your ancestors have protected it, for it is the only remainder of our ancient way of life. Its power is overwhelming, and if left in the wrong hands, will lead to our wars again. The shifter rightfully belongs to you to use within the guidelines of our laws, for it may only be used to excommunicate a convicted criminal." He saw the fear welling up in Zayo's eyes. "If it is not used properly, then the realms will collapse. Guide our hearts truly in the usage of it."

Zayo thought for a moment, then he said to Oorahno, "How does it work?"

Oorahno remained solemn. "Before you operate it, you must know what it does. When you push the activator, just enough cosmic energy is energized so as to shift a gateway or bridge to the sixth realm, the realm of hell, which is the only fitting place for such criminals. As soon as it touches the person who is to be excommunicated, it rips them from this realm forever. To the casual observer, it will appear that they are being imploded alive; if they were being imploded alive, then they would go the way of all righteous Caballians, and return to the emperor. But since criminals have forsaken the ways of the emperor, their souls must be committed forever to the guardian of darkness. The shifter will accomplish this for you." He saw Zayo sigh. "This is your first gift as our new king. Use it wisely during your reign, and our people shall always respect you as our protector."

Zayo hung the sabre from his vest, and accepted the shifter from Oorahno. He thought for a moment and said, "I do not mean to doubt you, but how do you know that they will definitely end up in the realm of hell, and not somewhere else, or perhaps even dead? If it kills them, then I am also guilty of murder." He then thought to himself, Father, teach me what to do.

"Booralta and I have discoursed on the principles of the shifter, both mechanical and metaphysical. It does not contain enough energy to implode a body, but the energy it does have is just enough to transport one person between two realms. The focal energy is a pure, good energy, just enough to remove the evil person; it is as if its energy source was based on the goodwill of our people. The principles of the shifter are what have guided Mehlanahr to progress in his studies; he knows the shifter better than I do."

Zayo thought about his words for a moment, then he reflected back to what Booralta had told him about Mehlanahr the day before. Mehlanahr had seen the young king's distress over his father's death, and knew that the only way for him to overcome it was to face it head on, and excommunicate the criminals as their laws prescribed. Zayo nodded at Oorahno, who left him. Then young king then lifted the rather heavy shifter, and made rather quick work of firing it at each one of the criminals.

Zayo left his father's platform, and it was doused with liquid philinium (which is very combustible) by some guards. From a safe distance, Zayo tossed a lit torch onto the platform, which almost instantly exploded in a tremendous fireball. No one was hurt, but it was a startling experience for them all. It did not take long before the bonfire died out, leaving behind only a heap of ashes.

The excommunications and the end of Kayloor's reign were over.

Once the bonfire was completely extinguished, there was a mandatory one-hour spell between it and the coronation of Zayo. A new platform was built by a group of artisans for Zayo during that time.

When Zayo stepped up onto the new platform, it was obvious to them all that he was occupied with self-doubt. What they did not see that was also troubling him was the fact that he was seriously grieving his father's death; he missed Kayloor more than any other Caballian at that particular moment. None of the Caballians expected him to experience such feelings yet because of his age; such related feelings and doubts do not usually surface until the Caballian is near his or her passage, around the age of thirty-five. Hindered by his troubled emotions in what simply seemed to be a question of moral correctness in performing the excommunications, Zayo was hardly prepared for his coronation.

When the silence and attention of the crowd was obvious to the young king, he gazed out upon them for a few long moments before he spoke. "My father would hardly be proud of me now," he said rather tersely. "Although the excommunications were in accordance with our laws, they were completely against his philosophy and everything he had taught me in my service as your crown prince. They only stopped the life of one person, but I excommunicated all of their lives, all five of them." He sighed desperately. "If Father were here, he would have reprimanded them severely, and perhaps clipped them, but he would not have given them their deserved excommunications. But what matters is the fact that if they were not excommunicated, the wars would have returned. Father had taught me, and I firmly believed, that I had the ability to love everyone for what they were—that is, until yesterday. I despised those criminals for murdering Father and attacking myself when I felt I was acting in the best interests of my family."

Suddenly, Zayo heard a voice say, "How do we know that you were not out for revenge upon the criminals for what they had done? Surely Kayloor's teachings to you were not for nothing."

Another voice cried out, "Our history has had some excommunications, but never five in one day."

Zayo was unable to identify the questioners. "I do not know what to say apart from this: if you do not accept the action I took, I will dispose of myself and leave you to your wars."

"You cannot be serious!" a third voice cried out.

After a long, deadly silent moment, a fourth voice called out, "How come none of you has asked why he did what he did? Dare to call him vengeful only if he refuses to answer that." Zayo's was able to pick up that the last remark came from Mehlanahr. This pleased the young king tremendously, as he knew he really did have a friend in Mehlanahr.

Zayo then said, "Everyone has lived for so long under my father's leniency that your spirits have grown weak, and you have forgotten the age-

44

old wisdom behind our laws for a philosophy that was new and untried, and at the time truly seemed like the best course of action to take. You have forgotten the wheres and whys of our laws, which are millions of years old."

Another Caballian then cried out, "Why did you excommunicate the guards?"

Tersely, Zayo replied, "One of them refused to listen to my command not to administer a clipping to someone who did not have identification upon entrance into Tokanar; that is treason. The other guard struck me with a whip when I stopped the clipping after my command was not followed. I have the right to stop such a punishment as the king, and even as the crown prince."

"This is not a question of the legitimacy of your birthright," someone else said.

"It is a question of who will or will not accept me for what I am and what I must become as a result of someone else's actions. As a member of the royal house, I am entitled to such judgments."

"Why?" a voice called out.

"Because I am the king."

"What makes you so different from any other Caballian?" yet another voice shot out.

"My individuality and my abilities entitle me to my job."

"What abilities do you have that no one else has?" someone asked.

"I do not know. But that is what I have been taught my whole life by everyone."

There were some snickers until Mehlanahr said, "It is unfair to test a twenty-four year old colt in such a manner. Everyone knows his education is incomplete."

Someone noticed that Mehlanahr was not yet a citizen, so she remarked, "Let Booralta be the judge of that."

"You are not wise enough to judge whether a person possesses knowledge or not? Our history dictates repeatedly that the king always knows when he is face-to-face with a criminal, and he does not need a shaman to tell him that someone did something very wrong and needs to be punished. All kings have shown this trait, even though Kayloor used it in a different manner than all others. Zayo shows a most excellent sense of criminal mischief—he made sure the punishment fit the crime as permissible by our laws. Sure, Zayo needed to be told who the criminals were that committed the treason against Kayloor, but he did not have to be told a single word as to who imploded our king; Zayo knew as soon as he faced him. Today is the first day of many years of a good king, one who will not willingly let himself be covered over by obscure happenings so as to shroud his judgment."

They finally began to agree with the fairness of Zayo's actions, and his direct judgment. Some mumbling began, but it was soon put to rest as someone asked Zayo, "Your judgment is acceptable to us as our king. But why did you argue with everyone but Mehlanahr?"

Zayo replied, "Yesterday, when my transport did not work, and I was injured, Mehlanahr was the only person who sacrificed himself to help my mother and myself perform our necessary duty in the dark hours of our lives. Without his help, I would not have been able to locate the criminals, which was a task that took us well into the night. Without his help, the criminals would have escaped excommunication for their crimes; I would not have been able to live with them...I would have been miserable the rest of my life just knowing that they lived, and I had the chance within my grasp to punish them for their heinous crimes."

"'Heinous crimes'?" someone repeated.

"Would you have dreamt it possible that such treason could be committed against Father, and that he would be imploded alive? Would it have seemed more unlikely that I would also be chastised the same day for performing my duty as the crown prince? When my mother saw my injuries take place, she was wishing she were also dead. Could you imagine such words coming from a mare who is pregnant? Could you imagine that my sibling will be a bastard, never fully knowing what a good soul our father was? Tell me, do you still think those crimes were <u>not</u> heinous? My mother is only one hundred and fourteen years old, yet she is a widow. What sort of condition is that for a queen? No other queen had ever become a widow before the age of three hundred."

Zayo's words had such a tremendous impact upon the Caballians that there was a markedly prolonged moment of silence. After what seemed as if it were an eternity, but was actually about ten minutes, they all began to kneel facing their new king. Zayo watched as all knelt, even his mother, who knew that it was time for Zayo to take the throne.

Once they were all kneeling, Booralta arose, and as he walked towards Zayo, he said, "It is time for the prophecy to be revealed." He climbed up on Zayo's new platform, and when he was ten feet from his king, he knelt, dropped his head, and waited. He could not speak another word until he was recognized by Zayo.

It was during a moment like this at a caucus of all Caballians that the king had absolute authority over all of them. When everyone had set comfortably on the ground, Zayo walked over to Booralta, and touched the shaman's right shoulder with his left hand.

Booralta stood up and addressed the crowd. "A new era is beginning for the Caballians," the shaman began, "one which will forever change how we live. For millions of years, we have lived as a people who distinctly separated the importance of scientific practices and theories from shamanistic beliefs and practices: how we did our work was distinctly separate from our philosophy of life. The stallion whom Zayo will call to be his adjutant is an engineer who will soon connect the gaps between travel and the differing realms. Do not be deceived when you see that he is not yet a citizen; even though he is only thirty-four years old, his knowledge, talents, and abilities will enable us to survive a war within the next fifteen years; this is imminent for our evolution. Your majesty, I ask you to call him, and to give him the collar; then I shall continue in the prophecy for your reign."

"As you request," Zayo replied. "Mehlanahr, come to me." The young king took the collar from his mother's possession.

Mehlanahr stopped ten feet from Zayo, knelt, and dropped his head. Zayo, knowing that Mehlanahr did not yet wear the vest of a citizen, called out, "Whose son is this?"

Without a word, Hohnoor and Bailaha walked up to the son, knelt beside him, and also dropped their heads. Zayo touched their heads and said, "Chemist and baker, I recognize you as Hohnoor and Bailaha of Tokanar." He touched their shoulders, and they stood up.

"Your majesty," Hohnoor stated, "I call this young stallion my son by the fact that he was born to my wife over thirty-four years ago. He has not yet been called to recognition as a citizen, and will not be until he is thirty-five."

"What do you call him?"

"Mehlanahr," Bailaha replied.

"Hohnoor and Bailaha, as the son of Kayloor, I hereby request that you release your guardianship of your son Mehlanahr so I may call him to serve me in fulfilling my destiny and leading our people to evolve into new and better ways."

"His heart knows what is right," Bailaha stated.

Hohnoor added, "He has already proven by his service to you that he is fit to be called to such an office."

"May our people always remember this moment in our history."

"Thank you, your majesty," they replied, and they left the platform.

Zayo touched Mehlanahr's head, and he said, "Son of Hohnoor and Bailaha, I call you now to serve with me as my adjutant."

"Your majesty," he replied, "I am not yet a citizen. How can I be worthy?"

"I am also not yet a citizen, yet our people accept me as their king. My friend, I need your help. Please do not deny me my dearest request. I have seen the honor of your heart, and I know it is deep. I know you will help me become a successful king."

"Son of Kayloor and Tarahnaha, I cannot refuse your call."

Zayo clipped the collar onto Mehlanahr's neck. The collar was of a pewter mesh, inlaid with twenty-seven evenly-sized crystals, each one of which was a different color from all the others; they each represented one hour of a day. It glistened and moved with the muscles of his neck as if it truly belonged there; it also highlighted his extremely handsome face. "As Hohnoor and Bailaha call you Mehlanahr, their son, our people will call you Sir because of your willingness to work with me."

"As you decree."

Zayo touched Mehlanahr's shoulder, and said, "Wait here until the master historian calls you." He then directed the master historian, "Please continue."

The shaman began an explicit prophecy. "We shall enter a war with aliens within the next year. This will cause greater grief for Zayo than the death of Kayloor. However, it will shine light upon a different war, one which will involve strangers. Mehlanahr's technology will be necessary to correct an imbalance, or rather, a chasm, in the realms, which was opened yesterday when Kayloor was murdered. I know this to be true because of the fact that a pegasus was born among our people less than an hour after Kayloor's death." He took the infant pegasus from Lahrohnaha, and held him up for all to see. "This is the son of Toorahgo and Lahrohnaha. He symbolizes the fact that we shall regain for our people the freedom we once knew, but at a greater level. If any harm comes to the pegasus, then we are doomed to extinction, for without him and Zayo's sibling, we will not evolve."

There were a multitude of mumbles among the Caballians as they tried to digest all of the shaman's words, but they could not. Zayo finally silenced them and said to Booralta, "How could Father's murder have opened up a chasm in the realms, one which Mehlanahr can correct?"

After pondering this question briefly, Booralta replied, "It is my duty to watch over the realms. Before my passage and during my internship, I was always reminded that the realms were a constant factor and could not be changed or disturbed by anything any of us said or did; that was knowledge which I accepted for many years. Once Mehlanahr began his internship as an engineer, I studied everything he did very closely. I must have spoken with Oorahno at least three days out of each week to check on Mehlanahr's progress. I watched it ever so carefully because even the slightest mistake on Mehlanahr's part would prove to be extremely costly to our people; thankfully, his work has been flawless. When I saw where Dahrohd's treachery would eventually lead us, I could not do anything to change it. Perhaps it was even done to test Mehlanahr's ability as an engineer, but I cannot be sure; it may be to counterbalance the pegasus.

"The treachery itself would easily have been upset by Mehlanahr's accomplishments, and would have been corrected. However, as soon as they began to plot to threaten Kayloor's life, the colt Andrux was altered into a pegasus, something which no doctor would have been able to discern. The moment that Kayloor was killed was a terrible moment indeed; his soul was ripped from all known realms, and cannot be found by any shaman. This has left a deep chasm—Kayloor's vacancy—and it cannot be corrected by any spirit in any realm because neither they nor we can normally leave the realm we exist in. Mehlanahr's technology has forged a path between realms, although it is not the same one where Kayloor is to be found to be brought to the correct realm, nor is it the same one that the shifter uses. When you will be required to use Mehlanahr's spaceship to remove the scourge that will come, then a long healing process will begin which will finally end the ancient wars. And when the healing has been completed, the pegasus and your sibling will permanently close the chasm."

"Why would Mehlanahr's spaceship need to be used?" Zayo queried. "My duty as heir is to mete out justice, just as I was required to excommunicate the criminals. Our people do not venture off of Equestra, unless it is a voyage taken by the master engineer and approved by our people."

Booralta knew that young Zayo was correct in asking the question he posed, and the shaman knew full well that he could not withhold any important information about Zayo's future reign because this was the time when the full prophecy had to be revealed to the people. "Your majesty," the shaman replied, "is it not true that every single king our people has ever had has shown a particular gift in an area which none of his predecessors have had, so that he can correct the most urgent portion of our history during his reign?"

"That is true, but what does it have to do with my question?"

"Your majesty, what I am alluding to is the remainder of the prophecy for your reign; hear me out."

"Then please tell me all."

"First, I must ask you and Mehlanahr to set down, because what I am going to tell you is something you would never expect to hear from my lips." They set down, and the shaman continued. "Your gift as king will be in your wisdom and judgment, which shall surely increase with each passing day. What a formidable king you shall be in one hundred years! But to ensure that you do not obtain too much power and authority as our king, your sibling will equally be Kayloor's heir, also possessing the birthright of nobility among Caballians!"

There was a gasp from the crowd as Tarahnaha fell faint; Pleeyedraha rushed over to her. Zayo was so dumbfounded that he could not accept what Booralta was telling him. "Shaman, if your aim is to teach me a lesson in humility, do you not think that my intervention in Mehlanahr's clipping yesterday was proof enough of such a thing? Please, do not vex me so...over millions of years, we have never had more than one ruler at one time."

"Do not listen to my prophecy now, but soon enough you will find out how wrong you were in ignoring my words to you!"

"Booralta, what you are telling me is such a drastic departure from our known history... how would you expect me to accept it so readily?"

"You have accepted the pegasus rather quickly. And you have accepted Mehlanahr. Are you so selfish that you are not able to accept the greatest aid you will ever be given in ensuring that our people evolve as they properly should under your reign?"

"Is it truly to be my reign, or will it be our reign?"

"Your sibling and the pegasus are the keys to completing the healing that you begin, and to finally ending the ancient wars; only then will our people be freed. Refuse to accept your destiny, Zayo, and you are denying our people the only possible chance we have at long-term survival."

"What does my sibling have to do with Mehlanahr?"

"It is true that Mehlanahr is your adjutant, and that no other king has ever had a co-existing rule with a sibling. But just as you need to hear my prophecy right now, your sibling will need to find its lost father. If your sibling and Andrux do not follow their instincts and pursue their destiny, then you will be the last."

"The last? The last what?"

"The last ruler we will ever have. If your sibling does not fulfill its destiny, then the wars will return to our people, forsaking all healing, and neither of you shall have an heir to the throne. Zayo, you must not allow this to turn into a greater tragedy than the alien war will be. If that does happen, then the wars will return, and we are doomed. Zayo, it is your duty as our king to prevent the wars from coming back. This will be the shared responsibility of you and your sibling. If Kayloor is not brought back to the emperor, then the realms will fall apart. Without the power of the emperor to help you, you shall never have an heir to the throne." Booralta looked as if he were quite exhausted from revealing his prophecy. In fact, he was so exhausted that he fell to one knee, and was quite short of breath.

Zayo knelt beside him. "Booralta, you must rest. What service can you perform to our people if you are sick?"

Booralta gazed upon the young king, and remarked, "How could anyone not be fond of Zayo the zealous crown prince? Kayloor was always so right to be proud of you."

"What are you talking about? Please come to your senses."

"I will rest soon." He stopped to catch his breath. Meanwhile, Pleeyedraha joined them, where she examined the shaman.

"Booralta," the doctor said, "the final breakdown of your nervous system is near."

"Pleeyedraha," Zayo said, "what is wrong?"

Her eyes were idle, but her mind was racing. "Your majesty, Booralta has been suffering from scleroses for many years. Medication has held the symptoms in check, but the disease has progressed throughout his nervous system."

"He may die?"

"He will die. Perhaps not today, but his day is drawing near."

"If that were the case," Booralta told her, "then I should have died yesterday. The final breakdown attempted to strike me yesterday at the moment Kayloor was killed."

"I knew something was wrong yesterday when you could not speak," Zayo told him.

"Your summoning of Pleeyedraha would have been useless. I could not delay your meeting Andrux or Mehlanahr. I will live long enough to finish my duty—to ensure that you are crowned. Then, the chasm will claim me at the next surge."

"'The next surge'?" Zayo repeated. "What 'next surge'?"

"The next power flux in the realms. It may be something like the great circle of the three moons, or it may be something like your sibling's birth."

"The birth of a foal will kill you?"

"No; what it is. When your sibling is born, it will tip the balance of power in the realms so that it is again in our favor. Until then, things are very dangerous for our people, and especially for you. But your sibling may not be the cause of my removal to the eternal realm. My death may be caused by something like the great circle. But I do not know for sure." Booralta took a few moments to catch his breath. He then stood up again, seeming to be quite himself, and he straightened out his vest. "Mehlanahr, son of Hohnoor and Bailaha, come to me."

Mehlanahr walked up to the shaman and said, "Historian, what service do you require of me?"

"Tell me of Zayo's strengths."

"I only met him yesterday."

"You served with him during a most despairing time in his life. You have seen a side which most people may never see—at least, not personally. Tell me what you saw in him yesterday."

"I witnessed a young king whose judgment of criminal mischief is indeed greater than anything I have learned from studying the history of his predecessors. I saw a young king who knows himself and his abilities, and who will not allow the grief of others to weaken either him or them. He knows what it means to be a king, and is ready to risk his life to protect those whom he knows serve the best interests of our people."

"What type of leader do you believe Zayo shall be?"

"What exactly do you mean by this question?"

"What do you feel are his dreams for our people?"

Mehlanahr had to think about this before answering. "We have had many kings in our history, all of whom each had a certain vision for where he felt our people should go. Zayo's vision is to put an end to the weakness that has overtaken our people—to repair the chasm which has been opened. Zayo's sibling will find the father it never knew, and in its own way repair the chasm in its life. Both are great visions which will mean sure success for our people if we work with them. I believe Zayo will succeed in rebuilding a greater place for us to live in, a greater reconstruction than either Pehsoorad or Polihdahr ever effected in their times."

"Can you prove this?"

"What other crown prince at the age of twenty-four has dared to challenge guards who would not listen to his command? Who else would run to help a mare through a difficult parting immediately after learning his father had been murdered? What other king would have dared to call an adjutant at his coronation who was not yet a citizen unless he truly believed he was doing the best thing for our people? His unselfishness has proven this."

"I have seen the same traits in everything I have heard of him from his father, and everything I have seen he will do as our king. Because of this, I instructed the master shoemaker to craft a crown with a peak in front of it to sit atop his blaze. I also instructed the master shoemaker as to the importance of the pegasus, and I instructed that the crown be alated."

"Has he done these things as you requested?"

"Indeed he has, and everything is ready. Now I give to you your first charge as Zayo's adjutant: You will take the new crown and sabre from the master shoemaker. You will place the crown upon Zayo's head. With the sabre, you shall pierce your left palm so as to cause a drop of blood to appear. You will use this drop of your blood to stain the blaze of your king after the crown has been placed upon his head."

"As you decree, historian."

BUILDING PLANS

The stallion who made Zayo's new crown and sabre was the master shoemaker, whose name was Ahrkoor. Ahrkoor was a very handsome stallion; he had gray hair, white fur, blue eyes, and odd black marks on his back in addition to those on his spine, legs, and ears. He was far from his youth, being about ten years older than Booralta. Needless to say, he was a forgemaster in Tokanar. It was not the first time that Ahrkoor had been charged with crafting a crown and sabre for a new king: he had already earned the black vest as the master shoemaker before Kayloor ascended to the throne. Kayloor's crown had been a most simple one, a bronze band half an inch in width about his head.

Zayo's crown was much more revolting, to those who thought that Kayloor's crown was a bit excessive. It was a gold band, three-quarters of an inch in width about his head, which formed a peak in front to sit atop his blaze, something like a mountain silhouette. In addition, Ahrkoor had attached a small silvery metal wing on either side just behind where each of his ears would be. This alated crown was lightweight, yet very sturdy.

The sabre was crafted in colors to match Zayo's crown, just as Kayloor's sabre had been. Whereas Kayloor's sabre had been bronze, Zayo's sabre had a gold hilt and a silvery blade, and was obviously very sharp. Mehlanahr accepted this new sabre and its matching crown from Ahrkoor, and brought these tools before his king.

Without a word, Mehlanahr placed the crown snugly upon Zayo's head. He pierced his left palm, made sure that a decent drop of blood appeared, and proceeded to rub it on Zayo's blaze. Once he had done that, he handed the sabre to Zayo, and knelt before him. "Your majesty," Mehlanahr said, and dropped his head.

Zayo replied, "My friend, not a single drop of blood is worthless, unless the person it came from was a criminal. My blood I have spilled for you, and your blood you have spilled for me. What greater friend could a person ask for?"

"The honor is in serving our people, and to prevent unnecessary bloodshed. Our job has hardly begun."

"Indeed," the young king replied.

There was not a single Caballian who missed Kayloor's presence more than young Zayo, who seemed to show it the least. His reaction so far had been to fulfill his duty as what a king should do—rather, what he thought a king should do. He felt as if he were living a bad dream. He was not yet ready to accept the fact that his father was dead, and would never be able to help him again.

Tarahnaha did not pay too much mind to Zayo, as her thoughts were consumed with her own problems. Her parents and uncle had been killed in accidents...they had been her nearest and dearest relatives. Her only other living relative now (besides her offspring) was her aunt, Dehnohraha. And now, her husband had been killed in some deep dark conspiracy. Where was his spirit? As she thought about her unborn foal also being his heir, she suddenly felt that Kayloor's spirit was somewhere where he could keep watch over her through all her difficulties. He had always been there for her when he was alive. What would he think of the sibling rivalry that was sure to develop between Zayo and her unborn foal? It was going to change so many aspects of their history. And Booralta said this foal would find its father.

Zayo and Tarahnaha were despondently detached during the lunch feast; it did not matter, because Mehlanahr had suddenly found a horde of admirers—all shapes and sizes, male and female, young and old. The coronation, however, was only the beginning of the celebration. The king and his adjutant were required to spend the next week traveling all over Equestra, learning the placement of each citizen, and how they all work together to make their society flow. This would begin first thing the next morning; the remainder of the afternoon was to be spent at Mehlanahr's house with his parents and sisters.

After waiting what seemed to be a long time after the feast for the Caballians to pick up their mess and get ready to depart from the palace grounds, Zayo ran up to his adjutant (who was in the depth of a conversation with Booralta and Oorahno), and said, "Mehlanahr, we have so many places to go. Where should we begin?"

Mehlanahr heard the king's rather excited approach; he turned to face Zayo, saying, "Yes, we have so many places to go today." He was about to say something else, but stopped himself short from what he was saying, realizing that the expression in Zayo's eyes was extremely distant. It was then that Mehlanahr finally acknowledged the seriousness of what had happened; it had started to faze him the night before, but he had pushed it aside—now he could not. He remembered everything that had happened at the passage the day before Kayloor was killed. The royal family had looked so happy as a young mare was given the blue vest of an engineer. No stallion had claimed her yet, but a rivalry started among some shoemakers, who found her ability to troubleshoot and repair transports very intriguing. She was going to be a valuable asset to them, because they molded many basic parts for transports. Her abilities touched everyone's hearts deeply, as if nothing could stop Kayloor's progress as their king. He had been a very dear king, loved by all Caballians, and seemingly hated by no one.

Wehrahn had mentioned something about Dahrohd's treachery being responsible for the treason behind the king's murder. Dahrohd had been a decent shoemaker and forgemaster. What had happened? Did his heart burn every time he raised the forgefire, and did the red flames remind him of Kayloor for some reason? It was all so senseless, Mehlanahr thought. A king with so much purpose to his life and reign to die such a senseless death. The adjutant began to weep aloud, knowing that the recent history of the royal family had been touched by so much death. Tarahnaha's parents...Neeyahr... Ahmehlaha...Kayloor. It was obvious that Zayo did not quite know what to make of it, and that Tarahnaha was so right in her desire to wish for a fast death for herself. Her entire purpose for living had been seemingly stripped away from her. Was it the ancient wars returning to them, though in a slightly different form? The wars would certainly return if the entire royal family were destroyed.

Booralta and Oorahno looked at each other, both of them feeling some of the sorrow which was affecting Mehlanahr. They knew what the adjutant knew, but with everything that had happened in the last two days, the young engineer was suddenly much closer to the royal family than most other Caballians. Mehlanahr could not explain, even if he wanted to, the depth of the friendship which was binding his allegiance to young Zayo. The young king had saved his tail (which may seem like a trifle), but when combined with the fact that Zayo later excommunicated two citizens who had tried to make Mehlanahr the victim of the old system (as it had been under Kayloor), it was suddenly the most important factor weighing against the young adjutant's conscience.

Zayo's approach was painful right now, but seemed as if it would be more beneficial in the long run; the Caballians would grow out of it. Mehlanahr shook away his tears, and tried to compose himself to say something; he quickly lost his courage, and decided to wait until later in the week.

Zayo removed the crown from his head. "Mehlanahr, can we begin making our plans?"

"Right away," the adjutant replied.

Booralta and Oorahno watched them trot away. Booralta knew that Zayo was not yet ready to accept his father's murder; when Zayo had matured some more, he would learn the motives behind Dahrohd's treachery. All would be revealed to Zayo in due time; Booralta knew it would not be too late to save their people from the wars.

Their planning went very smoothly, and so did the first few days of their travels, getting acquainted with all of the Caballians after the coronation. Zayo's enjoyment of his task removed him from thoughts of his father. By this time, they were more than a thousand miles north of Tokanar, traveling along the banks of the Sea of Serenity, and visiting everyone who lived in the fishing villages. They were called fishing villages, but it was actually a large collection of farms, most of which bordered on the Sea of Serenity. It was a beautiful rural part of Equestra, so expansive that the majority of Caballians lived in that rough geographic vicinity. There were many advantages to living there, but one of the greatest disadvantages was that there was one hospital located towards the center of the fishing villages, and that the residents who were far from it had to go without the availability of advanced medical care. There were a number of doctors scattered around who each operated independent offices, but a hospital was sometimes the only answer.

After making their way through this vast expanse, they entered the sloping mountain range, which separated the fishing villages from the extreme outskirts of Wateloqua. Wateloqua is the largest city on all of Equestra, having approximately ten thousand residents (Tokanar had roughly eight thousand five hundred), and occupying the largest geographic area. Like Tokanar, Wateloqua had a great abundance of plant life in it. Buildings were placed sparingly, in a random manner; they were connected in Wateloqua by circular roads that radiated from the center of town, which was landmarked by the oldest existing forge on all of Equestra. The circular roads were connected by a number of roads that criss-crossed across town, but there was no true pattern to those, because only one of them reached the central forge. Tokanar, for comparison, was more of a grid than anything else.

In their ancient cities, the Caballians had developed problems with noise, air, and water pollution. For the normally active Caballians, it had disastrous effects: their general good health had disappeared, taking with it their ability to run fast, and their lifespan was lowered to two hundred years. It was then, well over eight million years ago, that the king, whose name was Polihdahr, decreed that all of the cities would be destroyed and rebuilt as spacious parks, and that the chemists would begin immediately to work on finding a new, clean fuel source for their transportation.

After Polihdahr managed to slowly win the favor of the people, Equestra was painstakingly rebuilt as a garden planet. Their monetary system was abolished, including all barter, and Polihdahr decreed that the only way one person would be more important than another would be through the quantity and quality of the work they performed to benefit others. This was the beginning of the Caballian system of honor, and further enhanced the empowerment of the adjutant as a citizen of high honor.

Polihdahr was the king for almost 150 years before his death. Up until the day he died, he strove to mold the society to his visionary dream of what it should be. The last important decision he made was to redesign the educational system so that it had more substance and structure to it, and so that it would provide for the needs of every individual foal. The purpose of Polihdahr's changes were to nurture the student's natural abilities and interests in a combination of classroom studies and a hands-on apprenticeship. According to Polihdahr's plan, each foal would be brought to a nearby school on his seventh birthday for placement in a class with up to five other foals of the same age and a historian (teacher). They would receive formal classroom instruction until the age of twenty, at which time, the student would be tested by either his historian or a shaman to locate his exact strengths. Pending the results of such an exam, the student would be placed with a citizen of appropriate standing for his apprenticeship to a specific vocation. The apprenticeship would last until the student's passage at the age of thirty-five, at which time the student is formally and ceremonially accepted as an adult citizen.

Shortly after Polihdahr's death, the Caballians finally discovered a new fuel source in philinium, which burns very cleanly. When philinium is used as a fuel, the waste is converted—by necessary process to operate the transport—into a vital plant fertilizer. This achievement helped to speed up the regrowth of Equestra, and enhanced the development of Polihdahr's new cities.

Many thousands of years passed before Equestra was again lined with natural beauty, and the Caballians finally accepted the importance of Polihdahr's vision during his reign. The pollution disappeared, and their normal lifespans were regained.

GROWING UP

Once past the mountains, Zayo took his turn operating the transport. They had traversed the mountains and river a good hour after breakfast, and were hoping to reach Wateloqua by lunchtime; that was actually a half-day ahead of their schedule. Originally, they had hoped to reach Wateloqua by suppertime on this the fourth day of their travels. They had reached a lull in their conversation, so they each had their thoughts to themselves as they neared the intriguing city of Wateloqua.

Mehlanahr set there thinking about Zayo and the situation he was in. The young king was so absorbed in his duties and the importance of their trek that he would not mention his father unless someone else spoke of him first; even then, Zayo did what he could to keep all conversations about his father as short as possible. He just did not want to talk about it; he was not quite ready to deal with it. Booralta had been so right in what he said about Zayo.

Zayo set there thinking about what things would be like when his brother was born. It was an event that would certainly change his life as the king of the Caballians, especially because his brother would be a king at his birth. Zayo felt sure that Pleeyedraha would be the proudest one of all.

When they were about thirty miles outside of the city, Zayo slowly and instinctively slowed the transport so that it was now traveling at one hundred miles per hour; he had to because of their proximity to the city. As he set there thinking about his brother, he somehow slowed down even more so that they were only traveling about forty miles per hour; Mehlanahr said nothing to him about his slow operation of the transport, because it gave the engineer a chance to listen to the engine on a slow throttle. Mehlanahr's ears suddenly perked up, and he reached over and grabbed the brake to slow the transport down some more; when they had slowed down to about fifteen miles per hour, there was a sudden explosion in the engine of the transport. When it jerked to a stop, they were first thrown back into their seats; because of Zayo's height, his head cracked against the crossbar behind them. The cushioned seats acted as coils, and flung the occupants out of the transport. Zayo somehow found a safe landing spot in the middle of the grass, even though the strike on his head had knocked him unconscious. Mehlanahr fell into some brush, and was scratched up, but he felt all right; when he saw Zayo lying unconscious, his only thought was to see to the safety of the king. He felt some bruises, and knew that he could not carry Zayo the eighteen miles into Wateloqua. Mehlanahr knew right away that the philinium converter had exploded, therefore rendering the transport inoperable, including the emergency beacon.

Mehlanahr saw a trace of blood on the back of Zayo's head. He did not feel the rain, but it started to pour. After a few moments of some careful thinking, he thought he saw a transport moving towards them and Wateloqua. His gaze followed the transport for a few endless moments. When the transport stopped beside him, a handsome young mare deftly climbed out, with her black mane and tail sweeping across her bay fur. She wore the deep blue vest of an engineer, the same color vest that Mehlanahr would receive upon his passage. "Sir," she said, spotting the collar immediately, "please let me help you with your transport." She looked down at the ground, and saw Zayo laying there in his injured state.

Unable to hold back the tears, he replied, "If you would be so kind as to bring him to the hospital, our people would be most grateful."

She saw the shock in his eyes, and asked, "What happened?" as she noticed the blood on the back of Zayo's head.

"The converter in my transport exploded. He banged his head on the support bar, and we were both ejected. He is unconscious, but he continues to breathe."

She carefully picked the king's head up from behind, cradled it in her bosom, crossed her arms over his and around his chest, and held him up securely while Mehlanahr lifted his lower body, and they placed him in the back of her transport. As they got into the transport, she asked him, "You are to become an engineer and not a doctor or nurse? I find that rather surprising."

Mehlanahr regained his wits just thinking about his work. "I am a hyperspace student. I am currently studying with Oorahno."

"Everyone has been speaking of you, and what your placement will be on your passage."

"You are rather modest and outspoken from someone who lives in Wateloqua."

How did he know I live in Wateloqua? she wondered to herself. "I am a programmer," she replied. "Does that help explain my frankness?"

"What is your name?"

"I am Yehtraha." He is depressed, she thought, so I will tell him something that will hopefully make him laugh. "I must admit, that many of my friends and I pull straws to see who will have the advantage in gaining your attention after your passage, because it is spoken that you will be the most sought-after husband."

"'Most sought-after'?" he repeated, hardly believing his ears. "First of all," and he mumbled to himself, She speaks with fire, "mares can prod me all they wish. Secondly, I will do the choosing, and I will not choose a conspiring mare to trust. And last but not least, I am far from being ready for such a thing. I have my king to serve, my internship to finish, my passage to plan for, and a challenge to file."

Her voice laughed, but her eyes were amazed, which did not go unnoticed. "A challenge to give you higher ranking upon your passage?"

"I am to challenge Oorahno," he replied, his eyes smiling but serious.

"Forgive me," she replied, suddenly becoming as serious as he was. "I spoke silly words to you in the hope that it would enlighten what seemed to be a depression, but I misjudged your character. You are serious about your work and your life, and your fortitude will make you an unrivalled citizen. It is obvious that you will succeed in your challenge."

They entered the city at that point, so their conversation did not continue past Mehlanahr's thoughts. He had never before met anyone who was able to judge his character so quickly without any knowledge or forethought (Booralta could not be included in that category.) Even Tarahnaha still had many doubts about the success he was told he will have, despite Booralta's explanations.

He thought again about what Yehtraha had told him about her friends all pulling straws, and in trying to view it from her point of view, he realized how funny it actually was. But he dare not tell her that now, because he knew full well the purposes behind a stallion's position. He would not be prodded by anyone, not even Booralta, into making such a choice. Despite that, he was somewhat confused.

A short while later, they arrived at the hospital. Yehtraha ran from her transport into the hospital, while Mehlanahr went to have a look at Zayo, who almost seemed to be sleeping. Before he had a chance to think, a doctor and a nurse had come out. Mehlanahr quickly backed out of the way as the doctor checked Zayo and secured his head better before they were to move him.

Once she felt it was safe, she had Mehlanahr, Yehtraha, and the nurse carry the king into the hospital. Mehlanahr and Yehtraha were sent out of the room by the nurse, and the doctor began to examine Zayo much more carefully.

The nurse was sent out to speak with them about the doctor's preliminary diagnosis about ten minutes later. "Sir," the nurse said, quickly getting the adjutant's attention, "his majesty will have to remain here overnight."

"Why?" Mehlanahr asked. "How seriously is he hurt?"

"He fractured his skull."

"It does not take all night to mend a broken bone."

"Heptalaser is being performed on his head, but he is also suffering from a concussion. The treatment for a concussion usually requires twenty-seven hours. If all goes well, he will be able to leave here first thing in the morning."

Mehlanahr was obviously upset; he finally remembered himself somewhat and said to the nurse, "Please make sure that the best care is given to Zayo."

"I will tell Fooraha of your request." The nurse turned and left.

"Fooraha...Fooraha..." the adjutant mumbled to himself. "What would Pleeyedraha say now about a doctor I never heard of?" Yehtraha gasped, and he realized she was still setting with him. He told her, "You do not have to stay. I thank you for your willingness to help us when we truly needed it."

"What I did was nothing," she replied. "The road you were on is usually only used to travel to and from collected gatherings like passages, but my father's special request is what put me there today. I will not leave, because you are distraught over what has happened; someone to talk to will be best for you."

Her message sounded rather familiar to him, but in his present state of mind, he could not directly place it. "Stay if you wish, but that does not mean that I shall talk."

"Are you going to set here all day and night waiting for Zayo, or are you willing to leave this place until tomorrow morning and let your mind rest some?"

"If Pleeyedraha were tending to Zayo, I would not think twice about leaving; it would be the first thing on my mind. I know nothing of the credentials of the doctor who is tending to him."

Yehtraha tried to swallow her shock, but it was a very hard lump in her throat. "Sir, if I were to obtain some philinium from the refinery where your father works, I would be afraid to use it because I know nothing of his work."

"What are you saying, Yehtraha?"

"I am saying the same thing you are saying, Sir. Let me tell you a story about Fooraha."

"Please do," he remarked, wanting to hear what he could about this unknown doctor.

"She has always been known by all in Wateloqua as the best doctor alive on this part of Equestra."

"She is a healer?"

"There is only one healer alive, and she wears the black vest. After Pleeyedraha earned the black vest, Fooraha was placed with her for a spell to learn the ways of a healer, because of her talents as a doctor. She mastered the necessary skills to become a healer, also. Because she was so talented and did not have to work quite as hard as Pleeyedraha did to become a healer, she lacked the necessary belief in her own ability; that is why she is still a doctor."

"How would you know all this about Fooraha?"

"Do you or do you not believe what I am telling you?"

He felt rather ashamed for asking this question, and it showed. "I know that you would only tell me the truth, and what would help me, Yehtraha."

"Good. Can we leave the hospital?"

"I should tell Tarahnaha what has happened, so that she will not be surprised when we are delayed in our return to the palace. Is there a visiphone here?"

"Behind you, to your right."

He saw it, and went and used it. He did not go into any more details than he had to, actually being abrupt with Tarahnaha. He quickly returned to Yehtraha, where he said, "I should tell Fooraha that I am leaving, where I am going, and that I will be back here in the morning."

"Do whatever you feel you must," she said dryly. "You should know what your responsibility to Zayo is."

"Then I should stay here with Zayo?"

"Let your conscience be your guide in your decision. I told you what would be best for you to do, but you do not have to do it. You can be obstinate and stubborn, and totally ignore what I am saying to you."

He could hardly believe what he was hearing. "Why are you now talking to me like that?"

"I could not help but overhear your conversation with Tarahnaha. Why were you so curt with her?"

"I did not want her to get too upset about Zayo by talking about him very much. It will be a long time before she becomes accustomed to the fact that she is a widow."

"She has a son, and is very concerned about him. Would you deny her the right to know what she needs to know about Zayo? Or do you treat all others as if they were logarithms?"

Who does she think she is? he thought to himself. I do not know of any other Caballian who was ever so frank with me. Unless it is because that is the way she is, and she cannot help herself one bit. Finally he told her, "I hope that one day your frankness does not cause you any grief for what it is worth."

"Sir, what do you mean by your words?"

"Obstinate and stubborn, perhaps, but I do not have to put up with your chiding."

"Why are you talking to me so harshly when I was trying to help you escape your depression? You wear the collar of an adjutant, yet you speak to a citizen in that way!"

"Then why did you say anything to me about being curt with Tarahnaha?"

"If no one says anything to you about it now while you have the chance to think about it, then it will hit you like a shoemaker's hammer when you return to the palace. Being an adjutant is not a foal's game."

He must have been standing there for a good five minutes thinking about her words before he replied, "Yes, I am very upset over what has happened to Zayo. Neeyahr and Kayloor both died untimely deaths. What did young Zayo do to deserve such a fate?"

"Who is to say that he was not meant to be our king now? Or were you not listening to Booralta's prophecy at the coronation?" She saw his despairing glimpse, so she continued, saying, "Leave this place behind you for now. Zayo is in very good hands."

He told the nurse that he was leaving, that he would keep her advised as to where he would be, and that he would return in the morning. He finally left the hospital with Yehtraha, although he still did not realize how Yehtraha had learned Fooraha's story. But now, he did not care to know. It was not that important.

He was too upset about Zayo.

Mehlanahr and Yehtraha went to her house—she was living with her parents even though she was a thirty-eight year old citizen—where they were going to eat lunch. When they walked in, they saw her father, Gahrahnoor, who had come home for lunch from his job as a chemist. He was a handsome stallion, having black fur and hair, and brown eyes. "Father," Yehtraha said, a trite smile on her face, "I am finally back."

Gahrahnoor saw Mehlanahr but not Zayo so he said, "Sir, where is his majesty?"

"He is in the hospital," Mehlanahr replied. "The philinium converter in my transport exploded, and Zayo struck his head against the crossbar. He will be fine, though, once he recovers from his concussion. The hospital will let him go tomorrow morning."

Gahrahnoor looked at him rather gravely and remarked, "Is Fooraha tending to him?"

"Yes, she is."

"He is in the best hands outside of Pleeyedraha. Yehtraha," he said to his daughter, "I will prepare lunch for the three of us. You have time enough to show him Raivo's forge, where he can see to his transport needs."

"Yes, Father," she replied, and the two of them left her house.

Leaving the house, Yehtraha did not lead Mehlanahr to her transport, but began to walk away from it. Mehlanahr was thinking of asking her where the forge was, but before he did, he looked past her to see where she was leading him. She was walking towards the building that was closer to her house than any other, and was also much larger than any other forge on all of Equestra. Because there was only one shoe on the door, the forgemaster (who was Raivo) no longer crafted shoes or any other forge product, although his associates kept up with the demand for all shoes and products. Mehlanahr remarked as they neared the door, "Why is this forge so big?"

He truly has never been to Wateloqua, Yehtraha thought to herself. "This is the central forge," she replied. "Raivo lives here."

Mehlanahr suddenly remembered: this was the only ancient forge still in existence on all of Equestra. Mehlanahr thought that because of its age, the forgemaster could not use it to make shoes.

She led the way in, and after waiting for a few brief moments, a stallion (who seemed to be as old as Ahrkoor) came to greet them. When he saw Yehtraha, he smiled. "My dear Yehtraha," Raivo remarked, "how are you today?"

"Quite fine," she returned.

He looked at the adjutant, and saw that Mehlanahr was gazing at him. "Sir, I hope that you did not come here for shoes. I no longer have the strength for such tasks, and my associates have left for lunch."

Mehlanahr suddenly returned to himself. "I was told that you have a philinium converter available; I have need of one."

The shoemaker's eyes were full of questions. "Converters are crafted to last the lifetime of the transport. Why would you need one?"

"My converter exploded."

"By the three moons, how were you not killed?"

"I was bruised some, but Zayo struck his head against the crossbar, and has a concussion."

"Is his majesty in the hospital?"

"Yes. Fooraha is tending to him."

Raivo appeared to be relieved when Mehlanahr mentioned Fooraha. "Let me get that converter for you," he remarked, and left them standing there for a few minutes. He returned with a new one, and handed it to Mehlanahr. "Sir, may your journey continue to do well."

"Zayo will be in the hospital until tomorrow. What fortune can there be in that?"

"Sure, Zayo's journey as our king is somewhat imperiled by what has happened to him today. However, I wish for your journey to continue to do well. Many stallions envy your sudden fortune, and I doubt if there is a mare alive who would not wish to serve you. A king with such a good adjutant is sure to become a prosperous and favorable king."

"You are not a shaman."

"Perhaps not, but shoemakers are always referred to as the best philosophers among our people. Some are better disciplined thinkers than others, and it shows in the quality of their work."

"Who is the best thinker among the shoemakers?" Mehlanahr asked, sure that Raivo would explain to him why Ahrkoor wore the black

67

vest as a shoemaker, something he forgot to ask Ahrkoor when he and Zayo were in Tokanar.

"Ahrkoor is a very good thinker, which is why he wears the black vest. But it is not Ahrkoor—it is his understudy. I tell you, Mehlanahr, he is even more of a throwback to an ancient shoemaker, central forge or no. Shoemaking is the most ancient craft which still thrives in our society. Surely you have met Jayexeeyo."

"I met him in his house."

"I have seen him work before, and I tell you, I have never before seen a shoemaker who seems to learn by watching the movements of the flames in the forgefire. Our modern technology is not what he exactly cares for; he only works with transports because so many people depend on them. But like what the historians say of the ancient ones, he seems to have his mind bonded to some sort of magic."

Mehlanahr could not believe what he was hearing; he lived for technology, it being the most important aspect of his life. "I trust this is not a jest, Raivo."

"Sir, when you next need shoes, I recommend that you seek out Jayexeeyo. Watch him while he works, and you will learn about a stallion with as much potential as you possess."

As they walked out of the forge, Mehlanahr was already thinking of when he would next need shoes. He would insist on having Jayexeeyo make his shoes...Jayexeeyo, a stallion who had chestnut fur, chestnut hair, and black eyes. In his mind, Mehlanahr could easily picture Jayexeeyo muscling over the forgefire; he had always admired others who worked hard, especially shoemakers.

Mehlanahr and Yehtraha returned to her house for lunch. Lunch was ready for them; Yehtraha set down right away next to her father, but Mehlanahr did not. Instead, he said to the older stallion, "Sir, I am to share your table with you, yet I do not know your name."

"Forgive me," he replied, "I am Gahrahnoor."

"Gahrahnoor, I am honored." He set down with them.

"Sir," Gahrahnoor added, "eat as much as you wish. There is plenty more."

Mehlanahr had been reaching to grab some vegetables, but he stopped in his tracks and remarked, "Please call me Mehlanahr; I much prefer it."

"Whatever you wish, Mehlanahr," he chuckled.

The adjutant proceeded to take some food, so Yehtraha said to her father, "Will Mother be stopping for bread when she comes from the hospital?"

"Yes," he replied, "we do not have to stop."

Mehlanahr gulped his food, and put his hands down. "I did not realize your mother worked in the hospital."

Yehtraha gasped. "Forgive me," she said, "Fooraha is my mother." He comes from Tokanar, she remembered.

Mehlanahr was a bit surprised. Gahrahnoor changed the subject and asked him, "Who are you studying with?"

"Oorahno," he replied.

He thought about it for a moment, and then said, "What sort of work have you learned as a hyperspace student?"

"I have mastered all drive mechanisms."

Yehtraha could not hold back her surprise. "What is it like in outer space?" she asked.

"I cannot say that I liked it, nor can I say that I disliked it. Outer space was where I had to learn, and it presented a true test of survival to me. I used my available time to work on my own personal theories and designs."

That must be where he obtained his challenge to Oorahno, Yehtraha thought to herself. "What sort of theories have you been expostulating?"

"Dimensional travel much faster than the speed of light."

Gahrahnoor and Yehtraha both thought the same thought when Mehlanahr said that to them: that he was addicted to his work. "Then you spent all of your free time with your personal work," Gahrahnoor remarked.

"That is not true. Oorahno will not allow me to work myself sick."

By the time they finished lunch, Mehlanahr learned that Gahrahnoor was the analyst at the refinery in Wateloqua, and that Yehtraha had been working with her father for the past two months programming computers there. She had gone to the fishing villages early in the morning so as to deliver a new computer to the refinery there; it had much needed up-to-date programming in it, and was going to be used in a place that was still working with a very antique computer, one that was over a thousand years old. She had been returning from this when she found Mehlanahr and Zayo after their accident.

EQUESTRA

Yehtraha had already planned on spending the remainder of the afternoon in the refinery with her father. Mehlanahr decided that he would join them to visit the refinery, and look into more possible applications for his new fuel.

COMING HOME

Gahrahnoor, as the analyst at the refinery, was the administrative chief as well as the most talented among the chemists in Wateloqua; he and the chemical refiners all wore orange vests, and were collectively called chemists. There were many variegated distinctions among the chemists (as there were in all other fields), but all of them wore orange vests except for the master chemist, who operated the refinery in Laerion.

Chemists could be analysts (like Gahrahnoor and Toorahgo); they could be refiners (who were chiefly responsible for purifying things like philinium); they could be miners (who were responsible for locating and procuring necessary things like raw philinium and/or other chemical elements, as well as various metals and waxes); or they could be classified as guards (who were responsible for distributing everything produced by a refinery). Guards, however, were just as important as were analysts and miners; they had to see to the distribution of all chemicals and drugs to doctors, all raw metals had to be given to shoemakers, and philinium had to be dispensed for all transports. They also retrieved broken-down transports, bringing many of them to forges for new parts.

Gahrahnoor was responsible for the administrative work behind all of the guards' doings within Wateloqua; the master chemist moved them around and placed them accordingly to where they were needed. There were a number of guards placed at all gates of each city so they could make sure that no one left without enough philinium to make it back, because of the fact that the emergency beacon was known not to work without any philinium.

EQUESTRA

Approximately five hundred years after Polihdahr's death, the guards (who were already responsible for gate duty) were also given the charge of keeping track of all citizens who went in and out of the gate, so that people would be much easier to locate if they were really needed. After there were a number of problems with students who were not yet citizens because their mentors could not find them, they were thereafter all required to travel with identification until their passages. The punishment for being caught without identification was set at a clipping, because it was that important to the Caballians. Almost a thousand years later, when there were so many truant students that the king could not clip even half of them, the caucus (which was called by the king) decided to allow the guards to help king fulfill his duty, and all be armed with sabres so as to do so. The whips were given much later, after someone tried to interfere with a guard clipping a truant. Ever since that time, guards were always known to be commissioned servants of the king.

The refinery in Wateloqua was quite close to Gahrahnoor's house; it was two buildings past Raivo's forge. Mehlanahr spent most of the afternoon with Gahrahnoor and five of the refiners, discussing with them production possibilities and applications of the fuel he was planning on using in the new spaceship he was building with his new engines, the one which he would use to challenge Oorahno. The adjutant already knew that it would work in his engines, but he needed to know more possibilities of applying it to everyday life on Equestra.

During the remainder of the afternoon, Mehlanahr learned more of what Yehtraha had been doing at the refinery, and just how important it was that the likes of chemists, engineers, and shoemakers work with each other to achieve optimum results. It was an exciting afternoon for Mehlanahr, and he learned more being there than he ever learned from studying the records and hearing others' stories during his field trip.

When they were finished at the end of the day, the three of them walked back to Gahrahnoor's house together. It was raining, so they walked quickly, not wanting to get too wet, even though it felt good. Gahrahnoor walked straight into the house.

Mehlanahr stopped in front of the house, gazed at it blankly for a moment, then set down in the wet grass and the rain, staring at the house. His mind was a million miles away, thinking of the coronation. When Yehtraha realized that he was not right behind her, as he had been for most of the walk, she turned around to see him setting down in the grass. She did not know what to say to him, or even that she should say anything to him, so she left him there, and went into the house.

Yehtraha found that her mother was already home and had begun to prepare the supper in the kitchen. She watched her mother for a few moments, feeling that her mother was more elegant than ever; it almost seemed as if her mother had found a spark of confidence. Apart from that, Fooraha was an elegant mare, having the same bay fur and brown eyes as her daughter, but having golden hair. She wore the green vest of a doctor, something that she was very proud of. Yehtraha finally walked into the kitchen, poured herself some water, and set down. "Mother," she said, "what can I do to help Mehlanahr?" Although they were colored very similarly, Yehtraha's features and build were more similar to her father.

Fooraha's sparkling eyes glazed upon her only offspring, and she smiled. "I am sure that Mehlanahr is having a difficult time adjusting to his new position as the adjutant. He is probably blaming himself for Zayo's injury. Right now, during their travels, he has sole responsibility for Zayo, and neither of them is a citizen. Do you truly believe that Mehlanahr was prepared? He understood that much during the coronation when he questioned Zayo's choice. But understanding something and accepting it are two different things. That was the biggest lesson I learned when I thought I was ready to become a healer."

"That is not quite what I meant. He seemed to accept my help quite graciously, but his mind is lost somewhere. I tried to reach out to him, and to have him think about other things, but it was not successful. It is enough that he is so consumed with his studies that he is going to soon challenge the master engineer, but he is also so consumed with his duties to Zayo. It seems so unhealthy. Even as we speak, he is setting outside, getting wet in the rain."

"He is facing a very difficult time in his life right now, if I am right. Every person goes through it just before their passage; you went through it. He has to learn how to reach out and connect with everything and everyone. Today was testing enough on him for such questions to come up to him. I tell you, Yehtraha, I do not think that anyone would wish to be in his position."

"Perhaps I should have left him in the hospital to work it out for himself."

"What was best for him at the time?"

"I thought I did the right thing."

"Then you must hold fast to your beliefs, and what you believe is right and wrong. It is up to others to judge whether or not they accept what you feel is true. Sometimes you are all by yourself, and the only comforts are your thoughts. But more often than not, you find out that others believe as you do, because you were taught as they were taught."

"He became so absorbed in the workings of the refinery today that I am sure I did the right thing."

"He must be allowed to work through his struggle, so that he will see that everything he does is interdependent with everything everyone else does. The new adjutant needs our support, but especially now, he must also be granted the freedom of some privacy."

After their conversation, Yehtraha left her mother, and went and set in the workroom, a small room which was used for tasks like making candles. She had brought some warm water with her, and she set down and set to making some candles. They needed them, because they did not have any enough for the spare room, which was where it was expected that Mehlanahr was going to spend the night.

A half hour later, just as Fooraha was finishing all preparations for supper, there was a knock on the door; Gahrahnoor answered it. When he saw Mehlanahr standing outside, soaking wet from the rain, he was somewhat disturbed, and quickly ushered the adjutant into the gathering room. "Sir, feel free to groom here."

Mehlanahr smiled at him. "Truly a friend would dare to tell me such a thing, Gahrahnoor. But before I accept your offer, I would like to speak with Fooraha and Yehtraha."

"Come with me," he said, and he led Mehlanahr into the kitchen, where they found Fooraha by herself. Gahrahnoor left as quickly as he had entered, leaving Mehlanahr with the doctor.

"I am pleased to finally meet you under clearer circumstances," he told her. "I give you my thanks as well as the appreciation of the royal family."

Fooraha smiled at him. "I am pleased you decided to join us for supper."

Mehlanahr saw the amount of food, and remarked, "Truly three people could not eat so much food."

"Perhaps not, but I was concerned as to why you were detained. It would be impolite to ask straightforwardly."

That is the secret of Wateloqua, he thought to himself, and smiled. "I did think about visiting someone else for supper, but I must apologize to Yehtraha before I can eat."

"To apologize?" she wondered.

"Yes. Please, Fooraha, where is she?"

"I am sorry, I should not question you like that. She is in the workroom. You may show yourself there."

He wonderingly looked at her, and remarked, "Where is the workroom?"

She pointed at the back door of the kitchen. "At the end of the hallway through that door."

"Thank you," he remarked, and he left the kitchen.

Yehtraha heard his light footsteps as he entered, and she looked up from where she was setting to see him there. She stood up and said, "Mehlanahr, I am glad that you have joined us for supper. I am glad I have this opportunity to apologize to you."

"Why?" he wondered.

"I was too pushy in trying to get you to leave the hospital before...it was not my place to do such a thing. When I saw you set down outside, I thought you were truly upset by my words. Honestly, I had not intended any harm. How dare I infringe upon your relationship with Zayo and Tarahnaha? Sometimes I say things without any forethought."

Mehlanahr could hardly believe what he was hearing. He suddenly felt a little strange, and could not help but gaze upon her; he quickly shook it off. "Just as you speak the truth now," he said softly, "you spoke the truth earlier. I was so upset with myself and concerned about Zayo that I had forgotten all about what matters the most, and that is that our people truly would all forsake what they can to help Zayo, some more than others. Raivo helped to shed some light on it for me—he is such a great stallion."

Yehtraha noticed the look in his eyes, and was pleasantly surprised. She smiled, and could not help but shake her tail a bit. "I also love the forgemaster. Much of my early years were spent listening to his stories and wisdom. It was almost as if I had found myself another grandfather, and I was always very proud of my friendship with him."

"I must apologize for venting my frustrations and aggravations on you earlier in the hospital. Thank the moons for your persistence. If you had not stuck with what you felt was best, I would have moped around the hospital all day, and I did not need to do such a thing. I learned so much more about possible applications for my work. I am also beginning to understand how you are very much like your father, who is a very impressionable stallion. I am grateful that I met such a wonderful family to help me when I became out of sorts over an accident which I know was a fluke."

"All other families here are just as good as we are. It is the way of residents here in Wateloqua, that we look after everyone here, and be concerned about everything of any importance. That is why Raivo is such an important forgemaster, even though he no longer makes shoes."

"I am grateful for the chance to clear up many aspects of both my professional and personal life."

"I can understand the professional aspect, but the personal aspect? Something about that eludes me."

"Zayo and I have traveled quite a bit within the past few days, and I have met so many people. Tokanar was more than I ever thought it was, and I live there. The fishing villages were an incredible experience. We will finish our trip here, then continue on to Laerion. The rest of the trip will be easy, because I was finally forced to integrate my whole life with everyone I met; doing that, I realized that the time for me to claim a mare will be right on the day of my passage. I thank the moons for the people that have taken the time to assist me through this difficult part of my life."

"Who is she?" Yehtraha asked, but quickly remembered he was forbidden from making a claim until he wore the vest of a citizen.

"Surely all will find out when the time is right," and he smiled at her.

At that moment, Gahrahnoor walked into the workroom; he had heard Mehlanahr's answer, but he thought Mehlanahr was speaking about his work. "Are the two of you hungry?" he asked them.

"I am famished," Yehtraha replied.

"I feel awful," Mehlanahr stated, "looking as I do when I am asked to set at your table." His mane and tail were still dripping wet, and his fur was all matted; he looked completely unkempt.

"It is only rainwater," Gahrahnoor replied. "The worst it will do is make you somewhat uncomfortable."

"Would you rather eat by yourself?" Yehtraha asked him.

Mehlanahr finally said to them, "I will eat now. However, after supper, if one of you would be so kind, I need to be brought back to my transport so I can change the converter and bring it into town so Zayo and I can begin as early as possible tomorrow morning."

"Why not leave the transport to Raivo and obtain a new one?" Gahrahnoor asked.

"That would take several days. Besides, I already retrieved a converter so I can fix it myself."

"What about yourself?" Yehtraha asked.

"Since I must go out into the rain to fix my transport, then I should wait to groom until I have finished all my necessary duties."

"You will come back here when you are finished," Gahrahnoor told him, "take care of yourself, and spend the night. Then, Fooraha will bring you to the hospital in the morning, and you can get Zayo discharged from her care right away."

After a delightful supper which was more pleasant than lunch because of Fooraha's presence, Gahrahnoor brought Mehlanahr to his transport. Gahrahnoor had seen engineers work on transports many times, and he knew that such work as changing a converter took at least forty-five minutes for a handy engineer; some of them took well over an hour. The chemist set himself down to wait, and watched Mehlanahr as he worked.

When the adjutant stopped his work after ten minutes, Gahrahnoor immediately thought he had run into problems. "I will call for Yehtraha to meet us here," he remarked. "She can give you a hand with that."

"Why should you disturb her needlessly? I am almost finished."

"What more do you have to do?"

"Watch," he remarked, and he climbed into the operator's seat, and started up the transport very smoothly and quickly. "I had to make sure it started up. Otherwise, I would have had to pipe through some philinium."

"I thought you were studying astrophysical engineering."

Mehlanahr laughed at him. "Gahrahnoor, just as all chemists are chemical engineers first before specializing as guards, miners, or refiners, I am a mechanical engineer first and foremost. When I mastered the basic mechanics of transports and all appliances, I moved onto astrophysical propulsion, which I have also mastered. My talent is in propulsion. Why should I have any difficulty with a philinium converter?"

"It pleases me to see you in such good spirits; you were so upset by Zayo's injury earlier."

"You would have also been upset."

"I am glad you did not stay in the hospital."

The remainder of the evening sped by once Mehlanahr had groomed himself. Gahrahnoor, Fooraha, and Yehtraha had never seen him so properly groomed before; Yehtraha had first met him after he had been standing on the wet road in the pouring rain.

After breakfast the next morning, Fooraha and Mehlanahr each drove their own transport to the hospital. Zayo was so glad when he saw his adjutant; the king had already eaten breakfast and groomed himself, and was ready to go.

EQUESTRA

Late in the sixth day of their travels, Zayo and Mehlanahr finished crossing the Sea of Serenity, and were a distance north of Laerion, which had a population of 7,100. Since it was well past suppertime, and it was dark and nearing bedtime, they decided to sleep on the side of the road in the yellowgrass, and in the rain. After eating and grooming as much as possible under the limited light of the transport, they fell asleep. Not long afterwards, a second transport pulled up and parked near theirs. A stallion stepped out, lay down in the grass near them, and went to sleep.

Zayo was the first to wake up in the morning, and when he noticed the much older stallion was sleeping with them, he was surprised. Zayo thought he was about four hundred years old just from looking at him; he was actually three hundred and ninety-seven. The stranger suddenly woke up, only to find the young king looking down upon him. Zayo saw the smile in his brown eyes, and was not too surprised when the stranger said, "A very good morning to you, your majesty. I trust you slept well, and that you are feeling fit."

"Good morning," Zayo returned. "You know who I am, but who are you?"

"I am called Karayo."

Zayo had heard the name before, but could not place where, or how, Karayo was connected to their society. "Please tell me why you stopped to be with us," and he set down next to Karayo.

"You did best not to search for an abode last night. I knew you would not reach me, so I had wished to extend the hospitality of my house to you, although it has not been much during the past month since my wife died. I live about two miles south of here."

"It is quite a change to meet someone who is not from Wateloqua."

"I do not know of anyone who did not appreciate the quiet hospitality of Wateloqua. However, in Laerion, people are sort of the opposite. Professionalism is the unspoken code here, and hospitality is most of what people talk about. Tokanar has plenty of each, but it is quite a change for you to see the differences Wateloqua and Laerion present to our society."

"How did you know where we were?"

"I am a shaman."

"Like Booralta?"

"Yes and no. We are both shamans, but very different from each other in what our specialties are. Dehnohraha is also different from Booralta and myself. As historians, we three are trained in the historical aspects of our society, each of us mastering certain epitomes. Historians who serve as teachers have mastered a various number of social aspects, and are taught to teach the young ones. Once in a while, a historian learns enough of all disciplines to be called master of an epitome. When that happens, the historian becomes an administrator in a school, because he is still at a stage where his epitome does not cover the spiritual aspects of all phases of life. But once his epitome expands to include spiritual, metaphysical, and realistic, and he shows that he can use it to educate all of our people, then he is recommended to become a shaman."

"You have not yet explained how the shamans are all different."

"I was just getting to that part, your majesty. In order to become a shaman, the person must show that he is not only cognizant of, but possesses complete knowledge of, all spiritual interactions within our social order. He must know what will happen to everything and everyone else through even a seemingly innocent event such as a birth or a death; whether or not a person grooms, or eats, or sleeps; what decisions a person makes in his personal and professional lives. Booralta, in knowing what is happening now, has the very powerful epitome of foresight; he can accurately predict many future events. Dehnohraha also knows what is happening now, but her epitome is to relate what she knows to everything that is happening now; without her, it would be as if the right side of your brain were completely separate from the left side of your brain—no feedback between the two sides, no learning. I also know what is happening now with full knowledge; however, my epitome is to relate what has happened in our past history with what is happening now, and to provide explanations for what seem to be events happening out of the blue."

"Why does Booralta wear the black vest?"

"Because his epitome is the strongest, the broadest, the most far-reaching. His talent is the greatest."

Before Zayo could ask him another question, Mehlanahr awoke, and set up. "A very good morning to you, Sir," Karayo said.

"Thank you, and good morning, whoever you are," Mehlanahr replied.

"I am Karayo. Both of you must have breakfast with me this morning." Once at the shaman's house, Karayo cooked up a steaming pot of oatmeal with brown apples, something which Zayo thoroughly enjoyed, because he loved brown apples.

Just before lunch on the eighth day, they left the southern gate of Laerion, and had the prospect of finding a rural house soon to be in time for lunch with yet another Caballian. But it took them about a half hour longer than they had hoped, and by the time they found a house, they were at the point of giving up on lunch. Mehlanahr's knock on the door was opened by an older mare with off-white fur, a black mane and tail, and dark, foreboding eyes. "A very good afternoon to you, your majesty, and Sir. You have arrived just in time for your lunch. Please come in and eat before the stew loses its flavor." She led them to the kitchen, where she deftly served up three piping hot bowls of stew along with some very fresh bread.

Their amazing hostess did not speak as they ate, although Zayo kept glancing at her, with the feeling that he knew her, but he could not place it. Once she finished her lunch, they were also finished, and she quietly got up and cleared the table. She put the remainder of her cleaning duties aside for the time, and she set down with them again. "I know that you are much more comfortable now with some good food in your stomachs; it is my pleasure to have such guests for lunch. Questions are to be asked, and I can answer them for you."

Zayo felt so comfortable with her that he forgot to ask who she was, as he had done with every other Caballian he had met so far. Mehlanahr was amazed that she seemed to know what they were thinking. It was obvious that she lived alone, and had never been married, although she was quite old. "You are a good cook," Zayo commended.

"Thank you, your majesty," she replied.

Zayo saw how she did not look directly into his eyes when she spoke to him. No other Caballian had ever done such a thing, especially in Laerion. There must be a reason for it, he thought. And he thought. Until he realized that she was blind. And then he knew who she was, and why he felt so comfortable with her. However, Mehlanahr proceeded to ask her, "What is your name?"

She was about to answer him, but Zayo put his hand on her arm to stop her; she was so surprised at his action that she said nothing. Zayo then told Mehlanahr, "This is the shaman Dehnohraha."

Mehlanahr was taken aback, but Dehnohraha chuckled a bit. "How did you know?" Mehlanahr asked him. "You told me you never met her before."

"Mehlanahr, I noticed her blindness. What other Caballian is blind?"

"Physically blind?" the adjutant queried. "Or spiritually blind?"

"Your knowledge pleases me," Dehnohraha told Mehlanahr. "You are proving why Booralta spoke so highly of you at the coronation. So much has happened to your life this week, and you are assimilating into what you are capable of doing. Most people would not have been ready for so much all at once; they would have needed at least a hundred years."

"Does that mean the personal or professional aspect?"

"The polishing of each, and the interaction of both. Continue what you are doing, and your passage will become one of the most-remembered aspects of Zayo's reign."

"You do not have Booralta's ability of foresight," Zayo commented. "How would you know of what will happen?"

"It does not take the gift of foresight to understand such things. When you see as much of what is happening as I do, then some foresight is available without the added gifts of Booralta."

"Then what do you call it?"

"I call it psychological influxes. The greatest aspect of my talents is psychology; I understand it very well, and know how to use it and work with it. I do it so much and unthoughtfully that all doctors and historians call me the 'psychologist' publicly."

"How is my mother?"

"She is doing well, but is eager for you to get home safely. The news of your injury has her somewhat frustrated."

"I did call her from the hospital the morning I left, and I told her I was fine. That was not enough?"

"Zayo, in the wake of your father's murder, every single thing looms a dark shadow over her soul."

"Did I tarry too long with Gahrahnoor's family?" Mehlanahr asked her.

"I daresay not. You acted quite admirably. You have created many friendships which will last your lifetime, and those with people from Wateloqua, who sometimes have difficulty assimilating with those from Laerion and Tokanar—that is the drawback to their way of life. But every city has its drawback. Remember your gifts and talents, and always utilize them. Patience will be yours by the time of your passage."

"What are you referring to by 'patience'?"

"The engineer."

Mehlanahr was shocked that she knew. But, then again, she was a shaman. This was important for her to know.

The week quickly drew to a close for Zayo and Mehlanahr. On the morning of the tenth day, they arrived back at the palace. As soon as they got out of the transport, Mehlanahr said, "Zayo, wait a moment."

Zayo remarked, "Would I be wrong if I said that I knew something was bothering you throughout our trip?"

"No, you are quite right. And it was not the accident. It was mostly about my duty as your adjutant, and secondly about being an engineer. You see, Zayo, if the guards had not been permitted to do such a thing as clip a truant, then you would not have been hurt."

"Guards are commissioned servants."

"But why them, and no one else? What makes them so special? And if you spread such a commissioning to all, then it will probably lead back to the wars. Zayo, I believe you should remove that power of authority from the guards."

"Things seem fine the way they are."

"The guards were commissioned because the king could not handle all of the clippings. After meeting all of our people, I believe that such a power should be limited to the throne."

Zayo thought about it for a long minute. And he realized the validity of what Mehlanahr was telling him: why did the guards have such commissioning above all others? "I have only one aide who has sworn his life to help me, and he is the only one who should be so commissioned to help me."

"Zayo, I was not asking such a thing."

"Perhaps not, but it makes sense. I will abolish that law for good, Mehlanahr."

"Thank the moons; you will not commission me to bear a sabre!"

"Hold it a moment," the king told him. "AI empowered you to be my adjutant at my coronation. During that time, you were required to use my sabre to shed your blood for me, as I shed my blood for you. I am going to empower you to carry a sabre and to carry out whatever clippings are necessary in your duties to the throne. If you so choose, you do not ever have to use the sabre. What if I am unable to carry out a punishment for some reason or another besides my death before my brother is capable of doing so? Then you would be so empowered to punish someone. But as long as I am capable, I am going to carry out all punishments."

"What about the truants? What if there are too many?"

"If there are any such truants—and there are hardly any—then they will be clipped at a caucus the next immediate morning, within the twenty-seven hours."

"Then the gate guards will have less to do—or more, depending on how you view it."

"Guards have abilities and talents as chemists which are not used enough for our society. People should be responsible enough to keep an eye on how much fuel is in their transport, and to leave word as to where they are if they are not in their usual place. I am going to remove all guards from gate duty."

"Zayo, this is going a bit far."

"Why should people be policed when they all deserve respect and honor as citizens? If we commit them to such a trust, then I am sure that the number of petty crimes will drop to none. Our people are all highly intelligent, and know and understand what is expected of them."

"If there are more people like the guards who tried to clip me, then how could they be deserving of such a sacred trust?"

"Who is to say they are not? The guards that tried to clip you were probably irritated enough at having to perform their commissioned duty in the wake of the king's murder...their frustration was probably what made them act as they did, and not listen to me. My father tried to prevent such crimes from happening again by his forgiveness, but they will only be stopped completely if we get to the cause. Our people are peaceful. Why should citizens with peaceful demeanors be forced to fulfill such a nasty duty as clipping another? They will trust each other more if no one had such a responsibility."

Mehlanahr smiled. "Zayo, I presented my opinion to you, and pushed you in all possible directions, so that you came up with your own opinion and reasoning."

"That is why I wanted you to be my adjutant. I am going to abolish that law today, and have the analysts reassign the guards so they can focus more on research in the refineries, which will help you with your new fuel for your spaceship. Then, I will commission Ahrkoor to craft a sabre for you, one that will be given to you on your passage."

"Right now, Zayo, your mother is waiting for you." They raced into the palace, where Zayo quickly found his mother in the kitchen preparing enough lunch for three people; it was obvious she was expecting someone. Her hands were empty, and she had stopped what she was doing for a moment when her son came running in and grabbed her in a tremendous hug.

"Zayo," she exclaimed, "thank the moons!" She eagerly returned his hug.

"Mother," he replied, "I have missed you terribly. It was fun being with Mehlanahr, but not the same as being here with you."

"What made you think such a thing?" she wondered aloud.

"Oh, Mother, when I visited Dehnohraha, and I realized that there is a special feeling of closeness among close relatives. Things are going to be so much better when my brother is born!"

"You think so, too, or did Booralta say something to you?"

"Booralta said nothing except for my 'sibling.' But so many people agree that I am going to have a brother, because of family history. Out of all of my ancestors, there has only been one who was not a stallion."

Tarahnaha laughed at him, glad that his zealousness was fully back after the testy coronation. She truly loved her son very much, the first manifestation of her bond with Kayloor. There was another, but the first was the most special. Zayo was starting to follow in the ways of all of the greatest kings of the Caballians; Tarahnaha saw it, and was very proud of him.

The king soon found out that his decision to abolish the ancient law required the approval of all Caballians at a caucus. Since there was to be a passage the next day, he was required to present it to them there. After a new citizen was given his vest by Booralta, everyone approved Zayo's decision.

BEGINNINGS

The day on which Zayo was crowned marked the first day of the first year of his rule. Days were to be historically counted after that: the first year would count up to four hundred and fourteen days (which is the length of an Equestran year), then the historians would start referring to the second year of Zayo's reign. Birthdays were known by the number of the day on which the person was born. Since the numbering began all over again with a new king, the historians had to refigure all of the birthdays of all students and interns so that they would greet their passage on the correct day. The same was done for Mehlanahr, who needed to know what day was now his birthday for his passage.

The Caballians had a system of referring to what day of the nine-day week it was. The day of Zayo's coronation, the first day of the year, was called firstday. Secondday followed, as did thirdday, and fourthday, all the way through ninthday. The day after ninthday was always called firstday again.

It did not matter that Kayloor had been killed on ninthday: no matter what day of the week he died on, the day beginning a new king's first year always began a new week, and was called firstday. That was how the Caballians properly recognized the current king's reign.

Toorahgo's family moved into the palace before Zayo and Mehlanahr returned to the palace. They were given two of the three spare rooms which were in the palace. One of them was for Ehspreeyetaha; the other was for Toorahgo and Lahrohnaha, and would also house Andrux until he was old enough to sleep on his own, which was usually at one year of age. Besides the other spare room, there was one other empty room, and that was the room that Mehlanahr would be staying in.

On the day that he and Zayo completed their travels, Mehlanahr moved all of his belongings from his parents' house to the palace. His new room was the room that had last been slept in by Neeyahr; it had been built to house a couple. Once Mehlanahr had taken over that room, there was only one spare room left in the palace, and that was not very good, not with two families already living there and the potential for another quite soon. Tarahnaha and Zayo therefore decided to build on a much larger addition to the palace, consisting of eight more rooms: one for Andrux, one for Zayo's brother, one for the second adjutant, and at least three for any other offspring. That would leave them several spare rooms, and would hopefully last a number of years.

The normal length of a Caballian pregnancy is fifteen months, or one Equestran year. At the time of Kayloor's murder, Tarahnaha was six months pregnant, with nine months before the expected parting. Now, as she entered her eighth month, her condition was obvious to the naked eye. This foal was her last physical connection to Kayloor, something which she accepted quite gracefully.

Since she had been examined in the hospital on the day that her husband was murdered, she had not been to see Pleeyedraha. She finally brought herself there twenty-eight days later, on firstday of the fourth week of Zayo's reign. She was greeted by Pleeyedraha, who had her student with her. "Good morning, your highness," the master healer said. "You are looking well."

"Good morning, and thank you, Pleeyedraha. I feel quite well. How are you?"

Pleeyedraha's eyes became very sad when Tarahnaha asked her that question. "I am not coping very well, Tarahnaha. What did he do to deserve such a fate? The king who was like a son to me because of our bond...shall I try to deal with it, or shy away?" She broke down into tears, and Tarahnaha took her in her arms. "I can mask my pain under my work, but how long shall it last?"

"The nights have grown very cold since he was taken from me, but there is a tremendous warmth inside of me. It is a very different feeling from when I was pregnant with Zayo. Zayo had his active spells, and his sleeping periods, but it almost seems as if this one does not sleep. It is not as active as Zayo was, nor does it seem to sleep, but it is a constant

86

presence that reminds me of how much I truly loved Kayloor. I used to think that Zayo could easily serve as our king without even an adjutant to help him, mostly after he finished school. But now that I feel such differences, I wonder if the foal inside of me is truly a greater blessing than anything else Kayloor did for our people. I feel you will rest easier when Zayo's brother is born."

Pleeyedraha did not know whether to laugh or cry when Tarahnaha said that to her. After making a noble attempt to collect herself, she said, "Tarahnaha, I would like Tahrmaha to examine you."

"Pleeyedraha, I did not mean to upset you so much by my talk of the foal, just that it has me excited now."

"No, Tarahnaha, that has nothing to do with it. I want her to gain more experience examining patients as she is learning how to properly diagnose as part of her studies."

Tarahnaha laughed, and hugged Pleeyedraha. "Then it would be a pleasure to have Tahrmaha examine me." The two of them left Pleeyedraha, and went into an examining room with the door closed.

Finally, Tahrmaha spoke to Tarahnaha. "Your highness, forgive me for not speaking earlier; it was not proper for me to do so until you were properly assigned to my care and released from Pleeyedraha's charge. Now that you are 'officially' in my care, good morning."

Tarahnaha was instantly charmed by the young mare's protocol, and a smile spread across her face. "Good morning. Pleeyedraha has been teaching you well."

"She tries, but sometimes I am so afraid of encroaching upon her position as the master healer that I do not take as much charge as she wants me to. She treats me as her equal, but I can never understand why."

Tahrmaha was so determined in keeping herself in a right relationship with Pleeyedraha that she was holding herself back in her studies. Tarahnaha eyed her for a moment, and observed a very beautiful young mare—not just because her dark brown fur, golden hair and brown eyes were well coordinated, but her face was perfectly chiseled, al of its features in perfect synchrony. Surely she would be a most extravagant mare by the time of her passage, but she was still young. "Pleeyedraha is right," Tarahnaha told her. "You show her abilities and talents which can be used for the benefit of our people, yet you are afraid to do what you can and learn what you can. You remind me of Fooraha."

"I am studying to become a doctor, not a healer."

"Why limit yourself when you have the obvious potential to become a healer? Pleeyedraha wants you to tap into everything that you are, and become what you are meant to be."

"She always tells me I have so much to learn, though I know that I have mastered nearly all disciplines required of doctors. When I finish the microsurgery, I will have mastered all."

"You are only twenty-eight years old, and yet you have subjected yourself to such a depressive state of mind? It seems to me as if you have learned nothing yet."

"What more could there possibly be?"

"Think of your passage, and what sort of placement you wish to attain by that time. Try to make yourself as good as Pleeyedraha believes you can be, even if you become the best on all of Equestra."

"Pleeyedraha is the best-"

"Pleeyedraha is very old, and is growing tired. Fooraha did not fully earn the right to wear the vest of the master healer. If you can succeed where Fooraha did not, do it. Pleeyedraha took you as her student at her great age because you showed so much talent at the age of twenty. Who knows, but that you may even become a superior healer to what Pleeyedraha is? That would be a great honor for our people."

"I do not wish to undermine Pleeyedraha's honor."

"You would never do any such thing, I am sure. If you earn the black vest, it will be because of your own merit. If Pleeyedraha chooses to publicly acknowledge your talent as being superior, then she would embrace a higher honor and wisdom. She needs you to help her achieve it as much as you need her to become a healer."

"Then I must continue in my best work here."

"Definitely. And within the next seven years, you will learn many other things, including the honor of being chosen by a stallion."

"Pleeyedraha's assessment of your cunning was so true."

"Kayloor and I were very much alike in our thoughts and aspirations."

"I do not remember much from when I met Zayo during his travels, but he seemed to be like you." She was curious about the new king.

"He may seem like that, but he is a dormant fiery story, ready to spring into action. He is extremely headstrong and full of guile, as well as being very zealous."

"Natural dominance," she remarked. "That is why he had to excommunicate the criminals."

"He always does try to push himself to the front of everything."

"That must be why he would not forgive them. He does not want anyone to ever undermine his authority as our king, because it is his talent above everyone else."

"Respect should be his, especially after everything he has had to live through recently. Pleeyedraha has certainly told you very much about Kayloor."

"She tells me about Kayloor, and about you; about Kuhoor, and about Ahmehlaha; and about Neeyahr." Tahrmaha stopped herself, and proceeded to examine Tarahnaha. She took her time, observing many aspects of their combined health through her scanner. Finally, she told the queen mother, "I have never seen such a healthy foal. If you so desire, I can confirm the sex."

"That is not necessary," Tarahnaha remarked. "It will be heir to the throne, so I know it is to be another son."

"As you say," Tahrmaha told her, shaking her head slightly.

"Why are you shaking your head?"

"You are the first pregnant mare I have ever seen who did not want any confirmation about your foal apart from its health. But as you say, it is not necessary. The foal is also Kayloor's heir."

Tarahnaha smiled at her. Almost immediately, she liked Tahrmaha very much.

By the end of the fourth week, Mehlanahr had finished all of the final details in the plans to build a new spaceship with the new engines he had developed. The new fuel he wanted to use was something Mehlanahr called feruminous pentoxade because of its atomic dynamics. It was a molecule which, before Mehlanahr began his work with it, was only a theorized possibility. Mehlanahr extrapolated many ideas as to how to obtain it; his enhanced theories were presented to the master chemist for refining. When the master chemist gave his firm (and glad) approval that included the usage of all resources in the refinery, Oorahno also allowed Mehlanahr usage of any and all materials and any and all mechanical assistance he would need; in short, Mehlanahr had all resources at his fingertips.

Oorahno himself had had a long, hard struggle to achieve the position of master engineer, although he knew that he would be foolish if he failed to publicly recognize Mehlanahr as being the superior engineer. Oorahno now knew that Mehlanahr would succeed in his challenge, and that the adjutant would earn the black vest on his passage, something that no other citizen had ever accomplished in remembered history.

EQUESTRA

The new engines were small, each one of them not much larger than a transport's engine; the ship would require three of them. They were set around a long cylindrical vacuum, which had a port to the rear outside of the ship; this cylinder was to serve as a channel for the propulsion. The hull of the ship was to be covered with a sealed layer of ferrulous penticoroxide crystals, which would protect it from all damage during dimensional transport.

Dimensional transferal and transportation is an extremely intriguing concept, mostly because of how physical objects are moved through energy. It was not as if the ship was going to physically travel from point A to point B or wherever else they planned on going; the principle was to exponentially transpose the combined energy of every single aspect of the ship's atomic dynamics by the speed of light. It was similar to removing an electron from one ionic atom and using a power with enough force of energy to move it to another atom, thereby ionizing it with its added energy. The necessary energy would be created by the implosion of a predetermined amount of feruminous pentoxide; the implosion would be so big and so fast that its energy waves would seem to momentarily rearrange the matter of the ship, carry it while it still existed as energy, and when it dissipates, the ship would seem to Arematerialize." The energy of the dimensional transfer was so great that it created a temporal wormhole, thereby enabling the ship to travel much faster than light. It was a fantastic theory which Mehlanahr was bringing into reality, one which was so vastly different from all other types of propulsion ever used by the Caballians.

The construction of the ship was completed by the end of the seventh week, and it had every single Caballian talking about it (word spread fast through the shoemakers!) At that time, the ship was forced to undergo six days of mechanical testing to make sure that all systems operated properly. Those six days were just about as flawless as could only be dreamt of. By the time they were over, Mehlanahr was told to take the seventh and eighth days off for himself. What he was expected to do was prepare for ninthday (the seventy-second day of the year) which, although it was the day before his passage, was the day on which they were going to test his new ship. The historians called it the final test of his accumulated training during his apprenticeship to determine his placement in society; it was a test given to every person the day before their passage.

Oorahno had nightmares of failure, though he quieted himself with the simple reminder that it was a great honor to die performing one's duty, as he would be doing. It would be a complete dishonor to himself if he were to refuse to accept Mehlanahr's challenge, because he would be forced to give up his black vest to the winner of a technical and mechanical debate among all engineers who felt themselves worthy enough to wear the black vest; as a public spectacle, such a debate would bring great shame upon Oorahno.

He would rather die giving Mehlanahr a true chance to earn it.

The day before Mehlanahr's ship was to be tested (two days before his passage) Booralta went to the hospital for a checkup. Booralta went there at least once a week for a checkup; however, he intended to see a different doctor on this day.

When Booralta arrived at the hospital, and was brought to Pleeyedraha's office by a nurse, the master healer had her student with her. "Good morning," he offered them both; it was mid-morning.

Tahrmaha smiled at him but said nothing. After a moment, Pleeyedraha said to him, "Good morning, old friend. How do you feel?" She offered a grand smile for him.

"In what context?" he asked her in reply.

Physical or spiritual, she thought to herself. "In whatever context you feel is important."

"One shall overpower the other, and do away with it completely. Then my spirit will be at peace."

"When will this come to fruition?"

"In two days, on the day of Mehlanahr's passage, the great circle of the three moons will transmit its power."

Pleeyedraha turned to Tahrmaha and told her, "You should get into something far more interesting than our conversation."

"Pleeyedraha," she replied, using her usual soft voice, "I request to remain."

Pleeyedraha's shock showed in her eyes. "Of what assistance could you possibly be?"

"I wish to gain more insight into gerontology, and the affectations of the physical and spiritual."

Booralta stood there, bemused by it all, but he said nothing yet. "Why should you be concerned about such things?" Pleeyedraha asked her student.

"Is it not true that a healer must understand spiritual affectations as well as physical, and what better patient to study than the master historian who is a revered spiritual leader?"

"Tahrmaha," she said dryly, and took a deep breath, "I cannot believe that you are taking charge over me like this. It goes against everything I taught you, against everything I thought you were to become. Perhaps it is not true, and you are not fit to become a healer."

"Just because you have your own viewpoint as to what I should become when I earn my citizenship, that does not have to agree with what I truly am, and what my heart is telling me is necessary for me to learn." She shook some tears out of her eyes, and walked out of the room.

"Booralta," Pleeyedraha said, despairing, "what did I do? What did she do? Why are things suddenly so wretched between us?"

"Tahrmaha is correct, I fear," he told her. "As a Caballian, she has a right to know when something of such vital importance to our people like my death is impending. As your student, she has the right to learn."

"Kayloor was taken from us, and I have nothing else. Tahrmaha is beginning to mature, and I am also aging."

"She is no longer a filly of twenty years old, so part of your teachings to her must be that she is equal to you and to all others."

"She is trying to move too fast as an intern."

"Is Mehlanahr moving too fast as an engineer? His challenge to Oorahno is to be carried out tomorrow, and I have never seen such excitement among our people. When Tahrmaha shows such maturations, you must allow her to grow as much as she possibly can, and even then give her as much breathing room as she truly needs."

"She is moving so fast that she thinks she can become a healer overnight. I have never seen such impertinence."

"No, Pleeyedraha, it is not impertinence. You have properly diagnosed her talents, as I did when she was twenty, so you must allow her to learn as much as she can while her talents are fresh. If the molds are not made properly now, then she will never amount to much of a doctor, for she will have lost all of her ambition because you thwarted it. You must let her ambition carry her as far as possible, even if it enables her to become a greater healer than what even you are. Perhaps she even has the ability to properly empower Fooraha into grasping all and becoming a healer as she should have."

"Why are you also chiding me?"

"No one is perfect. But you cannot always circumvent your weakness. You must work with your weakness, and turn it into your strength, just as you did when Kayloor was new. That is why you became a healer. Now, if you would excuse me, I came here today with the specific intention of speaking with Tahrmaha."

"She knew this?"

"No. But she knows herself, and that is a very important asset in her favor."

"She knows herself better than I know myself? How can that be?"

"If you had any idea as to what she shall become, you would not question me so." He walked out of her office and down the hall, and found Tahrmaha in her own office. "Tahrmaha," he said, standing in the doorway, "may I come in?"

She looked up at the shaman, and he set down in a chair next to hers. "Pleeyedraha is right—why should I come between two friends such as you are?"

He shook his head at her, and replied, "I came here to speak with you today."

"But if you are to die in two days, why waste your time?"

"You are incredible," he replied. "When forced to react, you react as any master would. But when you stop to think, you always doubt yourself."

"I am only twenty-eight years old. Pleeyedraha is more than four hundred years older than me...I have plenty to doubt."

"What do you doubt the most?"

"That I truly have the potential to become a healer, because Pleeyedraha fights it so much."

"Do you remember the questioning that took place during Zayo's coronation?"

"Yes, but that has nothing to do with me."

"Pleeyedraha is doing to you what our people did to Zayo when they questioned him."

"Our king would rather be dead than mistrusted in such a way, and I do not blame him one bit," she remarked, letting down her guilty guard for a brief moment.

"Oorahno had the same difficulty with Mehlanahr when the adjutant presented a greater talent than Oorahno had ever seen, far surpassing even his own."

"What are you saying?"

"I am saying that the seeds for our future have been sown, but are having difficulty taking root."

"I do not see how I fit in."

"No, but in ten years or so you shall."

"Am I so right to be so contrasting?"

"You are maturing. Do you remember the first time you examined Tarahnaha?"

93

"Her foal?"

"Yes. How healthy was she when you examined her?"

"Remarkably healthy."

"You scanned for everything, including the sex of the foal?"

"That is standard procedure. Whether or not it is disclosed to the mare is up to her."

"What did you think after she left?"

"I thought that my scanner was malfunctioning, and I had it inspected by an engineer to make sure it was not."

"It was no malfunction. Tarahnaha is truly going to be surprised, as are the rest of our people except for you because you know."

"Everyone is talking about it as if it were the greatest thing...Zayo's brother, indeed!"

Booralta had to laugh at her. "I could tell you so many more things, all of them about your future, but what would it matter?"

"Things like what?"

"The stallion that will eventually claim you and the great number of foals you are going to honor him with. How you will fare in your test as a healer. The places you will go, the people you will befriend, the healing you will help perform, and the things that will happen to you. So much, Tahrmaha...you will become a living legend, just as Mehlanahr is."

"What does it matter?"

"Not very much right now. But one day, such things will be the most important aspects of your life. Protocol prohibits me from telling you much more, apart from the fact that you will become a renowned mare, one who our history will always remember highly."

"Then it does matter quite a bit."

"Indeed it does."

"And I truly understand protocol. You have told me as much as you possibly could about my future only two days before you know that you shall leave our people. Is there a historian with foresight enough to be trained to follow in your ways, or will you not be replaced?"

"When the time is right, someone with the talent will surface."

She smiled at him. Tahrmaha was one of the few Caballians who truly understood the role the shamans played in their society. She even knew a bit more than Pleeyedraha.

There was a time when no Caballian bore a blaze upon their forehead. More than fourteen million years before Zayo, they had been a warring people, in the midst of a great number of civil wars. The wars started when they were at their population peak—approximately five hundred and fifty-nine thousand—and they ended up lasting nearly thirteen thousand years. There was no leader for all. They lived in thirty-two different sects, each operating as a city-state with its own beliefs and laws it chose to follow. The Caballians were omnivores who fought for food and territorial rights. Their squabbles were not serious when they first began, but as time wore on, aggressions grew more hostile, and the killing began in earnest. Intermarriages posed many problems as to what laws foals should follow.

Over fifteen hundred years after they began to kill each other, they focused their fighting on depriving each other of food. A great number of meat sources quickly became extinct, and most plant life was burned. These food fights lasted well over eleven thousand years, and their once-prosperous population had dwindled to a mere one hundred and forty-seven. But all of the Caballians, save for one stallion names Pehsoorad, were too proud to admit that their fighting would soon make the Caballians themselves extinct. They were all afraid; Pehsoorad, who had been known by the fact that he was a friend with everyone, called a meeting of all of the remaining Caballians and proposed a different idea to them: that they work together to survive, instead of being so selfish. He was so afraid of how they would react to what he was telling them that he thought for sure that he would be killed that day. Amazingly enough, he discovered that they were all very tired of what the wars had done, and they were not only willing but eager to work together toward a common goal. Because of Pehsoorad's willingness to step forward and show them all what they were doing that was wrong and help them overcome it, he was unanimously elected to be their moderator; he would be the one called if fighting did break out again. When Pehsoorad finally died, it was also unanimously decided that his only offspring, his son, would continue in his stead because he best knew the ways of his father. This has continued in their family through all generations to Zayo.

An angry stallion rose against the moderator almost two thousand years after Pehsoorad. The moderator, Hehlehf, had invoked some ancient magic, and ended up murdered (the only other ruler to be murdered besides Kayloor), but left a pregnant widow. When his offspring was born, it was during the eclipsing circle of the three moons, an occurrence in which the three moons line up and block the light of Omistu. Hehlehf's offspring was different in one aspect from all others: he had a blaze upon his forehead; he was named Doorehlo.

EQUESTRA

The day after Doorehlo's birth, a shaman by the name of Caidehlos persuaded them all to accept the foal as their moderator, and also to have a general protectorate placed on the foal's life. Because of this protectorate, Doorehlo's title was changed to king before he died. Additionally, because the Caballians were so frustrated at the fact that such treason could be carried out against their moderator, treason was also made a severe crime, and excommunication was instituted as the only appropriate punishment for crimes like treason and murder. The twenty-seven hour statute of limitations on punishments was added later on at another caucus under another king.

MASTER ENGINEER

As the analyst at the refinery in Tokanar, Toorahgo assisted in the development of Mehlanahr's ship. The master chemist, Taelo, who usually works in Laerion, temporarily moved to Tokanar with his wife two months before Mehlanahr's passage, because he and Toorahgo had to work together with Hohnoor and other researchers to make it a reality for Mehlanahr.

Not far from the refinery in Tokanar was the engineering plant, where is where every single one of the engineers works out of. Some of the engineers are assigned to work in each refinery, but they must answer to Oorahno over any chemist. Those engineers are responsible for working with both the chemists and the shoemakers, and handle any and all mechanical problems with local equipment and transports; they are somewhat like location workers who must answer to their main office. Oorahno and a number of other engineers worked at the plant on research and in teaching the students (who were required to make a number of location studies, including in space ships). It was at the engineering plant that they constructed the new ship of Mehlanahr's design. Part of the plant was a hangar for spacecraft, which housed the three other craft in use, and which was where they built the new ship. There was a tremendous door leading to a small outdoor clearing, which they used for takeoffs and landings of their craft. Once the new ship passed all of its preliminary tests, it was wheeled outside, and was ready to fly.

The following Caballians were to be a part of the maiden crew: Oorahno; Mehlanahr; Taelo; Toorahgo; Aldoor, Keelahr, Dehrahlax, and

Tehsoorahlaha (all engineers); and Pakoor (the doctor). In the other space ships, various other personnel were required; since this was promising to be a very short event, they decided to do without any unnecessary extras.

Oorahno was the eldest of them all, being three hundred and eighty-two years old. Aldoor was three hundred and fifteen; Keelahr was three hundred and one; Toorahgo was two hundred and ninety three; Dehrahlax was two hundred and seventy-one; Tehsoorahlaha was two hundred and sixty-two; Pakoor was three hundred and forty four; and Taelo was two hundred and ten. It was almost a haunting idea to them that the master chemist was the youngest citizen, and that the youngest member of their crew was challenging to become the master engineer.

Each person was assigned to a specific duty when they boarded the ship. Mehlanahr assigned himself and Oorahno to monitor the engines of the ship, because they were the only ones who had some knowledge of their inner workings. Taelo and Toorahgo were to specify the fuel distribution through the computer network, which was hooked up to all systems. Aldoor was assigned to atmospheric control. Keelahr was assigned to gravitational synthesis. Dehrahlax was the navigator, and Tehsoorahlaha was assigned to any and all communications, including in-ship. Pakoor was, for all technicalities, assigned to work in the sickbay. However, since no one was currently sick, he remained with everyone else in the main room of the ship.

All systems were started up and inspected for performance just before they were to take off from the ground: everything proved to be operating smoothly and efficiently, so they took to the air. Once they were in the air, they closely monitored all systems. Before they prepared for dimensional transport, they scrutinized all systems again, only to find that everything was running very smoothly; this made the whole crew happy.

Oorahno then announced that Mehlanahr's test would be a "short" trip to Akthura, because it was part of the nearest neighboring solar system. The flight trajectory was programmed into the navigational computer by Dehrahlax. Then, Taelo and Toorahgo had the computer calculate the required amount of feruminous pentoxade for the planned trip. Mehlanahr double-checked their calculations, only to find that they had the computer programmed correctly. The main engines were turned on, and in very little time, they were ready to be fired. The ship was placed in the required position.

At that moment, instead of checking the systems, Oorahno spoke to them all. "My friends, if I were to check the systems now, I know that they would all prove to be flawless. Booralta knows that this mission is going to succeed; all that remains is to actually experience what dimensional transport is like. I cannot change procedure and say do not inspect the systems before firing main engines, but I would if I could." There were some laughs before he continued. "It gives me great pleasure that I have been challenged by Mehlanahr. I do not know if I can say that he has been the ideal student," and he smiled at Mehlanahr, "because he was always testing me, and he was truant from his studies for a whole week while he ran around Equestra with Zayo." There were some more laughs. "Mehlanahr has superior knowledge, and I must present this to our people tomorrow at his passage." He paused, then continued. "Fire the engines." There was a slight shudder and a flash of light, then the engines died. "What happened?" Oorahno asked Mehlanahr. "What is wrong with the engines?"

Mehlanahr could not hide his smile. "Master," he replied, "the engines fired. You should be confirming our coordinates with Dehrahlax."

"If I knew better, Sir, I would say that the engines started up fine, but shorted out."

"The engines had already been started up," Mehlanahr said, realizing that Oorahno was rather excited. He inspected the path they had followed. "The shudder was caused by a combination of the firing of the engines and an ion storm which we passed through, and the flash of light was all we were able to grasp of the tremendous amount of energy transpired during the dimensional transferal."

Oorahno gazed at him. "Sir, if I may say so, such an ion storm would have severely damaged any other ship we have." He turned to the others and said, "Check all systems for ion damage."

A short while later Tehsoorahlaha replied, "All systems are within normal operating parameters."

Oorahno found this hard to believe. "Dehrahlax, what are our present coordinates?"

"Point one three by point eight seven," the navigator replied.

"Tehsoorahlaha, show me our surroundings on the view screen."

Looming right before them was a strange planet. Aldoor ran some quick tests, then he said, "Master, it is Akthura."

"Land the ship," Oorahno requested.

The ship landed, and they all got out, and immediately began to visually inspect the outside of it for any possible damage, of which they could not find any. It was not long before they were back on Equestra, and the ship was readied to be towed to the palace grounds. The test was over.

EQUESTRA

Very early the next morning, as the royal family was getting ready for breakfast, a loud commotion was heard outside; some people were obviously there for Mehlanahr's passage, and something was going on. Zayo grabbed his crown and sabre and told his mother, "I am going on ahead to breakfast. There is much more excitement than usual."

"We are only waiting for Mehlanahr to finish grooming. I will come with the rest."

Zayo walked out of the palace, and guessed that from the size of the crowd, all Caballians were already there. In the distance, he saw a strange craft being towed toward where the platform was. Zayo realized it was Mehlanahr's ship, and he went running up onto the platform. He got everyone's attention and cried out, "What is all this ado? I have never seen such excitement on the morning of a passage."

"Breakfast is ready," someone yelled out to the king. "What is taking your family so long to join us? You are a bunch of sleepers!" This created a loud uproar of laughter among the crowd.

Zayo laughed along with them and replied, "We are waiting for Mehlanahr to be ready. How could the breakfast feast be eaten without him?"

"It is common knowledge that he challenged Oorahno yesterday," someone else yelled out. "Since that strange craft is being towed to the platform now, it is obvious that the challenge was successful. No other has ever challenged for the black vest before they were forty years old. That is what the excitement is about!"

Zayo looked towards the palace, and saw his mother and adjutant coming. "I am famished!" the king cried out. "Where is all the food that is rumored to be here?!"

Mehlanahr heard Zayo pushing their excitement, and saw him on the platform, so he ran up to his king's side. There was an uproar of laughter from the crowd. He was immaculately groomed, his hair was perfectly braided with rainbow ribbons, he was wearing his collar, and his composure was fully confident. "You cannot be hungrier than I am," the adjutant told Zayo. "I thought that the food would have already been distributed."

Zayo saw the expression on Mehlanahr's face, so he quickly decided, I am going to play a game with him. "Mehlanahr, while all of our people were out here working hard to distribute the food, you were so busy grooming yourself. What could be more vain?"

"How could I be given the vest of a citizen if I am all matted?"

"That is vain, is it not?"

100

"Yes, Zayo, it is vain. But I want everyone to see just how much of a perfectionist I am in my work."

"There is only one way to solve this problem. Since I met you, I have been trying to determine what the color of your fur is. Tell me what the color is called, and we can all eat breakfast."

Mehlanahr looked at his oddly-colored and dappled fur, and he realized that Zayo was playing a foal's game with him. The only way to win it was not to play it, but to start a superior game. He replied, "Zayo, I truly wish I could answer that question."

"That is ridiculous," the king replied, knowing that the adjutant had caught on. "Tell me. Please."

Mehlanahr frowned. "Zayo, out of all of our people, there is only one who knows the true color of my fur, and it is not me. It is the mare I wish to claim after I am given a new vest."

This statement did the trick, as all of a sudden, there were a bunch of whispers going around about who the mare might be. "Mehlanahr, you know this game very well. However, you never made a mention of it to my mother or myself. What is your game plan?"

"I just told everyone: I am going to claim the mare that properly identifies the color of my fur."

"Many mares will probably say something like golden brown," Zayo remarked; the whispers suddenly ceased.

"Gold is not the base color," Mehlanahr replied. "That would be an incorrect answer."

"Excellent food for thought, and an excellent game. It is time to eat."

Breakfast was soon finished; there was not much of a mess to be cleaned up, and it was quickly done away with. Zayo donned his crown, and went back up on the platform. They were all silently waiting for him to speak to them, so he began. "Never in my life have I ever seen such excitement at a passage!" he exclaimed. "And never in our history have we had a citizen make a claim to a black vest on the day of his passage!" The people started to cheer, but Zayo put his hands up, and they quickly fell silent. "Because of this, Mehlanahr will receive his vest from Oorahno, rather than from Booralta. Where is the master engineer?"

Oorahno was still wearing his black vest, as everyone noticed when he stepped up onto the platform with Zayo. Once he was on the platform, he was ten feet from his king, so he knelt and dropped his head. Zayo walked up to him and touched his left shoulder. "Master engineer, please tell our people about Mehlanahr's challenge to you."

Oorahno arose and replied, "Your majesty, in order for me to talk about the challenge and the test, I must also go into details about his education."

"You have all morning to tell our people. And they are eager to hear it. Take your liberty."

"Fifteen years ago," Oorahno began, "Booralta brought an introverted twenty-year-old colt to me, and asked that I accept him as a student of engineering. After my introductory conversation with the colt Mehlanahr, I was as convinced as the shaman was that Mehlanahr had a remarkable talent but he needed to learn how to better express himself towards others. So I decided that, instead of teaching him some engineering basics during the first few months, I would take him around to different job locations and have him view what many of our engineers were working on. Once he met many of them and felt quite good being with them, as if he were one of them, I started asking him questions as to how the whole picture fit together. His answers to me then amazed me, as he showed an extraordinary ability to piece together many different details which he had picked up from the many different jobs. I realized that, from allowing him to see as much as I did, he had taught himself most of the basic rough details. It was then that I changed his work somewhat, and began to explain to him many of the finer details as we went along. He absorbed these details as many of you ate your breakfast this morning—he had one gregarious appetite for technicalities.

"When our students were all tested to move into their advanced internship specializations, Mehlanahr proved to possess mastery of all internship disciplines. I proceeded to test him more deeply to see if he was capable of moving into advanced professional studies at his remarkably young age, and he showed a special talent in astrophysical engineering, which is the same field that I earned the black vest in because it is the most difficult. I then requested reports from the other engineers on their students; there were three of them. Their results were nearly as good, and from my overview with Kayloor, we felt it was best to train the four students in a real-life environment, and we began the countdown for the five months we would spend with them in outer space. That was a situation where they had to learn enough engineering to survive, and they learned more about what their futures as engineers would be like. Mehlanahr found that he could not avoid the others, but that he had to work with them as well as socialize with them, and he overcame many of his inhibitions to become the fine outspoken stallion he now is.

"He proceeded to master everything I could have possibly taught him about my own specialization, so I had him proceed with something I was never quite able to put any time into—individual research. He many so many previously unknown discoveries during his research, the most important being completing the physical and chemical theoretical background behind what was once a wild dream of mine—the possibility of dimensional transportation. I always had some idea as to how it should work, but I never knew if it was worthwhile to attempt it. Mehlanahr scientifically proved that such travel was easily possibly with our technology, that it would require far less fuel than all other forms of transportation we have, including the type of spaceship we were on, and that it would enable us to travel much faster than the speed of light itself— he showed me his research, and pointed out to me that with the speeds we would be traveling at, time would seem to stand still.

"I then asked him to attempt to design a new ship with a system that would be capable of traveling at the dimensional transport level. He finished those plans just after we returned to Equestra, so we proceeded to enable him to build his new ship, and to see if it worked. The ship was deemed space worthy four days ago by all engineers and Taelo, and we agreed to test it in actual interstellar flight yesterday. I never would have thought it possible, but within the space of two hours, we completed a round trip to Akthura and inspected all systems of the ship to find that it was still in perfect working order. We even passed through an ion storm, and emerged unhindered and undamaged, which utterly amazed me. I had some guards tow the ship here for everyone to see it, and it still looks as if it has not been used. I tell you that I walked on the surface of Akthura yesterday and breathed its air. It is because of the success of this new technology that I must relinquish my black vest to an intellectually superior stallion. And it is him that I am proud to call Master Engineer, as you all should be." He removed the black vest, and took the white tassels off of it. He accepted a blue vest from Tarahnaha, put the white tassels on it, and slipped it on. He then took the black vest with the blue trim in his left hand, and said to Zayo, "It is time for Mehlanahr to receive his vest, your majesty, if you would be so kind."

"Not quite," Zayo replied. "Since this is his passage, he can only be given the black vest if there are no questions from our people."

The crowd became rather boisterous, and it took some time for Zayo to silence them. He finally did, and they began to ask questions in a more civilized manner. "Oorahno," someone said, "how can we be sure that this showing is not just a fluke? This may be the only accomplishment he makes in his life."

"Whether it is the only accomplishment he ever makes," Oorahno replied, "or whether it is the first of many, has nothing to do with the fact that he has proven himself to be a far superior engineer than what I am or could even hope to be. Many people tell me that I have above average intelligence, but I tell you that Mehlanahr is a genius. His accomplishments thus far have already vastly changed the field of engineering; it cannot be compared to what it was fifteen years ago, because our ideals have all changed for the better under the light of his breakthroughs."

"What does he know about the responsibility of the black vest, let alone the responsibility of being a citizen?" someone else asked.

"What did he know of being an adjutant when Zayo called him?"

"That has nothing to do with it," someone else cried out.

"Why not? He has proven to be an excellent adjutant, something which he knew nothing about before he met Zayo the day before our king's coronation. In the same way, he will fit right into being the master, and will take all of his knowledge and expertise with him and be willing to share it with all, and teach us all ways to become better engineers. I know that he has already taught me very much about myself and what I am capable of; before his broad vision pushed his goals forward, I had thought that my vision was the greatest. He has the talent and the ability, and I do say that I must give him the black vest. It is my right to make such a request, just as it was his right to make a challenge to me for it when he saw that he was way beyond me in his work. Just as he has proven to be a good leader by serving Zayo, he will prove to be a good master by serving all engineers. I also say that a better engineer could not be found among our people, even in me. He is the best engineer, and it is his right through his merit to wear the vest of the master."

"These breakthroughs you have spoken of are of the utmost importance to all engineers," someone stated. "How are they important to everyone else and our society in general?"

"His talents and abilities are as an engineer, and his discoveries are going to be applied to every other aspect of our lives; first on our list are our transports, second are the visiphones, and third are all other mechanical devices which have proven to possess the capability to benefit from the new technology."

"Such technology cannot affect shoemaking," someone called out.

"When it will vastly improve our mining methods, it will indirectly affect all shoemakers. The metals which are mined will be much purer. It will improve our refining techniques. Our farming techniques, our healing techniques, and our artistry, in addition to every single appliance that affects all of our lives."

All of a sudden, a pleased laugh was heard, and many others followed it. Finally, someone said, "If he spends so much time in his research, how could he possibly have time to be adjutant, and how could he have time for a family since he stated he is going to make his claim today?"

Oorahno looked around at the people, and thought about the question that was poised. He then answered, "Most people view their work itself as a great challenge in their lives. To be a competent master, the work itself is not a challenge, but a means for progress. The challenge in his life, and to few others, is to enable all of our people to make progress and to evolve into what we have the ability to become. Just as I knew when he first became my student that he needed to be exposed to many people to realize his full abilities and talents, Zayo knew that he would earn his position as adjutant when they made their travels and he met everyone. That is my definition of a stallion driven not by hopes for his self, but for every single one of us. He knows and understands what means the most to all of us, because he feels the same things in his heart. His feelings run deep as do all of yours, but he more readily shows them. Self-expression is no longer a problem for him; it is how he shares his talent with all of us. Tell me that is not the definition of a true master, and I will tell you that you are wrong."

A great cheer was heard arising from the people, and it continued for quite some time. By the time the noise died down, Zayo told Oorahno, "The questioning is over. They are obviously pleased with your answers. Thanks in excess for sharing your wisdom."

"Your majesty, is it right for me to give him the vest now?"

"Yes, we must proceed. Mehlanahr, come to me!" he commanded. Before they had a chance to think, Mehlanahr had run up to the platform and jumped up on it, stopping to kneel ten feet from his king. Zayo saw him there, and smiled. He then called out, "Ahrkoor, come to me." The master shoemaker soon was kneeling beside Mehlanahr, and he had a new sabre in his hands. Zayo walked up to the shoemaker and touched his shoulder. "Master shoemaker, is that the sabre which you were asked to make?"

"Yes, your majesty." He stood up, and held out the sabre for Zayo to take, which he did.

Zayo studied it carefully for a moment, thoroughly pleased by the looks of it. It was crafted of pewter, and had twenty-seven tiny crystals embedded in the hilt; it had been designed to match the collar, and certainly was a tool fit for an adjutant. "Thanks in excess," Zayo remarked, and the shoemaker left the platform. "Oorahno, it is time for the vest." Zayo walked up to Mehlanahr and touched his shoulder; the adjutant stood up, but said nothing.

Oorahno smiled, tears in his eyes. He felt so distant, as if it were all a dream. When am I going to wake up? he thought. Shaking somewhat, he walked up to Mehlanahr, who removed his light blue intern's vest. Oorahno then slipped the black vest over Mehlanahr's head as Mehlanahr slipped his arms through. "Master," he stated, and added, "Sir." He knelt before Mehlanahr, but did not drop his head; that was only done for the king.

Mehlanahr touched Oorahno's shoulder, and the older engineer stood up, took the light blue vest from Mehlanahr, and stepped back. Zayo walked up to his adjutant and stated, "My friend, you have been like a brother to me. Just as you have been charged with the duties of the master engineer, I hereby give you your final charge as my adjutant: you are to carry a sabre with you at all times. Not because I am afraid of what might happen, but because none of the guards are allowed to bear such tools. Only you and I, and when the time is right, also my brother and his adjutant." Zayo grasped the blade in his left hand so that it would not cut him, and held the hilt out to Mehlanahr, with its weight supported just atop of the hilt by the back of his right hand. Mehlanahr grasped the hilt firmly, and Zayo let go of the blade. He then took it and tucked it into his vest.

Before Mehlanahr had a chance to leave the platform, people began to line up outside of his spaceship wanting to be given a tour of it, and see for themselves what he had created.

The next two hours were near mayhem, as everyone wanted to congratulate Mehlanahr, and to see his spaceship. For as many people who walked into it and looked around, there was not a single blemish upon it. When Mehlanahr finally got a moment to himself, it did not last long; Zayo interrupted him. "Mehlanahr, did you find a winner for your game?"

"She has not approached me," he replied. "In fact, no one has approached me with any attempt at an answer."

"Everyone knows it is a game. Perhaps they feel you are not serious."

"They are probably pulling straws, trying to decide who will approach me first."

Zayo started to laugh when he heard Mehlanahr mention a filly game. "Do you honestly believe grown mares would do such a thing?"

Mehlanahr then told him, "Zayo, they can be very contentious when they are fighting for the honor of being chosen. But she knows who she is."

"Well, I feel that the only way they will be forced to play your game will be if I got everyone's attention." The two of them walked up onto the platform, where Zayo quickly quieted the crowd. "Mehlanahr is ready to make a claim, but no mares have responded to his game yet. No one will go home until he is married."

A roar of laughter arose from the crowd. Mehlanahr then told them, "My life cannot go on very much longer until I claim her for my heart. My game is open to every mare between the ages of thirty-five and fifty who is not yet married—all those who tend to pull straws over being claimed." Some shrieks were heard from some mares, shocked that a stallion knew their game. "I know that there are fifty-three of you pulling straws, and I will hear all answers before you will know who the winner is. I am going to pull the final straw when I make my claim." Some of them began to run up to the platform, so he added, "Please line up single file, and please whisper your answer so no one else will hear."

He listened to their answers, one by one, counting them as they went by. He counted fifty-two of them. He then said, "Nearly half of the mares who came to me told me that they were already set on another; you will be good wives for those stallions, because you truly believe in them. Some of you also told me that you are unprepared for such a thing. Thankfully, none of them were the one I want. Everyone else who came up did not give me the answer I wanted to hear. But only fifty-two mares dared to come up. The one I want to claim, who is usually very friendly, has suddenly become shy." He saw Yehtraha standing in the crowd, and saw that she would not move. "Yehtraha," he continued, "please come here."

Yehtraha did not want to go, suddenly becoming very nervous, but as many people started to urge her to go in response to his bold claim, she could not stay where she was. She decided to play her own game in return as she walked up onto the platform and knelt ten feet from Zayo. Zayo walked up to her, touched her shoulder, and said, "I did not summon you here; Mehlanahr did. Why did you kneel?"

"Out of respect to my new master," she replied as she stood up. "I am an engineer."

"For the sake of our people, please respond to his public claim."

"Yes, your majesty." She walked up close to Mehlanahr, so close that he could see her blush.

Mehlanahr then said to her, "I am awaiting your answer."

She then knew it was time to put on a show for the people, so they could see the honor she expected from Mehlanahr. "Do you truly believe I am so impatient as to go running to a foal's game? If you believe that I should be your wife, then stand up for what you believe, and approach me with dignity instead. Make your claim with honor. I cannot believe this silly game that you started! I thought you were far more intelligent than you are showing!"

He then shot back to her, "Just as I thought when you told me you were pulling straws! You did it to cheer me up, and I did it to cheer our people up." His voice softened. "What have they had to enliven their spirits since Kayloor was murdered? Oorahno's speech was so theoretical and tedious many foals fell asleep. I knew that the spaceship would certainly enthrall them, so I had to do something else to make sure they would know why I needed to claim you. Games are always a fun way for people to become involved. Consider this our first duty performed together: we gave them a hepta treatment for their spirits."

She laughed and said, "You reacted just as I knew you would. Thank you for being so consistently philosophical. I could not come up before, because every time I pulled straws, I lost. My friends tell me I spend too much time with my computers."

"So that is your answer?" he asked her, somewhat shocked. She shook her tail at him, but would not say another word. He saw the glimmer in her eyes, and he felt a sudden charge of energy, he let out a daring whinny at her as he suddenly reared up. The crowd roared their approval, and he came down, embracing her and kissing her as the sky suddenly grew darker. As the sky lightened up again, a number of cries went out from the crowd.

Zayo got their attention and said, "What happened?"

Karayo ran up onto the platform and knelt ten feet from Zayo. Zayo touched his shoulder without a word, whence Karayo stood up and stated, "Booralta died during the eclipse. The power surge claimed him."

Zayo watched as his mother gave Mehlanahr and Yehtraha their white tassels. He then asked, "What about Booralta's vest?"

Karayo then said somberly, "He instructed me to claim it until a superior talent emerges." Karayo watched as Pleeyedraha walked up to the platform and handed Booralta's black vest with red trim to Tarahnaha. He removed his red vest, and exchanged vests with the queen mother.

Zayo watched as everyone cleared off of the platform, including his mother. He heard some murmuring, and saw some movement among the crowd. Soon, he saw Taelo walking up to the platform. He stepped up on it, and knelt ten feet from Zayo. Zayo touched his shoulder and said, "What troubles you?"

"This is no trouble," Taelo replied after he stood up. "I have been successfully challenged for the black vest, and it is time for me to relinquish it."

"Who has challenged you?"

"Hohnoor, because he did all of the chemical research for Mehlanahr's new fuel, something which I was incapable of doing because I did not know how to do it. Having proven his superior knowledge with the success of the new spacecraft, he has earned the right to be called Master Chemist."

Zayo summoned Hohnoor, and a loud roar of approval arose from the crowd as Hohnoor exchanged vests with Taelo.

After a wonderful lunch feast, the spaceship was towed back to Tokanar, and everyone left to go home. As the last few people were leaving, the moonsflowers budded. Their flowers would open the next day, and would last for a month before the plants went to seed.

EXPLOITATION

Karayo went home to Laerion, and packed up his belongings to move to Tokanar. He wanted to be readily accessible to Zayo. He did not have to worry about his family, because he was a widower, and his foals were grown. He found an adequate house in Tokanar that was large enough to accompany visitors when he would have them, but small enough to feel like home; it was about the same size as his current house near Laerion. It was near the center of town, and was not too far from either Ahrkoor's forge or the hospital. This made it an ideal location, much more accessible than Booralta's house had been. Booralta had enjoyed his distance from Tokanar when he did not have visitors, because it freed him for his necessary meditations.

The house Karayo was moving into was empty because it had been previously occupied by Dahrohd; Dahrohd's wife had moved back to her parent's house in the fishing villages when her husband was excommunicated for his treason against the king. Part of the reason Karayo was moving into this house was because it had been lived in by Dahrohd. He wanted the people to know that the treachery was gone, and that it was safe to walk in and about that house. They were afraid of the terror which had seized Dahrohd and his friends and persuaded them into committing the criminal atrocity of high treason and murder. But did they actually think that such a thing would soak into the walls and the floor and the ceiling, and all fixtures in the house? Karayo was the master historian now; it was time he taught the people that their fear was unfounded.

It was also a good way to help Zayo grow from the shadow of his father's death—make him go to the house lived in by one of the criminals to speak with the master historian when he needed to. It was not an extremely brilliant plan, but it would have its desired effects on all. That was what Karayo was counting on.

Mehlanahr quickly began his work as the master engineer in earnest. It took him a full day to review the work records of all engineering personnel. The next day, he set and figured out some methods to make any and all improvements in their existing technology with his newly proven theories. Then, he restructured the chain of duties among the engineers so that they would be able to implement his plans. His was a grand plan with so much enthusiasm from all others that it seemed as if it truly was the best way for their people to progress.

Yehtraha's work was restructured so that now she would work directly out of the plant. Mehlanahr saw in her records that she was a better computer programmer than Dehrahlax was, so he changed her duties to update the computers so that they would include significant updates of Mehlanahr's theories: his discoveries were going to be applied to whatever they could improve, which was nearly everything.

For starters, they updated the plant. As they neared completion of the reprogramming of the computer systems in the plant, Yehtraha was making a name for herself; not just because she was Mehlanahr's wife, but because her abilities as an engineer were as good as her mother's healing abilities. It did not take long for everyone to learn who her parents were, nor did it take long for people to begin equating her success with her marriage to the adjutant. It was obvious to all that the two of them worked extremely well together.

Shehronaha, who was the foremost expert on transport repair, headed their work on transports to enable the emergency beacon to be used even when there was no available power source; it was to have its own power source.

The power source for the new beacon was not philinium, but a refractor which normally subdued all impulses sent to it from the plant (which were sent the same way Mehlanahr's ship traveled). When the refractor was reversed, the impulses returned to the plant computers, and was translated as being an emergency—their emergency beacon. The impulses were driven on a principle similar to that of the dimensional transport—there was no time delay from point to point, so through the computers in the plant, they were able to detect where all transports were at a given moment. The angle of refraction in each transport was slightly different from all others. This replaced a task that had originally been performed by guards, while at the same time improving the beacon so that it would work at all times.

Similar to the refractor was a new technology which they were employing in the visiphones, which more accurately matched the picture with the spoken words. Tehsoorahlaha, who was the foremost authority on visiphones among the Caballians, spearheaded this.

Once Yehtraha finished reprogramming the computers in the plant, Dehrahlax took to performing all of the mechanical tune-ups on their telescopes and scanners. He updated all of the mechanisms so that they would work better with the newly reprogrammed computer system. Even though Mehlanahr knew what Dehrahlax's capabilities were as an engineer, and was fully confident of his success before he started, seeing the finished results was much more impressive; Mehlanahr was very happy. Dehrahlax then resumed what were usually his normal duties while they were on Equestra: to continually make comprehensive scans of nearby solar systems, and all of the areas in between. One of the first things he tried to learn were the effects of the ion storm on their solar system (the ion storm that they had met during the challenge).

Mapping was usually a relatively easy task, and at first it appeared to have been made much easier by the infusion of the new technology. When he began mapping on the two hundred and twentieth day, Dehrahlax thought that the effects of the ion storm would have been only slightly residual, but as he progressed that day, he located a new object between Equestra and the area in which the ion storm had taken place. At first he thought it might have been missed by their earlier technology, which was not completely accurate, but when he reviewed his own records from the early part of the last training mission, he realized that the older records were quite accurate despite their technological inadequacies. Because of the object's location, he knew that it could not be a comet; he hypothesized that it was an asteroid, and proceeded to run a spectral scan on it so as to determine its composition. The results of this were quite mystifying, as he could not isolate any known molecular structure; a few elements were detected, though not in as much quantity as they would have been in an asteroid. He reviewed the spectral scan at least a hundred times, both mentally and with the computer, but could not isolate any known structural type for an asteroid. The only hypothesis he could come up with was that the object was alien in origin, and if that were so, then also that it was not a

112

natural object, but that it was created by an intelligent being somewhere other than Equestra. He had the scanners set to record everything he was researching in that sector, and he put the machinery on the automatic mode. Then, troubled by his discovery, he went to speak with Mehlanahr.

Mehlanahr was in his office with the door open, and he was working on some theoretical work when Dehrahlax walked in. "Master," he said to the adjutant, "I have finished my research on the area affected by the ion storm," and he set down across from Mehlanahr.

Mehlanahr put his work down and set back. He saw the questions in Dehrahlax's eyes, and said, "My friend, something is troubling you."

"You would not believe me if I were to tell you my hypothesis." The expression in the adjutant's eyes told him he had absolute faith in him. "Mehlanahr," he continued, "I have discovered an asteroid that is not an asteroid, but appears to be alien in origin."

"What has your spectral scan revealed?" he queried, knowing it was standard procedure.

"I was unable to isolate any known molecular structures, and only a few known elements were found to exist in any quantity. Those include carbon, hydrogen, oxygen, and nitrogen."

Mehlanahr was shocked. "What sort of asteroid would have an atmosphere?" he wondered aloud.

"You mean the elements?"

"Atmospheric composition. It should sound familiar."

"Sir, if it is what I think it is, then the only ones who could have created it are sentient aliens."

"Then we had better be prepared. Aliens will be here soon."

Zayo was so happy with how his people were now progressing that he felt as if nothing could stop them. It was a great feeling for him to be on top of the world, serving his people as the king that everyone said he would become, including Booralta. It was true that he was now doing as much at his young age as what nearly all of his ancestors had done in their entire reigns, so he felt confident in the fact that he had indeed mastered his job soon enough. It was also true that he possessed knowledge pertaining to every single aspect of his job, including how to preside over passages and weddings. But his knowledge was raw; that pertaining to passages and marriages had never been applied, so therefore he lacked most associated wisdom which a king gains through serving in such a position.

Considering all of the struggles which he and his mother had been forced to live through recently, coupled with the success of his adjutant's challenge and passage, Zayo now had plenty of reasons why not to talk about his father. Zayo existed in this bubble as he was throughout the time that the computer system in the plant was being updated, and even up through the day when Dehrahlax made his discovery. This was Zayo's frame of mind when Mehlanahr called him on the visiphone and asked him to come to the plant. Mehlanahr did not give him any details, but the urgency in his voice made Zayo realize that it was imperative that he go to the plant immediately. Mehlanahr had never before spoken in such urgent tones with Zayo, and the king's only thoughts as he drove to Tokanar were that there had been a terrible accident somewhere involving the implementation of Mehlanahr's new technology. Zayo felt that his adjutant's new technology was the greatest thing to happen to their people in eons, and it grieved him to think that there could possibly be a flaw somewhere.

Thoughts like this were what had inhibited Oorahno somewhat in accepting Mehlanahr's technology for what it was; Zayo had much more limited thoughts, and did not yet fully understand that the unexpected could happen at any given moment, so he did not even think of the prophecy made at his coronation on his way to Tokanar.

When Zayo reached the plant, he ran inside, half-expecting someone to greet him with some terribly tragic news. But no one stood between him and Mehlanahr's office, so he bolted through the open door, nearly running into Dehrahlax. Zayo pulled himself together to speak as he stopped and stood there momentarily, then he said to his adjutant, "Mehlanahr, what is so urgent?"

"What would you possibly think, Zayo?" Mehlanahr dared.

"One of two things: either someone was seriously injured, or something has caused you to stop your work."

Mehlanahr shook his head and replied, "Please set down, Zayo."

Zayo set down, though rather reluctantly. "Does this involve Dehrahlax?"

"Yes, it does. He made a discovery a short while ago which is of major importance to our people."

"And so your work has stopped?"

"No, our work is continuing; right now, the system is on the automatic mode, mapping every movement."

Zayo appeared to be calming down. "That is standard procedure, is it not?"

"Mapping itself is standard, but what the scanners are mapping is the discovery you need to be told of." He stood up and started to walk toward the door. "Come with me; Dehrahlax too. I am going to show you what Dehrahlax discovered when he was studying the effects of the ion storm we traveled through during my challenge." He led them out of his office, and to the main room, where the scanners were. Mehlanahr had Zayo set down, showed him the pictured, then said, "What do you see here?"

Zayo set there staring at the picture for perhaps five minutes, then he remarked, "Is that object an asteroid?"

Mehlanahr and Dehrahlax both smiled at his thoughtful answer. "At first, I thought it was an asteroid," Dehrahlax replied.

"That is," Mehlanahr added, "until he ran a spectral scan on it. The molecular composition of it is entirely alien except for some elemental gases which are found in our atmosphere."

Zayo continued to watch it as it seemed to change its path on its own power, without any outside impetus. "An asteroid does not do that. Could it be some sort of alien spaceship?"

"That is what I believe it is."

Zayo thought about this for a moment, then he said, "What about what Booralta said of the alien war at my coronation? Perhaps this is the beginning of things to come."

"That is why I called you here immediately. I wanted you to learn of this as soon as possible. If they land their ship here, how are we to handle the situation?"

"If you determine that they are going to land here, let me know where they shall be landing if you can, and we will meet them. Perhaps we can have them leave immediately instead of allowing the war to happen."

Mehlanahr shook his head. "If it could only be so easy, Zayo, there would be no problem at all! That alien object is to be the greatest challenge you will have to face for our people. They are going to cause a war. But Zayo, we have the technology to prevent them from landing on Equestra."

Zayo knew right away he was referring to either implosion or excommunication. "We cannot do such a thing when they have not committed a crime."

"Our discovery of their presence is the beginning of the exploitation. We cannot stop exploitation; without it, there would be absolutely nothing. And no need for the pegasus or your brother."

"But Mehlanahr, there must be a good way to end this for all involved."

"Zayo, did your father die for nothing?"

"His was a senseless death."

"He was murdered because he did not stop some negative exploitation which had infiltrated our people."

"'Negative exploitation'? Who?"

"Who was responsible for the treachery according to Wehrahn?"

"Dahrohd. But what does that have to do with it?"

"The seed for discontent was sown somewhere along the line—I do not know where or when—and it grew into a rotten unyielding tree that only wanted the waters of our souls to absorb into its system."

"What?"

"They had to kill your father because he was inefficient about doing the job he should have done to prevent the wars from returning."

"How would you know such a thing?"

"Who walks around the palace saying that his father was an inefficient king during his reign, and that he pushed his father to become a better king but his father fought it? Who, Zayo? Is it possibly you?"

Zayo shuddered helplessly. "I did not realize that my words had such an impact. When I say things like that, they are thoughtless words without any forethought or emotional strife in them."

"Are you so sure? Often the words that just spit out of our mouths best represent our deepest thoughts and feelings...that is why such a value is placed upon a person's dying words."

Zayo could hardly believe his ears. Mehlanahr suddenly seemed to know everything. He looked back at Dehrahlax, who obviously thought that their conversation was extremely interesting, but kept his own thoughts to himself. Zayo soon realized that Mehlanahr was right, although he did not understand why, as Mehlanahr knew would happen.

"What are we to do?" Mehlanahr asked when Zayo said nothing.

Zayo finally replied, "What can we do if they have not done anything to us? We have no laws against their entering our solar system, just as we have no laws against asteroids. Until they commit an actual crime, I can do nothing except allow the exploitation which they present. If their craft is going to land here, let it land here. I am sure they cherish their freedom as much as we cherish ours."

"What if they commit crimes against our people and seriously disturb our society?"

"They are going to disturb our society no matter what; what can we do to prevent them from being free sentient beings? What we can do is protect ourselves by making them subject to our laws when they arrive here. They are going to bring exploitation to us, so we will push some of it on them in the form of our legal system."

116

"What if they do not understand when and why we punish criminals?"

"If they do not understand, we will teach them. Even if they do not speak the same language as we do, they probably follow some semblance of order in their daily lives. If and when they commit crimes, we will punish them for it. If they do not like how they are treated here, they can always leave."

Dehrahlax could not help but laugh at Zayo's words. "Your majesty, your words follow simple reasoning but are true in your approach. I believe your ideas shall work."

"If only I had such a boost of confidence from you, Mehlanahr."

"Zayo," the adjutant cried, "if I do not make you consider all sides of the given situation, who shall? We must be prepared as best as we can for their approach and imminent arrival."

Mehlanahr immediately rearranged the working schedules of Oorahno and Dehrahlax so that they would be able to monitor the alien craft twenty-seven hours a day, every day. Oorahno and Dehrahlax were each to take a shift during the night hours, and Mehlanahr was to work during the day. Mehlanahr was glad that there were no passages to occur for almost two weeks; if there was a passage, they would have to have someone monitoring the aliens (and miss the passage).

Early in the morning on the second day after the alien craft was discovered, when Mehlanahr was taking over scanning duties from Dehrahlax, it settled into orbit around Equestra. Mehlanahr immediately contacted Oorahno and Zayo. About twenty minutes after Zayo's arrival, it began its descent into the Equestran atmosphere. It did not go straight down, but made a descending arch. They followed its progress until it landed in a spot not far off the road connecting the palace and Tokanar. Zayo then called a number of guards to come to the plant, as well as Karayo. He also summoned all of the engineers who were in the plant to meet with him in a rather large briefing room in the plant, which had been designed for special lectures. In front of this rather large crowd, Zayo told them all of their situation with the alien craft, and asked them all to travel with him to see this craft and try to make some preliminary determinations as to the intentions of the aliens. Before anyone really had a chance to stop and think, they were off, each one in his or her own transport.

It took them twenty-five minutes to arrive at the general vicinity of the landing, which was in the midst of a large moonsflower field. The transports were left one mile away from the alien craft, then they set out on foot (all fifty of them) to get a glimpse of the aliens. The Caballians were all rather curious as to the type of exploitation which it was they were being exposed to by these aliens, and they did not know any better to be afraid of what was unknown to them; Zayo was the only one who showed any bit of hesitation, but he quickly overcame it.

As they neared the alien craft, they saw three of the aliens, who seemed to be carrying some sort of tool or weapon in a lackadaisical manner until they saw the Caballians, at which time they held them much more aggressively; the Caballians immediately knew that the aliens were holding weapons. Zayo and Mehlanahr had their sabres in their vests while the rest of the Caballians were unarmed, so the strange aliens stopped about ten feet away from them. They were shorter and much smaller than the Caballians, and walked on two legs.

Without even thinking of the possibility that the aliens perhaps spoke an alien language because of their alien origins, Mehlanahr said to them, "Please put the sticks down."

One of the aliens pointed its weapon up and fired a shot into the air; a shot of what, the Caballians could not tell. Mehlanahr stepped forward with Zayo right behind him, and before he knew what was happening, one of the aliens said to him in the same language, "Step back with the child," and he pointed his weapon at the two of them.

Mehlanahr stopped, but instead of stepping back, he repeated what he said at first. "Please put the sticks down."

Another alien, who had heard the commotion from their craft, left it and made its way over to its comrades. "Who is firing his gun without my command?!" he queried of the other aliens.

"Captain," the guilty one replied, "they approached us, and we only meant to warn them away, and not to harm us. What defense do we have against Centaurs?"

"Chan," the captain replied, "be fair. This is their turf. Put your guns down."

"Thank you," Mehlanahr replied when they had set down their weapons; the alien referred to as "Captain" was utterly surprised when he heard Mehlanahr speak the same language. "Who is serving you as your leader?"

"I am the leader of this expedition. I am Captain John Hancock, representing the Third Colonizing Party. We have traveled long and far from a planet we call Earth."

Zayo then said to the alien leader, "This is Equestra. What are your intentions?"

There was a bit of surprise at Zayo's protectiveness. "Our intentions are good. Our mission is to explore this part of the galaxy, and to possibly colonize a livable planet."

"What is wrong with Earth? Does it still exist?"

"It certainly does exist. We are an adventuresome and curious people, and we seek to learn more about what exists elsewhere in the universe." It then struck him that he was speaking to the shortest Caballian there, who seemed to be the youngest physically. "You have had your questions answered. Who are you that you speak before all of your elders?"

"I am Zayo," he replied, not even thinking of his title.

"Is that your name or your title?" he asked, and his comrades snickered, not believing that Zayo was serious.

Zayo suddenly reared up and whinnied at them. When he set down, he said to them with fury in his eyes, "I am the king of the Caballians!"

Hancock looked at his men and snapped, "What did I tell you about being fair? You're all space sick! Shut up and listen to them if you wanna ever get home!" They silenced themselves, though almost not soon enough. "Your highness, forgive them. It has been a long, hard trip, and most of the life-support systems on our ship were failing. We had no water except for emergency rations for each man per day, and they are somewhat giddy over the rain."

Mehlanahr saw the look in Zayo eyes, so he said, "You shall address Zayo as 'your majesty,' as is proper since he became the king when his father was killed."

"Death is an experience awaiting us all," he remarked.

Zayo looked at the alien and remarked, "My father was murdered. The first king to be murdered in millions of years. We are a people of forty thousand; it should not have happened."

"The motivation behind a crime often eludes the best thinkers." He saw Zayo's shifting expression, and felt that he was bitter over it; he decided it best to change the subject. "I would assume that my men are under your jurisdiction as long as we are here."

"You will be advised of our laws, and will be told if anything is unreasonable here."

"When will this be?"

"This afternoon. I would also like you and your men to come with me to the plant for lunch, then we shall head to the palace grounds where we will have supper. Tomorrow morning we will meet in a caucus, and allow all of my people to question you. If you do not like it, you are free to leave. But there is a certain way things must be done among the Caballians, and the caucus is one of them. All of my people have the right to know about you and to speak with you. That is the reason why you came here, is it not?"

Hancock was impressed with young Zayo, and agreed to his caucus.

Several engineers did not stay for lunch at the plant while the aliens were briefed on the Caballian legal system and laws. Zayo and Mehlanahr were pleased with how things were progressing with the aliens because of the amazing fact that they spoke just slightly different dialects of the same language, rather than different languages, as the Caballians had first assumed.

Shortly after lunch, the administrator in the school in Tokanar went to speak with Karayo. His name was Vehdoor; he was two hundred and eighty-three years old, and was recognized by his brown hair and fur and chestnut eyes. He wore a red vest with white tassels, and had three offspring, two of whom were citizens, the youngest being in her early thirties. He went to speak with Karayo because he was disturbed by the arrival of the aliens.

When Karayo opened the door to Vehdoor's knock, he was rather surprised to see him standing there, but he ushered him in, saying, "Welcome, my friend, and good afternoon. Come in and set with me." He led Vehdoor into the den, where they set down with some water. "You are here because the appearance of the aliens has you disturbed."

Vehdoor gulped down some water. "Yes, I am very troubled. Their appearance means the beginning of an extremely difficult time for our people."

"What makes you believe evolution is to be so difficult when it is a natural tendency?"

"When it means our people have to change the ways they learned to follow under Kayloor, and when the harbinger of what it is means that the seriousness of it will force young Zayo to face his father's murder, then it is to be difficult times. You remember how hard it hit Tarahnaha, Pleeyedraha, and Mehlanahr. It is going to hit our king like a shoemaker's hammer, because of how it has hit all of our people already. That is not to be a difficult time?"

Karayo was somewhat surprised by what he was saying, so he asked Vehdoor, "How difficult is it going to be for Zayo?"

"Difficult enough for him to be forced to mature at a very early age."

"That is all?"

"I would even say difficult enough for him to have to travel to their planet to get rid of them."

Karayo's eyes opened wide in astonishment. "How did you ever come to such a conclusion, Vehdoor?"

"My wife, who is an engineer, told me during lunch that the aliens were extremely disrespectful to Zayo, and brought out the fury in him. She also said that many systems on their spaceship were damaged beyond repair, which means they cannot use it again."

Karayo was shocked and amazed. "I believe that your true talent is surfacing. I would like for you to spend the next week working with me, during which time I shall test you—though you will not know for sure exactly when you are being tested—to learn the extent of your ability."

"Why? My work as an administrator is highly satisfactory; you have said so yourself."

"Yes, you have mastered your epitome. But if you are learning how to relate your epitome to everything that is going on around within the specific focus of our history—past, present, or future—then you are truly worthy of becoming a shaman."

"If I am to study with you, then who will serve as the administrator?"

"I believe that it is time for Daykooraha to become the administrator in Tokanar, and for you to begin refining this foresight you have shown me today."

"How can you be so sure of such a thing?"

"I recognized Booralta's talent the same way one hundred and fifty-three years ago."

"We will know in one week if I am worthy of becoming a shaman?"

"Yes. Your final test will be on sixthday next week."

"I hope that will not be the test for the black vest."

"No, I do not think so. It should take you much longer than one week to develop the talent necessary to become the master. When you progress that far, I will let you know."

"If I progress that far."

"You have moved this far on your own, my friend. With proper training and assistance, you will become the master historian before you die. From what you have shown me today, I believe you are to become Booralta's successor."

SLEEPLESS

Before they left their spaceship to go to lunch at the plant, the aliens were advised of the law which allowed only Zayo and Mehlanahr to carry any type of tool or weapon, so they had to leave their guns behind. After being advised of the Caballian laws by Zayo while they at the plant, they insisted on returning to their spaceship to obtain their clean dress uniforms, which they did just before going to the palace for supper.

Since they arrived at the palace in the mid-afternoon, Captain John Hancock made a special request of Zayo. "Your majesty, you must forgive us, you have not caught us at our best."

"What do you mean?" Zayo said, unconsciously wrinkling his nose.

"Our water supply on our ship ran out a month ago, and we were unable to recycle any more of it. We have been living on emergency water supplies, all of it being used to drink. Our waste disposal was not operating at full capacity, and we could not repair it."

"Would you be able to return to Earth if you wished?"

"If we had not found Equestra within a week of when we did, we would all be dead. I will not force any of my men to use that ship again, even if it means that they are doomed here."

"We have plenty of water here, and I am sure someone will be able to help you fix or replace whatever is not working on your ship."

"That is a very kind offer, but we have a more immediate health problem."

"Tell me what it is," Zayo replied. "I do not mean to be rude, but I have no idea what you and your people are supposed to live like."

"We need to bathe, and wash and change our clothes."

"'Clothes'?"

"The garments we wear, just as your people wear vests."

Zayo realized what he was talking about and replied, "Feel free to have your men bathe here in the palace. I am sure that with the time left today, you will be quite ready for tomorrow's caucus."

"Thank you, your majesty."

The fresh, wonderful air of Equestra was beginning to have a tantalizing effect on the humans, and they soaked it up, along with the rain showers that fell intermittently, which in itself had them ecstatic after their drought.

At the caucus the next morning, the Caballians asked hundreds of question of the humans. The humans were not as naturally colorful as the Caballians were; the most colorful of them was Captain Hancock, who had dark brown skin and black hair. There were a total of fifty-three humans who had been on their spaceship.

The humans answered the questions quite happily, because they were all polite questions not asking too much information, yet they revealed what seemed to be enough of human nature. They quickly proved themselves to be much different philosophically from the Caballians, which made for a very interesting morning.

There was one intriguing fact which the Caballians learned from the humans: that on Earth, they had animals which resembled Caballians in many aspects, animals they called horses. This piqued the Caballians' interest, especially when the humans kept on saying that the Caballians were sort of a crossbreed between humans and horses; the very thought of such a thing was quite hilarious to the Caballians.

Toward the end of the caucus, however, the humans, especially Captain Hancock, began to get pushy and arrogant towards the Caballians; this was part of the reason why the caucus ended. They got so pushy that Hancock demanded that his first officer, Ian MacBain, be brought to Earth by Mehlanahr that afternoon so that he could make his report to the humans there. The Caballians acquiesced, but only to keep things peaceful.

It took Mehlanahr less than an hour to completely prepare for the proposed mission to Earth. It was no problem for him to obtain the engineers and the chemist he wanted to serve on the ship, but when he asked Pleeyedraha to recommend a doctor, he ran into a problem. Pakoor, who had been a part of Mehlanahr's challenge, had had enough excitement, and wanted to stay away from spaceships for at least ten years. Pleeyedraha did not want to go because of her age; she knew that the excitement would affect her greater than it affected Pakoor. Finally, she made a rather unorthodox decision: she decided to send her student, feeling that Tahrmaha was ready for some real fieldwork. Tahrmaha only agreed to go because Pleeyedraha requested it.

Zayo insisted on going; he wanted to find out what the dimensional transport was like, because he had heard so much about it. Ian MacBain was to be the only human going to Earth. He gave hardly any thought as to how the Caballian ship would be received; it was certain to be different from how the humans received their own.

The trip was to be made in the afternoon of the two hundred and twenty-third day, the same day as the caucus. What took the most time was the location of Earth, but Dehrahlax finally located the star that Earth orbited. Once it was found, it was rather easy for them to program the computers for the dimensional transport; this took perhaps ten minutes. Once this was done, they took off.

The trip was much smoother than the first trip had been because of the absence of the ion storm, which made it an absolute pleasure. When they found themselves in orbit around a rather strange blue planet, MacBain was rather surprised, but said nothing; he obviously recognized it as being Earth.

Once their orbit was settled, Tehsoorahlaha assisted MacBain as he had to call his supervisors, and let them know where he was, why he was there, and obtain permission to land. The engineers were all quite at ease with what was happening during the trip, and knew exactly what had to be done; Zayo and Tahrmaha were equally intrigued by the workings of Mehlanahr's new technology and how they could travel through space in the blink of an eye. The crew was not too surprised at Zayo's interest, because they had seen it plenty of times in the plant, but they were enamored by Tahrmaha's participation, which far surpassed Pakoor's efforts to be interested in the new technology.

It took him some time, but with Tehsoorahlaha's help, MacBain was able to tune in to the correct frequency needed to communicate with Earth. "Earth Control," he said, "this is Commander Ian MacBain of the Third Colonizing Party. I repeat, this is Commander MacBain of the Third Colonizing Party. Do you read me?"

The Caballians were quite surprised at how he was calling his home planet, but they kept absolutely quiet, as they wanted to hear his conversation. Some static was heard, but soon enough, a response came through. "Affirmative, Commander MacBain. This is Alameda. What is your present location?"

"I am in orbit, Earth Control."

A bit more static came through. "Commander, please be more precise. We are having difficulty locating your ship."

"Earth Control, I am in orbit. I am on board an alien craft, because our ship was nearly destroyed by an ion storm. Our present location is amidst the Delta T satellite sector."

There was a long silence. "Commander, we have located what appears to be an odd comet, which much be the alien ship. Welcoming preparations are being made at Cape Canaveral."

"Earth Control, such preparations are not necessary."

"Standard procedure," came the reply.

"Earth Control, standard procedure is that you follow my recommendation in this matter...or does my rank mean nothing?"

"Commander, please verify your security code."

"Alpha-Omega Three, Barnard I, current mission. Service number five two five three Alpha four one two nine zero zero zero one zero Omicron. Security clearance Alpha, five eight seven nine two six Shakespeare. Admiral Van Housen, am I finished yet?"

The voice on the other end recognized the humor, and his laugh was heard over the radio. "Commander, you are free to proceed directly to Cape Canaveral."

"To meet with Admiral Gray?"

"Affirmative."

"Roger. Will proceed directly to Cape Canaveral."

"Roger, Commander. Welcome home."

It took the Caballians twenty minutes to locate Cape Canaveral and to land there. They landed in what seemed to be a rather clear area, and as soon as they did, Dehrahlax made a complete scan of the surrounding geographical area. Aldoor made a scan of the atmosphere and gravity. Oorahno carefully checked all systems of the ship. Once Mehlanahr was satisfied that it was safe for them to leave their craft, he gave Zayo his approval. Then, the young king said to MacBain, "How are we to proceed?"

"Your majesty," he replied, Athey are waiting for me inside. I would like for you to come with me. I am sure they would enjoy meeting you as much as your people enjoyed meeting my men."

"I will not go by myself," he remarked. "All of my people shall accompany me."

Zayo decided not to carry his own sabre, but to allow Mehlanahr to carry the only sabre among them. They left the ship, and were met by an armed guard, who lowered their arms when they saw that the only armed Caballian had his weapon tucked away—Mehlanahr's sabre was in his vest. No words were exchanged as they were escorted into a large briefing room; all but two of the guards left the room. MacBain and the guards sat down around a round table; the chairs were too small for the Caballians, so each one of them went beside a chair and set on the floor, putting them on the same level as MacBain.

Shortly after they settled down, another human entered the room. He also wore a uniform, although it was much more highly decorated than any uniform that the Caballians had seen before; it was Admiral James Gray, who was the highest ranking official at Earth Control. Commander MacBain recognized him, arose from his seat, and saluted the Admiral. Gray returned his salute, then queried, "Commander?"

"Aye, Sir?" he asked back.

"You will have to forgive me, Commander, but I cannot remember who you are."

"Sir, I am Commander Ian MacBain, executive officer to Captain John Hancock of the Third Colonizing Mission as commissioned by yourself. Our mission-"

The Admiral suddenly remembered, and interrupted him. "Your mission, Commander, as I do remember, was to inspect first hand the scientific basis for the fluctuations at Barnard's Star."

"Aye, Sir," he replied, a smile on his face. "But Barnard's Star is not its proper name."

"No?"

"No, Admiral. It is Omistu."

"I see, Commander." He sat down, and MacBain followed him. "How many planets are there?"

"Two, sir. The inner planet, called Equestra, has three moons, and is very much like Earth."

"Commander, I did not know that your mission involved landing on the planet."

"Sir, our ship was damaged beyond repair, and we had no way to repair the main recycling system. Even on emergency rations, our water was virtually gone."

"What about the backup systems?"

126

"Many of them were destroyed in an ion storm, which we were lucky to survive."

"Have repairs begun?"

"Admiral, our ship is beyond repair. It is not fit for any beast to use, except perhaps for scrap."

"So you saved your own lives."

"Admiral, the Caballians understand our plight."

The Caballians had been intent on the interchange between Admiral Gray and MacBain; at this point, Tahrmaha finally spoke for them. "Before the two of you deliberate on your problems any further, my people require some water. Where can we find it?"

"Who may you be, young lady?" Admiral Gray asked her.

"I am a doctor," she replied bluntly. "We require water, if you would be so courteous."

Zayo looked at Tahrmaha, and at the Admiral, but said nothing, because she was right. It was rather obvious that the humans did not understand the importance of hospitality, and he was very thirsty. The Admiral sent for some water, and it was quickly brought. After the Caballians had quenched their thirst, the Admiral spoke again. "What is your name?" he asked Tahrmaha.

"I am Tahrmaha," she replied. "I do not know who you are, or why you speak as you do, but my people consider the offering of a drink after a long trip a courtesy to any guest. Remember that, if we are ever to return here. It is for our health; we were beginning to dehydrate in your dry climate." The Caballians were all pleased with her tactful response. Tahrmaha's obvious sharpness of wits, intelligent charm, and charisma made her seem remarkable, Zayo thought. Since she was Pleeyedraha's student, perhaps she knew something of Kayloor and Pleeyedraha that Zayo had never learned. He kept this thought in the back of his mind, where he would not forget it. After a pause for another drink, Tahrmaha said, "Thank you for the water. It was refreshing."

"You are welcome, Tahrmaha," he replied, quite affected by her charm himself. "Caballians of Equestra, who has led you here?"

"Ian MacBain," Mehlanahr replied.

"Yes, yes, I know that, but which one of you was responsible for overseeing your mission here from Equestra?"

"I was," the adjutant replied, a curious look on his face.

"Then perhaps you could possibly tell me about your people."

"Who are you?" Zayo asked the Admiral. "You are the host, so is it not proper that you introduce yourself?"

"I am Admiral James Gray," he replied sarcastically, "the commanding officer of Earth Control. Does not protocol dictate that I speak with your elders?" He looked back at Mehlanahr momentarily, then his eyes fell on Oorahno, who was the oldest Caballian in the room.

Zayo became infuriated, and let out a sudden whinny. Mehlanahr then told the Admiral, "Before you show any more disrespect to our king, I implore of you as his adjutant that you apologize immediately and cease your sarcasm, otherwise we will encourage him to take punitive measures."

Gray fell into his seat. "I am sorry," he quickly apologized. AI did not know you were the king. I thought someone here was your father."

All of the Caballians saw the fury spark in Zayo's eyes, and they were not surprised when he jumped up with a whinny and ran out of the room. They followed him in close pursuit as he ran out of the building to the outside of their ship; he did not enter it, but stopped, as he was just letting off some steam.

Shortly thereafter, Admiral Gray and Ian MacBain followed them. Zayo then said to Gray, "Dare you insult me again with your ignorance and I shall excommunicate you immediately. You know nothing of my people or myself, so save your cynicism for your own people. I may be young, but I am no fool."

Admiral Gray nodded, then said to MacBain, "Did you bring your reports with you?"

MacBain looked rather surprised. "Admiral, with all due respect, we cannot deliver any reports until our mission is completed. Captain Hancock felt that you would have been pleased with a preliminary report."

"After the last mission was destroyed at Pluto, I thought the two of you would have had more sense."

"If it were not for the Caballians, you would not have any report, preliminary or no. We felt the best way to make a preliminary report was to let you see for yourself that we encountered friendly aliens whom we can communicate with without any linguistic barrier. If that is not good enough, perhaps you should forget I ever came back."

"Mister, remember who you are speaking to! Earth Control is going to be hounding me for some sort of written report from you, especially since they know you're back. What do I have to do, go get the reports myself?!"

"What is more important, regulations or alien contact?"

"Both are available."

"The written reports are not available...they are on Equestra."

"What good are they doing there?"

"Awaiting completion."

"Commander, do I have to put you in the brig?"

"As if it would do any good! Admiral, our men have not even had a chance to become accustomed to the Equestran day. We only arrived there yesterday."

"Yesterday?! How long did it take you to get here?"

"Less than an hour."

"Blasted!" He recollected himself, then he spoke to Zayo. "Your majesty, as you were kind enough to come here so that we could receive this news, would you be kind enough to help me expedite matters on my end?"

"How so?" Zayo asked.

"I would like to return with you to Equestra so that I can collect all of the reports from their voyage."

"You are asking for a round trip or one way?"

"Round trip, if it would not be a problem." Zayo started to ponder it, but was soon disrupted by a ringing sound. Admiral Gray excused himself for a moment to answer a telephone. He mumbled a few words, then listened carefully for a few minutes; the expression on his face could have been guilt or shock. A childhood friend of his, Doc Lawson, had just been assassinated by a revolutionary terrorist faction because of his connections. This terrorist, who was known as Fagan around the world, had his headquarters in Ireland.

When Admiral Gray finished with his short telephone call, Zayo granted his request to bring him to Equestra. Their return trip to Equestra was smooth. As soon as they had landed, Gray remarked to Zayo, "Your majesty, it was a remarkable flight. I wouldn't expect to be able to understand your technology, but I was curious as to how your engineers were able to produce a realistic gravitational field within the ship."

Mehlanahr, who was standing near Zayo, replied, "Were you able to detect any acceleration while you were in the ship?"

"Nothing I would have expected from an interstellar flight."

"And you wish to know why?"

"Does it have anything to do with the gravity?"

"Absolutely. Between the atmospheric pressure being released from the ceiling vents and the cradling gyroscopic rotation, a true feeling of gravitational pull is affected."

"How could you do this if the control room is at the center of the ship?"

"It is not the center of the ship. It only seems like that because the ship must alter its shape for when it is traveling through an atmosphere as compared to when it is traveling in the vacuum of space."

"Then how did I feel the gravity when we were traveling through the atmosphere?"

"The gravitational pull you felt at those times was the actual gravitational pull of the planets."

"But how do you overcome the inertia of acceleration?"

"It is counterbalanced by the cradling gyroscopic rotation, the speed of which is determined by how fast we are accelerating or decelerating."

Gray was amazed. He thought to himself, The ship rotates and I didn't feel it. When he stepped off of the ship and stopped to inspect his surroundings, he could hardly believe his senses. He took in a deep breath, and felt almost as if he had taken some uppers without the down crash; he remained at the peak of the mountain. He was brought to the palace, and after he had ample opportunity to speak with Captain Hancock, he spent time with Zayo, who explained to him Caballians laws and their judicial system. Zayo also told the Admiral that he was expected to abide by their judicial system as long as he was interacting with the Caballians. Gray acted as if he had his full attention on what Zayo was telling him, but actually he was far from it. Gray knew that there were many things neither he nor the colonists would ever learn about the Caballians from the Caballians, things he was very eager to learn for his own personal satisfaction. He came up with many ideas of his own, and he mentioned some of them to Hancock later that afternoon.

The colonists had set up a temporary encampment of tents not too far from the palace. Admiral Gray, however, ate dinner with the royal family, and spent the night in the palace in a spare room as a guest of the royal house. However, with all of the events that had happened that day fresh on his mind, the Admiral found it impossible to sleep. After a couple of hours of tossing and turning, he arose, and began to wander around the palace. It was not just to spend excess energy that he had built up, but he was a very curious person. He walked through the hallways peeking into the closed doors—which all opened very silently—and viewing their sleep. Everyone was asleep except for Mehlanahr and Yehtraha. He saw them move into each other's arms, and as they kissed, a bright light from their room prevented Gray from further watching their procreation. He staggered back to his own bed as quietly as possible, temporarily blinded by the light he had seen. And he finally did sleep well.

BLIND

As Gray struggled to wake up early in the morning, he saw the light of the dawn through his closed eyelids. When he opened his eyes, he still saw the same light, but absolutely nothing else: the light had effectively blinded him. He remembered the laws Zayo had told him about the day before, including the one dealing with the invasion of privacy during procreation. Gray thought to himself, How could they name excommunication as the only fit punishment for such a crime when he was already effectively blinded? The blindness certainly seemed to be enough to him. Unless— unless it was considered treason to disobey a law set by the king for the safety of their people. The law preventing the invasion of privacy during procreation was intended to protect their people from the blindness, and also to promote an unrestrained relationship in a marriage. Due to the biological alchemy of the Caballians, the light of procreation was connected to sensory excitement and increased circulation in the genitals. Those involved were not blinded because of their slightly altered alchemy during the act, but if you were not a party to it, you were not welcome, but blinded. Most people had enough sense to let well enough alone. To cherish privacy during procreation was part of the freedom enjoyed by Caballians in their daily lives. Gray somehow did not understand such a concept; the other humans had understood it very well. Gray called for help.

It was not long before Zayo came running into Gray's room. As soon as he was in the room, he asked Gray, "What is wrong?"

131

"I can't see! I can't see!" he exclaimed.

"Calm down," Zayo replied.

Gray recognized Zayo's voice. He tried to calm down, and said rather calmly, "I woke up this morning, and couldn't see."

Zayo did not know what to think. "I shall call a doctor to assist you, if you feel it will help."

"Yes, please." Gray thought he was going to obtain the doctor from the colonists.

It was not long before Pleeyedraha entered his room and said to him as she walked up close to him, "I am here to assist you as you need help. Zayo has advised me that you cannot see."

"No," he replied, suddenly realizing he had a Caballian doctor. "Who are you?"

"I am Pleeyedraha, and I am the master healer."

"You must be a good doctor."

"I wear the black vest." She paused a moment. "I am here to inquire about your eyes, not to discuss my standing as the master healer. May I examine you?"

"Yeah, sure," he replied, knowing that his was a serious predicament.

Pleeyedraha was able to quickly key in on human physiology, because it was not too different from Caballian physiology. Her examination did not take too long. "What sort of lights have you been looking into to damage your eyes?"

"I haven't abused any lights," he retorted.

"I am trying to help you. If you do not wish for my help, why did you agree with Zayo's recommendation to send for a doctor?"

"He offered, so I thought he would have sent for the human doctor. I did not know he would actually call you."

"You were afflicted, so young Zayo sought to procure the best possible care on all of Equestra. My people have never before encountered any type of alien, not in millions of years of our history, so I do not see why you should have expected Zayo to think of your own personal doctor. He is not a king for your people. He is the king of the Caballians, and it is his duty to serve every aspect of our lives. Why is it important that he suddenly change everything he is to serve aliens such as yourself?"

"Why not? We now have to follow your laws."

"To what extent are you subject to our laws?"

"For as long as we are to have anything to do with your people."

"If you kept to yourselves, and made sure that everything you did would not affect any of my people either directly or indirectly, then I am sure Zayo would leave you to our own people. But when every action you take involves any or all of my people, Zayo is involved. You slept under this roof last night, so what you did last night affects my people. Your blindness affects my people."

"I am the one who is blind! What could it possibly have to do with your people?!"

"Do not lie to me! Think of what caused your blindness, then say it has nothing to do with my people!"

"None of your people blinded me. What can you do about my eyes?"

Pleeyedraha was noticeably irritated with him. "I will ask you one more time...what sort of lights have you abused?"

"None."

Pleeyedraha picked up all of her equipment and supplies, and flew out of the room and into the den, where Zayo set waiting for her. She set near her king, and buried her face in her hands. She was so frustrated. "Pleeyedraha," Zayo said, "what happened?"

She looked up at him, and tried to shake off her anger. "Zayo, he is a chronic liar, and he is so selfish. He is avoiding what caused his blindness."

"He seemed quite interested when I offered to send for a doctor."

"He did not want me—he wanted a human doctor."

"A human doctor?"

"Yes, because he knows that we would have discovered what caused his blindness. He was blinded by a light. Twice I asked him what lights he abused to blind himself, and twice he told me he does not know. What can I do with an uncooperative patient?"

"Humans are quite different from us."

"I studied his physiology very closely, and there are not very many differences between humans and Caballians. I know what blinded him."

"What was it?"

"The photocytic cycle."

Zayo was shocked at what he was hearing. "Pleeyedraha, are you sure?"

"There is nothing else on this planet which could have caused it, unless he had something with him which enabled him to inflict the blindness upon himself."

"If it was the photocytic cycle, then this human disobeyed our laws."

"Certainly. I do not know of any couple who would invite another to witness such a thing, in wanting to preserve their sight."

Zayo still could hardly believe what he was hearing. "I was taught about the photocytic cycle in school, and about how it relates to the conception of a foal. But truthfully, I never knew whether it was a reality or if it was one of the fables."

Pleeyedraha nearly laughed. "If you do look at it from the perspective of a fable, then it most certainly romanticizes the conception of a foal. I tell you, though, that it is a vital aspect of our reproductive alchemy. Without it, there would be no next generation."

"Why would he have inflicted such a blindness upon himself?"

"Why not? Tahrmaha told me that your group had difficulty obtaining water, and that she had to nearly demand it, so do you think that he would demand some sort of attention from us in return?"

"Then you are not really sure what caused his blindness."

"I believe it was the photocytic cycle, because what reason would a sentient creature have for self-inflicted injury?"

At that moment, there was a knock on the open door to the den, and Zayo and Pleeyedraha looked up to see Karayo standing in the doorway. "Your majesty, and Pleeyedraha," he said, "good morning. May I join you?"

Zayo saw his mother turn and walk away behind Karayo. "Good morning," the king replied.

"Good morning," Pleeyedraha added. "Your timing is good. Please join us."

He entered the room and set with them. "The human is blind."

Karayo eyed the young stallion carefully. "He...was not blind when he came here?"

"He appeared to be quite normal yesterday."

"I came because I heard of his arrival."

"What have you heard?"

"The other humans are agitated over his presence. It seems almost as if he is an unwanted visitor."

"Unwanted, but not unwelcome?"

"Humans are strange creatures. Pleeyedraha, have you examined him yet?"

"Yes," she replied, Abut he would not tell me what caused his blindness."

"Do you know what caused it?"

"Most certainly. It was caused by a very bright light."

"What sort of light?"

"Either a self-inflicted injury, or the photocytic cycle."

Karayo was deeply disturbed by her words. "If the others are so agitated over his presence, then it was more likely that his blindness was caused by the photocytic cycle. The only way to prove this is for us to question him again."

"You are sure that it was caused by the photocytic cycle?" Zayo asked.

"Sure enough, but we need to force the truth out of him. Otherwise, there is no way to prove it."

"Even if we are sure it was the photocytic cycle?" Pleeyedraha gasped.

"These are alien creatures with a different philosophy of living than our own. There is less predictability in their actions."

The three of them walked into the room which the Admiral had slept in, and they found him sitting where Pleeyedraha had left him. Zayo walked up to him and said, "Admiral, how do you feel?"

Gray was almost glad to hear Zayo's voice. "Why do you ask? You know that I am blind."

"Was Pleeyedraha able to help you?"

"I had thought you were sending for the human doctor."

"I sent for the best doctor I know. Pleeyedraha has earned her position as the master healer."

"All she did was examine me and ask me some questions."

"You were unwilling to answer all of her questions."

"Unwilling? How about unable?"

"Unable because you know they would have implicated you? Or did you cause the blindness upon yourself?"

"Why would I want to harm myself? Besides, I have nothing with me which I could have used for such a thing. I have no weapons or tools with me, and there is nothing in this room which I could have used for such a purpose. If I blinded myself, it would be the end of my career."

"Admiral, I have brought someone else here to talk to you."

"Who is it?"

"Karayo. He is the master historian of my people."

"'Master historian'?"

"A shaman."

"What on earth is a shaman? Another kind of doctor?"

Karayo stepped forward. "I am a parapsychologist as well as a historian," Karayo replied. "I know the wheres and whys of my people, and everything that has affected and is affecting their lives."

"What do you want to talk to me about?"

"Your blindness. Zayo and Pleeyedraha are extremely concerned over your problem. Tell me the story behind it—what caused it."

"Why? You would never tell me everything about yourselves."

"We have nothing to hide. Honesty is our way of life. You only just arrived here, yet already you are making assumptions about us."

"All I know is about the laws that were explained to me yesterday. Zayo gave me reasons behind all of them, but some of the reasoning seems to indicate that you are afraid of something."

"I told you, we are not ashamed of what we are. Rather, we are proud of our existence."

"I do not believe it. With laws such as the one forbidding the invasion of privacy during procreation, you have something you are hiding."

"Did you ask?"

"About the reasoning?"

"Yes."

"Most certainly. Zayo told me that the freedom of expression unhindered was the reason behind it."

"The freedom of expression unhindered is the root of our very existence. Zayo is only a youth. What sort of answer would you have expected from him on such a law? He understands it completely, but does not realize that certain givens do not apply to you because you are not Caballian."

"His approach to us is certainly very limited."

"He is doing what he can to protect our people from the dangers which your exploitation presents. He has no duty to you or your people. It is difficult enough for him to fulfill his duty to our people because of his age, yet you expect so much more of him. Even Tahrmaha took the time yesterday to explain to you why our people require water, without demanding a reason why there was not water waiting for us upon our arrival. You should have explained your misconception rather than demanding we are hiding something."

"What are you saying?"

"I am saying that the reason behind not invading privacy during procreation is much more than illegal, it is alchemically dangerous. Zayo is still too young to have learned all of the details behind this, although much was told to him in stories. Zayo has done his best to protect you as well as our people."

"How on earth could procreation be alchemically dangerous?"

"Perhaps it is not so in humans, but it is in Caballians. You must remember that we are as alien to you as you are to us. Pleeyedraha, would you please explain to him the photocytic cycle of procreation?"

"There are photocytic cells in our reproductive organs," she stated. "When they are stimulated by an increase in circulation and sensory excitement, their glow is blinding to anyone whose photocytic cycle is not stimulated. If another Caballian were to witness such a thing, they would most certainly be blinded. If two Caballians were to procreate without being married to each other, they would become blinded. Also, if a photocytically active married couple knew that they were being watched, the existing psychological restrictions on their actions would prevent any hopes of reproducing, just because they knew the third party would be blinded."

"You mean that your people cannot reproduce if they are not guaranteed privacy?"

"Exactly."

"We are a people of forty thousand," Zayo added. "This dimension of our reproductive evolution has kept our population down."

"A built-in population control?" Gray wondered.

"If we had not evolved in this way," Karayo said, "Equestra would be at least as populated as Earth is."

"That law is to protect your biological rhythms."

"I wish you would have asked about it," Zayo remarked.

"I assumed that your people would have hidden something."

"Instead, you deceived me into believing that you would follow our laws. I trusted you, Admiral. You have absolved that trust."

"But your majesty, I could not sleep without an idea of what your people are like."

"Now, Admiral," Pleeyedraha said, "I am going to ask you one more time: what light caused your blindness? I am quite sure you know."

"It was that damned photocytic cycle!" he retorted.

"If the couple you witnessed were to learn of this," Karayo added, "they would demand that you be punished for your crime."

"What sort of crime is it to satiate one's curiosity?"

"When you disturb a couple's lives in such a way, it is a very serious crime. If it prevents them from reproducing for the rest of their lives whereas they would have had two or three foals, it is a serious crime. Preventing life is just as serious as ending it against someone's will. We consider it to be just as atrocious as murder."

"Don't you people have a lenient bone in your bodies?"

"I was generous enough when I told you of our laws yesterday," Zayo replied. "You said you would follow them. You now expect me to forgive you for breaking one of them?"

"It was a misunderstanding. If you return me to Earth, it will never happen again."

"You will never see Earth again," Karayo added.

"What?!"

"If I let you return to Earth unpunished," the young king continued, "then the rest of the colonists will also think they can get away with breaking one of our laws. If one of them murders one of my people, must I return him to Earth? If any criminal is returned to Earth, there is always the chance that they will return here to haunt my people. That will not happen. You agreed to follow our laws, and since you broke one of them, you must be punished for it."

Gray was uncontrollably upset. "You dumb ass! How dare you undermine the work I must bring back with me?!"

Zayo became livid. "That is treason. Your excommunication will take place this afternoon."

Their commotion was heard throughout most of the palace; Mehlanahr heard it, and hurried to find out what was going on. He entered the room as soon as Zayo had stated the time for Gray's excommunication. "Your majesty," he said to Zayo as he entered the room.

Mehlanahr saw the fury in Zayo's eyes when the young king looked at him and replied, "You are welcome here."

"Excommunication," Gray mumbled. "That must be some sort of a gross misunderstanding."

"Karayo, can you summon two guards for me, and make the announcement?"

"Yes, your majesty," he replied, and he walked out of the room with Pleeyedraha following him.

"Zayo," Mehlanahr remarked, "what is going on?"

"This human committed a serious crime, and he is to be punished for it."

"You explained our laws to him yesterday. What could have possibly happened?"

"Curiosity killed the cat," Gray quipped, "and satisfaction brought him back. I was curious as to your methods of procreation, so I set out last night to find out for myself. What happened is now that I am effectively blind, caused by your damned photocytic cycle."

Mehlanahr was shocked. "You are irate because you did not follow our laws? I am the one who should be irate here. You attempt to disturb my life in such a way, then you expect to be punished lightly for it?"

"Mehlanahr," Zayo said, "I had not wanted you to find out all of what he had done, because I know it would upset your life for some time."

"Zayo, even when you are photocytic, you can see and hear a door move unexpectedly."

All of the Caballians rushed to the palace grounds, especially those who lived far away. After Zayo painfully explained his crime to all of the Caballians and the colonists, Gray was excommunicated with the shifter.

Zayo went to his adjutant's office, and was surprised when he saw that Mehlanahr had the company of none other than Captain John Hancock. Mehlanahr saw the young king, and said, "Thank the moons you are here, Zayo."

Zayo gave the human a puzzled look. Hancock then said, "I asked him if I could go back to Earth with him to speak with the others about this, and he told me that I would have to speak with you, so I waited for your arrival."

"Why, Mehlanahr?" Zayo asked.

"He said it was important that he go back to Earth," the master engineer replied. "I did not want to tell him yes without asking you."

"We have been wounded deeply by an alien, and now you still wish to help them all you can. Why?"

"Zayo, what do you think the human would have thought if they had met Kayloor instead of you, and then had seen him killed? They would have thought us to be barbaric. Perhaps Gray was also an exception. There may as well be many good humans."

The trip to Earth was very smooth. This time, when Hancock radioed down to verify their landing, he was asked to land at Alameda by Admiral Van Housen. Whereas Gray was a very ordinary-looking man with gray hair and gray eyes, Vice Admiral Shane Van Housen was a sharp-looking individual, and could easily be picked out in a crowd. He had short (crew cut) stark white hair, icy blue eyes that pierced like daggers, and facial features that showed his Native American ancestry. But Van Housen had earned his rank through action, not through politics (as Gray had done).

Zayo had not removed his crown since the caucus ended; he had forgotten he was wearing it. Mehlanahr thought nothing of it as they left the ship. They were caught by a wonderful breeze, much unlike the heat they had encountered at Cape Canaveral. An escort of six guards met them, and brought them to a rather large building that was there; it was an office building four stories in height, much taller than any building on Equestra. The Caballians had never seen stairs before, so when they were brought up some stairs to the fourth floor, they were so struck by the experience of stairs that they did not pay much attention to the room they were entering.

It was a large briefing room, which consumed a full half of the fourth floor, as well as a large portion of the third floor. It was large enough to hold a hundred humans (seated), and there was easily room for another fifty humans to stand in the center. It was a rotunda of an auditorium. The rear edges of it were at the fourth-floor level, and the center of it was at the third-floor level. It was ideal for briefings concerning missions.

Captain John Hancock had been in this very room once before, when his crew was given its last full briefing before departing for Barnard. Hancock sat down in a front row seat, and all of the Caballians reclined in front of the row.

Just as they were getting settled, Vice Admiral Shane Van Housen hurried in, and ran down to the center. He saw Hancock, and walked up to him. "Captain," he said, "I am truly sorry to have detained you and your guests; I should have been here to greet you." He looked at the Caballians, and his eyes settled on Zayo for the purposes of his crown. "Commander MacBain has told me some information this morning. I trust I did not inconvenience you by having you come here instead of to Cape Canaveral?" Zayo shook his head no. "I am Vice Admiral Shane Van Housen. Is there anything which you require—any refreshment—before we continue?"

"If you would be so kind," Pakoor said, "some water would suffice." Van Housen summoned the water immediately; as soon as he did, the Caballians all began to laugh, except for Pakoor. The doctor looked at Zayo, who was laughing the hardest. "Your majesty," he said, "I have never before been mocked for seeing to the health of any person. Why now?"

"It is not you, Pakoor," the young king replied, still pleasantly amused. "No slight to your honor was intended."

Shane darted a look at Zayo and said, "I was told that you appreciate courtesy. I did not know that you mock it."

"It is not a mockery," Zayo replied. "Admiral Gray had killed whatever faith I had found in Hancock's attempt at outreach."

"Gray has always been a fool. If he were not a military man, he would have fallen in with the revolutionaries. It would not surprise me, though, if he had his connections."

"Revolutionaries?" Mehlanahr asked. "Are they the same as traitors?"

The water was then brought in. Van Housen allowed them to drink some of it before he answered Mehlanahr's question. "I have not forgotten your question. There are many kinds of traitors."

"I meant the type that would commit treason against their king."

Van Housen had to think about this before he could answer. "In that sense, then they are very similar. Whereas that type of traitor would likely make an attempt against his king's life, the revolutionaries assassinate anyone whom they feel is impeding their progress."

"Is it possibly that such people killed Doc Lawson two days ago?"

"Who is Doc Lawson?"

"I do not know—I only heard Admiral Gray speak of him on some sort of communication device. He was also mumbling something about Fagan."

I was right about Gray, Van Housen thought to himself. "Hancock, anything that is said about Fagan will not leave this room."

Hancock wrinkled his forehead. "Admiral, all I could possibly feel bad about is what we missed during the last ten years. Sounds like a civilian conspiracy, or possibly terrorists."

"He is a terrorist, Captain. Unfortunately, Gray has been involved in it, although I have no proof to that. That is why it cannot leave this room."

Hancock laughed. "Sir, I do not believe you will have any more problems with Gray. His career is finished."

Something happened on their planet when Gray went there, he thought to himself. A Caballian was heard clearing his throat, so Van Housen quickly asked, "More water?" They all took more, then he continued. "Hancock, please introduce your friends to me."

"I do not know most of them, Sir."

"I will introduce my crew," Mehlanahr said. He named them all, and indicated each person as he said their name. He also introduced

Yehtraha as his wife. Then he said, "My king, Zayo, wishes to speak with you."

The Admiral was obviously perplexed. "Who are you?" he asked Mehlanahr.

Van Housen was still standing, so Zayo asked him, "Do you think it would be better if you sat with us, in the circle?" Shane sat down in a hurry, bringing out some snickers from everyone. "That is Mehlanahr," he told Van Housen. "He is the master engineer among my people, and serves me as my adjutant."

"Your majesty, is Gray still on your planet?"

"How concerned are you about Gray?"

"Only professional concern. Personally, I despise the man. He is a coward if I ever saw one."

"He was arrogant and oblivious to the laws and honor of the Caballians."

"Meaning what? You said was, not is."

"I know exactly what I said, and what form and tense I inferred. Did MacBain tell you everything that happened the first time I was here? Of how rudely Gray treated me?"

"He did not have to mention that. I have reviewed the tapes."

"Tapes?"

"It is policy to record all briefings. And frankly, I listened to that particular tape five times; every time I did, it set me further against Gray in my opinion of him. He severely broke several regulations in the context of that conversation."

"When Gray first came to Equestra, I spent valuable hours with him, explaining to him all of our laws and our judicial system. But instead of his heeding my instructions, he put them to the test, and broke two of our severest crimes."

"What is your policy in such a situation?"

"As with any criminal, the punishment must be administered within twenty-seven hours of the occurrence of the crime."

"So you punished Gray."

"It was my duty to punish him. He had agreed to follow our laws, which also includes being subject to the appropriate punishment if merited."

"Where is Gray now?"

"There is only one punishment acceptable for the crimes he committed. That is excommunication."

Van Housen was jarred. If he is as sincere as he seems, Shane thought to himself, then...what the devil did he do with Gray? These aliens are much more complex than I originally thought. I must do what I can to obtain their friendship. After a moment's thought, he said to Zayo, "Could you please explain to me what excommunication is in the way of a punishment?"

Zayo replied, "The last time I dealt with criminals, they had committed murder, but our laws prohibit murder. The only way to stop criminals who commit capital crimes is to remove their existence from our realm of existence, and place them in the realm where all criminals spend eternity, where they can no longer harm innocent victims. If someone cannot serve a good purpose, and their soul shows that it is owned by the ruler of the realm of hell, then they have consigned their lives to that realm; by their acts, they request that to be their home. When their request is made, I am required to send them there by means of the shifter, which shifts their lives from this realm to the realm of hell."

Van Housen thought about his words, then suddenly thought to himself, So the punishment fits the old saying of go to hell, it actually sends them there. He withheld a laugh as he thought about what a strange character Gray had been. He then looked at Zayo's sabre as it hung from his lavender vest, and thought how it seemed to be a vastly superior make than that of any human craftsman, and the metals it was made of were different from the metals which were readily available on Earth. "If I may be so candid," he said to Zayo, who nodded, "if you are prohibited from executing criminals, they why do you carry a sabre?"

Zayo then said to him in a serious tone, "If any of my people were to show you or your staff disrespect, then I must be prepared to clip their tails, something we consider to be very humiliating." He paused a moment before continuing. "You are genuine, and have seen to the needs of my people; we were touched by your goodness when you offered us something to drink. You are not so concerned about your job as to allow it to infringe upon the well-being of others."

"My job is to ensure the well-being of all personnel who work here. That is also why Gray did not truly earn his position."

"Are there other leaders here on Earth?"

"There are so many—so many I cannot count them all."

"In your reports to them, let them know of our desire to be friends."

JAYEXEEYO

Six days after the caucus, on the two hundred and thirty-first day, Karayo was nearly finished with his initial questioning of Vehdoor. "It is time to put it all together and use it," he told his student.

"Kayloor never told Zayo about Dahrohd and Jayexeeyo."

"How does this affect Zayo?"

Vehdoor laughed; it was an easy question. "Zayo will not rest until he is told the whole story in its entirety."

"You are probably right about that."

"The only person who can tell him the story is Ahrkoor. The master shoemaker is old, and should have died ten years ago, but he continues to will himself to live, knowing that he has to fulfill his obligation to Kayloor's heir."

"His obligation?"

"To tell Zayo about Dahrohd and Jayexeeyo. Ahrkoor rarely makes shoes anymore. It was a tremendous strain on him to make the crown and the two sabres. Zayo will need new shoes soon. When he goes to Ahrkoor, he will learn the rest of the story, then Ahrkoor will die, and leave the black vest to Jayexeeyo."

Karayo was rather upset at the thought of Ahrkoor dying. "Do you have any idea how soon?"

"Within two days."

"If Ahrkoor does all this in two days, then indeed you are worthy to be called a shaman, the one with the talent of foresight. However, you will continue to work with me for several months because there is still so much for you to learn before you are fully capable of working on your own."

As Zayo awoke early in the morning two days later, he was direly thinking of his dead father, and what Kayloor would have done with the humans if he were in Zayo's shoes. It was very difficult to imagine such a scenario; Kayloor had been very lax, yet he had such experience which Zayo was far from, and Zayo knew it. But Zayo also knew that it was physically impossible to regain Kayloor; all of his essences were gone, although the lives that he had touched remained. He remembered this and much more about the father he had loved with undying passion and adoration. But as he arose from his bed that morning thinking of Kayloor, he suddenly remembered what he had thought of Tahrmaha when she had gone with Mehlanahr to Earth as a doctor for his crew.

Zayo's bed, like any other Caballian bed, was simply an interwoven mat of straw which had all ends hidden, and which lay upon a two-inch-thick cushioning made of a loosely woven fluffy material which, in texture, was rather similar to cotton, although it was yellowish. The beds were made by spinners.

While Zayo prepared himself breakfast, he realized that it was his turn to get food enough for everyone. The kitchen was so empty that, apart from what was barely enough for his breakfast, there was not a single grain of oat, let alone any type of fruit or bread. In order for him to have lunch and for everyone to have supper and breakfast the next morning, he had to fetch enough food for everyone.

After he ate his breakfast, he set to making candles for the palace. After that, he would head to Tokanar, obtain new shoes for his hooves, stop in the refinery and have his transport refilled with philinium, stop at a food distributor and obtain produce and grain, and visit a baker and obtain bread. Then, he wanted to stop at the hospital and find a way to speak with Tahrmaha about what she remembered of Kayloor. If he placed himself right, and deliberately took his time at every stop he had to make, then he would get to the hospital in time for lunch, and he would be able to eat with everyone there instead of by himself. Having prioritized his duties for that morning, he set out.

The northern forge in Tokanar, on the palace side of the city, was Ahrkoor's forge, the forge always used by the master shoemaker because of its proximity to the palace. Zayo had always had his shoes made by Ahrkoor, and had never gone to the forge when he was not there. Again, he was planning on the best shoes that he could get anywhere on Equestra. How could his plans possibly go wrong?

Shoemakers are perhaps one of the strangest breeds on all of Equestra. They, more so than any other Caballian, believe in the rich tradition that their work holds, and work in a very archaic manner. They consider it taboo to attempt to modernize their methods, because the way that they work is time-tested and proven to be the best. Many other ways had been tried, but none of them were ever quite as successful. Not only that, but some of their practices seemed rather ridiculous.

One of the oddest peculiarities of a shoemaker and his forge (this because there has never been a female shoemaker among the Caballians, as the fable goes) is that when he becomes the forgemaster of a forge, then the first thing he begins work on is to craft his own handmade set of tools, so that he will fully understand and appreciate the quality of the tools that he uses. When he has done that, and is ready to begin crafting shoes, he makes a pair of shoes right away, but that first pair is <u>never</u> given to anyone else, or nailed onto anyone's hooves: they are affixed to the entrance door of the forge on the outside, and are symbolic of the fact that the forgemaster is ready and able to make shoes for all others. If there is only one shoe on the door, then he still works, but only his associates craft shoes. If there are no shoes on the door, then no one dares to enter the forge because the tools are not ready.

Zayo saw the familiar shoes on the entrance to Ahrkoor's forge, the shoes which had hung there for over two centuries, and showed no sign of any rust, although they did seem slightly worn by the weather. The king entered, and found himself in the working area that he had visited many times before. However, the last time he had been there was with his father, and it now tugged at him even more that he had to speak with Tahrmaha and Pleeyedraha.

Zayo heard someone working near the forgefire, but he could not see who it was; the sound continued even after Ahrkoor walked up to him. "Your majesty, good morning," he said.

"Master shoemaker, good morning." He stopped and looked around very carefully, trying to place in his mind that everything was the same as it had been the last time he was there.

"Is something wrong, Zayo?"

"I do not know," he sighed. "Something is missing, but everything looks exactly the same as the last time I needed shoes."

Ahrkoor was puzzled by Zayo's comment. "Perhaps it is because not everything is quite exactly the same as it was the last time," he offered. "I am always moving things around."

"I expect that-" he began, but a sudden deadpan look stole over the young king's face. "Never mind, Ahrkoor. I guess I am just not feeling too well today." Zayo shook his head, trying to break away from whatever it was that was plaguing him.

Ahrkoor placed his hands on Zayo's shoulders. "I have known you since you were new, Zayo. Ever since your first set of shoes. Your parents were always proud of you, and our people are fast becoming proud of you. But why should you weigh yourself down with such deep troubles when life is difficult enough? Come—let me make some shoes for you. Do you have a hangnail poking your frog?"

Zayo managed a slight smile, but remained troubled. Even as the old shoemaker worked, removing the old shoes, cleaning out the crusted mud, trimming the hangnails which sometimes plagued the frogs, and filing the hooves so that his legs would align properly, the king remained sullen. New shoes were quickly crafted for his not quite full grown hooves, and they were precisely attached. When Ahrkoor finished, he saw that the king's eyes were still downcast. "Zayo," he said, "how old are you?"

"Twenty-five," he replied.

"I am about four hundred and fifty, perhaps some more...I forget how many. I remember Kuhoor as the crown prince. I have lived through so many difficult times, and so many happy times. But seeing you suffer like this is far worse than anything else I have ever lived through. Though I am physically losing strength, my inner strength...my love for my job and our people...has enabled me to continue to make shoes, and even your crown, my king." He knelt before a seated Zayo. "I have willed myself to do what I have accomplished in my lifetime, but seeing you like this tears my heart apart. I feel my strength fading from me as I kneel here looking at your distressed eyes."

"How could I possibly help you? I need you to help me."

"How long shall you retain the foolish foalish yearnings which you must release yourself from? Zayo, it is fine to look up to our people, but there are times when you cannot depend on anyone to do what you yourself must do." He stopped himself, as he was growing short of breath from his attempt to reach Zayo.

"Perhaps you should do what Raivo did...give up making shoes."

147

"Making shoes has nothing to do with the comatose heart of a king!" he suddenly exclaimed, and began to rasp for breath as his weak lungs were in dire need of a rest.

"Comatose heart?!" He helped Ahrkoor to lay down, as he was in a very bad way.

"Those who loved Kayloor...truly loved him. Pleeyedraha...has been hit the hardest, Zayo. She will die soon. How many people can take the pain of a murdered king whom they loved more than life?" His breathing stayed shallow, but he continued. "Zayo, I will die before I give up on your father. He did not deserve death!" Tears welled up in his eyes, and began to roll down his face.

Jayexeeyo, who was Ahrkoor's understudy, heard the elderly stallion wheezing and yelling, and he came running from where he had been working at the forgefire. When he saw Ahrkoor laying on the floor, he knew that the master shoemaker was in serious trouble.

"You expect me to forget my father just so that I can live?" Zayo pondered aloud.

"Not forget him, but stop depending on him. You are young enough to break away. Zayo, you must make the Caballians your people, instead of leaving them all as Kayloor's people." He stopped suddenly, almost unable to breathe.

"Why not you?" Zayo retorted. "You cannot break away?"

Ahrkoor looked over, and saw Jayexeeyo. "Master," Jayexeeyo said, "do you wish for me to tell him?"

"Tell him everything," Ahrkoor whispered, "and when I am satisfied, I will let go. Then you shall claim the black vest."

Zayo heard every word he told Jayexeeyo. "Many others have far more experience. I am only fifty-four years old. It should go to someone more experienced."

Ahrkoor shook his head no. "Jayexeeyo, you are a better shoemaker than I am. You learn by instinct, not by tutoring; you are the only shoemaker alive who possesses the ancient gifts," he whispered. "Your hands have such a remarkable feel for their task that I believe you can cure founder. No one will ever discredit you, because they know in their hearts that you are the best. I know Raivo will support you."

"Yes, Master." Jayexeeyo had Zayo set back down. "Your majesty, you must listen to a long story." Jayexeeyo knelt before him; he was very young, and was as red a chestnut as Kayloor had been; he was not yet married. Physically, he was the exact opposite of Mehlanahr: developed muscles throughout his body from heavy labor; refined bone structure in a face which was very scholarly; sparkling black eyes; and large pointed ears which curled over forward somewhat and were embraced by thickly curled, almost frizzy, shoulder-length chestnut hair. His chestnut beard distinctively set off his face. He looked like a shoemaker from a foal's fable, being very agile and powerful.

"I thought I was taught all stories and history in school," Zayo remarked.

"You know nothing of my life or education, or of what Kayloor and Ahrkoor did for me."

"Then please tell me."

"If Ahrkoor had not had a student at the time that I turned twenty, I would have become his student. But instead, I was brought to another."

"You are from Tokanar, though."

"Yes. I was finally placed with Dahrohd."

"The criminal?"

"Back then, he was not a criminal. He was a relatively new forgemaster with good skills. After my internship, Ahrkoor tested me himself. As it turned out, I had spent more of my internship teaching Dahrohd command presence, composure and confidence than he had spent teaching me basic skills, and he was a forgemaster! This was the beginning of his dishonor and disgrace."

"Then you were placed with Ahrkoor after your passage."

"I was, but not until after both Dahrohd and I were questioned by Ahrkoor and Kayloor. Ahrkoor, Dahrohd, and myself all vowed that we would never mention anything of the disgrace that Dahrohd had done to anyone but the king himself. Now Kayloor and Dahrohd are both dead."

"Why are you telling me? You are going against your promise to my father."

"Our vow was not to Kayloor, but to the throne. And for his majesty's sake, we can never renounce it. But Dahrohd...he did not keep his vow to the throne. Kayloor should have punished him then for treason...if he had, he would still be alive. But Kayloor was lenient, and forgave him of the violent misdeed he had done."

"How did Dahrohd not keep the vow?"

"He told Maroola and Wehrahn. They grew angry at Kayloor's unwantonness to act, all three of them, so they decided then and there to speak with Kayloor about it. Dahrohd brought the imploder with him...Booralta told Ahrkoor and myself that it was only intended to be used to clear away any bodies when Kayloor grew furious and killed one of them for treason! But when Kayloor did not grow mad, Dahrohd did."

Zayo looked at Jayexeeyo thoughtfully. "How did you come to know my father's story so well?"

"I told you, Dahrohd was my teacher."

"What was Dahrohd's disgrace that brought about the vow?"

"His inability to teach me fully how to be a shoemaker."

"Still, why is this important to me?"

"Zayo, you alone have the ability to lead our people away from Kayloor's mistake with Dahrohd that affected us all. Ahrkoor cannot escape it because he was so intertwined in it...he is too old to handle the stress of it. Speaking of Kayloor ever since his death has always made him short of breath."

"Zayo," Ahrkoor whispered, "Zayo, come to me."

Zayo barely heard his whisper, but he ran to the shoemaker's side. "What is it, Ahrkoor?" he asked.

"Lead the Caballians away from Kayloor's error...make them your people, willing to follow you. You are the hope of the future. Jayexeeyo is also young, and can work with you throughout your reign." He began to cry again. "Every time you see Jayexeeyo, remember your father's murderers...it is easy to do. But most importantly," and he caught as deep a breath as possibly, "always remember your father's undying love and sympathy for our people, and use your own love as an important ingredient of your reign." Ahrkoor exhaled the last remnants of his life.

Jayexeeyo removed his own gray vest, and took Ahrkoor's black vest with gray trim and put it on. He then imploded Ahrkoor's body. Jayexeeyo was now the forgemaster as well as the master shoemaker, so the first thing he did was to remove Ahrkoor's telltale shoes from the door. As soon as he had done that, Zayo said to him, "What will you do now, Jayexeeyo?"

"Your majesty, I have a lot of work to do. I have to melt down everything that was Ahrkoor's, and make my own. His tools, molds and stocks will not suit another forgemaster. They were his identity, and I must make mine."

Zayo was liking Jayexeeyo more and more. "I must not detain you then. May I call you my friend?"

"If it pleases you."

"But does it please you?"

"What would please me is if my king would heed everything that he was taught today, and use it to his advantage. He was given a very good tool today for his kingcraft, a tool much more important than any sabre or crown."

"Perhaps you should have been my adjutant."

"Never, Zayo! I hold too much love for Kayloor...it will take me years to fully adapt to another king."

"That is a shoemaker's jest!" Zayo cried, recognizing his torment immediately.

"Perhaps, my friend, but how else will I get you to leave? I do have work to do."

"Would you have accepted such a position?"

"That is hypothetical. Besides, Mehlanahr is more worthy."

"Why is that?"

"He is always there when you need him, despite his work and his family. Most Caballians feel that their family ties are the strongest." He began to pick up all of the loose shoes that lay in the forge, and started placing them in the fire so that he could melt them down and separate the metals. Jayexeeyo saw that Zayo was not moving, so he remarked, "You are not my student. I have taught you all that I possibly could that would be of any value to you."

"I am still despairing over what my father did."

"I do not think that you will find any more answers here."

Zayo finally left the forge, much more distressed than when he entered it not long before.

The refinery was quite close to Jayexeeyo's forge, so Zayo went there next. A guard put enough philinium in his transport to last at least a month. Zayo said nothing of Ahrkoor's death, but instead, set out for Karayo's house to obtain some answers which he could not get from the shoemaker—or so he thought.

Once Zayo had settled in Karayo's company, he drank some water. Then, Karayo asked him, "Where is Kayloor?"

"What?" Zayo replied with a start, not having heard Karayo quite right.

"Where is Kayloor?" he repeated.

"He is dead," Zayo replied.

"Do you believe it?"

"Of course I do!"

"Then why are you chasing after a dead stallion whom you know was imploded? His shadow remains in memories."

"What is wrong with learning from others' perceptions?"

151

"If it is something which they feel is worthwhile to tell you, and that you will understand it, then they will tell you on their own whim. Just like you could not press Jayexeeyo to tell you more than he had to tell you."

Zayo was nearly speechless. "How did you know I was speaking with Jayexeeyo?"

"Is Ahrkoor dead?"

"Yes, but that does not answer my question."

"You spoke with Jayexeeyo and learned Dahrohd's story because Ahrkoor was too weak to tell it to you himself."

Vehdoor had been setting with them, listening to their conversation, when he finally asked Zayo, "Is it also true that the black vest is now worn by Jayexeeyo? That he is the forgemaster, and has closed the forge until he completes his tools? And that you are uncomfortable with what you were told?"

"Yes, those things are all true," Zayo shrugged.

Karayo saw Zayo's uneasiness, so he said, "Vehdoor was trying to help, Zayo. He is learning to fulfill his role as a shaman. He told me two days ago that all of these events would happen today."

"Is there any way that I can find someone to help me break free from my father's shadow?"

"Ahrkoor was very close to Kayloor, and so he knew things which he told you for their importance to you. There are others who knew your father very well, and have been suffering since his murder. Speak to them."

"Pleeyedraha?"

"Perhaps. But remember this: just as you learned that you had to use discretion with the humans, you must use discretion with our people."

"But Mehlanahr told me that our people appreciate me for my openness."

"Your openness about yourself is what he meant. But use discretion when you speak about your father. It took you quite a while after his murder to be able to hold a conversation about your father. Many people still cannot, because the crime has severely wounded the honor and pride of our people. Things like that take much time to heal."

"It will take many years," Vehdoor added.

"The wound must be healed," Zayo replied. "Can a healer like Pleeyedraha help?"

"Pleeyedraha was too close to Kayloor to be of such use to you. But, I tell you this: your queen will be a healer. This will make you greater than Polihdahr."

Zayo suddenly realized that Vehdoor was going to be able to replace Booralta. "Why would such a thing matter?" Zayo wondered aloud.

"You are the king," Karayo said mockingly, trying to instigate Zayo. "You can make the big decisions now. You have silenced six criminals, and our people are becoming afraid of your shifter."

"That is as bad as a shoemaker's jest!" Zayo exclaimed. "But Jayexeeyo gave me a better tool today. How can I learn to use it?"

Karayo was pleased. "Now you are listening and learning, my king. You are learning of the love that exists between our people and their king. Kayloor had the tool, but he used it too often, even when he should have used the shifter or the sabre."

"I saw Ahrkoor die! That is not enough?!"

"Ahrkoor wore the black vest, and now someone else does. There was only one witness to the transferal, and that was you. It is your responsibility to make the announcement to our people right away."

"Why the hurry?"

"Why not? You were eager to get the excommunications over in a hurry, so you should show much eagerness in something much more honorable."

"What is so honorable about a death?"

"Ahrkoor lived a full life, and gave the black vest to who he felt best earned it. Celebrate the honor of Ahrkoor finishing his task, and celebrate the honor of a black vest being given to someone who truly deserves it."

Without another word, Zayo used Karayo's visiphone to make the announcement to all of their people. When he was finished, he rejoined them and said, "Karayo, why is it that I do not feel as if I can separate myself from my father's shadow?"

"Make yourself the king, Zayo. Make no mention of your father to our people unless it is necessary. Allow your experiences to take the place of all that is currently shrouded by Kayloor. Create new memories to soften the harsh ones. But, never seek to make your own experiences as harsh as possible so as to cover Kayloor's memory with bitterness. Let your reign become a pleasurable memory for all. As you sought to prevent Mehlanahr from being clipped, you must also seek to help every other Caballian to the best of your ability."

I will not ask Pleeyedraha, Zayo thought to himself. I will ask Tahrmaha.

EQUESTRA

It seemed like a very long trip to the food distributor. All the way, Zayo was pondering his conversation with Karayo even more than he had wondered about what Ahrkoor had said to him. Karayo's words troubled him, even though they were good words; it would take him some time to understand it all. But this could not be blamed on his youth, or his innocence, or his lack of wisdom; he was actually very insightful for his young age, and understood much more than many older citizens.

Zayo remained very somber as he loaded the food into his transport. He had bitten off more than he could chew this day as he delved into the very epitome of the Caballian society—or had he? Zayo was not experiencing the first time he had thrown himself into the heart of a situation, but every other time had been for a different reason altogether. This was the first time he was being forced to realize the strength of the Caballians' hearts. But it was not all as simple as it sounded, because he was being prodded into maturing much faster than he would otherwise have matured. He then proceeded to the bakery, where he obtained enough bread for the next day.

At the hospital, Zayo walked around a bit, but soon found that most of those who worked there were eating lunch, so he went to the hospital's kitchen to look for Pleeyedraha. She was not there, so he turned to walk out, but he did not get very far before Pleeyedraha walked through the doorway with Tahrmaha; Zayo was right near them. When Pleeyedraha noticed his presence, she nearly jumped at the sight of him. "Pleeyedraha, I have been looking for you," he said.

Pleeyedraha had spoken with Karayo about ten minutes earlier, and had learned that Ahrkoor and Jayexeeyo had spoken with Zayo about Kayloor just before Ahrkoor died. She shook her head. "Zayo, I know that you are upset over Ahrkoor's death."

"I set out this morning in search of remnants of my father," he told her.

"There is nothing for you here," she told him, trying to hide her pain.

"That is not true! Pleeyedraha, you were the only thing like a mother he ever knew! I have known you almost like a grandmother!"

"What sort of nonsense is this, Zayo?" she asked, holding back her tears.

"Forget it. I should not have come to you. You cannot help me, as Karayo said you would not be able to."

She tried very hard to keep her composure. "Zayo, you are troubled. I know that Ahrkoor was a good friend of your father's."

"Ahrkoor has nothing to do with this. He is gone. There is another wearing the black vest. Jayexeeyo imploded the empty corpse. Would you have liked to have done it?"

"Zayo, your mother is better adapted to dealing with this than I am."

"If I expose to her what I must, then she will also die, just like Ahrkoor died—of a broken heart! She is pregnant, and I cannot risk both of their lives."

Pleeyedraha could hardly believe the level that Zayo was speaking at. He was suddenly so changed from several days ago...what had happened to him? And what else was happening? "We must go somewhere else to speak, Zayo."

Tahrmaha looked at them, not knowing where she belonged—with her teacher, as she usually was, or by herself for a short while. "Pleeyedraha," she said, "is there anything you wish me to do?"

"Proceed with your lunch," the elder doctor stated.

"No," Zayo told the young intern. "You have shared some of Pleeyedraha's experiences with my father, and you must know what makes a king think if you are to follow Pleeyedraha in her ways of being an excellent doctor."

"I am not a psychiatrist," Tahrmaha rebutted, trying to remain quite decent despite his obvious changes. She had seen him when he was acting like his father, but now, for the first time, she was seeing the fire that Tarahnaha had told her of. "Shamans are trained in mental disciplines."

Zayo was shocked: she had actually dared to challenge him with such a diplomatic challenge! But he quickly adapted and said, "Pleeyedraha knows my ways, and has taught you quite a bit. I would like you to share your opinion of her knowledge with me."

"Pleeyedraha was Kayloor's nurse. You said so yourself—'the only thing like a mother he ever knew.' Forgive me, Pleeyedraha, but Zayo is still hideously suffering from his father's grasp."

Zayo was very annoyed at Tahrmaha's rebuttal, but he could not do anything about it; he had asked her a question, and she had answered it honestly. Pleeyedraha then said, "When will the two of you show some mental reserve and grow?!"

"Tahrmaha," Zayo said, "you still did not answer my request. I want you to speak with us."

155

"I will not assist you in chasing the lost glory of Kayloor," she told him. "I have people's lives to help before I could possibly consider what might have been if someone were still alive."

"You have worked closely with Pleeyedraha."

"I work and study with Pleeyedraha, but never with Kayloor. And he never imposed himself on our work relationship. Why must you? I will speak with you alone, when I am not working. But I cannot allow my relationship with Pleeyedraha to impair my relationship with you. Why did you grow angry with me when I did nothing to offend anyone, except perhaps Pleeyedraha for outstepping my bounds? What a temper you have!"

Zayo hung his head in shame and walked out; what had he done to Tahrmaha? She was right. He had absolutely no reason to grow angry with her. And he had no reason whatsoever to be angry with Pleeyedraha, because she had kept his family alive. If it had not been for her, he would never have been born.

Tahrmaha and Pleeyedraha went outside to see what had happened with Zayo. When he saw them, he began to cry very loud and distressingly. The two of them walked back into the hospital and into Pleeyedraha's office, where Pleeyedraha closed the door behind Tahrmaha so that no one would disturb them. They set down, and after a brief moment of silence, Pleeyedraha said, "Tarahnaha was becoming so concerned about him, because he had not yet released himself from his emotional ties to his father—until now. Today is the beginning, Tahrmaha."

"What did he want with me, Pleeyedraha?"

"I am not sure. But he probably feels that because you know me as well as you do that you also became well acquainted with Kayloor. It is not hard to come to such a conclusion. His motives, however, are his own, just as his father's were."

"Was it right of me to challenge him so?"

"Was it right of him to come here and test you so?"

"Why should he have come here, if only to lose his temper? You were Kayloor's nurse; that is easy to understand. I have only been a spectator every time that Kayloor came here to speak with you. Zayo does not understand such a thing?"

"Zayo is understanding too much today. Too much for his unsolved emotions. I tell you, I would have expected such an outburst from a stallion who was near to his passage. Twenty five?" she finally mused, bewildered by the whole situation.

"You mean the emotional breakthrough?"

"Yes." Pleeyedraha stopped to think a moment before she continued. "We have the situation all wrong—expecting too much of Zayo at his age; wanting him to understand and do everything that a king is supposed to do, something that usually takes about fifty years of training."

"I disagree with you, Pleeyedraha."

Pleeyedraha was rather shocked; this was the first time that Tahrmaha had disagreed with her in her opinion of the royal house. "Why?" she wondered.

"Why was he so upset with Dahrohd at the coronation?"

"Because Dahrohd pulled the trigger on the imploder."

"What killed Ahrkoor today?"

Pleeyedraha was stumped. "I really do not know why."

"It must have been Dahrohd. Is it true, that Dahrohd was Jayexeeyo's mentor before his passage?"

"Yes, but-"

"But nothing. Immediately after Jayexeeyo's passage, he was placed with Ahrkoor as an associate shoemaker. Why, if not to further teach him what someone else could not have taught him?"

"That is a supposition."

"Then why did Ahrkoor not take Jayexeeyo as a student when he turned twenty?"

"He had another student at the time."

"He probably wanted to take Jayexeeyo as his student, but could not because of his obligation to the student he had."

Pleeyedraha could see where she was leading. "Tahrmaha, Ahrkoor was very old."

"Perhaps, but I think not. I think something happened which we do not know about, something which connects Dahrohd, Jayexeeyo, Ahrkoor, and Kayloor in something very disturbing."

"Tahrmaha, that is a supposition."

"I believe Ahrkoor would not let himself die until Zayo had learned the full story, whatever it was. You saw for yourself that he is wearing new shoes, and it was he who made the announcement concerning Ahrkoor's death, and the transferal of the black vest to Jayexeeyo."

"How would you understand such a thing, Tahrmaha?"

"How true are you to our king?"

Pleeyedraha's face took on an odd expression, one which Tahrmaha had not seen for a long time. "Zayo's reign and Kayloor's reign are two different realms."

"Yes, but for Zayo's reign to be successful, he must know what caused the demise of Kayloor."

"Why?"

"I saw Zayo and Mehlanahr work together for a short time when you wanted me to go to Earth with Mehlanahr, and never before in my life have I seen such a friendship...they unwittingly command each other's respect. They do not even have to think about it. The same thing must be true of people like Ahrkoor."

"I was Kayloor's wet nurse."

"But what have you done to help Zayo since his father's murder? You are so caught up in your own distress over your 'son' that you have forgotten what is most important to our people, and why you wear the black vest."

Pleeyedraha was shocked: was the same thing happening to Tahrmaha? Finally, after collecting herself, she asked her student, "You have always plagued me with a question."

Tahrmaha was surprised at Pleeyedraha's sudden change in approach. "I have already taken too much of a liberty with you. You do not deserve to have me push you around like this."

The elderly gray mare suddenly smiled. "You have answered my question."

"What question?"

"Now you ask?"

"Curiosity. Too curious as always, though this time too talkative. Please forgive me."

"I will tell you what my question was if you bring Zayo in here. He will be interested."

Tahrmaha was perplexed. "You are not trying to teach me medicine. What is your point?"

"Tahrmaha, are you afraid to speak with him?"

"Yes—I mean, no—I mean, what did I do to deserve this chastisement? You must be collaborating with Zayo."

"You have become such a stickler for details that not even Zayo's temper can get past you. I know of no other Caballian who would dare to do such a thing! And to add insult, you made him feel ashamed!"

Tahrmaha shook her head—she could hardly believe what she was hearing. She showed some tears, and wiped them off with her wrist. "Pleeyedraha, tell me this is not true. What have I done?"

"You have done nothing wrong."

"Then why do I not feel good about it? Something must be wrong."

"Are you willing to accept it?"

"I must apologize to him."

"Apologize for what?"

"I must apologize," she repeated, and left the office. But she returned a few minutes later, obviously disappointed, and said, "Pleeyedraha, I am going to get some lunch."

"Did he lose his temper again?"

"He was not there."

Pleeyedraha was so perplexed at what was happening that she could not bring herself to be as upset as Tahrmaha was. "I do not know about my appetite, but I should also try to eat."

GROWING PAINS

What was waiting for them in the kitchen was a rather unwanted surprise: Zayo was setting at a table there finishing his own lunch. Tahrmaha immediately shied away from looking at him, and went about eating her lunch at another table. Just as she and Pleeyedraha were finishing their lunch, Zayo went to their table, and set with them. "Pleeyedraha," he said, "I still wish to speak with the two of you."

"I will not speak yet," young Tahrmaha stated.

"Why not?" he queried.

"I must apologize to you for making you feel so ashamed. You are my king. Even though you are younger than me-"

"Three years is nothing," Pleeyedraha injected.

"-I am not accustomed to someone losing their temper at me when I have done nothing. But I failed to remember your circumstances."

"Contrarily, you remember them all too well," he told her.

"You do have a photographic memory," Pleeyedraha reminded her student.

"It was not my place to say what I dared to tell Pleeyedraha in front of you," Tahrmaha continued, "that you are still hideously suffering from your father's grasp."

"No," he remarked, "you were right. I came to the hospital because I knew that I needed help to heal from my inner wounds. Karayo cannot help me through it all, and neither can Mother. Pleeyedraha, you are a healer, so why are you afraid of your duties as such?"

160

"Are the two of you so right and I so wrong?" Pleeyedraha wondered aloud.

"Pleeyedraha," Tahrmaha said apologetically, "I said some things without thinking."

"They must be true. Tell Zayo what you told me about the black vest."

"'What have you done to help Zayo since his father's murder? You are so caught up in your distress over your "son" that you have forgotten what is most important to our people, and why you wear the black vest.' Pleeyedraha, what was your question before?"

"I was wondering if you always showed me such respect because of Kayloor, or because of the black vest. But now I know that it was because of the black vest."

"I have doubted that lately, which is why I have been so wretched. But for me to disagree with you about the cause of Ahrkoor's death...that is very serious."

Zayo returned to his original request of Tahrmaha. "I would still like to speak with you about your differing opinions, those which seem to clash with Pleeyedraha. Especially since you disagree over Ahrkoor's death...we must speak about that." She nodded, so he added, "Tahrmaha, where can we speak alone?"

Pleeyedraha agreed, so Tahrmaha replied, "In my office."

Tahrmaha had been assigned her own office to study in as soon as she had begun her studies with Pleeyedraha; she brought Zayo there. There were two chairs placed across from each other for consultations, which is where they set. She saw the pained expression in his face and said, "Why are you hurting so much over Ahrkoor's death?"

"With Ahrkoor went a great part of my father's legacy, as much as Pleeyedraha holds."

Tahrmaha let the silence hang for a while before she said anything else to him. "A great part of Kayloor's legacy was lost on the day that you excommunicated Dahrohd."

Zayo was surprised at her words. "Do you really mean what you are saying? Much was lost on the day that Father was killed."

"Why did Dahrohd kill your father? And why is Ahrkoor dead?"

"Just because they are both shoemakers..." he began, not wanting to tell her anything about the treachery.

"No, Zayo, I meant what I said. It must be more than just coincidence that Ahrkoor died right after he made shoes for you."

"Ahrkoor has always made my shoes."

"Then tell me why the black vest was given to Jayexeeyo."

"Because he is the most worthy. That is why he was Ahrkoor's understudy."

His eyes bore a slightly devious expression, so she shook her head in disapproval. "Zayo, it is dark and disgusting, but you must face it. I believe that you learned something important today; you obviously cannot deviate from sincerity, because your eyes give you away. Something happened between Dahrohd, Jayexeeyo, Ahrkoor, and your father, something covering a number of years. It is true that Jayexeeyo was the first and only student that Dahrohd ever had; it is true that Jayexeeyo was placed with Ahrkoor to teach him more; it is true that Jayexeeyo has worked successfully with Ahrkoor; and it is true that Dahrohd murdered Kayloor not long after Jayexeeyo's success with Ahrkoor was publicized by Raivo, who predicted accurately that Jayexeeyo would next wear the black vest."

"What happened between them that could have possibly affected my father?" He was starting to work up a sweat.

"The things I am telling you must be true, but there is a reason why you are trying to push me away from it. What would I think of my king if he pushed me away from believing what I know is true? Dahrohd must have been such an ineffective mentor for Jayexeeyo that he was disgraced by both Ahrkoor and Kayloor, but was given a second chance by Kayloor because it was not irreparable damage. Dahrohd had a weakness, but he was afraid to report it to Ahrkoor because the master shoemaker had enough with his own student. When Ahrkoor had to take Jayexeeyo after his passage, Dahrohd must have been even more upset at his own flaws. And when Raivo publicized Jayexeeyo's success with Ahrkoor, Dahrohd must have felt completely undignified. He had failed at the job which the master had trusted him with, and then had to set back and watch Ahrkoor succeed where he could not."

"Dahrohd could not understand that he laid a good foundation for Jayexeeyo's education, nor could he accept the lesson of humility which my father tried to teach him!" Zayo shot back at her. "That is why he had to be excommunicated for his crime, and why we could not live with him in our society! Our lives are built on honor and humility! You should know that better than anyone else, knowing Pleeyedraha as you do!" He began to sob so loudly that she could not make him hear her.

When Zayo quieted down about ten minutes later, he was so upset and worn that Tahrmaha washed his face for him. This helped him feel

162

much more decent. She then said, "It is about time you had a good cry over your father. Pleeyedraha and Tarahnaha were becoming concerned about you."

"You did it deliberately..." he said chastisingly. "How could you feel good about doing something so cruel?"

"How cruel could it possibly be to prod you so that you get out of your depression and begin to heal?"

"Whatever happened to humility?"

"True, our lives run on honor and humility like you said, but when there is a criminal like Dahrohd who does not know how to put honor and humility together, he turns it into arrogance. His arrogance is what killed your father. Arrogance like that is what we cannot live with in our society. Your father was right in that we must be humble recipients. When someone else turns it into arrogance, the only way to meet the arrogance is not with humble acceptance (because there is no place for it), but with action to stop it. That is why you had to excommunicate him. What else would you have done?"

"What else could I have done? And what can I do?"

"Your father built his reign on humble acceptance and love. But if you proceed to build your own reign on just action, you will end up dead like your father. Your reign must encompass both, and use both for the good of our people."

"None of my ancestors have ever had to do such a thing."

"That is why you are to have a sibling, and that is why our people are going to evolve for the better. You will be a great king, because you have learned the lesson of Ahrkoor today. That is why your talent will be in wisdom and judgment. Polihdahr was a king of action, but what did he truly know about humility?" she asked, almost mockingly.

What do you know about being a king? Zayo thought to himself, yet he realized he suddenly had a newfound respect for Tahrmaha as a friend. "Why are you daring to tell me these things?"

"Booralta came to speak with me two days before he died, and he told me that I will become a living legend just like Mehlanahr is, that I will become a renowned mare."

"Sure," he said, mockingly. "If you continued to speak to me like that, I may take it for treason."

She held back a laugh at his wit, and she changed the subject. "I cam impart a secret with you, but you must not tell a single soul, not even Pleeyedraha or your mother."

Zayo was deeply mystified. "What sort of secret?" He then thought to himself, She knows every secret there is. Is this why Father always enjoyed speaking with Pleeyedraha? Ahrkoor died today, leaving Jayexeeyo to be my shoemaker. Since Pleeyedraha is very elderly, I should start myself with a new doctor. Even though Tahrmaha is too young to become the master healer after Pleeyedraha, I believe she will be a very good doctor. I will allow her to be my doctor.

"Everyone believes that you are going to have a brother, but they are all wrong."

"My mother is pregnant with my father's heir. Why will I not have a brother? Will he die before his birth, or soon after his birth?"

"Because the foal within her is not male."

"But how could he—I mean, she—be heir then?"

"What about Lehwohraha?"

Throughout the rest of the afternoon and supper, Zayo remained silent, not even speaking to his mother, which was highly unusual. He was thinking, contemplating everything that had happened to him that day.

After supper, he went and set in the den by himself. No one followed him right away, so Tarahnaha followed her son. She walked in after he had set down, and she said, "Zayo, may I set with you?" He looked at her standing in the doorway, but said nothing, so she entered, and walked up to him. "May I set with you?" she repeated.

He could not stop a few tears from falling down his face, and he replied, "I need to speak with you more than anything else in the world, Mother."

She turned back to close the door, then she set down next to him. She watched his heavy eyes shed some more tears, then she took his head and held it against her breast. "Zayo, I was very happy this morning until I heard your announcement, but most of my happiness has not left me."

"Why?"

"The kicks are growing ever so stronger. The life is so strong...there is something special about it."

He remembered what Tahrmaha said, but pushed it to the back of his mind. He nuzzled his head against his mother's breast. "I thought I had grown too old for this."

"I will always be here for you until you are married."

"Of course my sibling is special. Father has left a living reminder of himself."

"Zayo, it is much more than that. Before you were born, you would put up tremendous fights, then you would sleep afterwards. But your brother acts as if he does not want to sleep. He is always moving, always doing something. It is very difficult to explain. He is just as strong as you were, but in a very opposite way."

"He could not have been fighting as much as I have been today."

She held him at arm's distance and said, "What have you been fighting?"

"I learned some insight into Father's death from Ahrkoor and Jayexeeyo." She shuddered when he said this, so he knew not to tell her anything else about it. "I know that Father is dead, but until today, I kept a spot in my heart which I was hoping he would return to. But he cannot. Humility and action must be intertwined—neither one alone is enough for our people."

Tarahnaha could scarcely comprehend what she was hearing. "What are you talking about, Zayo?"

"I was not too kind today, Mother. I pushed Tahrmaha into telling me her views of Father. I acted when I should have been more humble and accepting. I should have been more accepting of what Ahrkoor told me, and of his death."

"Zayo, how could you do such a thing to her?"

"Mother, not even you—nor Pleeyedraha or Mehlanahr—was able to prod me into facing Father's murder and accepting it for what it is. But Tahrmaha did, and I cried more than I ever cried in my life."

You cannot fight a ghost, Tarahnaha thought to herself. "You must learn to build your own memories over the bitterness."

"But I could not do it without facing the bitterness, and knowing exactly what it was that I needed to build over. But now I know, and I will never forget it."

He is changed, she thought to herself. How did Tahrmaha do it? Then again, why did he do what he did? In ten years, though, she will probably become his queen. I am sure Pleeyedraha would be touched deeply by such a thing. "Thank the moons that you will never forget your own father."

"You are jesting!"

"Yes," she said, smiling. "But you could use a good jest. It has been a long day."

The human colonists were being treated most excellent. A system was set up for them where they were allowed to travel around the planet;

this included their learning how to operate transports. In this way, they were given open invitations to visit with whomever would welcome them, which turned out to be all Caballians who were not at the time involved in work that could not be stopped. Thusly, the humans were given a means by which to obtain a deeper look at the Caballian cities and social structure.

The humans felt that they were beginning to warm their way into the Caballians' hearts because they were being given much more trusted freedom than they had ever had before. John Hancock thought this to be a very interesting factor; he thought that the Caballians were trying to be cute or devious. It should not have affected the humans as long as they were being treated well by the Caballians, because it was taking time for them to adapt to each other. But the humans were in a hurry to get home, seeing as how Commander MacBain had already gone home.

Laerion, Tokanar, and Wateloqua are all within a reasonable proximity of each other; the Sea of Serenity in the midst of the three cities is a tremendous life-giving prospect, especially with the numerous rivers and creeks, which flow into it. The civilized part of Equestra, which includes the rural farm areas, covers about one-third of all land on the planet surface. At least three-quarters of the entire planet is livable. There are some very agreeable areas on the far side, in which the rain occurs in bursts, and plant life flourished, especially where the pink ivy completely grows over the tremendous amount of ruins left behind by a distinctly ancient Caballian way of life. Gone with that were most of the native animal life forms; there were still insects, and birds, and water creatures of many various kinds, but the land shows only Caballians in the civilized areas. What animals were left remained hidden on the far side among the ruins, staying as far away as possible from the Caballians.

There is a sea on the far side which connects to the Sea of Serenity by a narrow strait on the southern magnetic pole; the southern magnetic pole would have been livable had it not been for the constant heavy rains which fall there, making it quite uncomfortable. The sea on the far side is called the Unknown Sea. There are a good number of chasms and caverns at the bottom of the Unknown Sea, and there are a good number of islands in it. Many of the islands are nothing but rocks, but a small number of them are sizeable and livable, no doubt that they may have been inhabited at one time.

Toward the southern end of the ruins and inland quite a ways from the Unknown Sea was a deep, long, craggy valley, one which was avoided by the Caballians and was commonly referred to as the Pit of Promiscuity.

There were some strange elements in this valley which were nowhere else to be found on Equestra; the common fable is that was where all Equestran life forms were created. Whatever the cause was, it was forbidden for any Caballian to go near it because of the effects which the strange elements had on them, and all other living creatures, who dared to enter the valley. Not only that, but whoever did enter it never remembered what happened while they were there; only the shamans knew.

The Pit causes psychological changes, but the large Cave of the Magical mists (located to the north of the ruins) was fabled to cause physical changes. In ancient Caballian fables, the Cave was the source of the ancient wars: when the ancient emperor's son was killed by Caballians his corpse was placed in the Cave, and a stone placed in front of the Cave's opening, but two days later the stone was found rolled away, and the body was missing, only to have it rumored later that day that the emperor's son was seen in the piper forest alive and well.

The northern magnetic pole of Equestra is covered with a vast forest known as the Piper Forest; every single tree that grows there is a piper tree. Unlike most other trees, they grow hollow. They propagate when small branches either fall off or are broken off from larger trees. When the branches fall off, they leave round holes where they had been attached to the parent tree. Large branches on large trees have many holes in them, and resound the wind that blows across the holes. The collective music of the piper forest produces a hypnotic effect which tranquilized every single creature who ventures within. Also, the trees have the ability to move around, as long as they are not stopped by other trees' roots. They move slowly, however, so it is not readily discernible to the naked eye that they actually move. When someone falls under the hypnosis of the trees, they have a chance to move around him, and he becomes hopelessly lost trying to find his way out of somewhere that seems to be totally different from when before he was hypnotized.

The humans were taking advantage of their freedoms on Equestra, and were visiting anyone they could possibly think of—that is, anyone except for Karayo, Vehdoor, Dehnohraha, and Zayo. Since Admiral Gray had been excommunicated as a criminal, the colonists had been thinking of every way to avoid the shamans and the king. This was rather easy, because John Hancock was not required to speak with Zayo every day.

But the humans did not trust any of the shamans, because they felt that the shamans mingled in their affairs. Not only did they avoid them, but they avoided asking any questions about their purpose in Caballian society, which would turn out to be their gravest error. It was this sort of human ignorance which had led to Gray's removal, and was certain to lead to more problems with the Caballians if it was not corrected. But no one had yet "discovered" this problem, so it would remain uncorrected until it would actually found to be a problem affecting the Caballians.

The colonists, however, asked very many questions about the pegasus, Andrux. All they were told in response were bits and pieces of what Zayo had told the Caballians at his coronation. A few Caballians recommended that they ask Karayo for more information concerning the young alated colt. But the humans would not go and speak with any shaman, so it was always dropped after the recommendation.

The colonists received a communication from Earth extending to them and all of the Caballians a welcome to a planned memorial for Admiral James Gray at Cape Canaveral. Zayo politely told John Hancock no, that they could not celebrate a criminal's memory, even though he had done good things, too. He had committed a crime on Equestra that was intolerable. Zayo also told John Hancock (very diplomatically) that they could not afford a trip to Earth to bring the colonists to the memorial.

Family and friends of James Gray attended the memorial. Everyone fit into the picture except for three rather odd guests. They were not known by anyone else there offhand—no one recognized their faces, and they did not sign the guest register—but they claimed to have been close friends of James Gray. If anyone had actually known who they were, they would have been arrested immediately. It seemed like such an innocuous association, but no one knew exactly what was behind it all.

Two of them—Doc Reeve and Mr. Court—were top henchmen for the revolutionary Fagan. Doc Reeve had taken the job in Ireland as the top veterinarian for the breeding farm where Doc Lawson had turned down the job. Mr. Court was a mercenary who currently made his living by helping Fagan to rope together all of the more influential revolutionaries and setting them on a collective route—to do Fagan's bidding. Those who were there paid no attention to Doc Reeve and Mr. Court; otherwise even Admiral Van Housen would have recognized at least one of them.

With them was another character who had a normal habit (which he broke for the memorial service) of remaining far away from the public eye yet still remaining very powerful—Fagan. Fagan was an odd man, one whose warped ideas for the world were shrouded by a vast cover of quite decent morals, which he used to enhance his own plans for the world.

At the memorial service for Gray, many highlights were made of the accomplishments he achieved during his lifetime (omitting his blunder), coloring a wonderful image of a powerful man for all who were there. The idea was to impose the feeling that they had lost a great deal with his removal; he had dedicated his life to Earth Control. The point was made that he had been sent to hell at the hands of aliens encountered at Barnard's star, but absolutely nothing was mentioned of the crime he had committed to merit his punishment. It seemed fine for the public image that Earth Control wanted to maintain, but it painted a much too pretty picture for anyone who knew nothing about it. This left Fagan and his friends with the wrong idea of what the Caballians were like, and they took this with themselves after the memorial was over.

On the two hundred and sixty-ninth day, Zayo brought himself to Karayo's house because he wanted to find out how much the humans were taking advantage of their unlimited travels. "They have been taking full advantage of their freedom," Karayo told Zayo, "and have visited every sort of Caballian except for four particular people."

"Who?" Zayo asked.

"Dehnohraha, Vehdoor, myself, and yourself."

"Why would they do such a thing since they wanted to learn about us?"

"Since you excommunicated the criminal, they doubt the credibility of any shaman."

"So much they do not understand! I have been patient with them, but they continue to test me. I may really lose my temper with them."

"It would not surprise me if such an outburst did occur. But you must remain diplomatic with them as long as they are not truly committing any crimes against any of our people."

"But why would they avoid the greatest historians in our society? I will go to speak with John Hancock tomorrow, and I will ask him."

Hancock was surprised when he saw Zayo in their encampment early the next morning, but he said nothing about it. He went to Zayo and said, "Good morning, your majesty."

"Good morning," Zayo replied. "It has been some time since we last spoke."

"Forgive me, but my men have been working hard, and I have hardly had time to breathe."

EQUESTRA

"I know that your men have been making many visitations among my people, traveling all around Equestra."

Hancock spat out, "We have been working on designs for a new ship to take us off from here and bring us back to Earth!"

Zayo remained calm. "It is no secret that you dislike me for excommunicating Admiral Gray; I know that is why you are working even harder to leave. You have put on a decent front for my people to lead them to think that your people are working with us, when meanwhile you are only using what will help with what you want to accomplish."

"We do not wish to become too much of an inconvenience."

"There is no inconvenience in friendship. The only inconvenience arises when the friendship disappears. We had a good start, but what has come of us now? You try to make me look like a fool."

"That is not true!"

"Then why are you growing upset? Perhaps there is another reason why you are pressing to leave so soon."

"My men are sick and tired of how they have had to live since they came here. Our tents are dilapidated and falling apart."

"When you first came here, it was your spaceship with the water shortage. I believe it is your morality. It frustrates me that when your people are presented with excellent circumstances, they become dull and lose their edge. Do you really need a struggle to keep you going? You are so comfortable with what you are that when the opportunity avails itself for your people to progress, they actually seem to regress back to what they were. I have offered the assistance of my people so that we can progress together, and learn from each other, but you seem to be fighting this. Tell me, what can I do?"

"I am sorry," Hancock replied, "but I disagree with your analysis. My men have pushed forward onto unknown ground, and they are making the best of it. As you have your social attachments, we need ours; we need our own establishment to survive. Before, our establishment was our ship. Now it is our community, which we wish to make as strong as possible for the time that we will be here."

"Why do you wish to do this, if you know that you will be leaving?"

"You are denying us the comforts of civility while we are staying here?"

"No. I am questioning your intentions, which are misappropriated. You have proven yourself to be ignorant."

"How could our intentions be wrong? We have done our best to work on our friendship."

170

"I may be only twenty-five, but I am not stupid! Your people have deliberately stayed far away from the greatest resources of Caballian philosophy and history."

"Which is what?"

"Our shamans."

"Those storytellers implicated an innocent!"

"We possessed medical proof of his crime. What you have failed to understand is that Caballian justice follows a logical pattern. The only time emotional patterns may affect the outcome is when the emotions are my anger and frustration at the crime for the very fact that it happened at all! I carefully explained all of our laws to Gray, and he deliberately abused them, just because he was curious. Do you understand the psychological harm it caused to my household to know that they cannot successfully procreate because of this? Is it too much to ask that each person be granted freedoms that will not be harmed by any others? Is it too much to ask that we be allowed to reproduce?"

"Even your people have proven to be criminals at times."

"Crimes arise from misunderstandings. I grow upset when people do not make an effort to prevent misunderstandings. Gray encouraged his own punishment by deliberately 'misunderstanding' my interpretation after he assured me that he fully understood our laws, yet he knew nothing of the ways of my people."

"Your majesty, why must you continue to do this to me?"

"If your people wish to remain here for a time as welcome colonists, then they should work harder to understand the Caballians, just as we have worked hard to understand you and your people. Which one of my people has not opened his house or knowledge to you or any of your people? Tell me one, and I will clip his tail."

Hancock shook his head. "Your people have been too kind, and we truly do not know how to reciprocate such kindness."

"One day, perhaps not in your lifetime, your people will return the favor in another form. That is the meaning of friendship."

171

MERAHLAHA

Tarahnaha, like all other mares, was exquisitely beautiful in her pregnant state. She had always held great respect for Kayloor in her heart, but even after his death, it was still growing. In fulfilling one of her most primitive yet most important roles as Kayloor's queen, she was effectively relocating her self-esteem. Psychologically, she was devastated when Kayloor was murdered, but the new life growing after his death pleased her and every other Caballian more than any other happiness. She was very close to the parting day now, and had stopped working as an agricultural technician about a week before; she wanted to remain with her son as much as possible.

Relatively early in the morning of the two hundred and seventy-third day, Tarahnaha was escorted to the hospital by Zayo for a checkup. When Pleeyedraha saw Tarahnaha, and gave her a quick check, she admitted her into the hospital because Tarahnaha was ready to part that day. Zayo, who did not want to miss the parting, stayed with his mother throughout the day. Late that afternoon, Tarahnaha finally parted from the foal, which amazed her to the fact that it was a filly. Her new daughter was a very comely new foal; she had chestnut fur like her father had had, and also had light brown hair. Born a queen, she had the same type of blaze upon her forehead that Zayo did. She bonded to Tarahnaha, and stood up on very shaky and wobbly legs. Tarahnaha named her new daughter Merahlaha.

Zayo went to the visiphone, and called a caucus for the following morning to celebrate his sister's birth.

Everyone was on the great lawn outside of the palace before breakfast the next morning; breakfast was ready well ahead of time. As was the usual custom, the farmers brought a wide variety of fresh produce for breakfast. A steady supply of water was provided by a number of pumps scattered over the lawn; there must have been at least a hundred pumps, all of which were connected to the Sea of Serenity, which could be seen from the palace. Just as farmers brought the food for everyone, they collected the solid wastes afterwards from the transports to use as fertilizer.

After breakfast was over, Zayo went onto his platform and began to address the crowd. "When I was crowned, Booralta has prophesied that the foal my mother was pregnant with would also be my father's heir, and that I would be required to share the throne with it. Many of us assumed that, from the history of my family, that my sibling would also be a king. As I announced yesterday, I have a sister, who is a noble queen. Her majesty's name is Merahlaha, and the time has come for her to be presented to you as our queen."

He saw his mother standing near the platform with Merahlaha in her arms and he said, "Mother, please bring her majesty to me."

As Tarahnaha climbed the platform with her daughter in her arms, Merahlaha awoke from her nap. She was cuddled against her mother, and her eyes opened slightly. Tarahnaha held Merahlaha out to Zayo, who gently took his sister in his arms. He thought his sister was the most beautiful filly among their people, and he cherished the fact that she resembled their father so much. He was very careful as to support her as his mother had instructed him. When Tarahnaha saw that he had her properly, she fell back to a distance of ten feet, and knelt. Tarahnaha had her hair properly braided with purple ribbons which did not match the color of her fur or the color of her hair, but were considered beautiful because of what they represented.

Merahlaha did not yet have her hair braided, because a foal's hair is never braided before it is one month old. Some murmuring began, but Zayo was quick to cry out, "Silence!" As soon as he had done so, his sister let out a whinny, and he smiled. "This is her majesty Merahlaha, our queen, who is Kayloor's heir to the throne." He held her up and brushed her hair out of her face, so that they could all see the blaze upon her forehead. As soon as he had done so, he carefully reclaimed full support of her. "Merahlaha is as much Kayloor's heir as I am, and it is our duty to rule equally and fairly. Her majesty will not be shown any partiality because of her age, but she will be given all the due respect of her office throughout her lifetime. Even though she is new, her judgments and instincts are to be trusted as being those of a truly noble queen. I hereby charge every one of you to teach her as much as possible about her father in every possible way. Anyone who spoils her in her early position of power will be clipped, and possibly brought up on charges of treason. I also charge you that, in addition to teaching her the teachings of our father, you will teach her to use those teachings in her rule so that she will serve you as best as she possibly can as my sister."

Tarahnaha heard her daughter begin to whinny, and she thought to herself, What are to be the implications of their joint rule? In the past, one ruler had always been enough. Tarahnaha heard her hungry daughter again, and she heard their people begin to clamor for more words. She finally arose from where she was kneeling, took her hungry daughter from Zayo, and immediately let her suckle. She said to Zayo, "Let me talk to them; that is what they want."

Zayo silenced them for her. Tarahnaha then began, "The legacy of Zayo and Merahlaha is only beginning. Many things are changing for us; they have been changing since Kayloor was killed. I am amazed by the legacy that has been growing since the birth of the pegasus. Mehlanahr has given us a new technology, which has become an important asset in our dealings with the humans." She saw the humans in the crowd; she knew all along that they had been there. "Would a king without Zayo's sense of judgment have been able to prevent the humans from completely upsetting our way of life? I think not. I praise my son for what he has done in that capacity. He has exhausted all possible efforts to maintain a balanced relationship with the humans. It does not surprise me that my son is successful thus far." The noise suddenly began to grow, so Zayo took over.

"Do you refuse to accept my sister as your queen?"

"It is obvious that her majesty has the blaze," someone else said.

The noise from the crowd soon died down, and slowly turned into cheering.

KIDNAPPED

John Hancock was frustrated. He was frustrated that his men had to work hard to rebuild their ship. He was frustrated that he could not explain to Zayo why it was important that they spent so much time repairing their ship. He was frustrated that, even at the pace that they were working at, it would take them years to finish their task. His frustrations grew tremendously when he learned from his crew that the ion storm had caused them to travel through a wormhole. They had no idea where in the universe they were, but it was definitely <u>not</u> Barnard. The Caballians knew where Earth was and how far they were from it.

Hancock was dismayed at the coldness which the Caballians had displayed in excommunicating Admiral Gray for a crime. They had not given him a chance to speak on his own behalf, not a second chance to work with them, not a chance of forgiving him. But perhaps—perhaps there was a way to amuse his men and to alleviate the tension which had been building up. He came upon a scheme which would answer both their being marooned on Equestra and the coldness of the Caballians.

He patted himself on the back for his ingenuity.

Early on the morning of the two hundred and seventy-fifty day, which was firstday as well as the day that the Caballians went back to their jobs after the caucus for Merahlaha, the humans set out the trap of their plans. It was set up on a road that ran westward from Tokanar toward a

175

few scattered farms; they were going to capture a couple of Caballians traveling on that road.

They set up three transports to block the road, none of which had yet been updated with the new beacon. Whoever was driving along the road would be forced to stop. Such was the case with Shehronaha, who was traveling to an appointment to repair some farm machinery. One of the humans possessed an imploder, and they used it to get her out of her transport, and to tie her up securely and gag her so that she could not speak; she could not walk or move her legs very much, and she was having difficulty breathing through the gag. They put her in the back of her transport, and they left her while they waited for another.

After more than half an hour, Jayexeeyo came driving down the road and was stopped in the same manner. He had been traveling to visit with his parents and infant brother since it was his day off from his work. He was tied up and placed in the back of his transport, which was very difficult for the humans to accomplish because he was so strong. As soon as this was done, the humans cleared the road. Two of the transports that had been used for roadblocks were taken back to their settlement. The other one led the two transports containing Jayexeeyo and Shehronaha towards the far side of Equestra. The humans brought them to the Pit of Promiscuity, which they reached that afternoon.

Calls went out for Jayexeeyo and Shehronaha but went unanswered, as no one knew where they were or what had happened to them. Karayo was not too sure yet; he could not go to Zayo until he had full information. However, he did call Zayo on the visiphone, just before dinner, to let the king know that he was suspicious of the humans. Karayo also told Zayo that he was hoping to have complete information by the next morning, which was a passage. The shaman was planning on arriving at the palace early so he could meet with the king.

Jayexeeyo and Shehronaha were abandoned in the Pit of Promiscuity alone, together. After they managed to untie each other, and had fallen victim to the effects of the forbidden valley, they fell asleep for a short nap. They awoke, unaware of each other's presence, and each one of them found their own transport and drove it back to Tokanar, reaching the city later in the evening. Shehronaha went to her temporary lodgings with a friend, and Jayexeeyo went to his house, and they went to sleep for the remainder of the night, neither of them remembering meeting the other.

Very early the next morning, long before the break of dawn, Jayexeeyo and Shehronaha both awoke in their separate abodes and remembered being kidnapped and brought to the ruins, yet they each remembered nothing of the forbidden valley or of ever meeting each other. However, they both knew they needed to speak with Zayo immediately about the actions of the humans. Since it was a passage day, they both left Tokanar extra early; his transport followed hers all the way to the palace. He felt tired as he got out of his transport and walked towards the palace door through the first light of dawn; as he reached her transport, she climbed out, took a misstep, and fell on the ground. He ran to where she fell, and he said, "Are you hurt?" After he said that, he took a look to see who she was. Her platinum hair, dappled cream-colored fur, deep blue eyes, and dapper face struck him; he remembered her from her passage. She was the engineer who was given her vest the day before Kayloor was killed. On that day, Jayexeeyo had spoken with some other shoemakers about her placement by Oorahno to repair transports, and as they were all wishing they could avail themselves of the services of such a handy engineer, Jayexeeyo somehow decided that he would earn the black vest to prove his honor to her, then he would claim her so he could have her work with him.

She grabbed her right front hoof, and attempted to pry the shoe off. "My foot," she replied with tears in her eyes, seeing someone standing over her but not recognizing who it was, "it turned. It hurts a lot. Could you summon Pleeyedraha?" Her eyes drifted and rolled, as she somehow knew her life was imminently in danger.

Her shock from the pain was very obvious, and so was the swelling. Without a moment to lose, Jayexeeyo set to work on her foot, gingerly popping the shoe off of her foot with his fingers; she was quickly relieved at the release of pressure on the frog, which was throbbing with pain. As he felt the joint, his heart was in his throat; she had foundered, and all he had was an untested method he had developed which had the potential to save her life. He was desperate to make it work and save her life, because he was devoted to claim her. She felt even more release of pain as he massaged her coffin bone and coronet; his strong fingers were able to gingerly rotate the coffin bone back up to where it belonged. Shehronaha was lucky that her coffin bone had not pierced the frog. As he soothed her injured joint, his gentle massage released endorphins, which removed the pain and the irritation of the inflamed laminae, and also pulled her from her shock. When he was done, he told her, "Do not get up yet."

177

She looked at her benefactor, and then recognized who he was. "Why?" she asked. "I know I hurt my foot bad, but how bad is it?"

"You foundered." As he went to his transport she grimaced and thought to herself, No one can treat founder, I am dying. He took out a file, a jar, and a new ready-made shoe from his transport. After he carefully cleaned and filed her hoof in a rather odd manner, he opened the jar and brushed a dark brown aromatic liquid on her soft frog, and proceeded to put the shoe on her hoof backwards to give her extra stability and support in the heel. "You may stand up now, but gently."

She carefully stood up, and was utterly amazed at how her foot felt when she stood on it. "A backwards shoe?" she wondered aloud.

"How does it feel? Walk on it."

She gingerly took a few steps. "My foot always bothered me since I was young. It has not felt this good in years." She felt herself blush, realizing she was smitten with the most eligible stallion on all of Equestra; she looked up into his devoted eyes, and suddenly, a chill went up her spine. "I feel as if I know you already."

"Are you all right?" he asked her.

She thought back to the day before and said, "No, I am not all right. I must speak with Zayo."

"I am also here to speak with him, about something that troubles me deeply. It is sad, but he and Mehlanahr must remove the humans today."

"The humans! That is what happened to me! They tied me up, and brought me to the ruins on the far side! I missed my appointment!"

"You were not the only one. I, too, was savagely kidnapped. It took twenty humans to hold me down while they tied me up and threatened me with an imploder. I wanted nothing to do with their conspiracy, because it was my day off, and I was to meet with my family."

"Twenty humans? You are strong."

"I am only one person."

She saw the deepening look in his eyes as he said that and she thought about how good her foot felt; she then realized his purpose. Shehronaha saw he was becoming puzzled, and his ears were standing up as she seemed to be daydreaming. "I am sorry," she said. "I meant no alarm, even though my foot caused alarm for you. No one has ever cured founder."

"I was not alarmed; I knew what to do for you. Tell me how your foot feels, and you will know why I wear the black vest."

"My foot has never felt so good. But it also matters how you feel, because you express yourself through your work."

"All that matters is that your foot is better, for if I did not help you, then I only succeed in dishonoring myself."

She laughed at him. "You are so vain!"

"That is not vanity. That is self-preservation. I worked very hard to earn the black vest, so I must continue to work hard to retain it." He saw the expression in her eyes become one of longing, and he knew he had won her heart. He saw that she wanted to speak, but she could not get the words out. At that very moment, he just wanted to grab her and kiss her; he held it back. "While we are here, I will tell Mehlanahr that you are relocating to Tokanar. So many engineers are always coming in and out of my forge for transports and transport parts, that having you work there with me will free up many other engineers for other duties, plus it will allow me to maintain your feet properly."

"An engineer working in a forge?"

"Why not? Do you have any idea how many broken-down transports are picked up by guards and brought to me each day just because a forge is considered to be a hub for transport repair and maintenance?"

"Perhaps we should speak with Zayo first about the humans."

"Yes," he agreed.

"It is odd, but I cannot remember yesterday afternoon. How did I get untied?" He thought about it deeply for a short while, and as he did, his conjecturing made him shudder. When he finally realized what had happened, he started to weep. Shehronaha was shocked, but she did the only thing she could think of: she grabbed his hands in hers. "How could something pain you so deeply?"

He was ashamed to look her in the face. "We were dishonored by the humans. They have caused irreparable damage to the two of us. What happened to us should have never happened to anyone."

"What could have possibly happened to distract you from what you have done for me?"

He saw the gratitude in her eyes, and he calmly continued. "The humans left us in the forbidden valley together, which caused both of us to forget even meeting each other. We must have untied each other, and were forced to break the law." She could not help but shriek at his words. "However, we were not blinded, so we are meant to be together."

"That is a crude way of finding out whether or not something is meant to be."

"Do you still feel it in your heart?"

179

"Of course I do."

"We have a bond in our hearts because of it, and that will never change, especially now that we have realized it."

She smiled at him. "You are so dear."

He looked behind himself, and saw that just about all of the Caballians were gathered for the caucus. Looking back at her, he caressed her face. "Are you prepared to publicize our bond today, Shehronaha?"

She hugged him and said, "Try and stop me, Jayexeeyo."

Jayexeeyo's knock on the palace door was answered by Zayo. "Good morning," Zayo said to both of them.

"Your majesty," Jayexeeyo said, "good morning."

"Good morning," Shehronaha also said.

Zayo let them in. "The passage will begin soon," he told his guests.

"Before any passage," Jayexeeyo replied, "we must speak with you and Mehlanahr."

Zayo saw Mehlanahr walking in the hallway with Yehtraha, so he said, "Mehlanahr, come with me."

Mehlanahr took leave of his wife, and followed Zayo, Jayexeeyo and Shehronaha into the den. Mehlanahr closed the door behind them. Jayexeeyo then said, "The humans must be removed from Equestra today."

"What happened?" Mehlanahr asked.

"They kidnapped us yesterday, and left us on the far side by the ruins, in the forbidden valley. They were all conspiring against our morale and honor. I know kidnapping itself is not a crime, but we were painfully and crudely tied up. I missed spending the day with my parents and brother, and Shehronaha missed her appointment."

Zayo then said, "How do you know you were left in the forbidden valley?"

"How else do you explain memory loss? Neither one of us remembers yesterday afternoon. We remember being kidnapped and brought to the ruins."

"A kidnapping is not a crime, because no Caballian has ever kidnapped another. However, since you firmly believe they caused you to unwontedly break one of our laws, then they are the ones who broke that law. Yet since we cannot be sure which of the humans it was who broke the law, then you are correct in surmising that they must be extricated today."

"I will see to it," Mehlanahr said. "My father can muster up enough guards to bring them in the spaceship." Mehlanahr then saw a very sad expression on Zayo's face. "What is wrong?"

"It pains me that such a thing had to happen to two wonderful people, both of whom my father held high esteem for. He always admired how Jayexeeyo was able to learn so much with Ahrkoor. And the night before Father died, all he did was talk about Shehronaha's passage, because there was so much incredibly positive competition as to where she should be placed. Oorahno very nearly placed you with a shoemaker," he told her, "but then decided you needed a bit more experience before he would make such a move."

"Mehlanahr," Jayexeeyo said, "I want her to be placed with me today."

Mehlanahr held back a laugh as he noticed a passionate glance between them. He saw the questioning look in Zayo's eyes, then he said to Jayexeeyo, "I can only do that if Zayo allows you to marry her right after the passage."

Zayo watched as Jayexeeyo took Shehronaha's hand in his and he said, "Jayexeeyo and Shehronaha, you must tell our people why you want this."

"We are prepared," he replied.

"Good. We must go outside now; we are late for the passage."

After a stallion by the name of Dotoor was given an orange vest and placed as a chemist in Laerion, Zayo summoned Jayexeeyo and Shehronaha up onto the platform. She stepped up onto the platform gingerly as he helped her. The humans saw them as they knelt together ten feet from Zayo, and were shocked. Firstly, the humans did not think that they would make it to the caucus; secondly, the humans felt that the Caballians knew what had happened. Zayo touched their shoulders and said, "Master shoemaker and engineer, please let our people know why you did not answer their calls yesterday." They stood up; he then whispered to them so that no one else could hear, "Tell them what you feel is necessary."

Shehronaha nodded at Jayexeeyo, so he spoke. "We were painfully tied up by the humans against our wills, kidnapped, and brought to the ruins on the far side. They dumped us in the forbidden valley against our wills, where we were forced to break the law." Many gasps were heard from the crowd; the humans were in total shock.

Zayo quieted the crowd down and said, "Since they have not willingly committed a crime, but were the victims of an attack against our morale and honor, Jayexeeyo and Shehronaha have not committed a crime. The humans committed the crime by forcing them to break the law. I shall attend Mehlanahr and Hohnoor to extricate them back to Earth today." Zayo took a deep breath, and continued. "Despite the atrocious acts which were committed against them, Jayexeeyo and Shehronaha desire to be married." He looked at them, and stepped back.

They looked at each other, holding hands. Jayexeeyo said, "She foundered this morning."

Shehronaha added, "He cured my founder and removed the pain from my foot." A loud roar of approval went up from the crowd when she said that; no shoemaker had ever before cured founder. And now, everyone fully knew why he was the master shoemaker.

"I need to keep a close eye on it so it does not recur before it is fully healed," he said after the crowd quieted down.

"He needs my assistance with transports so he can focus more on his craft."

"It is time for her to settle down."

"It is time for him to have his own family."

That last remark stirred up so much emotion in him that he reared up and whinnied at her. A loud roar of approval went up from the Caballians as he swept her into his arms and kissed her. But hardly a moment passed before Pleeyedraha was also up on the platform, kneeling ten feet from Zayo. Zayo touched her shoulder. She said nothing to him, but walked up to Jayexeeyo and said, "Master shoemaker, how are you able to cure founder? And how is your wife able to walk without pain, and not be lame?"

"Master healer," he replied, a smile on his face, "I am honored. As you are the best doctor on all of Equestra for total health, I am the best shoemaker for foot health. I know our feet better than you do. When she foundered this morning, and I felt the downturned position of the coffin bone after removing the shoe while inspecting the joint, I immediately began a manual manipulation of the coffin bone back up off of the frog, which had not been punctured, though it is soft. You know that when a shoemaker knows how to massage a foot properly endorphins are released which remove pain and inflammation in any acute injury. I also ensured that there was no damage to any ligament or tendon before I allowed her to stand up on it. And because founder involves the coffin bone rotating not just down but forward, I filed her hoof accordingly, slightly shifting the line of gravity back, and applied a shoe backwards, so as to provide more support in back, and so as to help prevent the joint from foundering again."

"Who taught you this method?"

"It is my method, which is why Ahrkoor insisted that I wear the black vest."

She looked at Shehronaha and said, "May I examine your foot?" Shehronaha smiled, and proudly held her foot up. Very methodically and very deliberately, Pleeyedraha inspected her foot with her scanner. When she had finished, she said, "The joint is stable, and there is minimal inflammation. I see residual evidence of the founder, but it should completely heal over time."

"That is why I need to keep an eye on it," Jayexeeyo stated.

Mehlanahr approached with their white tassels, handed them to Jayexeeyo and Shehronaha and said, "May today always be remembered in our history, for after millions of years, we finally have a shoemaker with the ability to cure founder. You saved your wife's life today, and it is important knowledge. I am honored to call you my friend."

Before anyone was able to leave the caucus, the guards captured all of the humans and started to bring them to the plant. Since it was Pakoor's day off, Pleeyedraha asked Tahrmaha to attend as the doctor for the mission to Earth; it was expected to be a short mission, so she did not mind going.

It was not long before they arrived at Alameda, where it was late in the evening, and growing darker. There was a noticeable chill in the air, but the Caballians shrugged it off when they stepped into it. The humans were under heavy guard; every single guard had an imploder in his hands by Zayo's charge. Soon, a number of human guards came and took the colonists from the Caballians, and put them in a special holding area where they would remain until their fate was decided. As the Caballians were left alone outside their ship for a few moments, Mehlanahr said to Zayo, "Is it imperative that all of us attend you in your conference with the Vice Admiral?"

"You do not wish to go?" Zayo wondered.

"I have work I must attend to here. The humans nearly destroyed the kitchen, and the sickbay is damaged."

Zayo knew it was important that everything was working on the ship. "How long will repairs take?"

"If I have enough people to help me, perhaps an hour. By myself, it will take all night."

"I want at least one person with me; all others will assist you."

"Who will you take with you?"

"Tell me who you can spare."

"I need my crew to work on the systems, and I need all of the guards to move heavy equipment. Since none of our people are injured, I can spare the doctor."

"What if someone is injured?"

"Zayo, it is very unlikely. Besides, Tahrmaha will be bored here."

"Then I will take her."

After all of the other Caballians went back into the ship, Mehlanahr dismissed himself from his king and went into his ship with his crew.

Zayo and Tahrmaha did not get too far towards their destination before they were greeted by a group of guards. These guards, who were all heavily armed, began to escort the Caballians towards where they had to go, but before long, they veered away from there and headed in another direction. Zayo turned, and found that he could no longer see Mehlanahr's ship, so he focused on the task at hand.

Guards were a usual occurrence at Alameda, but even in the faint artificial light available, Tahrmaha could see that the guards' uniforms were ill sized. She had never before seen this in humans, and had thought that they prided themselves in the conformed suppleness of their garments, but these guards were markedly different in that aspect.

The Caballians were led into a building quite far from the one in which they had previously met with the Admiral. It was an airplane hangar, with a plane in it, ready to go. Zayo then said to them, "Where are we going to speak with the Admiral?"

The humans turned their guns towards them, and all of them laughed. "You are not going to deal with the Admiral anymore," one of them replied. "There is someone more powerful who can deal with you and your wild, delusional plans for controlling Earth."

"I do not have to answer to any of you."

"You will do as you are told, or you will be killed. It is that simple."

"Kill me. I have nothing to lose."

"So you believe you are a martyr. We will see."

"I am the king of the Caballians, and I serve only my own people. Return me to Vice Admiral Van Housen, before I lose my temper."

The person he was talking to stuck his gun in Zayo's face. "You dare to talk to me like that, when I hold the gun in your face?"

"You will not kill me," Zayo said boldly.

"Perhaps not yet. Besides, Fagan is waiting for you."

He is a hypocrite, Zayo thought. And the young king was quite right in this assumption. But Zayo did not have much of a choice in his current position; he would have to wait until the time was right to correct the situation. He then said to Tahrmaha, "As long as I breathe, I will fulfill my duty. I did not intend for you to be caught in a threatening situation, but please help me in making the best of it until we return home."

"Yes, your majesty."

"I trust that Mehlanahr will follow up on his duty to me."

"Merahlaha is safe, considering the worst may happen to us. And I know my duty to you."

"Thank you."

"Enough of this!" one of the humans finally said. "The two of you will not stand here planning your escape!" Zayo and Tahrmaha were shot with tranquilizers, and almost immediately fell unconscious. They were placed in the airplane, which immediately left the hangar and Alameda.

As the Caballians were finishing the repairs on their ship, a commotion suddenly sprang up among them as they noticed a group of humans collecting outside. Mehlanahr saw that Vice Admiral Van Housen was with them, but that Zayo and Tahrmaha were not, and it troubled him; he ran to meet the odd group outside. He went straight to Van Housen who, when he saw Mehlanahr, said, "Sir, I was informed that Zayo was to meet with me right away—an hour ago. What is the delay?"

"Admiral," he replied, maintaining his composure for the moment, "Zayo left us with a consort an hour ago to meet with you. How could he have not reached you yet?"

Van Housen suddenly snapped a few brisk orders to those around him, and the crowd quickly dispersed. "A full security search is being carried out."

"How long will it take?"

"Perhaps an hour, at most."

"Many things can occur within an hour. Where is my king now, and where is my doctor?"

"I honestly do not know. We are employing our best attempt to find out."

"I am still responsible for Zayo's welfare. These guards will stay here for the time to assist you in the search for our king. If Zayo and Tahrmaha were injured, I will need another doctor; I must obtain one while I still have time to do so."

"I have many doctors here."

"Not that are trained in Caballian physiology. I apologize for my brazenness, but I must do what I can to ensure that my king lives. If not, then I have failed my king."

Van Housen saw that Mehlanahr's eyes had tears in them. "You know and understand your duty so well, yet you are a stallion of deep feelings."

"I am no different from the rest of my people."

The Admiral smiled. "As soon as we locate your king and his consort, I will contact you personally."

"I must take leave of Earth for perhaps half an hour. I will return with more people who will be better suited to help me find, perhaps, and aid my king if something is wrong."

"You are not too sure whether or not something is wrong."

"I know something is wrong, but I do not know the cause yet. If my king is injured or killed, I must be prepared to take proper action."

"What of the doctor he is with? Sure he will help his king if he must."

"Tahrmaha is one of our best interns. If something happens, I am sure she knows her duty."

"She is young. Perhaps they only wished for some time alone."

"No, Zayo would never deviate from his duty and break a law, especially such an important task as dealing with the colonists. He was very upset with them, and was eager to see to the proper reprimand for their actions against my people."

"Their actions <u>against</u> the Caballians? I find that hard to believe."

"Zayo was prepared to explain everything to you. His intentions were honorable, and commendable."

As soon as the spaceship took off, Mehlanahr made some phone calls for people he thought would be best suited to help him. Pleeyedraha agreed to help him, as did the remainder of his engineers who had not gone on the initial trip, except for Shehronaha. Tarahnaha, Yahno and Nehmayaha were appalled when they heard the news, but they knew that Mehlanahr would do everything in his power to bring their offspring back safe.

When Pleeyedraha arrived at the plant (shortly after the spaceship had landed), she had Pakoor and several nurses with her, as well as some more sophisticated portable equipment, which was not already built into the ship. Mehlanahr's first words to Pleeyedraha were, "I requested a doctor, not an entourage."

"If you need a doctor for Zayo," she replied, "then you may very well need a doctor for Tahrmaha. And if we cannot bring some nurses, perhaps we can recruit some of your engineers to help us."

"With the space limitations we have, you and your staff will be required to stay in the sickbay throughout the journey." He brought them into the crowded ship, and they left immediately.

Within a half hour from his initial departure, Mehlanahr was back on Earth. Van Housen knew they were back before they landed, and he radioed Mehlanahr after their landing to apprise the adjutant of their ill luck in the search so far.

As soon as the security alert had been issued, all outgoing flights had been postponed, and all incoming flights were being redirected to Moffett. Alameda was being scoured, every square inch of it, and nothing was going to stop Shane Van Housen from searching it. Even he was becoming bent on finding Zayo and Tahrmaha because they disappeared so mysteriously. The security was usually good enough, but what could have possibly happened? It did not make any sense. How could two Caballians, who were so obviously different from humans, have disappeared without a whisper? The humans had some videotaped records, all of which showed Zayo and Tahrmaha for a few brief moments with an armed escort. Where they went was not known, but one clue was left: the uniforms had either been borrowed or stolen. The possibility of spies at Alameda haunted the Admiral. Who were they, and what did they want with Zayo and Tahrmaha?

All incidents which had occurred between the Caballians and the humans thus far had not remained top secret, a fact which all involved knew very well. It was true that all interactions with the Caballians had taken place with top brass except for the colonists. But Van Housen was regretting the route Admiral Gray had insisted on taking, since it made too much public at one time. What had he overlooked? The colonists, since their return to Earth a short while ago, had remained in detention, so there was no leakage there, no way they could have possibly started any incident on Earth.

Van Housen could not get Gray out of his head. From what Shane had learned, Gray had committed espionage on Equestra, the crime he was punished for. This was not known anywhere else on Earth, except to top officials of the UN, who could all be trusted. Who else was there? What else was there? The foremost public spectacle was the memorial for Gray, which the Caballians had refused to attend because Gray was a criminal.

EQUESTRA

The memorial had been open to all friends of Admiral Gray. Shane had known all of them except for three men, who he did not remember seeing before; they spoke with no one that he could recall. He sent the video records of the memorial downstairs to the holography lab, and was told within twenty minutes of the results: they had positive IDs on two of the three men. The first one was Mr. Court, a mercenary known to occasionally be in collaboration with Fagan. The second was Doc Reeve, who was known to be one of Fagan's top assistants, as well as the veterinarian for his Ireland ranch. But they had no record of the third man, and could not let Shane know anything about him. But Shane was positive that the third man was Fagan. He verified where the supposed location of Fagan's ranch was. He then took the holograms, and went running out to the Caballian ship.

Mehlanahr met Shane Van Housen outside the ship, and immediately brought him into the Caballian spaceship. Shane only stopped for a moment to be amazed at the interior of the ship, and the number of Caballians he saw there. He then said, "Mehlanahr, I am positive Fagan is seeking vengeance for the excommunication of Admiral Gray. He...somehow managed to attend the memorial that your people refused to attend."

"Your problem here on Earth has managed to kidnap my king and doctor? Have you no control over the situation?"

Shane shook his head. "I want to try to rectify it...I owe you that much."

"Where is he?"

"I believe he returned to his ranch in Ireland."

"Show me what you have."

Shane showed him the holograms. After that, he showed Mehlanahr on a planetary map the Caballians had made where Ireland was. It happened so fast, but he did not notice that the ship lifted off from the ground. "When do you plan on taking off?"

Mehlanahr laughed at him. He looked at the sensor map and said, "We are very close to Ireland now." He observed how busy Dehrahlax and Oorahno were, and he added, "We have already begun to search for them."

"How long do you think it will take?"

"It depends. Some of your buildings are made of strange composite metals which our sensors cannot penetrate. If they are in one of those buildings, it will take time to adjust our sensors."

Zayo awoke with a start, only to find himself laying in an uncomfortable position. He did not recognized his surroundings as he viewed them from his vantage point on the floor, but he saw Tahrmaha out of the corner of his eye, so he set up and looked at her a little closer; she still slept. He looked around the room they were in, and he saw that it was a very small room with metal walls; one of them had a door in it. The room was barely big enough for the two of them to have room to walk around. Zayo got up, walked over to the door, and tried to open it. But it would not open under his grasp, and he could not figure out what the concept of a locked door was. He turned back around, and saw that Tahrmaha was waking up, so he walked back to her and set beside her.

She looked around quickly and saw him, so she set up facing him. "Your majesty," she said, "how do you feel?"

"I am fine," he replied, "except that this is a terrible time for you to be so formal. The door will not open, and I do not know how else to get out of this room. I have had enough of this human desire to kidnap...it was bad enough with Jayexeeyo and Shehronaha. But they actually had a desire to kidnap me...I cannot understand why. I am irritated, and I will punish them for trying to steal our freedom."

"That is not a very good feeling, especially since we value freedom so highly. To go where we want and do what we do within the moral confines of our laws is the greatest appreciation we have for our society."

"Those were words my father often spoke."

"Pleeyedraha is fond of quoting Kayloor's wisdom."

"It makes me proud to be his son and heir. I loved everything about my father. Why did they have to kill such a good stallion? Was he too good?"

"Look at yourself, and review your own life so far. You have inherited your father's good aspects, plus you have inherited your mother's strength and courage."

"I really was not asking...I was talking to myself."

"Are you telling me that you do not need consolation?"

"Right now we should not be wasting our time discussing my father. We should be thinking of how we will get home."

After a moment of thought, she asked him, "What sort of trick is it that the door will not open?"

"I have never seen anything like it before, nor have I ever heard of deliberately fixing a door so that it will not open."

"Then how will we ever get home if we cannot leave this room?"

189

He grabbed her hand and replied, "Know that I do not wish for any harm to befall you. You should be home on Equestra, safe with your parents, instead of being lost on a strange unknown planet. None of our people belong here. I had only intended on doing the right thing when I brought the humans back here. I never thought that there would be any risk to myself with my adjutant."

He is different, Tahrmaha thought to herself. Becoming more like Kayloor each passing day. But they are so different from each other...Zayo is strong and does not back down from a challenge, but his father would never force his ways of justice upon anyone. Zayo will not leave Earth satisfied if he does not punish the humans for kidnapping him. "I have no doubt that you will seek out and punish the humans who did this to us."

At that moment, they heard someone playing with the door. As soon as they turned to see who it was, two humans walked in. One of the men was carrying a gun, and the other was not. The unarmed one spoke. "Good morning, and welcome to my ranch."

Zayo and Tahrmaha stood up. "That is how you refer to a prison?" Zayo asked.

"You are dangerous," the stranger replied. "I cannot allow anyone to interfere with my plans for humanity. But I could not just have you assassinated, because you are far too valuable for that. So, once I have extracted my price from the United Nations, I will let you go—if you cooperate with me."

"I am not a criminal, and neither is she. Why are you keeping us here?"

"You are the king of your people, and you are out to conquer humanity. But you cannot do that, because that is my role. Don't you see? You are interfering with the progression of my plans."

"I am not a conqueror. I am a judicator."

"Then why did you kill Admiral Gray, and why have you returned the others here to Earth?"

"They have committed despicable crimes against my people."

"Like what?"

Zayo did not like being interrogated in such a way by a stranger, so he remarked, "I do not have to answer any of your questions."

The other human clicked his rifle. "You consider yourself to be a martyr?"

"You are a stranger, and I cannot recognize your authority. You have proven nothing to me, especially as to why I should answer to you. I am a king, the king of the Caballians; I serve the best interests of my people, and am required to answer only to those directly involved."

"Then why do you answer to Van Housen?"

"Because he has proven to me that he is out to serve the best interests of both of our peoples. I respect his position."

"I am Fagan!" he riled. "I have controlled the destiny of mankind for the past fifteen years, and I will continue to do so! I am the greatest visionary this world has ever known!"

"You are no leader. If you were, you would have proven your accomplishments instead of losing your temper over a statement of fact. You and I have nothing in common; we have nothing to discuss."

The rifle was aimed at Zayo, and the man holding it said, "Fagan, when you give the word."

"Mr. Court," he replied, "in a moment." He then said to Zayo, "Do you really want to be a dead king?"

"There will be no importance in my death," he replied.

"I told you to cooperate, but you are not cooperating."

"Zayo," Tahrmaha said, trying to control her fear, "do not let him make you look as if you are as foolish as he is."

"Tahrmaha, please," he replied, "what would happen if I were to be murdered, like my father before me? Mehlanahr and Merahlaha will avenge my death, and they will protect our people from humans and any other aliens whom they might encounter."

"Your sister is but a new foal."

"Mehlanahr is resourceful and cunning. And one day Merahlaha will grow up, and will be a formidable queen for our people. They will also have Andrux to help them."

"Zayo, you are hardly of age, yet you are contemplating your own death! You are far more valuable to our people alive. What would they think if you were to be killed within a year of Kayloor's murder? People expect that both you and Merahlaha will be with them for the next four hundred years."

"I will not die. Booralta said I will have many princes."

"You have one more chance to save yourself," Fagan yawned. "You will entertain me."

"You are envious of what enjoyment I am getting out of this ridiculous argument?" Zayo chided.

"Do not mock me! I have the gun pointed at you, and I know that Mr. Court is not afraid to use it!"

"What do you seek, entertainment on the aspects of being a king?"

"Hardly. I want you to demonstrate, with your consort, how your people go about attempting to reproduce."

Zayo's eyes were glaring mad. "Kill me," he whispered coldly.

Fagan laughed at him. Tahrmaha was now visibly frightened; she could not bear the thought of Zayo being killed at his young age, and their people living under Merahlaha. "Zayo," she exclaimed, "that would mean interstellar war!"

Before Zayo could answer, a shot rang out, and drove straight into the center of his chest. He fell to one knee, maintaining eye contact with Tahrmaha, and he said, "I cannot travesty your life in...such a...way...better off dead." His voice broke off, and he slumped to the floor, unconscious.

Tahrmaha glanced at his wound, then she looked up at her captors and said, "He is dying. What will you do with his body? Consume it, as you consume animals? Or will you actually have the decency to let it be returned to Equestra, where it may be properly burned?"

Mr. Court put down his gun. "But he killed Admiral Gray, and...and he made things hard for the colonists," Fagan said, laughing nervously.

"Admiral Gray was punished for committing treason against Zayo," she continued, figuring it was best to tell Fagan as much as possible before she, too, was killed. "He had promised to follow our laws while he was visiting Equestra, but he broke that promise, and attempted to alter the life of Zayo's adjutant. He deeply offended Zayo's generosity and upset the trusting nature of my people. He was fully warned, but he did not heed the warning."

"The laws must have been too complex. He probably did not understand them."

"You do not understand that we are vastly different from you. If Zayo had just done as you asked him to do, both of you would have been permanently blinded by the action of the photocytic cells in our reproductive organs. Zayo would rather die than risk your safety, or anyone else's safety. We have laws to protect our people from this, and those were the laws that Admiral Gray abused. He was blinded before he was excommunicated for said treason."

He looked at her and retorted, "You are trying to manipulate me, but it will not work."

"I only speak the truth. It is up to you whether or not you accept it. And it is up to you whether or not you retain us. Hardly does it matter, because you will eventually be punished for what you have done to my king."

192

"Maybe you have a point," he said, growing weary of what he was up against. "Mr. Court, bring them to the mainland."

"Where, Fagan?"

"Anywhere where you will not be seen."

COMA

Four humans brought Zayo and Tahrmaha to an empty beach on the mainland by helicopter. Little did the humans know that Zayo was not dead yet; Tahrmaha knew that if Zayo received medical attention within the hour, he would certainly not die. If his injury was left too long, it would eventually kill him.

The four humans dragged Zayo out, and lay him on the beach. Tahrmaha stayed near Zayo so she could keep an eye on him. Mr. Court stayed with her for a moment while the other three returned to the helicopter. He saw Zayo's chest rise and fall, and he said, "He is not dead yet?"

"He will die if he does not get medical attention," she replied.

"I will help him," and he pointed the gun at Zayo.

"It is not enough that my king is suffering?" she asked; she grabbed his gun, and pushed it away so that it was not pointed at anyone.

He wheeled around to point it at her, but she caught it, and ripped it out of his hands, throwing it a long distance away. "What are you doing?!" he yelled.

"You will not help him die. Rather, you must be punished for deliberately hurting him with the intention to kill him; that is treason."

Mr. Court started to run away, but she quickly overtook him, and grabbed him. As a witness to his attempt to kill Zayo, she was allowed to capture him under Caballian law, so she mercifully took his neck in her hands, and moments later, he collapsed, unconscious. As soon as his friends saw this, they took off in the helicopter to return to Fagan.

Tahrmaha returned to Zayo, where she turned her full attention to him, using what few supplies she had with her to tend to the wound in his chest. The bullet had not gone very deep at all, just through some muscle, and had deflected off of his breastbone; the shock had knocked him unconscious. Zayo was lucky this time, very lucky.

About twenty minutes after she finished tending to his wound, the helicopter returned. This time, however, there were six men, including Fagan. All of them got out of the helicopter. They were all armed, except for Fagan. He led the party to her, and he said, "I have had it with you."

She stood up and replied, "You freed us. Why have you returned?"

"How dare you question me like that? First you were bragging to me about how morally correct your people are, then you turn around and kill Mr. Court. How dare you?"

"Treason against the crown of Equestra is a crime of which both you and he are guilty of, a crime which is punishable only by excommunication; he is not dead, only unconscious. There is no reason for what you have done to my king."

"Yes there is—if we didn't do it, no one would. You had to be stopped."

"You had no reason for kidnapping us, harassing us, and attempting to kill Zayo."

"No one will ever catch me. No one has ever caught me for anything I did. And you are going to pay for what you did to Mr. Court."

"Mehlanahr will not rest until you are properly punished."

"Mehlanahr. Mehlanahr. Who or what is Mehlanahr?"

"Mehlanahr is Zayo's adjutant."

"It will be too late. When I am through with you, you will be much closer to death than your king is. HA!"

Tahrmaha was tied up and beaten unconscious, most of the trauma being to her head. Then, Fagan proceeded to rape her. Due to her head trauma, her photocytic cells were unable to react as they normally would have. Fagan then beat her some more until she was on the borderline of death.

They took Mr. Court, and left Zayo and Tahrmaha there. Left for dead.

Dehrahlax found the beach where Zayo and Tahrmaha were. Just before the Caballian spaceship reached their location, he noticed the helicopter leaving them. He turned the scanners on to follow it and its occupants, and they landed on the beach. Mehlanahr stepped out by himself, but when he saw Zayo and Tahrmaha laying there in their injured states, he ran back into the ship and had Pleeyedraha and her staff tend to them. Within ten minutes, Zayo and Tahrmaha were in the sickbay, and were being treated for their injuries. Their ship left the beach, and followed the path which the helicopter had taken.

They caught up with the helicopter as it was landing on the island, and he landed next to it. All of the engineers and guards raced after the humans; they were all carrying imploders except for Mehlanahr. The humans had left their rifles in the helicopter in their hurry to escape, but were now caught empty-handed. The six humans were rounded up and could not escape as the Caballians encircled them. There were perhaps forty Caballians there, an exorbitant number for the size of the ship which they had used; it was worse with the colonists in it.

"What is the meaning of this?!" Fagan shot out when he saw that he was surrounded. "You are trespassing on private property!"

The Caballians passed glances at each other, and they all ended up looking at Mehlanahr, who said to Fagan, "Who hurt Zayo?"

"Who are you?"

"I am Mehlanahr," he replied calmly, "adjutant to his majesty Zayo, and master engineer of the Caballians."

Fagan looked at his captors, and thought to himself, I had better play the moral game with them. They will fall for the bait, and will not outwit me. "Did you hear me, Mehlanahr? I said you were trespassing on my private property. That is a crime here."

The Caballians were all puzzled by his comment. Fagan was pleased by this until Mehlanahr asked him, "Who are you?"

"I am Fagan!" he exclaimed. "I will have every one of you assassinated for this treachery!"

Van Housen was right, Mehlanahr thought to himself. He is as bad as Kayloor's traitors. "Fagan, tell me who hurt my king."

Fagan saw Mehlanahr's hand on his sabre, so he said, "Mr. Court shot him."

"Who is Mr. Court?"

"He is in the helicopter, but he is unconscious."

"How did he become unconscious?"

"He was overwhelmed by that female who was with your king."

Tahrmaha fulfilled her duty, Mehlanahr thought, and smiled. "Why did she capture him?" Mehlanahr continued to ask.

"What would I know of what Mr. Court did? He was a mercenary."

"Where were you when she captured him?"

"I was here."

"If you were here, how did you find out that Mr. Court was unconscious so that you could retrieve him?"

"The men who were with him fled her threat, and came immediately to me."

He returned to get vengeance on Tahrmaha, Mehlanahr thought to himself. He then said to the Caballians, "Keep them here until I return." He turned and walked into the ship, heading towards the sickbay. He walked right past Shane Van Housen, who was trying to stay out of the way. When Mehlanahr saw both doctors and all of the nurses working feverishly on Tahrmaha, he knew right away that she was hurt very bad. Zayo was laying on another bed, waking up, so Mehlanahr went to speak with him.

"Mehlanahr," Zayo said when he saw his friend, "you must find Fagan. He—he has committed treason."

"The man who hurt you—Mr. Court—is unconscious. Tahrmaha captured him for what he did to you."

"Where is Tahrmaha? I wish to speak with her."

Mehlanahr looked over his shoulder at the hustling doctors and nurses, and some tears escaped his eyes. Zayo followed his adjutant's gaze, and soon recognized where he was. "Tahrmaha is dying."

"No! That cannot be! Tahrmaha cannot die!"

Mehlanahr was deeply distressed by Zayo's words; he suddenly realized that Tahrmaha was Zayo's link to his father and Pleeyedraha. "Zayo, she was hurt far worse than you were."

"How did she get hurt?!"

"I do not know. But we are holding some humans outside whom I was attempting to question before, one of them being this Fagan that the humans fear."

"Fagan is going to be excommunicated," Zayo said very calmly. "He said that he has controlled the destiny of humans for the past fifteen years. Called himself the greatest visionary, and said I was interfering with his plans for humanity."

"He said he will have all of us assassinated for our treachery against him."

"He must be responsible for Tahrmaha's injuries."

"That is hypothetical until you have solid fact."

Suddenly, Pleeyedraha's voice called out to them, "I can identify the culprit from a cell identification. The genetics belong to Fagan."

"Tahrmaha needs you more," Zayo said to her, as she stepped up to his bedside.

"I have done all I possibly can. Her condition has stabilized somewhat; she has a slight chance. But Pakoor is better suited at treating a patient with head trauma than I am."

"What sort of head trauma?"

"She is comatose." She saw the ghastly expression on Mehlanahr's face, and she saw Zayo let some tears go, but she continued. "She was severely beaten and raped by someone who wanted her dead."

"No!" Zayo whinnied. "How can this be?! She was an innocent bystander who was performing her duty by serving as a doctor on this mission, which was supposed to be very short! If she dies, what do I tell her parents?! For the sake of our people, Tahrmaha cannot be allowed to die!"

Mehlanahr grabbed him by the shoulders and said, "Now you know how I felt when we had the transport accident! It is no fun being helpless, and knowing that especially as our king, you cannot do a thing about it! But if she cares for you as much as you care for her, then she will not die! Friendship shows how strong two people can be!"

Zayo calmed down some. He then said, "I need to take action now with Fagan, but once we return to Equestra, I must follow her request and encourage her to heal. I cannot allow this to kill me."

"Shane Van Housen is on the ship."

"Good," Zayo said, standing up. "He will witness how we handle criminals." He left the sickbay, with Mehlanahr following him.

Upon passing Admiral Van Housen outside of the sickbay, Zayo said to him, "Admiral, come with us."

Shane was shocked upon seeing him. "Your majesty," he said, "you are fine?"

"I am fine, but Tahrmaha is critical and comatose. Fagan tried to kill her, and I need for you to witness how I handle such a criminal. Are there any laws here on Earth forbidding me from excommunicating him?"

"You are our guests here, but since Admiral Gray is the one who started this problem, you are definitely within your jurisdiction to mete out justice your own way."

"Thank you." Mehlanahr handed him the shifter, and Zayo led them out of the ship. When the other Caballians saw the king, they were ecstatic until he said, "This is no time for celebration right now. The daughter of Yahno and Nehmayaha is critical and comatose, and

198

Pleeyedraha does not know if she will survive her injuries." He saw the six prisoners and said to them, "Fagan, do you know what the punishment is for what you did to me?" At that moment, Mr. Court woke up in the helicopter and walked out of it, joining Fagan.

"What did I do to you?" he asked. "I never held a weapon in my hands."

"You masterminded the scheme to kidnap Tahrmaha and myself, and you ordered Mr. Court to shoot me with his gun in an attempt to kill me because I refused your order to fornicate! Treason and attempted murder are crimes both deserving excommunication."

"You are crazy!"

"Then you were so upset over the fact that Tahrmaha captured Mr. Court for me that you sought revenge on her."

"That vengeful bitch had no right! She deserved everything she got!"

"To be tied up, beaten until she was near death, and savagely raped?"

"You did not see me do anything to her, unless you were faking being unconscious."

"Our master healer performed a genetic test, which identified you! Rape is also a crime deserving excommunication!"

"For what it is worth, it was fun! I always wanted to make it with a horse, but a centaur was even better!"

Zayo moved so quickly hoisting the shifter up into the air and firing it at Fagan so fast that no one knew what had happened until he had disappeared. He then looked at Mr. Court and said, "For your attempt to murder me, you will also be excommunicated," and he fired the shifter at him. "I am satisfied," he said to Admiral Van Housen.

Shane felt some relief and he said, "If you would be so kind as to keep these prisoners in your custody long enough to bring them with me back to Alameda, I would be so grateful."

"Granted." They went back onto the ship.

Shane then said, "Why did you return the colonists?"

"They plotted and performed a conspiracy against the morale and honor of my people, as they tied up and kidnapped two citizens, a stallion and a mare, and brought them to the forbidden valley, where they were forced to fornicate against their wills."

"That is everything?"

"Procreation outside of marriage is dangerous and illegal, and is punishable only by excommunication. I should have excommunicated the colonists, but since there were so many of them, and I could not be exactly sure as to who played what part, I extricated them instead."

"You did not excommunicate your own people for that?"

"Of course not. They were the victims, forced into doing something they never would have done otherwise."

Once at Alameda, the prisoners were led off of the ship. Zayo then said to Shane, "Admiral, we will take our leave of you here."

"It has been a privilege to meet you," he replied. "Perhaps one day we will be ready for more of a friendship between our peoples."

"Not in your lifetime," Zayo replied. "But do not give up your work. Other humans have much to learn from you."

"Thank you. It has been an honor to learn from you."

"I wish we could part under better terms, yet this is the best we could do. We must get Tahrmaha to the hospital."

"I will always cherish what I have learned from you."

"I thank you for your assistance. You are the most wonderful human I have met, and I call you my friend."

As their ship took off from Earth, Zayo contacted Yahno and Nehmayaha to meet them at the hospital. He also contacted his mother to let her know he was fine. When the ship landed on Equestra, it was near suppertime. Tahrmaha's condition was stabilized enough so that she could safely be brought to the hospital, which they did cautiously but quickly. Soon after Pleeyedraha and Pakoor had her settled in and connected to monitoring equipment, they were summoned out of the room by a nurse, who brought them to the waiting area; Yahno and Nehmayaha had just arrived. Yahno said to Pleeyedraha, "How is she?"

Pleeyedraha could not hold the tears back, as she finally allowed what had happened to her student to affect her. AI wish I could give you good news," she said, Abut the only good news I can give you is that she is still alive."

Zayo walked into the hospital at that point. He saw the desperate expressions on Yahno and Nehmayaha's faces, and he said, "I know that Tahrmaha will survive."

Pleeyedraha was shocked. "Zayo, I know you mean well. Yahno and Nehmayaha, she was savagely beaten and raped by humans who wanted her dead. Zayo excommunicated the guilty party immediately, but Tahrmaha is in critical condition because she is in a coma. We have treated all of the obvious injuries to her head, so she seems to be asleep. But with a coma of this type, it is highly unlikely that she will ever awaken."

"Pleeyedraha, Yahno, Nehmayaha, Tahrmaha will wake up, even if I must risk my life to wake her up."

"Zayo, you know nothing of medicine."

"Perhaps not, but I know more about the spiritual needs of our people. There cannot be a tragic end to such a day as today was. The marriage of a couple cannot be at the cost of a life of another person; if it is, then they will never have any foals, for their marriage will be shrouded in darkness." He saw the looks on their faces and he added, "They tried to kill me, too. I was luckier than Tahrmaha; my injury was not as serious. Your daughter was very brave. I was the first one hurt, and she was a witness to it, so she captured the human who tried to kill me, and I was able to excommunicate him."

Yahno looked at him and said, "Why would they try to kill you?"

"They were savages," Zayo replied calmly. "Under threat of death, they ordered us to procreate. I told them to kill me; I would not satisfy their primitive lustings. I will not break one of our laws for the sake of my own life, because those are the laws which I must uphold to protect our people. If I do not, then the wars will return here to Equestra."

"Pleeyedraha," Nehmayaha said, "we wish to see her."

Yahno and Nehmayaha entered Tahrmaha's room very quietly; after they did, the nurse walked out to leave them alone. They were shocked by all the monitors that she was connected to, because she seemed to be asleep. They would have thought her to be asleep except for the intravenous feeding tube in her neck. They set next to her, and before they knew it, they had fallen asleep.

When Zayo returned to the palace, his mother was glad to see him safe, yet she was extremely saddened by Tahrmaha's injuries. Kayloor had always spoken highly of Tahrmaha to his wife, and Tarahnaha understood why.

Throughout the first week of the coma, everyone was very hopeful that she would awaken at any time, but as time dragged on, their hopes sank lower and lower.

Zayo was, in all likelihood, the most depressed of all. He felt responsible for what had happened to Tahrmaha, because it was at his urging that he did not leave the ship alone. If he had gone alone, she would not have been kidnapped and injured; if he had gone alone, he might be dead instead of her being near death; if he had gone alone, who knows? Pleeyedraha felt just as bad, though, because she had asked Tahrmaha to go to Earth because it was Pakoor's day off, yet Pakoor ended up on Earth anyway.

About a month and a half later, on the three hundred and twelfth day of the year, Zayo ended up in Karayo's house. Karayo still had Vehdoor studying with him, but Vehdoor was much closer to being able to work as a shaman on his own.

Once Zayo had set down with some water, he said, "Why is Tahrmaha still in the coma?"

Karayo looked at his king carefully and retorted, "How did Tahrmaha get into the coma?" He saw Zayo's puzzled look. "My dear king, the problem is that you are only looking at the surface details, but not at what connects it all."

"What have I missed? I was there when Tahrmaha was hurt!"

"Certainly you were there. But how long were you unconscious? And what was said between Tahrmaha and the humans which you did not hear because you were unconscious?"

"How could I possibly know such a thing unless I ask her about it? I cannot ask her because she is in a coma."

"How did the two of you get free from Fagan's ranch?"

"They set us free after they tried to kill me."

"But since they went through much trouble to get you into their possession by kidnapping the two of you, they must have made it difficult for her to bargain for your freedom."

"What are you saying, Karayo?"

"I am saying that Tahrmaha probably said and did what she could to obtain your freedom. She probably told them you were dying, and that your body needed to be properly burned here on Equestra."

"Why would she say that?"

"Why not? She was upset that you were injured, and felt that the more she told them about our people, the better chance you would have of getting home alive. Tahrmaha also told him that you refused to follow his command because it would have blinded him, and you were trying to protect his safety."

"That was the main reason why I told him to go ahead and kill me."

"You can tell me Tahrmaha does not know that, yet it was easy enough for her to figure out what happened with Dahrohd, Ahrkoor, Jayexeeyo, and Kayloor, and how it was all connected with your father's murder? Give her more credit than that—she is very intelligent. She knows that your job is to see to the safety of others, and to keep the wars from coming back. She knows it all too well.”

“Why would Tahrmaha have done all this?”

“She knows what you mean to our people, and she knows her duty to you. I would believe that she was desperate to get you back here before you died, and that she exhausted every possible effort to see to that. I believe that is what happened before the coma.”

Zayo shook his head. “What does this have to do with her coma?”

“Just as she exhausted every possible effort to get you home safe, you must exhaust every possible effort to break the coma. That is how she will wake up from her sleep.”

“Every possible effort? I have done everything possible!”

“Not yet. The ancient magic was invoked when Jayexeeyo and Shehronaha entered the forbidden valley. It must be answered, otherwise Tahrmaha will never wake up.”

“How could I possibly answer magic?”

“There is one thing you do not know, Zayo: when the forbidden valley is invoked, so must the cave of the magical mists, otherwise our people will be destroyed by what has happened so far. It is an ancient riddle. Just like Omistu appears and disappears each day, the crops are planted and harvested, and Equestra has opposite magnetic poles, there is the forbidden valley and the cave. If both are not used equally, then the balance will be lost, and the wars will return. You are our king, and you must do what you can to prevent that.”

“Then two people must go into the cave, just like two people went into the forbidden valley.”

“Yes,” Karayo agreed.

“Then, after the caucus tomorrow morning, I will bring Tahrmaha to the cave.”

As soon as Zayo had called the caucus, he went to the hospital to speak with Pleeyedraha. He went straight to her office, and found her setting there doing some administrative work. “Pleeyedraha,” he said, “good morning.”

She looked up at her king, and she could not help but smile at him. “Good morning, your majesty,” she said. “Please, set with me.”

He set across from her, and took some water that was readily available. “I was just speaking with Karayo.”

“About Tahrmaha?”

"Yes. How did you know?"

"You have been here every day to see how she is doing, and to ask if she has awoken yet. Zayo, when are you going to relieve yourself of your guilt?"

"Tomorrow."

She was quite baffled by his answer. "What do you mean, tomorrow?"

"Karayo told me that there is only one way she will wake up. Because two of our people entered the forbidden valley and invoked the ancient magic, the reply to it must be summoned from the cave so that the wars do not over take us."

"What cave?"

"The cave of the magical mists, on the far side. To save her life and the lives of all of our people, I must bring her to the cave. After the caucus, I intend on setting out for the cave immediately, which is why I want Tahrmaha at the caucus, with all of the equipment and tubes removed from her."

"Is that what the caucus is all about?"

"Yes, because it involves Tahrmaha and myself leaving our society for a while."

"What if the cave kills both of you?"

"What if it does not kill us, but heals her? Pleeyedraha, there is no fear of my family ending with me because of Merahlaha. And if I do not bring Tahrmaha to the cave with the chance of our dying, then certainly all of our people will die. It must be done. Pleeyedraha, please bring her. It means very much to our survival as a race."

"Do you truly believe that Tahrmaha will awaken from the coma after being brought into the cave?"

"I most certainly do." I will die with her if I must, he thought.

As requested, every single Caballian was at the caucus, including a comatose Tahrmaha. As soon as they had eaten breakfast, Zayo went up onto the platform, and got their attention. "My people," he began, "the past four weeks have been an ordeal for all of us, because Yahno's daughter still sleeps in the coma. There is nothing more that Pleeyedraha and the rest of the doctors are able to do."

"Then why did you summon us here?" someone called out. "An address on her condition could have been given over the visiphone."

"You are right. However, I spent some time with Karayo and Vehdoor yesterday. Because the humans invoked the ancient magic of the forbidden valley, we must counter it by invoking the magic of the cave of the magical mists. I must risk my life to bring Tahrmaha there, because she risked her life to ensure that I returned here safely from Earth. If I do not bring Tahrmaha to the cave, then the wars will return to us, and we will all die. If I bring her there, she will awaken from her coma."

Some murmuring began, and someone cried out, "Where is Tahrmaha now?"

"She is here, in Pleeyedraha's transport."

Eight Caballians reached into Pleeyedraha's transport, and lifted Tahrmaha up out of it. They carried her up to the platform, and laid her at Zayo's feet. "Bring her to the cave," one of them said. "If the others do not agree, let them make war with us."

The murmuring quickly stopped, and a number of them began to shout for Zayo to bring her to the cave. He let it go on for a short while, then he got their attention and said, "If anyone disagrees with what I need to do to prevent the wars from returning, speak now, or forever hold your tongue in silence." There was dead silence.

After a few minutes passed by, some others clamored to the platform and lifted Tahrmaha up off of it. "Your majesty," one of them said, "where is your transport?"

"It is behind the palace, by the sea," he replied. They carried her over to it, and carefully laid her down in it. Some others reached into their transports, brought out some food, and put it into Zayo's transport so that he would have food for his journey. He ran after them, and as soon as everything was secure, he departed.

Once Zayo left, they reassembled, and Mehlanahr went up onto the platform, where he got their attention. "Where is the master historian?" he asked.

Karayo walked up onto the platform with Vehdoor, and they stopped before Mehlanahr. "Sir," Karayo said, "please let Vehdoor speak."

Mehlanahr backed away, and Vehdoor, for the first time in his life, began to speak to his people. "Zayo is going to be successful," he said. "When the ancient magic is invoked in the cave, Tahrmaha will wake up out of the coma. But it will not happen overnight.

"Zayo will be gone from us for several years. When he comes back and tells us what adventure befell him while he was in the cave, you will all be glad he went to save Tahrmaha's life. It is very difficult to accept so soon following Kayloor's murder, but it is what must be done. It is good that we have such a king, who is so ready and willing to act when he must risk his own life. Merahlaha is still new, so it will be up to all of us to do as Zayo would have us do if he were here. We all know what our king would ask from us if he were here. Let us not force Mehlanahr to act in his stead while he is gone, doing what he can to prevent the wars from returning. Mehlanahr's blade must remain unused for when Zayo will return to us. Then, we will be a proud people he is glad to return to. We must learn the confidence to believe that we know how to live without our king, so he will know that he can always depend on us to stand by him when we are troubled by humans.

"The humans are gone, and all that remains for us to fear are shadows. Will they get the best of us, or will we fight to break free from the shadows, as Zayo has been fighting to break free from Kayloor's shadow? We have yet to learn from his example. Since he is sacrificing his time and risking his life to save Yahno's daughter, it is only proper that, when they return to us, they will be greeted with such a celebration as could not even be matched by Mehlanahr's passage."

They all agreed to it.

It seemed to Zayo as if it were an eternally long trip to the cave on the far side. He ate while he drove, and stopped only to defecate and urinate, and to sleep when night became too dark.

He arrived at the cave late the next day. He managed to get her out of the transport, and had to drag her into the cave. He went in as far as he could see, and he settled her down on half of a very flat portion of the rocky floor, which was actually a large flat rock split in two with each half just big enough to lay someone on. He set next to her on the other half, and set there watching her.

Zayo must have been setting there for at least four hours before fatigue overtook him, and he fell asleep in a rather uncomfortable position.

THE GREAT CAVERN

As Zayo pulled himself towards consciousness, he felt that he had not slept so good since his father was killed. It was an enchantingly restful sleep, and he almost did not want to wake up, but he dragged himself to consciousness despite his reluctance. As his eyelids were about to open, he felt as if his body was strange to him, as if the cave had done something to him; he was afraid to look at himself. Once he mustered up the courage to open his eyes, he knew immediately that he was in a strange room in a strange building; it seemed to be Caballian in origin, yet it was far different from anything he had ever seen. The walls seemed properly made of stone, but there were no candles in the walls; there was an eerie glow emanating from the ceiling, which was much stranger than the artificial lights he had seen on Earth.

He was laying nearly flat on his back, so he slowly rolled his eyes from their upward gaze so he could look upon himself and try and decide why he felt strangely different. The first thing he saw of himself were his chest and abdomen muscles, which were suddenly so much more developed than they had ever been that he automatically assumed that he was, by the magic of the cave, now physically mature. He lifted up his left hand and looked at it, and saw that it seemed to be at least as large as his father's hand had been. He had been twenty-five when he brought Tahrmaha into the cave, but he had not yet begun to fill out; he had been rather lanky, like all others of his age. His arm muscles now seemed to be as well-developed as his chest muscles were; they were as refined as

207

Mehlanahr's muscles were, but they were built up more like a shoemaker. He pushed his upper body up off of the floor, and saw that the rest of his body was in the same muscular condition.

His bone structure was as developed as his muscles were; in many respects he seemed physically mature. He touched his chin, but it was still bald, so he knew he was still young. He set up, and looked around at his surroundings.

The first thing he noticed was a mare sleeping on the other side of the room. It seemed to be Tahrmaha, but she was now as physically mature as Zayo was, but in a much more feminine respect. Zayo remembered seeing pictures of his grandmother Ahmehlaha, and knew that she had been much more beautiful than his mother, but as he helplessly gazed at Tahrmaha, he realized that she was much more beautiful than Ahmehlaha, and much more intelligent. He wondered if she was alive until he saw her chest rise and fall at slow intervals. He shook himself from gazing at her so, but when he could not displace her beauty, he knew one thing: he would pursue her to become his queen.

Very slowly, he stood up, but as he did, he realized his legs were not at all shaky, but that they felt quite good to be used. He stretched his rather taut muscles, and when he was certain that the circulation was rushing throughout his body, he began to walk around the room very slowly. He studied the walls, looking for evidence of a door for about five minutes before he found it. He then set out to figure how to open it.

When he thought he had found the latch, he reached out to open the door, but was quickly stopped by the sound of screaming. He whirled around to see Tahrmaha screaming and crying at the top of her voice. Her words seemed to be gibberish until he realized that she was calling his name over and over again. He ran to her, and knelt beside her. "Tahrmaha!" he whinnied at her. She did not seem to hear him, so he whinnied her name several more times until she heard him, and tried to bring herself under control.

Her eyes opened, but were glazed. "Zayo, Zayo, he—he hurt me...he dishonored me. Let me die!"

He felt an urge to laugh, but knew better; he knew that the only way to break her delirium was to play a psychological game with her. "You are dead," he told her.

She rubbed her eyes, and suddenly saw herself; she saw that she was now a physically mature mare. Her head quickly turned so that she could see where his voice was coming from, and she saw his changed form. "I am dead?" she asked.

"You were spiritually dead. Now that you have regained control of yourself, welcome to the living."

"Then...were those humans all a bad dream?"

"They were not a dream, Tahrmaha...it was all real. Pleeyedraha and Pakoor did what they could to save your life."

"What happened?" she asked, realizing he knew something she did not; she set up slowly.

"The human Fagan wanted vengeance on you because you captured the person that tried to kill me, so he beat you until you were in a coma, and then he raped you. However, Pleeyedraha could not bring you out of the coma."

"Then how did I wake up? How many years has it been, and where are we?"

"I do not know how long it has been, and I do not know where we are, but I know how you woke up. Karayo and Vehdoor told me that the only way you would wake up from the coma would be for me to risk my life to bring you into the cave, because you risked your life to regain our freedom from the humans. After the humans invoked the ancient magic of the forbidden valley, the only way to correct the displacement and prevent the wars from returning was to make use of the cave of the magical mists."

"What happened to Fagan?"

"I excommunicated him as well as the human whom you captured, the one who hurt me."

Tahrmaha shook her head. She stretched out her body, and stood up very slowly. "We have been gone at least a few years," she stated. "But if you brought me to the cave of the magical mists, then how did we wake up here and not in the cave?"

"We shall find out," and he walked back to the door to open it.

When Zayo reached to open the door, Tahrmaha could not help but notice the finesse with which his muscles acted together. There were no jerky movements, but an absolutely fluid motion. She was so drawn in to his appearance, absolutely smitten. She quickly shook the thought out of her head, thinking. how close to thirty five was he, and would his body develop any more? How old was she, and had she missed her own passage? That gave her anxiety to even think about. Even worse, she felt a longing for him to claim her.

After a bit of a struggle with the latch, Zayo managed to open the door. She was on his heels as he stepped out of the room they had been laying in, and they began to walk down a narrow but dim hallway. They did not get very far before someone who appeared to be a Caballian stepped out of another room and turned in their direction. "Yea," the stranger said, "Yea, hearken ye steps."

Zayo and Tahrmaha stopped in front of him. "Good day," Zayo said, not knowing what time of day it was.

Tahrmaha observed the stranger, and noticed that he was somewhat different from the Caballians they had known. He had what appeared to be gill slits in his neck, webbing between his fingers, and webbing where his hair and tail should have been; the webbing was golden in color. His fur was black, and his eyes were slate. He had hooves, and his face appeared to be quite normal apart from some webbed fringes on his ears. Where his beard should have been was some webbing. He was fascinating to look at. "A merry day, much better that thou hast awoken. Dost thou fareth well?"

"We are confused," Tahrmaha said.

The stranger had a piece of rope tied around his waist; it was made out of seaweed. "Thou hast been through much travail," he said to them. "Thou mayest calleth me Beltadro. Ye premises suffice as mine abode. I am ye fisher, whence I discovered thee in ye alcove of yon cave."

"I am called Tahrmaha."

"I am Zayo; I am the king of the Caballians. Why were you in the cave? It is dangerous."

"Ye side of yon cave which ist on ye land ist imperiled. Ye side here in ye open waters ist safe. Thou were in ye air pocket betwixt ye two sides, so I safely pulled thee through."

"How could you have come up from the watery side?" Zayo asked.

"How not? I abide in ye waters, as do all Acaballians. How tis that thou dost not?"

"All of our people live on the land," he replied. "I have never seen nor heard of anyone living in the water. I only know the Caballians, not the Acaballians," and he clearly enunciated the difference.

Beltadro looked at them a little closer, and saw again that they had hair but no gills or webbing. "Thou art strange and different from all Acaballians. Twould be best if thou wouldst willingly meeteth ye Acaballians at public council on ye morrow."

Zayo and Tahrmaha were struggling to understand his speech; it was stranger than anything they had ever heard a human speak. "Where can we stay until the council?" Zayo asked.

"If thou wouldst be agreeable, thou canst stayeth with me."

"That is a gracious offer," Tahrmaha said. "We cannot refuse."

"Art thou hungry?"

Zayo and Tahrmaha had been so caught up in the physical changes that had happened to them that they had forgotten about whether or not they were hungry, and how long it had been since they had last eaten. They shook their heads in agreement, so Beltadro brought them to another room in his house. It was his kitchen, and it had a rather odd odor in it. He had his guests set on two carved stone chairs at the stone table. He picked up some food that had been sitting there, put the finishing touches on it, and placed their plates before them. He then set with them, and was the first to begin eating. It was food, but not like food that Zayo and Tahrmaha had ever eaten before in their lives. They were given utensils to eat with that looked somewhat like forks; Zayo picked up his fork and tasted the food in front of him. He liked it so much that he proceeded to eat all of it so fast that Tahrmaha was just tasting hers when his plate was clean. "That was fabulous," Zayo said. "Thanks in excess."

Tahrmaha tasted it, and proceeded to eat what was on her plate. "What type of food is this?" she asked after she had eaten it.

"Pickled coral from mine yards up yonder," Beltadro replied. "'Tis ye staple among Acaballians. Dost thou normally consume coral?"

"We eat what grows on the land, because it is much easier for us to obtain."

"Beltadro," Zayo said, "please tell me about the Acaballians."

Quickly, Tahrmaha said, "Zayo, it is rude to be so pushy upon our host!"

"What am I to do?" Zayo asked her. "Are we to sit here, and not ask any questions about where we are and how we got here? Protocol can be an effective tool, but so can questioning each other. Sure it is nice here, but I would like to know how we came to be here, and why. It is rude to attempt to learn our condition?" He turned to their host and said, "Beltadro, is it too much to ask for you to tell me about the Acaballians?"

"We have always lived on Equestra," he replied. "AInnumerable eons ago, we wert one people, Caballians and Acaballians. Whence came yon fighting and wars, those of us which wert Acaballian fled into ye sea to protecteth that which wast just and true; feelings wert that thy Caballians wouldst destroy thyselves. Four cities wert builded erein one capsule of air under ye waters, which ist wherein mine abode and all others exists, and where we now abideth communing. Said air capsule ist grand enough whence tis able to support ye population twofold of what erein exists."

Beltadro seemed to speak in riddles to them; Zayo and Tahrmaha were having a difficult time understanding everything he was saying to them. When it had time to settle into Zayo's brain, he said, "How great are the numbers of Acaballians?"

"Fifty thousand reside in ye air capsule. One hundred sentinels continually roam ye waters; sentinel houses exist in small air pockets in caves such as yon cave which thou wert slumbering nigh upon."

Zayo was dumbfounded at their numbers. "I always felt that forty thousand Caballians were a lot; you feel that fifty thousand Acaballians is a modest amount. You are a fisher...what does a fisher do?"

"Tis my duty to procure food for Acaballians. When my family shalt cometh, thou shalt learneth much more."

"How large is your family?" Tahrmaha asked.

"Ahkeelahara who ist mine wife, and three foals she hast borne for me."

"Zayo," Tahrmaha said, "where do you think we are?"

"I believe we are in the Great Cavern underneath the Unknown Sea."

"What of Beltadro and the Acaballians?"

"It is time for a reunification. Just as the Caballians could not have any divisiveness in working to solve the mystery of our disappearance on Earth, our peoples must not have any divisiveness if we are to evolve as we must. The Acaballians are the key to my success as a king. If we can earn their friendship, then it will be well worth it."

Tahrmaha was stumped. Even at a time as this was, Zayo was thinking of his duty as a king. If his plan worked, it would make him a great king.

Beltadro almost did not know what to say to his guests. Finally, he said, "Thy thoughts and ideas art best brought before ye council on ye morrow. Thou hast agreed with this."

"Forgive me," Zayo replied. "It was important that she understand what is happening before it expands beyond her scope. She is not a leader, but a doctor. You can understand this?"

"Tahrmaha ist thy friend or thy wife?"

"Tahrmaha ist mine friend," Zayo quipped, forcing himself to attempt to use Beltadro's idiom. "Among Caballians, we art too young to be of age for marriage, though never too young that such a though wouldst not enter our heads. There art many fine mares whom I wouldst consider before choosing one. And I am sure Tahrmaha wouldst be equally as selective in whom she agrees to join with."

Beltadro smiled. "Then Caballians practice much as mine Acaballians. Ye pubescent Acaballians art allowed to consider marriage whereafter ye age of facial growth in yon stallions."

"'Facial growth'?" Zayo mused.

Beltadro fingered his webbed beard and said, "Mine beard."

Tahrmaha laughed; it seemed quite humorous that they would be speaking about such a thing. Never in her life had she ever heard two stallions speaking about such a subject as Beltadro and Zayo had broached. But if Zayo truly wanted reunification, then every single aspect of each other's lives must be known among all.

Beltadro laughed with Tahrmaha for a moment, then he said, "Thou art people of good humor. Tis wonderful. Wherein it wouldst not trouble thee much, kindly tell mine ears of thy people."

"When the wars occurred among our people millions of years ago, it was never known among the Caballians that the Acaballians left them to live in the cavern; at that time, we were all called Caballians. The wars did not end until there were only one hundred and forty seven Caballians left. At that time, my ancestor Pehsoorad called a truce, and set the guidelines for how they were to live if they were to survive. During Pehsoorad's lifetime, he ensured that they did not fall back to their warring ways, because he believed that they were a worthy people, worthy of giving themselves a decent chance to live. When Pehsoorad died, his son was elected to continue his job in his stead. After that, it was his son's son, and so on, and so on, up to my sister and I. We are known to be Pehsoorad's descendants because of the marks on our heads," and he showed Beltadro his blaze. "My sister, Merahlaha as she is called, also has the blaze of leadership. I am called the king, and she is called the queen. When the time comes for me to marry, my wife will be called a queen, though not a noble queen with a crown as Merahlaha will be when she is grown."

"'When she is grown'?" Beltadro repeated. "How old ist she?"

"When I last saw her, she was a new foal."

"Why ist yon sister a queen? What of thy father?"

"My father was murdered by three Caballians."

"There exists three citizens in yon empire whom have murdered thy father...howin can thy soul rest?"

"We have laws to prevent such crimes from happening. They knew before they went near Father what would happen to them. They probably felt that since they were spiritually dead, it was not worthwhile for them to continue living at all. The only punishment for such a crime, according to the laws accepted and practiced by Caballians, is excommunication."

"Ist not such excommunication warlike?"

"The practice of excommunication is the only thing which instills the fear of returning wars into the Caballians' hearts."

"Thou art still a savage people."

"The Caballians cannot be judged by the fact that three people allowed themselves to turn back on the rest of us. It was only the second time in our history that one of my ancestors was murdered by people who were unsympathetic to my family's cause. I am sure that occasionally you have a vagabond or three among the Acaballians."

"Which ist true, we art not perfection. There art those of us whom desirest to live upon the land again."

"What ist done with them?" Zayo asked.

"Whence they art caught by a sentinel, they are subjected to psychotactic treatments immediately; none art allowed to leave the sea, for fear of being seen by our warring brothers, thine Caballians."

"The Acaballians work to preserve unity just as the Caballians do. It is amazing that, after millions of years, we have so much in common."

"Our peoples have had time wherein to grow and learn to abide. Tis not so amazing that thine and mine peoples have learnt the same successful way upon which to dwell. However, friend Zayo, said discussion must wait for council."

Not much else was discussed between Zayo and Beltadro after their lunch, which Beltadro had eaten somewhat late in waiting for his guests to eat with him. They excused themselves shortly thereafter, and left their host's house so that they could explore the cavern. Beltadro was not dismayed at their departure, because Zayo and Tahrmaha promised to return to his house for supper.

As they left Beltadro's house, Tahrmaha said, "Zayo, how long do you intend on staying here before we return home?"

He turned to face her, and could not help but smile. "Tahrmaha, I have so much work to do here before we return home. My soul will not rest easy until I know that steps are being taken for Caballians and Acaballians to be reunited."

She was worried, and frustration was all over her face. "Your majesty, I do not wish to impede with you and the job you must do, but there are some things which take precedence."

"Like what?"

"You are so excited over what we have stumbled into that I doubt if you stopped to think of how old you are."

He rubbed his chin and said, "I am not thirty-five yet."

"No, but have you forgotten already that I am older? I may already be thirty-five, and I may have missed my own passage!"

His face sobered up very quickly. "Tahrmaha, you are right. But please try to see it from my point of view. What did you think of Beltadro?"

"He is a dear soul."

"Exactly. However, if I understand him right, he is frustrated over the fact that our people have been divided for so long. I believe he risked his life by bringing us here...I believe that all other Caballians have been forbidden from finding out about the Acaballians—it is their way. He has risked his life to give you and I a once-in-a-lifetime opportunity, so I am not about to blow it all and cause a war with them. They fled to get away from the wars, and it is my duty to prevent the wars from returning. If we leave on behalf of your passage, then we will miss the greatest moment in our history by not doing what we can to heal the wound with our lost brothers. Beltadro has risked his very being for this moment...I beg of you that you postpone an equally important aspect of your life. It must be done for the sake of both of our peoples."

"Why, Zayo? Why must I sacrifice so much to help you and your reign? It means much more to you than it does to me."

"If we go back now, and you are in time for your passage, every single stallion who is of age will try to win your favor. Look at yourself in a mirror...you are more beautiful than my grandmother was. Then what? The wars will return for sure, and it will all be worthless. You and I have already risked so much for each other on Earth. Now, all I am asking is that you see this through with me."

"Zayo, you are not yet of age, yet you are asking such a thing of me! I cannot believe what my ears are hearing! What would our people think?!"

"If that is truly how you feel, and you are so selfish, then our being here is worthless, and you are not worthy of becoming a healer. If your needs are more important than the needs of all Caballians alive, then you are free to go. I cannot keep you here against your will. You must stay because you want to do the right thing for our people, and honorably earn your place in our remembered history. There will never again be such a moment as this is...I beg of you that you do not spoil it for something so selfish. So what if your passage is postponed? You will still receive your vest. But it is those selfish yearnings which will invite the wars to return. Is it worth the destruction of our race for you to instigate a fight among many honorable stallions who all feel they should deserve you? If I return with you, I can protect your honor because of my office."

"That is ridiculous!" she exclaimed, trying to deny it.

"That is what it amounts to. Either you are worthy of fulfilling your destiny, or your life and everyone else's lives are as good as over."

"Why can I not have a choice in the matter?"

"Tahrmaha, the very essence of what I am means that I have absolutely no choice; Father always stressed that upon me. I must stay here and do what I can, even if it means my death. Vehdoor was right."

"What do you mean, he was right?"

"He told me that I had to bring you to the cave in order for you to wake up out of the coma, which I did. If I had not brought you to the cave and invoked the ancient magic, then the wars would have returned in another form. Whether you want to or not, you are an important factor in this."

"How do you feel about this all?"

"How do I feel? Why should my feelings matter? It is my job."

"Why not? It is your life as well as mine. If you do not tell me how you feel about it as I have told you, then I will leave. If you tell me everything, I will stay."

Zayo was cornered by the one mare who had the nerve to corner him in such a way. "Not even Father was ever able to corner me like that," he replied.

"But Zayo, I do not do such things because I want to. It is there, and it must be done, and I am hardly afraid of your temper when I know that I have a valid point."

"Neither do I ignite because I want to...it is the very essence of what I am. Most couples never learn that aspect of their relationship; they can only see what is on the surface. Mehlanahr has an idea as to what it is all about, but-"

She interrupted him, saying, "You still have not told me what is on the surface. That is what I am blind to."

"When I awoke in Beltadro's house, and I saw you laying there sleeping, it took every ounce of my strength to control my hormones."

"Your pheromones are just as loud!"

"Now you understand how I feel. I have been fighting that as well as concentrating on my duty. If you give up on me now and leave, I will excommunicate you when I get back."

"What?!" she whinnied.

"Why not? If you leave, I will be unable to finish my job here. It is because of you and your coma that I ended up here, so you had best see it through. Your leaving would be grounds for treason, and I would prove it in front of our people."

"I still say you are too young to make such a claim!"

"What is worse, that or treason? And what can be done about it? We must circumvent an antiquated law to ensure that our people again become one. This is one instance where Father had the right idea. And surely you know what is more important."

Tahrmaha suddenly thought to herself, Why am I arguing with him? Let him use his excuse to make his claim. I am not the one who should argue with him about it. Tahrmaha composed herself, and said to him, "Why do I have to argue with you to get you to make your point clear? Or is it that you will only hear my side of the story if we are both yelling?"

"You forced me to say it. You should have let me be until I am thirty-five."

Tahrmaha suddenly realized her error. "It seems as if yelling is the only way to vent our frustrations," she said much more calmly. "The pheromones are trying to get the best of us."

"We cannot survive the struggle to mature without confronting all other reasons as to why we are here. How could you possibly feel comfortable with living out your life, knowing that our people are divided into alienated groups?"

Tahrmaha let out a little laugh. "It seems so petty; I could not help myself because it still haunts me to think of what happened on Earth." Self-control, she thought to herself, will help us to keep our sanity until we are home with our families. And he is right—I must fight it out with him. Thank the moons that this is what it has come to.

Once they had a chance to look around, the sights they saw were utterly amazing. The ground in front of Beltadro's house was very rocky, and seemed to show no soil; not far beyond the rocky area was an immense submerged field of coral growing, seemingly ready to be harvested. They knew that Beltadro was a farmer by what they saw. The field sloped down towards the darkened corner of the cavern, which is where it was met by the water. On the far side, the field seemed to go on and on for miles along the edge of the cavern. On the side opposite the end of the cavern, there ran another field of another type of crop, which ran into some exposed rocky soil. There were other buildings to be seen, all of them quintessentially Caballian, yet somehow different from what they knew.

EQUESTRA

The roof of the cavern was expectedly unlike the Equestran sky. It had an unfigurable glow about it that lit up the cavern almost in broad daylight, yet which was darker at the edges of the cavern, which seemed to fall into edges of questionable darkness and water. The ceiling itself was illuminated by the same factor as the rooms in Beltadro's house (which Zayo and Tahrmaha did not yet know): it was thickly lined with crystals and philinium; other minerals incited the philinium, which caused the crystals to glow brightly. It was an absolute miner's paradise, holding enough to keep their race alive for countless eons. Like the surface of Equestra, it had its own unspeakable beauty.

The cavern air was as damp as the surface atmosphere was. It was impossible for it to rain there, but their presence underneath the water kept their lungs healthily moist. Zayo and Tahrmaha took some enchantingly deep breaths, and felt even moreso a sense of belonging. Just the idea of what they had been brought into was astounding. Between that and his feelings towards Tahrmaha, he was quickly forgetting the pain he had suffered over his father's death.

As he was about to set out in the direction he wanted to go, he took her hand in his. She tried to pull it back, saying, "Zayo, please, it is difficult enough just standing near you."

"Please," he pleaded, "I feel insecure in such a strange place as this is; you are the only friend I have here. We will not speak, but use your imagination. We can walk all afternoon in silence if you wish. As long as I can touch your hand, and know that you are trying as hard as I am to keep your sanity, it will be enough to keep me honest. Besides, criminal longings grow stronger when you are forced to face them by yourself."

"But you have the same criminal longings."

"Are we to fight it alone in such a strange place as we are in? I need to be reassured that we have a common cause to believe in. It will help me remember my duty."

"But the things that I think and feel when you touch my hand...it is as if the thought is criminal enough to destroy my soul."

"We have a tremendous job ahead of us, and we need to be able to provide each other with spiritual support if we are to be successful in reuniting our people. Just because we are not citizens yet means that we cannot publicize our commitment, nor establish a physical bond. But we can be best of friends who are committed to helping each other."

She relented, saying, "I am a doctor, but I never heard of such a thing."

"Before my father was killed, I had sat with him on a number of questionings to see if couples were prepared to publicly come together. People meet and become friends under all different types of circumstances, but the key factor in every relationship is that a couple must be committed to helping each other, and they must be the best of friends who can implicitly trust each other."

She relaxed, and they set out on their walk.

It was an absolutely quiet afternoon for Zayo and Tahrmaha. In their walk, they pretty much stuck to the fields, viewing the buildings from a distance. Zayo knew that, until the council, it would not do for either of them to be readily seen by any Acaballian; from a distance, they could not be recognized as not being Acaballian, so it did not matter to those who saw them in the distance.

By the time they returned to Beltadro's house, Ahkeelahara had been there for nearly an hour. Beltadro had become somewhat concerned about his guests, but was grateful when they finally returned. The supper that Ahkeelahara had prepared for them was just as invitingly delicious as the pickled coral had been. Acaballian food was a far cry from oatmeal and apples, but Zayo loved it just as much.

CORBO

Zayo and Tahrmaha had nothing they could braid their hair with for the council. Neither of them had their intern vests on. Additionally, he had left his crown and sabre behind. When they found out that they were to eat breakfast at the council, they really and truly felt depleted. It would have been easy to accept if they were among people they knew and loved, but they had absolutely no idea of how the other Acaballians would accept them, or even if they would survive the morning, considering the lengths that Acaballians went to in avoiding the feared Caballians.

Many eyes were on them as they ate breakfast, and as soon as it was consumed, they could hear more of the whispers. Before they knew what was happening, they were surrounded by a vast number of sentinels. With all of their weapons poised to strike Zayo and Tahrmaha, she was frightened, but he kept his composure. They stood up to face the sentinels.

"Spies," one of the sentinels said. "Thou are cometh to destroy ye cavern and ye Acaballians. Thou must be excommunicated."

"May I have the honor of speaking with your governor before I am to be removed?" Zayo asked. "If I am to be removed here, please allow me to do so with honor."

"Thou art strange," another sentinel said, "but thou art correct. Thou deservest to be treated as an honorable stallion. Whereupon they intentions proveth to be false, thou shalt die."

"I thank thee. I also claim right of honor for my consort."

Some of the sentinels were ogling Tahrmaha. She noticed it, and she realized just how right Zayo had been. "Right of honor to be bestowed upon a vixen?" a female sentinel asked. "Thou hast best not hold any deceit within thy heart."

"Is she entitled to right of honor or not?" Zayo asked.

"We cannot deny right of honor to thee, vixen or no. Thou art wise. Thou shalt confer with yon governor." The sentinels escorted them to high ground where, upon a platform, set a stallion who served as their governor. The governor was a rather diminutive stallion compared with Zayo, although he was similar to most other Acaballians, who seemed to be for the most part the same height and weight as Caballians. He had the refined appearance of many Caballians, and had an extremely intelligent look upon his olive face. His fur was gray, and his eyes were black; his webbing was silvery. Around his neck he wore a rope-chain; hanging from this was a diamond-shaped piece of white marble which, if it were to be compared with Zayo's blaze, was the same size and shape, though more refined. The sentinels knelt before the governor; the one who was between Zayo and the governor said, "His excellency Khasadro."

"Your excellency," Zayo said, but Tahrmaha remained quiet.

"Right of honor hast been granted thee," Khasadro replied. "Thou mayest speak all thou desirest ere eventide."

"Your excellency," Tahrmaha said, "right of honor it is to be in such a magnificent place as this is."

Zayo was surprised to hear her speak, and whirled his head around, saying, "Tahrmaha, please allow me to be diplomatic."

Khasadro was quick to stand up. "Sire," he said to Zayo, "dost my eyes deceiveth me, or art thou of the royal realm?"

"Excellency," Zayo said, turning his head back to the governor, "I am not a shaman; I do not understand what is the 'royal realm'."

"Upon thy head ist ye symbol of ye true leader. Twas given to me whenceupon I proved my wisdom and guidance upon beloved Acaballians, yet thou wast born with said symbol on thy head. Wert I so foolish as to ignore ye birthright of leadership?" He lifted the rope off of his head, and went to put it on Zayo's head, but Zayo stopped him.

"Excellency," Zayo said, "I do not doubt that thou art genuine. Thou knowest thine Acaballians; I know the Caballians. Wouldst thou be so quick without learning more?"

Khasadro was utterly impressed with Zayo. "Thy majesty," he said, wanting to give Zayo the respect which he truly deserved, "thou hast been spoken of erein many eons." He put the marble back around his neck. "Mayest I touch thee?"

"Wouldst I never be offended," Zayo replied, and he stepped closed to Khasadro. The governor proceeded to touch Zayo's hair, moving it off of his blaze, and viewed the blaze with quiet reverie. He soon took his hand back when his eyes were satisfied, and he said, "How wast thou art come nigh upon ye council?"

"Beltadro hast brought us here from yon cave which seest the land upon ye other side. He has given us food and shelter, and is a true friend."

"Whereupon dost thou knowest Beltadro?"

"Whereupon we awoke within his abode after falling asleep in the cave. Beltadro brought us to the cavern, for the purpose of rejoining our peoples, risking his own life and livelihood."

"Why?"

"Hast Beltadro shown thee any deceit? Hast he attempted to hide us, or keep us for his own benefit?"

"Tis a remarkable attempt. Whereupon it hast been millions of years since yon exile, yea mine Acaballians art forbidden contact with thine Caballians, Beltadro is rightly fearful." He began to pace around on the platform. "If thou wert not of yon royal realm, thou wouldst be excommunicated, as wouldst be Beltadro. Ye fables have earned thee thy lives."

Khasadro set back down in his seat. "Who art thou, and who art thy vixen?"

"I am Zayo, the king of the Caballians. My friend is Tahrmaha; she is a doctor."

"Zayo and Tahrmaha of yon Caballians, I wouldst be honored for thee to set with me during yon council."

"The honor wouldst be ours, to abide with yon Acaballians for a spell. Whereupon the end of said council, we shall depart to return to our people, the Caballians. Departure shall make my heart weak, longing for when I shall be with thee again."

"Tis a great honor that ye think so highly of yon Acaballians."

"Whether Acaballian or Caballian, thou art a worthy people, worthy of thine heritage."

Tahrmaha looked at Zayo with perplexed eyes, because she was amazed at how fast he picked up the Acaballian idiom; she figured she had best learn it also. Khasadro had his chair moved to the left, and two other chairs were placed on its right. The chair to Khasadro's immediate right was now in the center of the platform, and Zayo proceeded to set there; he had Tahrmaha set on his right. The only things Zayo was missing were his crown and sabre, Tahrmaha thought to herself. Other than that, he seemed to be right where he belonged—in charge of the platform.

"Pray do tell me of thy fables concerning Zayo," Tahrmaha asked of Khasadro.

Khasadro laughed a hearty laugh, which pleased Zayo and Tahrmaha. "Thou needest ye history lesson," he replied. "I requireth yon able storyteller," he called out to the Acaballians.

Shortly thereafter, a stallion came forwards. He was quite old as compared with many of the other Acaballians. His fur was golden, his eyes were chestnut, and his webbing was black. "Excellency," he said to Khasadro, "heretofore I request ye right to fable."

Khasadro would have normally granted such a request, but now that he had Zayo sitting with him, he was afraid to reproach the king. "Thy majesty," Khasadro said to Zayo, "tis thy honor to grant such a request."

"Excellency," Zayo replied, "though I am the king of the Caballians, I know nothing of thy ways. Pray that thou wouldst be the one who shalt give proper consult to thine Acaballians."

"Thy word art great here, and doth carry all final decision." He turned to the storyteller and said, "Sheladro, thy request ist granted. Mind thee of whom thou speakest to; mind thee ere not forget anything of import, lest his majesty wouldst not fully comprehend thy honored fable."

Sheladro began his story. "Many eons ere, shortly thereafter ye time upon which yon Acaballians hadst fled into yon waters and cavern for to escape yon wars, yon Acaballians wert afraid perchance Caballians wouldst seek us out, yea, destroy us, by thy destructive ways for Equestra. Perchance to save yon lives, yon Acaballian governor took with him his wife and went hither to stay with yon Caballians, and spread ye word that ye Acaballian sect was extinct. Perchance our governor wast unable wherein to stop yon wars, yea his son succeeded."

"The son of thine governor from yon eon?" Zayo wondered.

"Ye same, sire. Ye son of yon governor wast called Pehsoorad."

"How wouldst thou know such a thing?" Tahrmaha asked.

"Yon descendent of Pehsoorad, called Hehlehf, went nigh upon yon cave to learn more of yon ancient magic. Yon governor hadst left ye cavern and gone to abideth with yon Caballians so to protect all of Acaballian sect from destruction. Hehlehf discovered that yet we abideth, which wast considered forbidden knowledge to all Caballians then; whenst he wast discovered, ye sentinel followed him out of yon cave onto ye land and excommunicated him after twas known that his wife wast with foal. Yon sentinel knowest not that Hehlehf was descended of yon governor.

EQUESTRA

Yon ancient magic of ye cave hadst changed Hehlehf so that whilst his heir developed, twas marked so as to prevent it from suffering said fate of yon father. Thy people knowest naught of Acaballians and ye sentinels, so therefore thou not knowest yet we abideth still, whereupon thou wast brought here by Beltadro.

"Tis not allowed for a sentinel to touch thee, for ye mark upon thy head wast put there whereupon yon sentinel hadst removed thy ancestor. Thou art protected by yon misdeed, for thy family hast returned sanity to yon brethren. Thy family hast fought to save said brethren from yon warring ways, which ist thy sworn duty for thy people. Ye ways of yon governor and his family hast been most honorable. Thou art of ye mixed blood, so therefore thou art ye greatest among us. Thou art of ye governor, and of peace, and of all other things Caballian and Acaballian. Thy family hast proven themselves for to be yon able leaders, which ist why ye governor Khasadro wearest thy symbol. Now that thou knowest thy history, thou canst learneth yon fable." He paused for a moment, saw that Zayo and Tahrmaha were ably following him, so he began to tell them the fable.

"Whilst Equestra wast but ye new planet, twas inhabited by strange beings which controlled all ye metaphysical and ethereal happenings. Equestra wast yon power central to yon development of ye universe, and twas home to yon creatures whilst twas new. Wheretofore ye time came for yon formation of Equestra to settle into ye stationary planet, most of yon creatures fled into Omistu, which wast powerful enough for to support ye ancient powerful life forms. Therein wast ye accident, and three of yon ancient ones wert killed greatly. One wast in yon forbidden valley, one wast in yon cave, and one wast in ye moonsflowers.

"Ye ancient ones in yon forbidden valley and yon cave wert but twins, their power split as if by right and left. One wast good, whilst ye other one was evil. Ye good one occupies yon cave, and ye evil one occupies yon valley. Ye third ancient one occupies yon moonsflowers, yea controls yon moons. Tis ye reason for ye ancient magic in yon places.

"Whilst there be ye continuing battle amongst ye twins, which ist why ye balance needest be retained, ye moonsflower controller ist settled and by far more powerful. Ye twins continue to battle, as in ye most ancient times. Once twas ye battle so bitter amongst ye twins yet ye moonsflower controller hadst intervened, and hadst done so much to stop ye twins from said fight, yea he left ye remnant of his power in yon cave. Ye remnant wast picked up by thy ancestor Hehlehf whenst he passed

224

through yon cave. Said power ist why thou art our leader, and we needest follow thee to our lives' end."

Zayo was stunned; it was a remarkable fable, rich in Caballian folklore and ancient tradition. "That wouldst explain why Karayo told me that after the valley was invoked, the cave also needed to be invoked," he told Tahrmaha.

"Zayo, tis but a fable," Tahrmaha replied. "Ye twins art representative of yon Caballians and Acaballians."

Zayo laughed at her analysis. "What wouldst Karayo think of said fable?" he asked her. "Tis a beautiful story."

"Sheladro, our thanks are in excess," she said. "Thou art a worthy historian."

Sheladro smiled at the compliment which Tahrmaha paid him, and he ran away from the stone platform.

After Sheladro left the platform, the Acaballians began to make a great noise. Zayo said to Khasadro, "If I knew ye purpose of yon council, I wouldst not hesitate to achieve said purpose."

"Acaballian council is held but once per month," the governor replied. "Tis ye time for to communicate all tidings. Since thy present ist of great import, tis ye first order of business."

"Dost thou control what manner wherewith ye council ist run, or dost thy people democratize?"

"Mine Acaballians dost know nothing of political import. Therefore, they alloweth myself to make such decisions."

"Dost thou not allow thy people to speak their minds? Ye conscience of yon Acaballians ist what controlleth ye social dynamics by which thy people abidest. Guidest them truly, yea hearken to their needs and ideas. What thy people know ist of greatest import to thy life, and to thy world."

"Thou art king, yea, thou art strange. Tis not an Acaballian idea."

"How wouldst thou know if it wert or wert not an Acaballian idea? Dost thou listen to thy people? Or dost thou monopolize their lives?"

"I wast selected as yon governor; I know what tis best for yon Acaballians."

"Thou knowest of Acaballian ways, but not of Acaballian ideas."

"Thou art false!" Khasadro suddenly whinnied; this got the attention of all of the Acaballians so well that the place was deadly quiet. Khasadro felt he was right, and he set back in his seat.

"Thou wouldst deny me ye right of speech at council, when I am thy king?"

"Thou art yon Caballian king."

Khasadro saw some sentinels approaching and relaxed, but Zayo paid their actions no mind. "Thy fable sayeth I am ye son of yon governor of Acaballia, yon governor which risketh his existence for to save all Acaballia. Thy fable protects mine existence, and protects thy people from ye wars. Thou art seeming foolish...do not force me to turn thy people against thee. Keep thyself in one favorable and honorable light." If I had my sabre, I would clip him, Zayo thought.

The sentinels stopped in front of Khasadro, where the closest one said to him, "Excellency," but not another word.

"Ist there ye way wherein ye council mayest continue?" Khasadro asked the sentinel that had spoken.

"Excellency," he said again, "thou art underplaying ye role of his majesty. Thou must understandeth he ist marked because he knoweth best. Thou dost not desireth to invoketh ye twins."

Khasadro jumped out of his seat, quite upset, and said, "Thou art Acaballian sentinels! What hast affected thy minds?!"

The sentinel shook his head. "Excellency, thou art one good governor, yea, thou dost not understandeth; his majesty ist greater than thee. If thou dost not changeth thy mind, ye sentinels shalt upstage thy governorship this council, and supplicate his majesty Zayo to selecteth another."

"Thou art speaking for thyself!"

Tahrmaha sat there and wondered to herself, What did Zayo do this time to create such a disturbance?

"Thou claimest to be one true leader," another sentinel said.

"Thou art ye dictator," a third sentinel added.

"Thou art unfair," yet another sentinel said. "Thou cannot manipulate he whom wast chosen among all by ye emperor."

"Our predecessor erred in excommunicating Hehlehf," a fifth sentinel said, "for he sought to bettereth Caballians and Acaballians, though he knoweth very little of us. Thou shalt not forceth ye sentinels whereupon to disagree with Zayo."

"Thy king hast not proveneth his worth to thee!" Khasadro whinnied. "Why dost thou favoreth him so?!"

"Thou canst haveth thy wars," an Acaballian said, one who was not a sentinel. "Thou seekest yon wars by iring ye sentinels. Thy people knoweth things that thou dost not remembereth well. His majesty knoweth best...hearken to ye needs of thy people, Excellency. Thy sentinels do not wish to conflicteth with thee, nor with Zayo. Why forceth thy people whereby to chooseth between ye twins whenst thy people canst chooseth ye greater guardian, thou of ye moonsflowers?"

Khasadro removed his governor marker, and laid it upon the platform before Zayo. "Thy majesty," he said, his voice full of repentance, "thou art required by deepest need to ruleth ye council. Thy people needest to speaketh with thee...hearken to ye voices, that thou mayest truly learneth of all Acaballian needs."

Khasadro arose, and went to leave the platform, but Zayo stopped him by grasping his right shoulder with his left hand. "Thou art ye courageous stallion to fight thy ire and show thyself willing to be ye part of thy people...that ist what ye governor needest be," Zayo told him.

"Mine soul dost not deserveth to sitteth with thee."

"Thy soul deservest to be called mine friend. Thou hast learned humility. Pray do sit with thy people. I shalt be honored to hold council for thy people."

Tahrmaha was amazed that Zayo showed such restraint in dealing with Khasadro, yet she knew that friendship with the Acaballians was what he wanted more than anything else in the world. But at what cost to the respect he commanded from the Caballians? It frustrated her, yet she felt that he had some sort of scheme in his heart. All she could do was wait and see what it was, and keep silent unless she was spoken to. Zayo's matters did not yet directly concern her.

After Khasadro left the platform, Zayo picked up the governor's emblem. He handed it to Tahrmaha, and had her stand up. He picked up the chairs and threw them from the platform, far enough away so that they did not hurt anyone when the landed and broke. They were quite heavy, being made of stone, but Zayo was mad, and needed to vent his anger and frustration. Tahrmaha was grateful he did not have a sabre in his hand, because she knew he would have found a reason to clip Khasadro. When the chairs were gone, she gave the emblem back to Zayo.

The crowd of Acaballians grew somewhat restless when he threw the chairs, so he held up his hands in the air to get their absolute attention. "Thou art free!" he exclaimed. "Free from yon tyranny of wars and fighting, free from yon dictatorial governor, free from all that plagued our ancestors! Thou art a brave, noble, and beautiful people, full of life and zest, full of love and compassion, full of knowledge and wisdom, full of talents, full of all richnesses of yon abode! But thou art afraid of shadows!

Never in mine life have I met any person who was so afraid of yon existence and yon beliefs that ye remain so hidden from thy brethren!"

"Yon Caballians seekest to kill us all," someone cried out.

"Yon Caballians seekest to exploit ye cavern," someone else cried out. "Thou wilt eatest all ye pickled coral!" There were some muffled laughs at this, but they did not last long.

"Yon Caballians wilt destroy ye crystalline secrets," yet a third person said.

"Thou cannot fight against thyselves if thou art to be successful in thy fight against yon Caballians!" Zayo whinnied at them.

"Who hast called yon fight, yon war?!" another Acaballian cried out. "Tis ridiculous!"

"'Yon Caballians seekest to kill us all,'" Zayo repeated. "'Yon Caballians seekest to exploit ye cavern. Thou wilt eatest all ye pickled coral.' 'Yon Caballians wilt destroy ye crystalline secrets.'"

"Tis true!" another one said.

"How dost thou know tis true?" Zayo asked.

"Acaballians survived because yon ancestors fled ye wars. Yon governor wast required to endeth yon wars."

"Thou art afraid of yon Caballians! Thy fears art unfounded!"

"Yon Caballians art unholy!" someone whinnied.

"Thou art so afraid of yon shadow that thou art not worthy of mine time. Thou dost not deserveth to abide with yon moonsflower ancient power. Thou deservest yon twins and yon wars."

"Thou art tricking us!" someone else yelled.

"Thou art so afraid of yon shadow that thou art not worthy of thy heritage. Thou dost not deserveth to be called brethren of yon Caballians. Thou haveth no hearts!"

"Tis not true!" another person said. "Ye Caballians fighteth, whereupon Acaballia sought peace!"

"Twas millions of years ago! Let thy ancestors rest with yon erring ways. Release yon shadow, and encompass what is now true! Thou art a worthy people, as worthy as thy brethren. Thou art not as afraid of thy brethren as I am afraid of leaving here alive! I feel as if I wouldst be excommunicated for being here, thou I wast brought here unwillingly. Thou art stubborn and fierce. Do not use this to fight amongst thyselves about yon Caballians. Unite thy hearts, and tell thyselves that thou must learneth all things before taking ye wrong step. As thou gavest me right of honor, giveth right of honor to yon Caballians!"

"How dost we knoweth that yon Caballians shalt giveth ye Acaballians right of honor?" someone asked.

"I am Zayo, and I promise thee this: that whereupon any Caballian shalt show thee disrespect, said tail shall be cleft with mine sabre. Whereupon any Caballian shouldst invoke ye twins, ye criminal shalt be excommunicated publicly—publicly for all Caballians <u>and</u> Acaballians."

"How dost we knoweth that thou speaketh ye truth?" someone else asked.

"I am Zayo. Tis against my duty to all, for not only would it dishonor myself, but it would dishonor all."

A long period of silence followed Zayo's disclaimer. Then, one of the Acaballians dared to speak up and asked, "Art thou afraid of what thou dost not know?"

"No," Zayo replied. "I am afraid only of what I know will harm any of my people."

"Then tell us what we dost not know of thy Caballians." This request was highly favored by all other Acaballians, so Zayo got their attention and quieted them so that he could speak.

"Yon Caballians art a worthy people," Zayo began. "Our society ist based on honor. Whenceupon a person becomes of marrying age, he or she becomes a citizen, and ist given ye vest of citizenship. Ye color of said vest ist symbolic of yon person's vocation: red vests for historians, storytellers, and shamans; orange vests for chemists, guards, and miners; yellow vests for farmers—what thou wouldst call fishers; green vests for doctors and nurses; blue vests for mechanics; purple vests for my family; gray vests for shoemakers; and brown vests for artisans. It shall be Tahrmaha's day of recognition soon, as she is nearly of age to be given a vest. She wilt be given a green vest, for she hast studied to become a worthy doctor.

"Some citizens art more able than others to do much work for others. Those who art best art called masters. Wherein there exists one master for each color of vest, said master also performs necessary administrative duties for all citizens of said same vest color. Tis a great honor to be called a master, and ist only given to our best citizens. I have one adjutant whom ist sworn to serve me at all times, and who ensures that mine decisions art proper for all of our people; his name is Mehlanahr, and he ist yon master engineer of yon Caballians. Mehlanahr hast builded a vehicle with which to travel to other planets, and it has served me well recently.

EQUESTRA

"Whence, not long ago, strange aliens landed their own vehicle on our beloved Equestra, whenceupon ye exploitation wast much worse than any exploitation which may occur between Caballians and Acaballians, yet I wast able to prevent ye Caballians from fighting with them. Yon aliens committed crimes against ye Caballians, so I wast forced to bring them back to their planet in Mehlanahr's vehicle. In said voyage, ye aliens nearly destroyed Mehlanahr's vehicle, but he wast able to fix it greatly.

"Whilst I needed to return these aliens to their planet, I needed to explain their return to their leaders. As Mehlanahr and his crew wert repairing ye damages to his vehicle caused by ye aliens, I wast required to have Tahrmaha attend the matter with me, whenceupon ye other aliens kidnapped us, and imprisoned us against our wills. One of them hurt me greatly. Whenceupon Tahrmaha captured ye alien who wast guilty of harming me so greatly, she wast nearly killed by yon aliens for fulfilling her duty to me.

"Tahrmaha was nearly dead when she wast found by Mehlanahr and ye other doctors, and I was injured. We returned to Equestra, whereupon Tahrmaha remained in a coma. Because ye aliens had invoked ye spirit of yon forbidden valley, I needed to invoke ye spirit of yon cave so as to enable Tahrmaha to awaken from her coma. I wast also caused to sleep in yon cave. When we awoke from said sleep, we wert in Beltadro's house, not knowing how we arrived therein.

"Yon Caballians have fought bravely against ye evils presented by yon aliens, and art sworn to support my decision to save Tahrmaha's life in said way, through yon cave. Yon Caballians have united in a common cause, and have proven themselves to be most noble and honorable. Thou needest to do ye same; unite together in ye common cause. Not ye cause to keep thyselves secret and fearful of yon brethren, but ye cause to be reunited with yon brethren and healeth ye olden wounds. It pains my heart dearly to hear thee sayeth that thou dost not wisheth to know thy brethren at all. Tis much like ye twins. We must rid ourselves of ye shadow of yon twins and grow ye moonsflower shadow."

"Why must we be so quick to rejoin with yon Caballians?" someone asked.

"Why must thou be so quick to cry fear and hatred? Thou wilt see yon pegasus, and understand that yon Caballians have found ye way to freedom for all our people. As thou believeth that I am thy king, believeth that what I am telling thee about yon Caballians ist also true. Ye Caballians have outgrown ye wars. Now ye Acaballians must outgrow ye warring ways. Tis my duty to prevent yon wars from returning."

230

"Ye pegasus ist ye fable," someone else said.

"Then, as I know little of Acaballian fables, I require a storyteller to fable yon pegasus."

The fable of the pegasus was not told by Sheladro, but by another storyteller, whose name was Heraha. Heraha was an elderly mare, who seemed to be almost as old as Pleeyedraha was, and just as elegant. Zayo had her join him and Tahrmaha on the platform, from where she proceeded to tell her fable.

"Ye hath been told ye fable of yon twins and lineage," she began, "thy majesty. Thou hast learned much about yon Acaballians very quickly; thou art one intelligent stallion."

"I thank thee for thy broad compliment," Zayo replied. AThou art good with words; thou must have an excellent fable."

"Thou art kind. Whenceupon ye ancient ones wert powerful spirits, they had ye mystique and ye grandeur. Whilst Equestra stormed and formed in ye early days as yon planet, ye ancient ones watched ye formation of yon powers. Erein before they wert to leave Equestra, ye royal garden of yon ancient ones wast ye only remaining artifact still to abideth on Equestra. Ye royal garden consisted of ye moonsflowers and yon musical trees."

"The piper forest," Tahrmaha said.

"Aye, ye same. Ye ancient ones cherished ye trees and moonsflowers. Whenceupon ye ancient ones wert forced whereby to leave ye beloved Equestra, yon emperor sought out one new home for ye ancient ones within ye cavern of Omistu. Tis why yon Acaballians abide in ye cavern of Equestra, so as to remember ye ancient ones.

"Ye ancient ones wert of three types. One was like ye Caballians yet they wast unicorns, with horns upon ye heads whereupon thy blaze sits. Ye second one was seaspies like ye Acaballians yet they wast able to sing ye olden songs with as much music as yon musical trees. Ye third one wast ye family of yon emperor; he and his sons, who wert pegasi, and known to be yon ruler by ye wings and ye blaze."

"Heraha," Zayo interrupted, Ädid yon emperor have ye golden eyes?"

"Aye, how wouldst thou know such a thing? Only ye ablest storytellers knoweth such a thing."

"Ye Caballian pegasus has golden eyes. White hair, and silvery skin. His wings art indigo of ye moonsflower hues."

EQUESTRA

"Thy pegasus ist very much like yon emperor, thy majesty. Thou art indeed ye gifted king to have such a person alive from thy people."

"Ye pegasus is a young colt; he wast months old whenst I brought Tahrmaha to yon cave."

"Ye emperor ist great, sire. Twas he and his family who carried ye ancient ones to safety for ye cavern of Omistu. Whence an accident occurred, and ye twins wert split, ye moonsflower guardian wast left on Equestra, and died here, leaving ye ancient magic."

"Who wast responsible for splitting ye twins?" Zayo asked.

"Twas an accident; I know nothing more. Ist ye pegasus of thy family?"

"No. His birth wast caused by those who murdered my father. Ye actions of yon twins to overtake yon moonsflower guardian hast invoked ye greater power in ye pegasus, which ist why ye Acaballians must rejoin with yon Caballians. Otherwise, all of our people art doomed, for Omistu shall surely be destroyed by ye ancient ones if we do nothing."

"How wouldst Omistu destroy ye cavern?" someone else asked.

"As ye ancient ones wert killed whence they did not escape Equestra when they could, thou shalt be destroyed if thou dost not flee from thy warring ways. Leave ye shadow of yon twins behind."

"Thou seemeth to be very wise," an Acaballian called out. "If thou art true, and ye pegasus ist yon Caballian, then all Acaballians must realize yon wars art indeed over."

Zayo clutched the governor's token in his hand, and remembered what needed to be done before the council was over. "What dost ye Acaballians wish to do? Tis thy decision; do not give it to yon governor, for no individual canst speak best about all of thee."

It took a while, but their approval soon rose to a loud clamor. They all agreed that the wars were indeed over, and that the era of the pegasus had returned.

Tahrmaha did not know whether to be amazed or relaxed over the fact that Zayo was so far succeeding in his quest to reunite their peoples. She knew that he would not leave the cavern until he had tried his best, and she believed that he would not leave a failure.

A while later, when the noise began to die down, yet another Acaballian approached Zayo. "Thy majesty," he said, "if yon Acaballians art to join with thine Caballians, shouldst we know of thy laws?"

Some others heard his request, and word was quickly spread, so that the noise immediately disappeared. Zayo then said, "Thou art correct; we have many points to tend to." He walked around the platform for a moment, then began his description of Caballian laws. "Among mine people, we have laws which wert set by mine ancestors so as to prevent yon wars from returning to ye Caballians. Ye Caballians, when they art told of ye reasons behind ye new law, decide if it shall be beneficial for them, and vote upon it at a caucus, much like your council. Ye Caballians gather much more often than once per month; we gather to celebrate each person when they art of age and art to receive ye vest, we gather to celebrate marriages whenst they do not occur upon a passage, we gather whenst a caucus ist called—and which may be called by any person as long as they present sufficient reasoning for calling a caucus, and we gather to celebrate a new king, queen, crown prince, or crown princess.

"Ye laws, as agreed to by all Caballians, art as follows: Ye first law ist that all life is sacred, and that no life may be taken or harmed in any way, without exception. Anyone who violates this law ist excommunicated so as to remove ye evil ways and prevent them from spreading to others; tis like a disease whenst it begins, and can easily cause our wars to return.

"Ye second law ist that ye procreation ist blinding to all others who art not involved, therefore tis a sacred private practice sanctioned only for ye married couples. Tis because a couple cannot successfully reproduce if they know they are harming another. Ye violator ist excommunicated, for they art preventing life from beginning.

"Ye third law ist that ye marriage ist sanctioned for lifetime. Ye adultery, fornication, incest, and rape art forbidden, for they cause sickly disease and blindness. Thou canst only marry once in thy lifetime. If anyone requests remarriage or attempts illegal procreation, they art excommunicated so as to relieve ye unlawful yearning.

"Ye fourth law ist that the life of ye king such as I with ye birthmark of nobility ist not to be abused. Tis my sacred duty to serve all of thee, whence thou shalt also work with me. If anyone tries to undermine my job as thy king and play my role as ineffective, thou art committing treason if thou dost not attempt honorably to work with me. Tis known that I have been trained for my duty since my birth; therefore tis accepted that I know ye best way to prevent yon wars. If anyone decides to commit treason and upend my rule without consulting me and yon caucus, thou art to be excommunicated for being selfish.

"Ye fifth law ist that ye only person who mayest command a punishment ist myself. Tis because if ye people art allowed to punish ye brethren, tis causes conflict and leads to war. Wherein I am only allowed to commission others to carry out punishments if they art sworn to protect and serve my life. Ye only Caballian with such right ist my adjutant. If for some reason I am harmed and cannot punish ye person who hast harmed me, then ye witness ist allowed to fulfill ye punishment for me."

"What of ye sentinels?" one of the sentinels asked.

"Tis must be discussed with yon Caballians. Yea, if thou wouldst agree to protecting Equestra from yon aliens in peaceable ways without any force or weapons, thou wouldst be greatly honored by all Caballians, and held in high esteem. We must avail ourselves of all resources from ourselves as we have available; ye sentinels art capable of being chosen watchers. Since thou hast no reason whatsoever to prevent Acaballians from being seen by Caballians, and since yon wars no longer exist, thy weapons wouldst be useless. Ye sentinel mayest carry out a punishment, as well as all other Acaballians, if both my sister and myself art unable to do so. Ye privilege ist also for yon Caballians; however, like yon Caballians, thou must be either a witness, a storyteller, or a shaman to be able to fulfill said duty. Ye storytellers and shamans have ye ability to know all details of yon crime without being witness, which ist their talent above all others, so it must be trusted as being true."

"Tis satisfactory," another sentinel replied, and they all began to lay their weapons at Zayo's hooves, and the crowd cheered them on.

When they were all finished, and the crowd quieted down, Zayo said, "Thou art great people, ye sentinels. Thy honor ist remarkable. Yon Caballians shalt respect thee highly. Ye sixth law ist that each citizen ist responsible for ye duty to all others; therefore thou art expected to work unless thou art gravely ill, or thou art expecting to part from thy foal, or thou art dead, or any other legitimate excuse which ist pardonable. If thou dost not fulfill thy duty to thy job, thy tail shalt be clipped as high as possible so as to disfigure thy image for years." A number of them shirked to examine their webbed tails, and laughed.

"Ye seventh law ist that thy foals art required to learn enough knowledge so as to be respectable and responsible citizens in ye society whenst thy offspring ist old enough. Thy foals art to be brought to a school whenceupon they art alive for seven full years. When thy foal ist twenty years of age, tis time for ye young one to begin learning a vocation, so ye foal ist placed with a vocational mentor by a historian or shaman; yon foal couldst also be placed by ye storyteller. Thy foal shalt learn with ye mentor until ye age of placement, which ist thirty-five years of age. Whenceupon they offspring ist ye age of thirty-five, he or she ist given ye vest of citizenship, and is allowed to marry one citizen whom hast not yet married. Thy offspring art required to attend ye school or vocational training as much as thou art required to work thy job. If thy foal ist absent with no valid reason, thy foal and thyself art clipped; if thy foal ist over twenty years of age, then only thy foal's tail ist clipped, and thou art not to be faulted. Tis because when a foal ist old enough, he or she ist required to learn responsibility on ye way to filling ye place in society.

"Ye eighth law ist that all people art to be treated respectfully, as thou expects to be treated with respect. If thou showeth disrespect to another, thy tail shalt be clipped. Ye disrespect ist similar to ye treason, though ist for how thou treatest ye other brethren. If thou cannot live and work with ye others in an honorable and respectable way, thou shalt be marked for thy refusal to work with others satisfactorily. If thou wert sick and Tahrmaha wast thy doctor, and she refused to treat thee because thou art Acaballian and not Caballian, that wouldst be disrespect, and her tail wouldst be clipped." There were a number of gasps when he said that. "Ye embarrassment ist usually enough to aright ye offending party, and end yon dissent. If it does not, then thou art committing treason by not heeding yon laws, and art to be excommunicated before ye wars return."

Once he was finished explaining all eight laws to the Acaballians, Zayo allowed them to think about them for about five minutes before he said to them, "I have presented to thee ye Caballians laws, that which prevents yon Caballians from warring. Dost thou accept these, or dost thou require that they be changed to suit thy needs?"

There was a long moment of silence before a sentinel walked up to Zayo and said, "Thy majesty, thy laws art fair and broad. There ist no questions about them, for yon Acaballians art able to approveth them so as to suit yon needs to rejoineth with yon Caballians."

"Whom art thou?" Zayo asked.

"I am called Corbo, sire. Ye onliest problem wouldst be in adjusting yon Acaballian lives to assimilate into Caballian society." A cheer arose from the crowd, as they were highly pleased with what Corbo was presenting to Zayo.

Before the crowd died down, Zayo took a good look at Corbo, and saw a stallion with coloring he had never seen or heard of in his life. His fur was not a solid color, neither was it a flat layer of two colors, nor was it dappled. Rather, it was large patches of white and brown. His tail was white. His eyes were a lighter shade of brown, and his webbed hair was brown. Somehow, he was utterly fascinating to look at, and his confidence sparked his eyes. As soon as the crowd was quiet, Zayo asked, "What problems wouldst this entail, Corbo?"

Corbo smiled, knowing he had found favor with Zayo. "Thou art ye good king, worthy of ye sentinels' support. Ye sentinels wouldst be assigned to patrolling ye entire planet of Equestra. What of yon other Acaballians? Whither wouldst they be living and working?"

"Wherefore have they been living and working all of yon lives?"

"Within ye cavern, sire."

"Whyfore wouldst thou thinketh that I wouldst unsettle thy people from thy homes?"

"Then how wouldst we be assimilated into yon society?"

"Thou wouldst assimilate as much as yon Caballians wouldst assimilate. I ask only that each people sacrifice as much as the other to unify thy goals and remove thy hatred. I am sure that there art some Acaballians who wouldst insist on changing thy lives so as to abide with yon Caballians. Also, some Caballians wouldst desireth to abide in ye cavern. For example, since I have a sister who ist also marked with ye birthright of nobility, one of us would reside here in yon cavern once my sister Merahlaha ist of age to be able to rule enough alone. I wouldst insisteth that ye councils and caucuses be held together, with all Caballians and Acaballians present, that all Acaballians who art of age be given proper vests of citizenship at one caucus, and that all passages for new citizens and marriages be celebrated by all of our people."

"Thine ist one good idea, with much merit. However, what wouldst thy new people be called, Caballian or Acaballian?"

The way Zayo was speaking with Corbo, he suddenly felt as if he were racking brains with Mehlanahr once again. He missed his adjutant. "What do thine Acaballian residents desire?"

"To be made whole with yon Caballian race. Ye time for folly ist over."

"No," Zayo remarked, "I did not mean for thee to answer my request. I wish for thy brethren to tell me what they want." He lifted his head up, and said to the crowd, "Thy brother Corbo has made a recommendation. What dost thou think?"

A cheer went up for Corbo from everyone in the cavern. When the noise had a chance to die down, someone called out, "Ye new governor!" Many other Acaballians began to call out, "Governor!," so Zayo got their attention once again.

"Thy people do not need a governor wile thou art Caballian...however, tis a good idea so as to commission yon sentinels to watch thee while I must be in Caballia. I will be required to split my time between Caballia and Acaballia, so thou must trust thy sentinels and their duties to me and to you. If a crime occurs whilst I am in Caballia, then ye sentinels wouldst be required to arrest ye criminal and call a caucus to be held in Caballia, which thou wouldst all be required to attend. Twould make more sense to hold yon caucus in Acaballia, yet thy brethren in Caballia cannot reach here because they cannot breathe yon waters, and tis too dangerous for them to pass through yon cave."

"Thy majesty," someone called out, "we possess vehicles for traversing through yon waters, for tis impossible for us to travel long distances without breathing air. We canst spend three hours in ye water, but not much more. Our gills tire easily. Tis why we abideth in ye cavern."

"Then perhaps yon Caballians couldst adapt said vehicles for to travel to caucuses here when the need arises, and thou wouldst be able to attend caucuses in Caballia when the need arises. Fair is fair. Whoever calls ye caucus should hold it in yon country."

"Tis wise," one called out, and they all agreed.

"Corbo," Zayo said, "since thou art a sentinel, pray do tell me whose responsibility it is for to assign ye duties to yon sentinels."

"Sire," Corbo replied, "tis my honor since I have proven to possesseth ye greatest knowledge among ye Acaballian sentinels."

"Corbo, hearken, for tis my decree. Since thou art ye most honorable of ye sentinels, thou shalt be called ye master sentinel. Whenceupon thy people shalt receiveth ye vests of citizenship, thou shalt receive ye black vest of ye master, as does my adjutant. However, thy vest shall be of ye new color from all others. At yon caucus in Caballia, I shalt decree that ye sentinels be given vests of ye color indigo, ye color of yon pegasus' wings and ye moonsflowers, since thou art to protect all of Equestra from injury. Wherefore there art my guards in Caballia, said guards shalt also be given ye new indigo vests. Ye guards now weareth ye orange vests. Whence thou art called to become ye master sentinel on all of Equestra, ye guards shalt also be thy sentinels. Ye sentinels shalt learn some duties which art appropriated to guards, and thou shalt determine which guard duties art fitting for ye sentinels, and which should be delegated to yon chemists. Whence this takes place, thou shalt be one of ye greatest citizens of all Equestra, being ye master sentinel. No Caballian can discredit ye black vest, not even of ye sentinels, for thou hast proven thy loyalty to thy people this day."

Corbo knelt before Zayo, and bowed his head. When all of the others saw this, they cheered in favor of Zayo's decree. Zayo touched Corbo's head, which lifted right up, and he touched his right his shoulder with his left hand and said to Corbo, "Thou canst stand. Tis not my moment for command."

Corbo arose and said, "Thy majesty, thou art true."

ADVENTURE TO HOME

Tahrmaha stood near Zayo, watching all he was doing and listening to everything he was saying with great admiration. She remembered all of the prophecies which were told concerning Zayo's reign, but she was only now beginning to realize the impact of Zayo's reign, and what a great king he was making himself. She felt ashamed that she had mentioned going home for her passage, and wished that she had never said anything about it, but she knew if she had not, and she had missed it by staying in the cavern more freely, then Zayo would have wondered why she did not tell him about her passage.

When Corbo left Zayo, the king called out to the Acaballians, "I was able to make ye decree for ye sentinels because they didst prove to me what their duties art. Whenst I have learned what import each one of thee holds for Acaballia, I shall be able to decree a vest for thee, so that thou wouldst be easily recognized by those who know nothing of thee. Ye best way for to do this wouldst be for me to visit each and every one of thee. Whence I have learned of thy purposes, I shalt know what a great people thou art!

"Whence I have finished meeting all of thee, then thou canst be acknowledged as proper citizens in front of all ye Caballians at ye caucus, not just ye residents of Acaballia. Ye meetings shalt require one week. At ye end of said time, we shalt meet again in council to discuss whenst thou shalt be able to attend ye council in Caballia. I know that I am asking much of thee, and that tis a tremendous step thou shalt be taking, though it shalt be ye greatest moment in all history whenst all Caballians meet together in ye caucus. Also, by ye end of said week, thou shalt let me knowest what marriages are to take place, so that they canst be administered at yon caucus. What other business must be properly tended to before ye council?"

"Placements," someone called out. "Some new adults art prepared to be given ye full duties."

Zayo held back his laughter. "If thou agree, ye placements shalt be postponed so that they canst be administered during ye caucus in Caballia."

"Ye new adults art ready now," another voice said.

Zayo got very serious and said, "Yea, hearken! Tis time for ye Acaballian passages!" A cheer went up from the crowd. When they settled down, he continued. "I do not know how thy placements are performed. I requireth some assistance." A young brown mare walked up onto the platform, and knelt before Zayo. Zayo touched her shoulder, causing her to stand up. "Tell me thy name and thy purpose here," he directed her.

"I am Pheerha. I have learned how to grow ye coral and pickle it, and to produce all other foodstuffs. Yea, there ist ye abandoned farm near ye school in ye city of Vayaar, and I desireth to relocate there and work it for my placement."

Zayo quickly caught on. He looked at the crowd and said, "If thy hearts agree, then Pheerha shalt become ye fisher in Vayaar." A loud roar of approval went up from the crowd. Pheerha ran off of the platform, excited. In the same way, six other young adults came up and requested placements for themselves, and they were all warmly accepted and approved. Zayo liked this, and was already thinking of how elements of placements could be incorporated into passages to make them much more exciting. He was glad he listened to them by not waiting on the placements.

Shortly thereafter, a young couple walked up onto the platform and knelt. They both had bay fur and webbing, and dark eyes. Zayo touched their shoulders, and they stood up. "What are thy names?"

"I am Tahzo," the stallion replied.

"I am Ehloorha," the mare replied.

"Tahzo and Ehloorha, what ist thy purpose here?"

"Thy majesty," he replied, "we knoweth that thou requested for all marriages to wait for Caballia. However, we have waited for ye month and ye council. Our hearts plead with thee for to allow ye joining today."

Zayo saw the expectant faces among the crowd, and he knew he could not say no. "Why do you desire this?" he asked them. He saw their quizzical faces, and elaborated. "Tell ye people why thou dost desireth to be married. Show thy hearts to them. If thy sincerity shows through, so shall thy emotions, and thy hearts shalt converge."

Tahzo pensively thought for a few minutes before he began. "Ehloorha ist my best friend among all Acaballians."

She replied, "Tahzo assists me in every way as we worketh together every day."

"Her spirit shineth like ye crystals above, and her beauty is as deep as ye Sea."

"His strength carrieth me and supporteth me in all endeavors."

"Her nurturing ist fertile for ye young foals we educate in ye school."

"His compassion hast prepared his heart."

"Her heart beateth loudly when she seeth me."

"His loins pulseth with energy in want of ye family."

In front of a shocked crowd, he let his emotions go, and he reared up and whinnied at her. When he came down and kissed her, there was such a roar of approval.

But, the Acaballians were accustomed to quieter marriages, and had never seen a stallion rear up from desire of a mare. As soon as the crowd quieted down, someone said, "What ist thy purpose?"

"That ist how ye Caballians art married," the king replied. "Tis ye old fable which sayeth that ye charged stallion shalt consummate his marriage ye same day, but ye quiet stallion may requireth years for to learneth how to become photocytic." He was amazed at how they all seemed to agree with him. Zayo then got what he wanted: an emotional energizing of the crowd, as they totally supported what they saw in the young couple. No one else would go near the platform, however. "Tis time for me to begin my visits with thee. Ye council ist over."

"How shalt thy majesty meet with all Acaballians?" a voice called out.

"In thy homes or jobs, wherever thou art. Ye only place I cannot interfere ist thine private procreation." There were many laughs when Zayo said this, as it seemed a very humorous thing to speak of, immediately after such a marriage. They were all eager to meet him up close.

Afterwards, Tahrmaha said to Zayo, "What am I to do whilst thou dost travel among ye Acaballians?"

Zayo laughed at her noble attempt to use the Acaballian idiom, and said, "Thou art enjoying this much more than thou expected. Thy soul wouldst feel deprived if thou shouldst not meet yon Acaballians with me."

"I am not thy adjutant," she said.

"I know very little of what ye Acaballians art like, so since thou art ye only familiar face in all of Acaballia, I desireth thy company. Besides, thou mayest discover different medical technology in Acaballia which shalt help thy career in Caballia."

Tahrmaha suddenly laughed, as she realized that his use of Acaballian idiom was improving tremendously. "If Pleeyedraha and Tarahnaha were to hear you speak like that, they would wonder if you were Acaballian yourself! You do have a humorous streak!"

"Thou mayest call it humor," he replied, "but determining myself to speak like them as soon as possible is the surest way of learning what they are all about, and how their society works. To truly understand who and what they are, and their purposes for living, I must make myself an active part of them while I am here. Besides, it would help if you made yourself known here, so they learn that you are an intelligent vixen, and not just a beauty as my grandmother was; she was only a nurse. Do not argue with your instincts; I know that you really do like it here."

"What makes you think that?"

"You did not just leave yesterday."

"You threatened to excommunicate me!"

"You cornered me. I am not allowed to counter your moves? Besides, you seem to enjoy ruffling my thoughts."

"When I disagree with them!"

"Why must you be so difficult so as to argue with me just to get your point across? The first time I met you, you were quiet and thoughtful. Was the head injury so bad?"

She grew furious at him. "The difference between then and now is this: I am passing through the psychological adjustment every person goes through just before their passage. I do not mean to be cruel to you, or to argue just for the sake of arguing. I wish I could speak with others who have gone through this, like my parents."

"That is why I want you to go with me this week, rather than just sitting in someone's house. You will meet many understanding Acaballians, who will know what is causing your strife because they are so similar to us."

"Do you really think so?"

"I also know that if I do not see your face every day this week, I shall surely feel deprived. I have a difficult job ahead of me, which was only made somewhat easier by this council. Right now, you are the only friend I have here."

"What about Beltadro and Corbo?"

"Yes, they are acquaintances. But they do not know me like you do. I need someone to ensure that my decisions concerning the Acaballians are fair and just. Please, Tahrmaha."

"Do you know when to accept 'no' for an answer from someone?"

Zayo laughed. "What do you think?"

Soon after Zayo and Tahrmaha left the platform, they were approached by a stallion, who glanced at their bare hooves and said, "Thy majesty, shalt thou travel with no shoes upon thy hooves?"

"Whom art thou?" Zayo asked the bay stallion with the chestnut webbing and the black eyes.

"I am Teldro, most distinctive farrier in Acaballia." Zayo and Tahrmaha were a bit puzzled, as they had never heard of a farrier before. Teldro saw their puzzlement, so he added, "I craft ye shoes."

Zayo and Tahrmaha could not help but smile at him. "What ist thy distinction?"

For a brief moment, Teldro had a hurt expression in his eyes (for Acaballian shoemakers are very humble), but as he pondered it, he quickly overcame it. "My shoecraft ist ye best in Acaballia."

Zayo touched his shoulder and said, "Since we art in Acaballia, and I have always had nothing but ye best shoes my whole life, thou art required to crafteth ye shoes for us. Where ist ye forge?"

"Right here in Patoron. We canst walketh."

Once in the forge, Teldro lit the fire, and they set down to talk. Zayo said to him, "What dost thou do for ye founder?"

Teldro shook his head and said, "If thou shouldst founder, then thou art required to spend ye life lame."

"How many times hast thou seen founder?"

"Many times. Tis ye rocks."

"Then I requireth something of thee."

"What ist upon thy heart?"

"Thou shalt work with ye master shoemaker in Caballia, Jayexeeyo, who shalt teach thee how to cure founder. Thence, Jayexeeyo and thyself shalt teach all Acaballian shoemakers to cure founder."

"Tis too complicated."

"Tis easy if thou shouldst understand how to use thy hands only— no tools."

"Alloweth me to speaketh with ye master Jayexeeyo first."

"As thy heart desireth."

243

EQUESTRA

Zayo and Tahrmaha ate lunch with Teldro while they waited for the forgefire to become ready. After they ate, Teldro made them the most comfortable shoes, and made their hooves feel so good, they felt as if they were walking on air. As they were about to leave the forge, Corbo entered and said, "Thy majesty, thou shouldst requireth my services."

"Corbo," he said, "how shalt thou assist me?"

"How shalt thou travel around Acaballia on foot? It shalt take ye year. I offer my vehicle, yea, thou dost not know how to operate ye Acaballian vehicle."

Zayo smiled and said, "We wouldst be honored."

What Zayo thought would take one week ended up taking thirteen days, not counting the day of the council. They learned all about Acaballian mechanics, farriers, miners, storytellers, doctors, nurses, purifiers, food processors, fishers, and hundreds of other vocations. As Zayo met them, he found out each person's standing in their society, much as he did when he traveled with Mehlanahr among the Caballians, though this time he was with Tahrmaha and Corbo. The Acaballians were thrilled that Corbo was escorting the king all over Acaballia in his travels, for to them, it placed Corbo in higher esteem.

On the day after they finished, a council was again held by the Acaballians. But this time, there was no governor, and no chairs upon the stone platform. Tahrmaha stood off of the platform, but very close to it; Zayo was up on it by himself. He garnered their attention and said, "My beloved Acaballians, thou art ye great and worthy people, as worthy as thy brethren ye Caballians! I tell thee, ye only difference ist thy country, whether tis Caballia or Acaballia. But thou art just like yon Caballians, and have welcomed Tahrmaha and myself dearly! Whenceupon I have met with each and every Caballian here in Acaballia, I have delegated a vest for each of thee, each one of a different color. All colors I have delegated, including indigo for ye sentinels, but not including ye color purple, which ist only for Merahlaha and myself.

"Thou art as ready as thou shalt ever be to be reunited with thy brethren in Caballia for yon spiritual assimilation; all of thee and all of yon brethren in Caballia shalt be required to assimilate as much. Many things shalt take place at ye caucus in Caballia, including ye right to challenge for highest honor among each vest color. Yea, this means that all of thee who shalt be wearing ye orange vest and all of yon brethren who also wear ye orange vest shalt have to proveth whom ist ye most worthy and honorable citizen among yon vocation, for ye right to wear ye black vest.

"If thou wouldst be agreeable, I recommend that thou dost begin preparations for yon journey to Caballia. Thou shalt be required to bring food enough for three weeks and all of thyselves, including thy newest foals; if anyone is to be left behind, ye caucus cannot be held. If anyone herein agrees to attend ye caucus, yea does not attend, that person shalt be excommunicated for treason against ye crown. Thou shalt depart from Acaballia in three days, and shalt follow ye most direct route to Caballia, to ye palace on ye southern end of ye Sea of Serenity. Tahrmaha and myself shalt depart today; I wouldst desireth for ye master sentinel Corbo to escort Tahrmaha and myself back to Caballia in thy vehicle."

It took a short while, but soon, all of the Acaballians were in agreement with Zayo. When he saw this, Corbo went up to the platform, and knelt before Zayo with his head lowered. When all of the other Acaballians saw his actions, they fell silent. Zayo walked up to him, touched his right shoulder, and said, "Thou art Corbo, known to all Acaballia to be ye master sentinel. Pray do stand." Corbo stood up slowly, and looked up. "Thou art courageous. Thou shalt be ye first Acaballian seen by yon Caballians in Caballia. Thou art worthy, for thou knoweth best what thy brethren art afraid of, why thou fearest yon Caballians. Thou knowest that I am thy king, and thou trusts my words to thee. For this, I need thee to serve me now, and bring Tahrmaha and myself back to Caballia to prepare the way for thy brethren here, whom shalt follow us in three days. Thou canst decline."

"Yea," Corbo replied, Athy majesty, hearken. I cannot decline. Thou hast presented to me ye great privilege, and thou hast allowed me to atone for yon sentinel's error."

"Art thou prepared to depart?"

"Aye, my vehicle hast been supplied with one week's supply of food."

"Why only one week, when thy brethren art to bring three weeks?"

"We shalt not needeth more. If thy people accept me, then I must showeth them that I am willing to eat thy food, as thou hast eaten ye food of Acaballia."

Zayo thought about it, and could not argue Corbo's point. "Thou shalt have thy way in serving myself in yon best manner."

"I thank thee excessively, thy majesty."

"I thank thee, Corbo. Thou art ye great stallion of high honor."

Andrux always giggled. From the time he learned he could make sounds with his vocal cords, he discovered the magic of laughter. By the time he was two years old, he was making remarkable but feeble attempts at flight. His wings fluttered as much as his voice did. For all those who did not live in the palace, he was an absolute charm, always free and easygoing without a care in the world. Then again, what cares did he truly have? He did not really remember anything about Zayo, and could hardly understand why everyone was always so upset about Zayo not having returned yet; that was part of the reason why he was always giggling.

Even on his sixth birthday, he was giggling; it seemed as if he would never forget how to laugh, or the magic he felt when he laughed like a sheepish imp. He was told many stories about Zayo, but did not understand most of them; he thought they were just fables, although everyone kept telling him that Zayo would return one day.

Why was everyone so upset about this person called Zayo?

Andrux had the ideal playmate in Merahlaha, who lived in the same house, and was nine months younger. Merahlaha did not giggle like Andrux did, but was very quiet. Whereas Andrux liked to play with the candle flames, Merahlaha liked to sneak around, and made sudden loud noises so as to startle everyone. Even though she annoyed many people, she enjoyed the crashing sound made by pitchers and glasses breaking on the floor when they fell. She was a royal terror and a haunt, and no matter how hard everyone tried, they could not completely stop her from doing whatever activities she felt like doing. Tarahnaha was very strict with the young queen, but no matter how strict she got, Merahlaha kept on trying to undo what her mother was trying to teach her. Many times, Tarahnaha would become frustrated, and would start telling Merahlaha of the day that her brother would return home and set her straight, as he set all of their other people straight. But like Andrux, she felt that the stories of her brother were more of a threat because her father was dead, and no other stallion could fill Kayloor's shoes.

Out of all of the palace residents, there was one person who Merahlaha knew would not stand for her noise tricks, and that was Mehlanahr. Mehlanahr did not threaten her with any stories of Zayo. Rather, he told her that if she continued to irritate everyone in the palace, then she would never become a queen, but that she would end up as dead as her father was. Merahlaha never said anything to anyone else, but she wondered what it was like to have a father. Mehlanahr figured she felt this way, so besides telling her that, he told her that if she made any noises around him, he would spread word among all of their people about how disrespectful she was, and that she did not deserve to attend school with the other foals when she turned seven years old. She knew it was a privilege to attend school, a privilege only given to those who turned seven years old. Mehlanahr would tell her that, if she ever wanted to see her seventh birthday, then she had better stop making noises with objects, and start making more noise with her mouth. The adjutant got so frustrated with her one day that he told her that if she made any more noise around him, he would clip her tail with his sabre. He told her that it was legal for him to do such a thing to a disrespectful person, and she believed it; from that point, she never made any noises when Mehlanahr was home.

About two months after his sixth birthday, while the palace residents were eating breakfast, Andrux ran from the table and jumped into the air. For the first time in his life, he was able to keep himself airborne for more than a few seconds; the seconds ticked by, and grew into well over a minute before he was completely exhausted and fell to the floor. As soon as he hit the floor, he erupted in a glorious giggle, which told his parents he was unharmed.

From that moment on, Merahlaha did not deliberately crash any more objects. Instead, she was now more interested in watching Andrux fly, so she had no time to crash.

Six years is a long time, Mehlanahr thought as he examined the stationary fixation of Zayo's transport on the beacon scanner. Vehdoor said he would be gone for several years. Vehdoor also said Zayo would live through a remarkable adventure. What could possibly be happening to my king? he thought to himself.

Mehlanahr turned away from the scanner, and pondered his predicament. Zayo had left when Merahlaha was new. He knew nothing of his sister's first words, or of her crashes. Her crashes! Mehlanahr thought to himself, What would Zayo think of such a thing? Tarahnaha said that he was not so devastating when he was young. But for her to enjoy scaring people? I have never heard of a foal so inventive to get attention...then again, I never knew a bastard like Merahlaha is. One day she will go looking for her father. And I doubt if she will find him, unless she learns the effects of his reign, and postulates what he was like from there. And Zayo is still at the cave. When will he decide to come back?

"Karayo," Vehdoor said, "Zayo's adventure is over."

Karayo looked at Vehdoor's unfaltering eyes, and replied, "Tahrmaha has awoken from her coma?"

Vehdoor saw Karayo's desperate eyes, and said, "This is not humor, Karayo."

"Six years is a long time. You told our people he would be gone for several years. All of them are growing desperate, my friend. And Merahlaha believes that her brother is but a fable."

"What do you believe, Karayo?"

"I believe that it is easy to misjudge the effects of the cave, and that you had no accurate way of predicting just what effect the cave would have on Tahrmaha. How can you be so sure that she has awoken?"

"Because there is a serious rainstorm collecting over the forbidden valley."

"A rainstorm has nothing to do with the realms."

"How not, Karayo? There has only been light rain in the valley since the humans put Jayexeeyo and Shehronaha there. That side of the planet should not have rain like we do here, but monthly rainstorms. The imbalance prevented proper weather in the valley. Now that it has been corrected, Zayo and Tahrmaha are on their way back here."

Karayo went to his visiphone, and called Mehlanahr at the plant, asking the adjutant to call a caucus for the next day. When Karayo returned to Vehdoor, he said, "Mehlanahr has been scanning Zayo's beacon."

"That is good. How far away are they?"

"The beacon has not moved."

"Karayo, I tell you that they shall return to us tomorrow. I do not know how, but they shall return. I know it in my soul. Our people said that when he returned, we would celebrate as never before."

"I asked Mehlanahr to call preparations for the celebration."

"Then what is the problem?"

"How are they to get to the palace from the cave if not by transport? It would take them weeks to walk it."

"Perhaps they are walking."

After Mehlanahr forwarded Karayo's request for a caucus to all of the Caballians, all of the farmers immediately began to gather together food enough for three meals for all forty thousand Caballians, which was standard procedure for a caucus. The bakers set to cooking enough bread ahead of time so that they would have enough for the next day. Everyone else did what they could to prepare for the celebration. Tarahnaha, Pleeyedraha, Yahno, and Nehmayaha were the most ecstatic of all.

Andrux could only giggle at everything everyone was doing to prepare for the celebration, because it was festivity planning at its peak, and it excited him to no end. Merahlaha, however, felt as if her world were about to come to an end—that all of the fables and nightmares would now come true, and that her life was not so good as she had thought it to be. She was so disturbed that not even Andrux's attempt to fly in the palace could break her doldrums. She was right about one thing: the Caballian world as they knew it was about to come to an end, and her brother was the cause of it. That was tough for a young filly.

Most of the food Corbo had brought with him was pickled coral; that was all that Zayo and Tahrmaha ate when they stopped for meals.

Since they exited from the cavern at the southern end of the Unknown Sea, they proceeded to traverse the strait which connected the Unknown Sea with the Sea of Serenity. Once they were in the Sea of Serenity, they set a direct course for the palace grounds, which would take them over land for quite a distance. They traversed much of this on the same day as when Mehlanahr called the caucus; they would arrive at the palace on the day predicted by Vehdoor.

They were not far from the palace when they were forced to stop for the night, because it was much too dark and dangerous for the vehicle to travel over the land safely. There were perhaps thirty miles between Zayo and his home.

Throughout the whole night before Zayo was to return, Mehlanahr was absolutely restless, and could not sleep a wink. Right now, the only thing that would satisfy Mehlanahr's soul would be the safe return of Zayo and Tahrmaha.

Mehlanahr thought of how long they had been gone, and knew that Tahrmaha should be at or near thirty-five years old; when was her passage to be? Pleeyedraha had told him once, but it had slipped his mind, pushed out by other details of his job which seemed much more important. Zayo must have grown quite a bit. Mehlanahr wondered what they looked like, and what, if any, physical changes had been wrought by the cave.

At the first symptoms of dawn, as many of the Caballians were already on the palace grounds for the caucus but were sleeping, Mehlanahr brought Zayo's crown (which Jayexeeyo had enlarged for his adult head) and sabre, as well as a new lavender vest, out to the platform and laid them in the center, where Zayo liked to stand. As he stood there and eyed the platform, Mehlanahr felt a tremendous gap in his life. The Caballians were accustomed to having a king, and for millions of years, had not lived without a king. But for them to live the past six years without Zayo and only an incompetent Merahlaha was a tremendous load for Mehlanahr to carry on his soul, being Zayo's adjutant. Mehlanahr was glad of one thing: the humans were gone from Equestra, leaving behind their junked ship and tents. At least they had not returned while Zayo was gone. At least no punishments had to be performed while Zayo was gone; Mehlanahr's sabre was still unused.

Vehdoor had called for a celebration like no other, to even surpass Mehlanahr's passage. Mehlanahr could feel that something big and important, something of the utmost historical importance, was going to happen when Zayo returned. What was it? Did it have anything to do with Tahrmaha? Was it something Zayo had engineered on his own? What could it possibly be?

Mehlanahr suddenly felt an insatiable curiosity, and knew that he had to be ready to act at the first sign of Zayo's return. He ran back into the palace and into his bedroom, where he braided his hair, and donned his collar and sabre. Now he felt more ready as Zayo's adjutant.

Yehtraha caught a sight of him rushing through his preparations, and laughed at him.

CRASH

Mehlanahr saw Merahlaha standing on the platform near her brother's crown. She had her hair braided with purple ribbons. She was a pretty young filly; her face was similar to her mother's face, her fur was chestnut like Kayloor had been, and her hair was a beautiful light brown. Her deep black eyes were the same eyes that Zayo had—deep, pensive, and rather brooding. She saw the adjutant as he walked up to her on the platform and she said, "Mehl, the caucus." She seemed a bit agitated, and almost excited, but it was hard to tell just exactly how she felt.

"Merahlaha, what is my name?"

"Mehl-ahnahr," she said deliberately, and shook her head. "Mehl, why do you always tell me that?"

"Because you are too lazy to say my full name, so you think you can decide to chop off most of it and just call me Mehl. You might think it is cute, but it is disrespectful, and I should chop off your tail as much as you chop off my name." His glaring eyes pierced into hers as he put his hand on the handle of his sabre, and he scared her good.

Her eyes suddenly became tearful, and she said, "I am sorry, Mehlanahr," saying his name slowly and deliberately.

He let go of the sabre handle and said slowly, "I do not care who you are—Kayloor's heir or not. If you want our people to treat you right, then you must learn to treat them good. How they feel about you is as important as how Tarahnaha feels about you; it makes all the difference as to what a good queen you will be when you are old enough." He saw the fear in her eyes sink in. "We must begin this caucus for Zayo. Your brother must be welcomed back with great celebration, like no passage you have ever seen. You were new when your brother left, and do not remember anything about him, but he is a better king than your father was."

She was shocked; he had never said so much to her about her brother during all of her young life. "Mehlanahr," she said, but she just stood there and looked at him.

"Yes, Merahlaha?"

"How come you never talk about Zayo?"

"You must find out for yourself what your brother is like. What I know about him and of his ways will not mean very much, but will seem like a lot of nonsense. I do not want to confuse you. He is good, and our people love him very much. I am sure that you will also love him, as much as you love your mother."

"How come you never speak about him, but Mother always does?"

"No matter how much I tell you, what I tell you will be a mere shadow of what he really is. I do not want to give you the wrong ideas, or try to tell you everything when it is impossible. Besides, some things are more important to you right now."

"Like what?"

"Like knowing why it is improper for you to call me Mehl. No one else has ever called me that—not even Yehtraha."

Zayo, Corbo, and Tahrmaha were up at the first hint of light. As soon as he had eaten breakfast, Zayo said to Tahrmaha, "My soul doth feeleth naked without ribbons and ye vest."

"Whyfore wouldst thou desireth ribbons?" she queried.

"Vehdoor, Karayo, and Mehlanahr art intelligent stallions. Tis likely we art to walk into yon caucus."

"Whyfore wouldst yon Caballians call ye caucus?"

"Ye caucus wast required for me to bring thee to yon cave. Since Vehdoor wouldst knoweth whence we shalt arriveth, he hast made his supplication to Mehlanahr for to call ye caucus. Yon Caballians shalt celebrate our return with much festivity, moreso than Mehlanahr's passage."

Corbo was amazed. "Dost thou truly believeth ye celebration shalt be grand?" he asked Zayo.

"I knoweth my people yon Caballians as much as I knoweth thee and yon Caballians in Acaballia; perchance better, because my life wast spent with them."

"How shalt thy people receive my presence?"

"Ye people shalt be festive, and shalt inquire as to ye adventure which befell us in Acaballia."

"How doth yon Caballians knowest thou wert in Acaballia?"

"My soul dost not believeth that they can see past ye ancient magic of yon cave; they can only guess. Yea, from ye outside observances of ye forbidden valley and yon cave, they shalt attempt to guess until they art told all."

"How shalt thou explaineth my appearance? My appearance ist different from thee."

"Thou art ye Caballian. Thy appearance shalt be explained whence I tell of Acaballia's history in my directives to them."

"Thy 'directives'?" Corbo repeated.

"Aye, my directives. Yon Caballians in Caballia cannot argue with thy presence, or ye fact that thou art my subject as much as they art. Tis not for them to disprove thee."

"How canst thou say such a thing without advice from ye Caballians?"

"Anyone who showeth disrespect to thee shalt have their tail clipped; anyone who showeth disrespect to what decisions I have made concerning yon Caballians in Acaballia shalt be excommunicated for ye high treason. Tis not for them to question how I treat others; rather, they should only be of ye mind that I am treating them properly as ye king."

"Wouldst lack of information lead to yon wars?"

"Caballia shalt learneth all they desireth upon ye caucus whence all Caballians from Acaballia meet with them, three days hence."

Corbo walked into his vehicle, and Zayo and Tahrmaha quickly followed.

Mehlanahr was easily able to obtain the attention of all of the Caballians. He then said to them, "I have called this caucus at the request of Vehdoor, who has said that Zayo shall return to us today. All of us have agreed that we would celebrate very splendidly when Zayo returns to us. But what exactly are we celebrating? Zayo's return to us? Tahrmaha's awakening from the coma? Or is there something we do not know about their trip to the cave of the magical mists? Vehdoor, please tell us what we do not know."

Vehdoor went up onto the platform, and stood on the left side of Zayo's crown, sabre, and vest; Mehlanahr and Merahlaha were on the right side of them. "Zayo is returning today, indeed! And Tahrmaha is awake from her coma!" Vehdoor was obvious excited, but everyone else was having difficulty catching on. "Anyone would consider it an adventure just to have to use the ancient magic of the cave of the magical mists. But after Zayo brought Tahrmaha into the cave for healing, they befell an adventure, whenceupon all shamans lost sight of them. They entered the cave through the only known opening. But they have exited a different way, having traveled all the way through the cave. Zayo's transport still sits at the mouth of the cave. What happened to them as they passed through the other side of the cave and exited from wherever they exited from is a great but yet unknown adventure, one which they will proudly tell us of as soon as they arrive. And they will incorporate their discovery into our lives."

"When shall they arrive?" someone called out.

"This morning."

"How shall they get here if their transport is at the cave?" someone else asked.

Vehdoor had to stop and think for a moment. "I truly do not know," he replied. "The ancient magic is very unpredictable, and it is impossible to tell even how they were able to leave the cave. Perhaps they may even be walking here from where they awoke."

There were a number of grumbles. If Zayo had brought Tahrmaha into the only known entrance, they would have left the same way; it was common sense. Vehdoor was somewhat unsure of himself, and rather untested as a shaman, which explained their uneasiness. The grumbling grew so loud, echoing irritation, that before long, not even Mehlanahr and Merahlaha were able to subdue them.

A half hour passed before Mehlanahr gave up trying to get their attention. The festive mood was now gone, and it seemed as if nothing could bring it back. Merahlaha was annoyed that their people would not listen to them, and thought that Mehlanahr was right when he told her she had to treat their people respectfully so as to be treated just as good herself. She felt very small, and could not look at any of them; neither could she look at her mother.

Ignoring the noise of the crowd, she looked out upon the horizon, her head full of wishful thinking. Wishing that she could learn how to be a queen and lead such a caucus in a respectable manner; wishing that she could meet the brother she never knew; wishing that she could meet the father she never knew. Wishing so many things, and feeling so lonely that she felt miles between her mother and herself. As she gazed out past where the Caballians were collected, she saw something moving on the horizon of land. Not knowing how to get the attention of the Caballians, she ran to

Andrux and said to him, "Andrux, I need to talk to them; he is coming. I need you to fly so they will stop arguing. Otherwise, they will fight. I must stop the fight; I am a queen."

He giggled at her request and said, "Is this your idea of crashing the caucus so that everyone knows you are here?"

She giggled back and said, "Yes. I need you to help me crash."

He jumped up from where he was setting and said, "I always wanted to help you crash. Now I will not get in trouble like you!" He quickly took to the air, and flew out over the Caballians. He flew past them, in the direction in which he saw Zayo's vehicle moving from. The arguing of the Caballians was quickly lost as they all began to wonder where he was going.

Was it truly Zayo?

"Sire," Corbo said to Zayo, "something ist in ye sky."

Zayo, who had as good a view of where they were going as Corbo did, watched it intently as it drew closer towards them. "Corbo," he said as they drew closer to the object in the sky, "stop thy vehicle."

He stopped, and Zayo jumped out of the vehicle just as Andrux fell from the sky to the ground, exhausted from the longest flight he had ever made in his life. Zayo ran to him, and quickly saw that it was the young pegasus. Andrux saw Zayo as the king ran to him; Zayo stopped and knelt beside him, saying, "Why hast thou come here? What of thy caucus?"

Andrux, for the first time in his life, did not giggle, but whispered to Zayo, "Help."

Zayo picked up the colt in his arms, and brought him to Tahrmaha. He laid the pegasus on the bed of the vehicle and said, "Tahrmaha, he requireth assistance."

Andrux whispered to Tahrmaha, "No," but she proceeded to quickly examine him.

Moments later, she said to Zayo, "Ye pegasus ist exhausted." She said to the colt, "Save thy breath, Andrux." She turned back to Zayo and said, "My soul dost believeth he requireth thy help, thy majesty."

Andrux coughed and whispered, "Merahlaha."

Zayo knelt beside Andrux again and said, "Didst my sister send thee here to me?"

"Crash...caucus...fight." Andrux nearly choked on his words.

"What crash? What fight?"

He coughed again, and sufficiently gathered his breath to speak better. "They are all...arguing...fighting...do not believe...that you...are coming. Merahlaha...told me...to crash...the caucus."

"'Crash the caucus'?" Zayo repeated. "What dost thou mean by ye word 'crash'?"

"You do not...understand...but you...talk strange. Mehlanahr...needs you now." He gave up talking for the moment.

Zayo looked out towards the palace, and saw that it was not far to where the Caballians were gathered, so he picked up Andrux in his arms, and began to walk to the caucus, carrying the young colt in his arms. Andrux was satisfied, knowing that he had done a remarkable thing in crashing the caucus. For the first time in his life, he fully flew his physical limitations. He had been airborne for five minutes, and had traversed two miles. It was no wonder he was exhausted. But he had found Zayo, and he was proud.

Andrux looked up at Zayo, and said to him, "You are Merahlaha's brother."

"I am thy king. Why didst thou risk thy life?"

"I knew I could reach you. I flew before, but not so far. I did not know you were so far. But I had to."

"Thou art brave, son of Toorahgo."

"You know my father?"

"I know thy parents and sister well."

"Why do you talk so strangely?"

"'Tis a long story, my friend. Ye story must be told to all of our people, so it shall wait until we art upon my platform."

When they saw where Andrux was heading, they all kept their eyes upon him. They were not able to make out any other people until Zayo started to walk back with Andrux. Merahlaha proceeded to clear a path between where her brother was walking towards the crowd and the platform so that he could reach it unhindered. As Zayo drew close to his people, and they were able to recognize him, they all began to cheer loudly for him, glad of his return. Tarahnaha joined her daughter and Mehlanahr on the platform (which Vehdoor had left). Yahno and Nehmayaha pressed to reach the edge of the platform so that they would be able to welcome Tahrmaha back.

Corbo pulled up alongside Zayo as they reached the crowd of Caballians. Some people reached out their hands in an attempt to touch Zayo, but as soon as they saw Corbo, they pulled their hands back. Some of them actually thought his webbing was repulsive, though Zayo and Tahrmaha felt completely different about it. When Zayo saw their hands pull away from Corbo before they could touch their king, he quickly whinnied, "What ist thy problem? Art thou afraid of thy brother?!"

His voice rang out among the people, much deeper and more mature than it had been, about as mature as it would get. The mere sound of his voice silenced their cheering. He heard the silence fall over them, and he stopped in his tracks. Corbo then said to Zayo, "Sire, tis not fair to thee. Perhaps thy judgment of thy people wast wrong."

"Where ist my sabre?!" Zayo called out. Mehlanahr picked up the crown, sabre, and the vest from the platform, and took off running in a full gallop to his king. Zayo handed Andrux to Corbo, turned around, and singled out every person who had pulled their hands away from Corbo. There were eleven of them, and Zayo did not miss a single one as he proceeded to name them all. "Ahfehtoor, Aryoolaha, Railoor, Ghaxooraha, Khihdulaha, Feranto, Yoor, Volnoor, Pirahaha, Behnoor, and Ehxtahro. Thou art disrespectful to thy brother Corbo. Thou shalt have thy tails clipped."

"Who is he?" someone asked Zayo.

"Whenceupon I mayest get to my platform, I shalt be able to telleth thee all. Thou art presumptuous. Thou hast forced me to punish thee before I mayest set my eyes upon my mother and sister. What dost thou knoweth about Corbo?" There was absolute silence among them. Some of them began to examine Corbo's obvious differences, while many others could not keep their eyes off of beautiful Tahrmaha, who was undoubtedly far more beautiful than Ahmehlaha had been.

Zayo looked up, and saw Mehlanahr standing there with the crown, sabre, and vest in his hands. "Your majesty," he said, "six years is quite a spell to be gone from us." He handed the lavender vest to Zayo, who slipped it on.

"Six years?" Zayo repeated. "It seemeth as though twas less than a fortnight."

As Mehlanahr placed the crown upon Zayo's head, it was obvious that Zayo was far more muscularly superior to Mehlanahr, and he was not yet thirty-five years old. "You have been gone for six years, and you have developed a strange way of speaking, stranger language than the humans used."

"My story shalt be told to all of thee, whenceupon I have clipped these eleven tails." Zayo righted his crown, took his sabre from Mehlanahr, and felt the hilt with his left hand. Now he felt more like a complete king.

"Ye criminals shalt precede me to my platform," Zayo told them, and pointed his sabre up the clear path. "Mehlanahr, thou shalt walk with Corbo and myself."

Mehlanahr saw Corbo, and managed a smile, although he wondered where the stranger came from. Zayo truly did have an adventure to describe, one which most certainly involved Corbo.

As the criminals walked on ahead of them, Corbo eyed all of their vests, the likes of which he had never seen before, but had only heard about. He gazed upon Mehlanahr's black vest, the likes of which he would be given as the master sentinel. Corbo saw that the blue trim on Mehlanahr's vest matched the color of some of the vests which people wore, so he knew that his black vest would have indigo trim the same color as the pegasus' wings. And Andrux had beautiful wings.

Corbo liked what he saw of the Caballians, despite the fact that eleven of them had shown him such disrespect. It made him feel good to know that Zayo was going to clip their tails; Corbo felt more like one of them with each passing moment. He knew that the Acaballians belonged to this world which Zayo was king of.

As the eleven criminals were shepherded onto the platform, Tahrmaha saw her parents, and ran into their arms. "Mother, Father!" she exclaimed. "How I have missed thee!"

Yahno and Nehmayaha were amazed at the elegant beauty of their daughter; never in their lives did they think that she would end up more beautiful than Ahmehlaha. They could not hold back their tears at seeing her awake from the coma which had struck her while she was on Earth. She hugged each of them dearly and said, "Tis no need to weep."

Yahno scrutinized his daughter and remarked, "Every bit of you seems to be recovered from the coma except for your speech. It is such a shame."

She suddenly realized that she had been using Acaballian idiom with them, so she forced herself to think back. "Forgive me," she said after some thought, Abut the coma did not induce my speech to change idiom."

"Then what was it?" Nehmayaha asked.

"When I awoke two weeks ago, enraged at what had happened to me on Earth, I was in such a marvelous place, yet I wanted to leave it immediately and make sure I was back here in time for my passage. But Zayo begged me to stay, and we ended up discovering such wonders as you would never dream of in your wildest dreams! The Caballians we met talked rather different, so to better learn their philosophy, we forced ourselves to master their idiom. It took us the better part of a week, but I would not trade my experience for the world! Corbo is like that—he speaks in the other idiom."

"Corbo?" her mother asked.

"The sentinel who escorted Zayo and myself back here so that I would hopefully be in time for my passage. He is a dear soul, as dear as Mehlanahr and Pleeyedraha are, and as wise." She stopped for a moment, then had a very serious expression on her face. "Tell me, did I miss my passage?"

"Your passage is not for another month," Yahno stated.

"Is Pleeyedraha still alive?"

"Yes," he replied, "but she is growing weaker. I do not believe she will live another year."

"Where is my mentor?"

Her mother indicated which direction Pleeyedraha was in, so Tahrmaha then said to them, "I must take my leave of you for now and see Pleeyedraha."

As Zayo walked up onto the platform behind the criminals, he saw Merahlaha, but said nothing to her; he would not speak to her until after he had punished the criminals. He eyed the criminals, seven stallions and four mares, and stared at their crooked line for a long moment before he turned to the crowd and raised his hands to obtain their absolute attention. "'Tis time for me to rejoin thee, but how dost thou greet me? Yea, I have returned with Tahrmaha, and my friend Corbo, who hast proven that he ist as ready to risk his life for my reign. And how dost thou greet my friend, whom ist Caballian? Thy hands reach out to touch me, but whenst thou seeth Corbo, thy hands art pulled back in fear of someone whom thou knoweth nothing about! Thou knoweth what ye law for disrespect commands as punishment; thou hast agreed to abideth by ye law, yea thou hast broken it today." All of the criminals looked at him in fear, knowing that there was no way to stop Zayo from exercising his right to punish them. "Ye criminals shalt turn so that thy tails art facing yon Caballians." They all turned around slowly, and their tails were lined up. Zayo quickly walked through the line, and made quick work of excising their tails. He cut all of them off at the high point of the tail, so that when he was finished, all that was left was the living stump which angled up from their bodies; the hair of the tails had hung down from this stump. The hairs of their tails were all flung to the floor in front of the platform.

Shamed as they were with their tails clipped, they all ran off of the platform to the back of the crowd, where no one would ogle at their punished tails.

Zayo saw his sister upon his platform, and walked up to her and said, "Whom art thou?"

She eyed him carefully, trying to figure out what he meant by his strange words; after a long moment, she said, "I am sorry, but I do not understand you. Can you speak more clearly?"

He suddenly realized he had been speaking in Acaballian idiom. He said to her, "In the midst of a caucus called to celebrate my return, you, a filly I do not know, are standing on my platform when I was required to clip a number of citizens for disrespect. Do you wish to have your tail clipped also?"

"I am Merahlaha," she replied, trying to provide an excuse for her being on the platform.

"I am Zayo," he returned, "and I was crowned the king of the Caballians the day after my father was killed. This platform was built by our people for my use."

"I am Merahlaha. Your sister."

"You are an uneducated filly. Who are you the daughter of?"

She was growing upset at his seemingly ridiculous questions. Who did he think he was? she thought to herself. "I am Merahlaha, of Kayloor and Tarahnaha. I am Kayloor's heir and your queen."

"I am Kayloor's heir and your king. I was crowned, you have not yet been crowned. Since you have not yet been given a crown, why are you on my platform?"

"Zayo," Tarahnaha shirked, "she is only six years old!"

"She is a queen," he replied, "and she must learn not to abuse her place among our people." He turned back to his sister and said to her, "Why are you on my platform?"

Merahlaha became frightened, and the tears began to fall down her face. "I do not know," she sobbed.

He knelt before her, and took her small hands in his large hands. "Then you truly do not know. If you do not know something, never be afraid of admitting that you do not know. It takes more courage to learn this than anything else you will ever learn, but it will mean more to you if you are to fulfill your destiny as our queen. Even just before he was murdered, when I was already twenty-four years old, Father would never allow me on his platform without his express consent. Until you are properly crowned, you will only be up here with my permission. That is the only way you shall learn what a privilege it is to be up here in front of our people." He took off his crown, and placed it in her hands. "When our people gave this crown to me, they gave me the privilege to control the use of this platform."

She felt the crown carefully and examined it, saying, "Why the crown?"

"If you are to be a queen, you must learn that it is a great honor to be in such a position among our people. The only way you will learn that is to live as one of them until you are crowned. You are queen in title for only now, but your duties shall be that of a crown princess. When the time comes for you to be crowned, then it shall be your privilege to share the platform with me."

She carefully placed the crown back on his head. She pushed his hair aside, and saw his blaze. Merahlaha choked back her tears and said, "Then I should not be here," and she tried to leave him.

Instead of allowing her to leave, Zayo picked her up in his arms and said, "Since I have just returned from a long trip, and I have a wonderful story to tell, I want you here with me."

She wiped her eyes and asked him, "Why?"

"Among all of our people, it is most important for you to learn why I was gone for so long, and why I only just returned today. Besides, I need an explanation from you."

She sighed and said, "What explanation?"

"What did you mean by telling Andrux to crash the caucus?"

"Mother tells me I always crash things."

"Why do you crash things?"

"I like to make noise."

"What sort of noise?"

"The noise of breaking crystal, or of banging doors and plates, or of clomping on furniture, things like that. I like noises. But I have not made any noise in months, until today."

"Why did you not make any noise for months?"

"Because I was more interested in seeing Andrux fly. He learned to fly, and I forgot about crashing for a while."

"Then what happened today?"

"Everyone started making a terrible noise. They did not believe that you were coming back today. Me and Mehlanahr could not stop them from making the terrible noise, so I asked Andrux to crash the caucus."

"How did you intend for him to crash the caucus?"

"I saw you, but no one else did, so I wanted him to fly to stop the terrible noise they were making. But he did not stop flying."

"No. He flew to me and told me you needed help. He was so tired I had to carry him back here. But that was a good crash, and you may have prevented a war. It is sad that our people must fight over whether or not I am coming back. What did Vehdoor tell everyone?"

"He said you were coming back, and that we had to greet you with a great celebration. But no one believed him because your transport is still at the cave."

Zayo realized what had happened. It was logical for them to assume that he would return with his transport because they only knew of the land entrance to the cave, but not the entrance from the cavern. He had left them for six years soon after his father's murder, leaving behind only an infant sister to lead them. They thought he was being selfish about bringing Tahrmaha to the cave of the magical mists, but naught they knew of what he needed to discover there in the cavern! It seemed more as if they were becoming selfishly possessive of his family. It was even more imperative that he fully describe his adventure to them. "What did you think?" he asked her.

"I thought—I thought that Mother always told fables about you, and that they were not true. I did not know I had a real brother."

"Why would you think such a thing? Mother has never lied to me."

"But I do not have a father, only a father's name. Who was Kayloor?"

"Kayloor was the king before us," he replied. "He was the best father on all of Equestra, and taught me so much. Since he is already dead, you must learn about him from the older citizens, who knew Father well in their memories."

"Why were you talking funny before?"

"You will stay with me as I tell my story, and you will learn how I learned a different idiom from some different Caballians who are as wonderful as all of these Caballians are. Corbo is one of the different people, and he came back with me to see everyone." Her world is about to get a whole lot bigger, he thought to himself.

Zayo walked over to his mother, and hugged her, saying, "Mother, how I have missed thee!"

"It has been a long six years," she replied, returning his embrace, "but I am so glad that you are alive, and so handsome! And Tahrmaha is so beautiful! I never thought the cave would have been so good to the two of you!"

Merahlaha squirmed, caught in the middle of their embrace, so Zayo set her down. "I wish that you could have seen everything I have lived through during the past two weeks! Never in my life did I dream that I would live as part of such an amazing epoch of our history!"

"Does this have to do with your new friend?"

"Indeed, Corbo has very much to do with it. I must tell our story to everyone at once, otherwise I will repeat it thousands of times." He walked back to the center of the platform with Merahlaha on his heels, but before he could say a word, Karayo came running up onto the platform, stopped ten feet away from Zayo and knelt with his head bowed. Zayo walked up to him, touched his right shoulder with his left hand, and said, "Master historian, what dost thou requireth of me?"

Karayo stood up and replied, "Your majesty, a superior shaman has proven his worth to our people, and he needs to be acknowledged as the master historian."

"Indeed, tis marvelous!" Zayo exclaimed. "Whom ist yon shaman?"

"Vehdoor."

Zayo looked out over the crowd and called out, "Vehdoor, cometh to my platform!"

Vehdoor was up there within moments. He knelt next to Karayo, and bowed his head. Zayo touched his shoulder, at which Vehdoor stood up. "Historian," Zayo said, "pray do tell my ears what occurred this morn."

"I requested that a caucus be called for you because I knew that you would return to us today. I explained as much as I possibly could to our people earlier, but they refused to believe me. It broke my heart to hear them grumble about you and your return the way they did."

"How didst thou knoweth I wouldst return?"

"Every inch of my soul felt it, especially when I saw the change in weather at the forbidden valley."

"Thou wert at yon forbidden valley?"

"No, but I like to observe changing weather patterns on Equestra. It helps me to compile facts for my job."

"What ist thy job?"

"I am a shaman."

"Karayo hast said that thou art prepared to become ye master historian. Ist that ye truth?"

EQUESTRA

"It is quite likely. Not even Karayo knew that you had left the cave of the magical mists. I was the only person who was convinced that you were indeed returning this morning."

"Karayo, this ist ye truth?"

"Indeed, your majesty," he replied, and he removed the black vest.

"Tis thy request that Vehdoor hast sufficiently challenged thee on ye merit and honor?"

"Yes, your majesty."

"Then, Vehdoor, tis thy honored right to be called ye Master Historian."

SEASPY ADJUTANT

Zayo walked back to the center of the platform, determined to tell his story. First, he called out to his people, "Before I begin my story, is there any other urgent business which must be tended to?" He heard many of them say no. "After my last caucus, I brought Tahrmaha to the cave of the magical mists. I fell asleep near her. When I awoke, Tahrmaha was still sleeping, but we were no longer in the cave. We were in a room which was quite unlike any other room I have ever been in."

"Where was the room?" Merahlaha asked.

"That is the amazing part of my story," he told her. "Millions of years ago, when our ancestors still fought wars, there were thirty-two sects among our people. One of these sects was the sect of Acaballia. Acaballia hated the wars with undying passion, so instead of staying to fight it, they fled to another part of Equestra."

"Where did they go?"

"Under the Unknown Sea is a large cavern, a cavern which is almost as large as the Unknown Sea itself. Acaballia fled into this cavern. It is so difficult to find the entrance that no other Caballian knew if any members of their sect still lived. Acaballians protected themselves from being found out by the other Caballians by sending their governor and his wife to the rest of the world. This governor told everyone that all of Acaballia was dead, thereby protecting Acaballia from all other attacks."

"Who was the governor?"

"I do not know his name. However, the governor had a son named Pehsoorad who eventually became the first moderator for our people; he was our ancestor, Merahlaha. We are related to the Acaballians.

"The Acaballians set up their own civilization inside of the great cavern. Tahrmaha and I awoke inside a room in one of their houses. Corbo is from Acaballia. For those of you who have seen my friend Corbo, it is obvious that there has been some slightly different evolution in them as there was in us. Where their hair was they now grow webbing; they also have webbing between their fingers, and gills in their necks which allow them to breathe water for several hours at a time. The way I was speaking before is how all Acaballian residents speak. It is a beautiful idiom, and is enriched by many of their own fables of our origins, and of the original residents of Equestra. They have a talented number of storytellers who have the privilege to fable; they are historians and shamans, and their knowledge is vast."

"Are their fables as interesting as Mother's fables about you?"

"Acaballian fables are so fantastic that they make my life seem like a pale shadow. Not long after the ancient wars were over, our people had a moderator named Hehlehf. Hehlehf was a very intelligent stallion, and of his own accord, discovered the existence of the civilization dwelling in the Acaballian cavern. However, it was forbidden for any Acaballian to make their presence known to any of us. When Hehlehf discovered their civilization and the sentinels who are much like guards, he attempted to flee through the cave of the magical mists. One of the sentinels followed him, not knowing that he was the moderator of the Caballians, whose duty it was to prevent the wars because he was not marked with the blaze as you and I are. The sentinel is the person who murdered Hehlehf, but not before Hehlehf's wife became pregnant. Hehlehf had been touched by the magic of the cave, so his heir was also touched, and was born with the blaze.

"I do not know how they ever found out, but the other sentinels learned that one of them had murdered the descendent of the governor who had preserved the existence of Acaballia. Acaballia still has one hundred sentinels, of which Corbo is the master."

"You woke up in Corbo's house?" Merahlaha asked him.

"No. Tahrmaha and I awoke in Beltadro's house; Beltadro is a farmer. His crops are nothing you would ever recognize; the greatest one is his coral, which is as much of a staple to the Acaballians as oatmeal is to us. But they eat their coral pickled, and it is the most delicious food I have ever tasted in my life.

"Beltadro's crops grow under some water at the edge of the cavern. In a pocket of air in a small cave near his crops, Tahrmaha and I were asleep under the spell of the cave of the magical mists, for it was the same cave; it has a second entrance near the cavern. He brought us back with him to meet his people because he saw my blaze."

"How would they know what the blaze is for?" she asked.

"The same way they found out that Hehlehf was the governor's descendent. Acaballia had a governor who presided over such caucuses once each month. The token of his office is a necklace of an emblem which is the same size and shape as my blaze. The monthly caucus, or council as they call it, was to meet the day after Beltadro found Tahrmaha and myself. Beltadro prudently would not answer any of my questions concerning Acaballian politics, telling me that if I wanted answers to my questions, Tahrmaha and I should attend the council meeting the next morning."

"So you went to their council?"

"Yes. Tahrmaha and I went to their council meeting. As soon as we had eaten our breakfast, we were surrounded by sentinels; it was obvious to all that we were outsiders because we had hair but no gills. They were about to excommunicate us, but I pleaded for right of honor before we were to depart."

"What is right of honor?"

"It means that if you commit a crime, you deserve to find out why, and to offer an explanation if you feel that it does not merit punishment. Tahrmaha and I were not there because we wanted to be there, but because Beltadro had brought us there. The sentinels brought us to their governor, whose name was Khasadro. I started to talk with him, but when he saw my blaze, he was amazed. They could pass the emblem from one person to another, but I was born with the mark of leadership on my forehead. Because of this, our lives were spared.

"As I proceeded to learn some of their fables concerning myself, I learned how it is illegal for any sentinel to touch me because of what one sentinel had done in murdering Hehlehf. They have fables concerning the pegasus, and the ancient people who lived on Equestra before the Caballians did. Khasadro, however, was a poor governor. He set up on his stone platform and would make decisions for all of his people without inquiring for their ideas and input. I questioned him about this so much that he ended up resigning his governorship!"

Merahlaha pondered this and said, "Mother was right—you are a tyrant!"

"I only want what is best for our people, Merahlaha. The Acaballians were so much like ourselves, that I knew my soul would not rest if all of our people were not rejoined and our different societies integrated. Therefore, I told them that if they truly believed I was as much of a king as they made me out to be, and that they accepted me to be their king as well, then they had best overcome their fears of us and meet with us in joint council. Imagine a caucus more than twice as big as this one is!"

"How many of them are there?" someone called out.

"More than fifty thousand. Tahrmaha and I spent thirteen days meeting with each and every one of them, as I did with you when I was crowned; since we did not know how to operate their vehicles, Corbo escorted us during those thirteen days, as well as escorting us home. And now, they are as dear to me as all of you are. Besides, this cold war of fear must come to an end. Because of this, I make this decree: that you will accept all Caballians who reside in Acaballia as your brethren as much as they are willing to accept you and our laws. They have made the first steps. They have accepted all of our laws, which included all of their sentinels laying down their weapons forever. They are willing to reach out and socialize with us. My heart wants to see this happen. Corbo came with me today to let you know that their expression of reunification was genuine, and that they are willing to forget the erring ways of our past so that they can work with me and all of you, because they are just as ready to accept me as their king."

"When do you intend for this to take place?" someone else called out.

"When do you want it to happen? Do you want the war to continue on and on while we stand here and deliberate our differences like incompetent political fools, or are you willing to accept my judgment in this matter?"

"What do you recommend?" someone asked.

"I recommend that the Acaballian residents are just as honorable as all of you are, and that they are prepared to meet with you to discuss this openly in a caucus. You would be fools to postpone the joint caucus, for it would only mean that you are afraid of your brothers. I have risked my life to get this to happen, even knowing that Tahrmaha might miss her passage, but it is that much more important to me and to all of you."

"When do they want to meet with us?" someone else asked.

"All of them wanted to come with me today, but I would not allow it—not before I had a chance to explain what is happening to all of you. Therefore, I told them, I needed to meet with you in a caucus before; I asked them to arrive here three days after I did. They are to arrive here in their vehicles in three days, all of them with three weeks' worth of provisions, most of it to be pickled coral, which I want all of you to taste— it is a delicacy you should not miss for your lives! When they arrive here for the caucus, they will be prepared to tell you all of their fables, so that you might learn how rich their lives are, just as rich as ours. We have so much to offer each other, and we should not miss out on such an opportunity in our history."

"If all of this works as well as you believe it shall," someone said, "then the sentinels would effectively be useless."

"I have spoken with them about this already. The sentinels would be more important to us than ever before. They know and accept that our laws forbid them from punishing anyone. They have agreed to protect all of Equestra from aliens who may land here. It was not difficult for the guards to disarm, but it was a bold gesture on Corbo's part. It is very difficult to stop a sentinel from being a sentinel, but there are some measures which can be taken to ensure peace. Since they have a specialized duty which can fit under no other vocation, I hereby decree that all of the sentinels shall be given vests of citizenship of a new color—the color shall be moonsflower indigo. Additionally, all of you who are guards shall exchange your orange vests for indigo vests in three days. Then, you shall no longer be called guards, but sentinels. Corbo has proven himself worthy enough to be the master sentinel. It is your privilege to challenge him for the black vest, which he shall be given."

There was a long silence before the Caballians began to cheer in approval of Zayo's recommendation. When it quieted down, someone else said to Zayo, "Since we are to give vests to all of the sentinels, we should also give vests to all Caballians from Acaballia who are citizens and interns."

Some cheering began, but Zayo silenced them and said, "If we are to proceed in that manner, then it shall be their right to challenge for any and all black vests which all of you happen to wear, just as it will be the right of the guards to challenge Corbo for the black vest as the master sentinel." There were a number of amused expressions. "This presents the potential of a number of challenges," he added, laughing.

"It will be a scramble to find the true masters," someone else said jestingly.

"Perhaps, but it is so much more fun than war!"

There was not a single Caballian who was not laughing.

Merahlaha said to her brother, "What was so funny before?"

He had to stop and think about it before he could answer her. "It is somewhat like how you had Andrux crash the caucus today."

"How?"

"You did what you could to stop the grumbling and complaining. Sometimes it takes a crash to get everyone's attention, like it did today. Crashing can be good if you use it to everyone's advantage. You cannot hurt people with crashing. And you cannot use crashing to stop them when they are doing their best to work with you."

"Why were you laughing?"

"Because I also had to crash today. To get our people to realize that Corbo was Caballian, I had to clip eleven tails!"

"That is a crash?"

"It certainly is, because it is not something I would normally do at a caucus. I only did it because they were bad and disrespectful."

"Mehlanahr threatened to crash me."

"Why?"

"Because I call him Mehl."

"He said he would clip you if you continued to call him Mehl?"

"Yes, he did."

"He was right. Would you like it if I called you Mer?"

"No."

"It is the same thing to him when you clip his name. But that crash is nothing compared to the crash that will happen in three days at the next caucus."

"Why will it be a crash?"

"Because fifty thousand Caballians are coming to meet with us, and they will be given vests as citizens of Equestra."

"Passages are boring!" she sighed.

"It will seem boring for you and I because I did most of my work already by talking the Acaballians into coming here. They were difficult to persuade."

"Is that what you do is persuade people?"

"Somewhat, if I know that I am right. I let them persuade me when I know that they are right. In three days, when fifty thousand citizens are given their vests, a number of them will feel that they deserve to challenge the masters for the black vests. The Caballians of Acaballia deserve a fair chance to wear black vests, especially if they truly are the masters on all of Equestra."

"What are we going to do while they do this?"

"That is not all that is going to happen. When the question of the masters is settled, then each one of the masters shall be required to meet with all vocational subjects and to learn everything about the current placements. You and I will be the two most bored people during the next caucus. I want you to meet some of their storytellers, and learn all of their fables concerning us. They know much more about our family than I ever knew myself. Not only that, but we will be able to talk, and learn about each other. I do not know anything about you, and I am sure that Mother has told you very much. You will tell me about yourself, and about Andrux, and about everyone who lives here. You will let me know what has happened during the six years that I have been gone."

"How? I am only six years old!"

"You know much more than everyone else does, because you are young and are probably annoyed with listening to everyone talk about your brother. You will tell me about yourself, and I will tell you about myself and about Father."

"You remember Father?" she whispered.

"Indeed I do, and you are very much like he was—quiet and thoughtful, with many ideas in your mind like crashes. He was the best father we could have ever had. He was always proud of me, and I was proud of my father, who was the king. But he did not always know when it was time to crash, and he liked to forget about crashing. I am sure if he knew you, he would have been very proud of how you crashed my return. He would have been proud that you did what you could to help our people, and to make sure that they welcomed me back with a party."

She did not understand all of his words, but she hugged him anyway. Tarahnaha, who had heard their conversation, said to Zayo, "My son, I spent many hours with her, trying to understand her, but I could not. How did you do it?"

"Oh, Mother," he said, tears in his eyes, "she missed me."

Tarahnaha still had much to learn about Merahlaha the crasher.

Merahlaha pulled herself back from her brother, and she saw that he had been crying. She wiped the tears off of his face and said, "I am glad that you came back. Can we crash now?"

He laughed at her and said, "If we crash now, you will not be able to help me crash at the next caucus."

"Why not?" Tarahnaha laughed when Merahlaha said that.

"You are not yet ready to crash the next caucus."

"I was ready today. It is easy to crash!"

He looked at her sternly, and she quieted down. Tarahnaha could hardly believe that Merahlaha was obeying him so quickly, yet she knew her daughter needed a father figure in her life. Zayo was young, but being an older brother could be a tremendous help since Kayloor was gone. "You have so much else you have to do before the next council," he continued.

"Like what?"

"Dost thou understandeth my speech whenst I speaketh in yon idiom?"

"What are you talking about? I think you are silly."

"You must learn to speak like that before the next council so that you will be able to understand the fables that the storytellers are going to tell you."

"How did you learn it?"

"It took me three hours to learn to understand them, but I told myself I could understand it, and it was much easier."

"I am not a good student," she said, holding her chin out.

"You are a terrible queen if I ever saw one."

She had such an insulted expression on her face that Zayo had to really force himself not to laugh. "You are a tyrant!" she exclaimed.

"It will be easier to teach you their language than it will be for fifty thousand of them to learn your language."

"You should have taught them while you were there."

"If we want them to be interested in us, then we have to prove to them we are genuinely interested in them and want to learn everything about them, especially their fables. Besides, they have a fable about the pegasus which you really must hear."

"How do they know about Andrux?"

"I do not know, but they do. Are you hungry?"

She did not have to think about it. "Yes, I am very hungry. Can we have some apples?"

He took her hand in his. "I know of something much better than apples which you will enjoy eating as much as I do."

"What?"

"Pickled coral."

"What is that?"

"That is what Corbo eats. I will ask him to let you try it, but if you want more of it, you must learn to speak his language and ask him yourself."

Corbo was on the other side of the platform. Zayo brought Merahlaha to him and said, "Corbo, dost thou possess more pickled coral?"

"Aye, sire," he replied, "but tis not yet ye lunch hour."

Merahlaha examined him as he spoke, and was trying to figure out was his gills were for. "What is that on your neck?" she asked him.

"Thy majesty, tis my gills. Zayo, I canst only give thy sister ye pickled coral if I couldst lead her to my vehicle. However, tis forbidden for me to touch thee."

"Who hast forbidden it?" Zayo asked him.

"Yon Acaballians."

Zayo held out his hand and said to him, "My soul wouldst not abideth well if thou couldst not touch me. Let ye physical touch remindeth thee of yon spiritual friendship."

"Thy ancestor," he grumbled, but said no more.

"Twas ye ancient sentinel, not thee. Thou shalt not condemn thyself for yon misdeed. Touch my hand."

Corbo was ashamed, but he slowly reached out his left hand to grasp Zayo's left hand. At first he gently grasped Zayo's hand, but when he felt the strength in it, he gripped it very firmly. Zayo smiled and said, "Thy hand hast not killed my body."

"Thou art very strong, my king. And thou hast said that thou hast not yet reached yon age of facial growth?"

"Twill be more than three years, Corbo." Corbo let go of his hand. "Dost thou possesseth more pickled coral?"

Corbo smiled, and held out his hand to Merahlaha. "Thy majesty," he said to her, "my soul desireth that thou dost eat ye pickled coral which ist in my vehicle."

She returned Corbo's smile, and gave him her hand. "Can Zayo come with us?"

"Aye, twould be favorable for my soul to be seen with both of thee. Thou art noble."

The three of them walked off of the platform together. Zayo looked out at his people, and saw that many of them were preparing to leave the caucus. He was glad to see them go, because it was over for now.

As Corbo led Merahlaha to his vehicle, she said to him, "If you say 'thou,' is that anything like 'you'?"

"Thy mind ist full of questions."

"You did not answer my question."

"Thou didst not answereth my question."

"Thou didst...answereth?" she repeated.

He nodded at her. "Thou art my queen."

"I am your queen?" she questioned, but he knew better than to answer that question. "You are Zayo's friend, so you are my friend."

Corbo was happy. He was starting to believe that the reunification was going to work for all Caballians, mostly because of Zayo's dedication to what he believed in. And he was starting to understand why Zayo was the king, and not someone like Khasadro.

Merahlaha loved the pickled coral, and ate so much of it that she felt tired.

After Corbo had moved his vehicle up close to the palace, he took some of the pickled coral out. As they walked into the palace, Corbo was amazed by the candles, and by their fragrance. It was very delightful and aromatic. Moments after they walked into the kitchen and set the pickled coral down, Mehlanahr came walking in.

Zayo saw that Merahlaha was falling asleep, so he said to her, "Merahlaha, you should go to your bedroom and take a nap." She did so very obediently without a word, leaving her brother in the kitchen with Mehlanahr and Corbo.

Mehlanahr then said, "Tahrmaha is so beautiful."

"I know," Zayo sighed.

"What else happened in Acaballia?"

"I had a duty to perform," he replied.

Corbo then said, "Thou are watchful here in Caballia over thy people. How shalt thou also watcheth thine Acaballians?"

Zayo replied, "Thou art ye master sentinel."

"Yon Acaballians needest more than ye master sentinel," Corbo continued. "Yon Acaballians requested ye new governor, yea, thou speaketh nay. Hearken, yon Acaballians needest thy representative for to be ye spiritual watcher."

"Merahlaha ist too young. I cannot leaveth her again."

"So that is what happened," Mehlanahr said. "They need you just as much as we do."

Zayo sighed sadly and said, "That is about the sum of it."

"What is your heart telling you to do now, to tend to their needs? I wish I could go there for you and become acquainted with the Acaballian natives as we did when you were crowned."

"Out of necessity," he replied, "and out of the need to get to know them and begin to learn their needs, I allowed Corbo to bring me to everyone when he volunteered."

"Could you have told him no?"

"Of course not. He is a hero to them, being the most honorable person in their society, next to their governor."

"Was there conflict between Corbo and the governor?"

"There was conflict between all of the sentinels and the governor. That is part of what caused him to resign—they felt that they needed a king more than an elected official."

"They are just like us—a proud people needing to retain their identity and their history."

"Hearken to our needs," Corbo said. "Thou hast heeded my words to thee in Acaballia...be mindful of thy feelings here."

Mehlanahr smiled and said, "Zayo, how did you feel when Corbo confronted you in Acaballia?"

Zayo thought about it and said, "I felt the same way I always feel when I seek advice from you." He then saw where they were pushing him, and he replied, "Our people will not allow such a thing."

"Why not?" Mehlanahr asked.

"Because they will feel I will have enough help with Merahlaha."

"Zayo, after living for six years without you, everyone here knows what it is like to be without a leader. At least they had me to look up to, to help them with passages and marriages. Acaballia has no one. It is the least you can do to help them. If you are as genuinely interested in their needs as you say you are, then you shall do it, and change our tradition so that we can embrace them more readily."

Corbo then said, "Telleth my soul which one of thy people shalt serve for ye Acaballians, and I shalt abideth with it happily."

Zayo replied, "It cannot be someone from here. It must be someone who knows the Acaballians, someone whom they already respect, yet someone whom I also respect dearly. They deserve their own representative to ensure that my decisions will embrace what they are, just as the Caballians here allowed me to select someone to discourse my decisions with."

"Then whom shalt thou select?"

"Hearken to thy heart, and thou shalt knoweth all. Thou art my friend."

Corbo thought about it, then he said, "My soul doth not feeleth comfortable with ye sabre."

Zayo told him, "When I commission thee, thou shalt be required to carry out ye punishments only when Merahlaha and I cannot."

"Zayo was gone for six years," Mehlanahr told Corbo, "and I did not need to use my sabre once. And even before he left, I never used my sabre."

Corbo smiled and said, "Then I shalt accepteth thy request," and he hugged Zayo.

During lunch, Zayo decided to allow Corbo to stay with Merahlaha and Mehlanahr while he went into Tokanar with his mother. She was setting to work, even though it was a caucus day. She wore a golden yellow vest, and her assistance was needed immediately as they were beginning work on crafting the vests for the Acaballians. Zayo gave his mother the number of vests they would need for each color. Zayo had to replace his transport, so he had his mother drop him off at Jayexeeyo's house; the shoemaker was not in the forge because it was a caucus day.

Zayo's knock on the door was answered by Shehronaha, who was somewhat surprised to see the king. "Your majesty," she said, "good afternoon."

"Good afternoon," he replied, as a young filly came running up behind her and grabbed her legs. "Is Jayexeeyo here?"

"Yes," she replied. She looked about, but did not see his transport. "Where is your transport?" She let him in the house.

"Do you have one I may avail myself of?"

"I have a new one at the forge I just completed."

"You are too kind."

Jayexeeyo walked into the den upon hearing their voices, and he sternly told his daughter, "Pohldeeraha, we have a guest."

She ran to her father and said, "Father, I play nice."

"When the king visits our house, we must welcome him."

"Yes, Father," she said, and she calmed down.

"How old is she?" Zayo asked them. He observed a comely young filly who had chestnut fur like her father, her mother's blue eyes, and her father's curly hair that was as light as her mother's hair.

"She is four," Shehronaha replied.

Zayo smiled. "Jayexeeyo, I need to commission you for a task."

The shoemaker smiled and replied, "My services are always available at your request."

"I just had a long discussion with Mehlanahr and Corbo, and they convinced me that I need to commission a second adjutant, someone to lead the Acaballians as my personal assistant, because Merahlaha is far too young to fulfill the duties of a queen."

Jayexeeyo pondered this and replied, "Have you spoken with Vehdoor?"

"I will once I obtain a transport. My mother brought me here on her way to make vests."

"Then I shall begin work on the collar and sabre first thing tomorrow morning."

"Thank you, my friend."

Leaving Pohldeeraha with Jayexeeyo, Shehronaha brought Zayo to the forge in her transport, and showed him the new transport she had just finished putting together two days before. "Your majesty," she said, "this transport is actually a prototype which Mehlanahr designed, and has far superior performance than the ones we are currently using. The philinium reaction chamber is sealed, and there is no converter in it."

"No philinium converter?" he wondered.

"No. The reaction chamber is thermodynamically sealed to the laser jet, which fires the drive. We were able to accomplish this because Hohnoor has fantastically improved the refining process. And it is far more efficient, and much quieter."

"What do you mean by more efficient?"

"A full tank of philinium will last twice as long as it did."

"You did not increase the size of the tank..."

"Of course not. That would not be practical. We also redesigned the cockpit, so that it provides easier access to all controls. And the new visiphone in it can be used while it is being operated."

"There is a new visiphone in it?"

"That was my idea."

"I love it! But have you tested it?"

"Mehlanahr and I took it for a test drive yesterday, and I did not want to part with it. I almost did not want to return home."

"But it is a prototype...you should keep it in the plant."

"What good would it do there? A transport needs to be used. If you do not use it, the philinium will eventually corrode. Besides, we have the master plans for it in the plant, and I have a copy of the plans in the forge. And for everything you have done for our people, you deserve it. Especially now, since you will be making many long trips to Acaballia. With the visiphone in it, it will help you keep in touch with everyone. We know how keen you are in communicating with our people."

Zayo took a good look at it, inside and out, and said, "It is beautiful. Thank you." He climbed into it, and started it up. He was amazed at the smooth sound of the engine. Shehronaha opened up the cargo bay doors for him, and he drove it out of the forge, and straight to Karayo's house.

When Karayo answered Zayo's knock on the door, he was a bit surprised to see the young king. "Your majesty, good afternoon," he said.

"Good afternoon," Zayo replied. "Is Vehdoor here?"

Karayo let him in and said, "You have impeccable timing. He is here packing up his belongings which he had forgotten several years ago when he moved out onto his own in Tokanar. How did you know he was here?"

"I did not know. But I knew that you would be able to tell me where he was if he was not here."

Karayo let out a little laugh. "What brings you here?"

"Actually, I need to speak with both of you."

Karayo went and got Vehdoor and brought him into the gathering room where Zayo was waiting. "Your majesty," Vehdoor said, "good afternoon."

"Good afternoon," he returned. "I need both of you to tell me what you think about Corbo."

Karayo eyed him carefully and said, "What have you done?"

"I allowed Mehlanahr and Corbo to persuade me into making a decision that will help the Caballians in Acaballia to assimilate." He saw the questioning looks in their eyes, and he continued. "I am going to commission a second adjutant, one who is from Acaballia, and can work with the people there."

"A second adjutant?" Karayo wondered. "No king has ever had two adjutants."

"No king has ever dealt with over ninety thousand Caballians, which is what the population of Equestra is, not forty thousand as we originally thought. And Merahlaha is far too young to handle any type of responsibility."

Vehdoor thought about it, and finally said, "I believe that this unorthodox decision which you have made will bring you great success. The Caballians from Acaballia have never had a king, and by your choosing one of them as your personal advisor, they will have greater confidence in you."

"I know they will," Zayo said. "When I was in Acaballia, and their governor resigned, they were all requesting that I appoint Corbo to be their new governor. But I do not want them to continue their ways of the governor, for he was too much of a dictator. If I commission Corbo instead, they will grow in their attempts to learn how we do things democratically. They have a great spirit about them, and I know I need to earn their favor. For as long as we are separate, then we are technically still at war, as we were millions of years ago. It is my duty to put an end to this, even if it means my death."

Vehdoor then told him, "You will not die, but you will grow stronger. Have more confidence in your ability. I believe you have uncovered the key for what it will take for us to evolve."

"Then you believe that Corbo will be a good choice?"

"Yes," he replied, "but never underestimate his knowledge. Corbo is as wise as Booralta was, though in a different way. He is an excellent choice to wear a black vest, for he has earned and merited a great amount of spiritual knowledge in serving his people. And the way he desires to serve you, our people shall always be grateful that you commissioned him."

"Then you do understand the place that the sentinels hold in their hearts."

"I believe I do. And I am thrilled that you earned their support, for they have trained their hearts to advance the needs of their people."

"Then you will support me at the next caucus. I have already commissioned Jayexeeyo to craft the collar and sabre."

REUNIFICATION

Corbo stayed in the palace the next three nights as a special guest. His waking hours were spent with Zayo and Merahlaha. Zayo and Corbo would only speak Acaballian idiom in front of Merahlaha, and were forcing her to learn it, which she did much better than she thought she would. She could not speak it very well, but she was able to understand them when they spoke like that.

It was no problem at all for Zayo and Merahlaha to get Corbo to try the foods they usually ate—oatmeal, bread, fruits and vegetables, and grains. Corbo loved apples, but was unsure of oatmeal, though he liked stews of all kinds. And bread—he thought that bread was the greatest invention next to pickled coral.

Zayo and Merahlaha took Corbo on a tour of the Equestra they knew, showing him Tokanar in all of its infinite detail, as well as all types of fields. Moonsflower fields, oat fields, fruit groves, and vegetable patches. And trees—Corbo loved trees. Everyellows fascinated him somewhat, but the few piper trees that he saw in Tokanar had him utterly astounded. He loved to walk around in the rain and get soaking wet. He liked the feel of grass beneath his hooves. He liked the smooth ride of the transport that Zayo was now driving. During his second day in Tokanar, Corbo jumped into the Sea of Serenity, and stayed under the water for about two hours before returning to Zayo and Merahlaha without having taken a single breath of air. When they saw him walk out of the water, and saw the water pouring out of his gills, they were impressed with his ability to breathe water in such a way as only Acaballians could do.

Corbo enjoyed his stay with Zayo and Merahlaha to the gill. As he attempted to teach his language to Merahlaha, he learned her language, and was better able to communicate with both of them. Zayo knew that he had found a great friend in Corbo, because the sentinel was genuine in his desire to reunite their peoples.

On the evening of the three hundred and eighth day of the seventh year of Zayo's rule, many of the residents of Caballia began to arrive on the palace grounds. A vast number of the transports were loaded with food, food which would last them at least a week; if it ran out, some of them could always go and get more. A number of bakers cooked up a vast quantity of special bread which did not grow stale, but rather, got better as it sat in the moist air. They all had their hair loose, but had plenty of ribbons in their transports, which they would use to braid their hair in the morning; they never slept with braided hair.

While the farmers and bakers had been busy preparing the food for the council, everyone else who wore a yellow vest spent every waking hour crafting enough vests for the residents of Acaballia. Zayo had told his mother how many of each vest they needed, so there would be no shortage; he had even taken into account the number of citizens who would be making their passage (even if it was a few days late). They also had to make enough white tassels for all of the married couples in Acaballia, which was nearly forty thousand people.

It was such a task to make all of the required vests that a number of artisans as well as farmers and bakers were recruited to help in the process. Each person was assigned to crafting vests of one color; one made red vests, another made orange vests, another made yellow, and so on. The black vest for the master sentinel was crafted by Zehnoraha, who was the master farmer. Because each spinner made only one color vest for the council, and did not have to change dyes while making the silk, they were able to work much faster. Each spinner loaded up his or her transport with the vests that he or she had made, so each transport full of vests contained only one color vest. There were hundreds of people working on the vests, but even so, each person was responsible for crafting hundreds of vests. To make sure that they were completed on time, all those who were scheduled to have a day off during that time worked; additionally, each one of them started work at first light, and worked well into the night, taking time only to eat, urinate, and defecate. Tarahnaha was thankful that Zayo and Corbo were able to keep Merahlaha occupied.

EQUESTRA

The spinners all arrived on the palace grounds well into the night. They left their transports near the platform, and fell asleep for the remainder of the night. They were exhausted.

Zayo was awake at the first hint of twilight. He was quick to bathe, groom, and braid his hair with purple ribbons. Even though he was still only thirty-one years old, he was very handsome for his age, far more handsome than many other more mature stallions. The only thing he was lacking was a beard. No matter how one looked at him, it seemed as if his beard was just missing off of his face, as eleven citizens were just missing their tails from their rumps. But there was not even a hint of facial growth on his chin, which looked very naked for how physically mature his body was.

He picked up his sabre with his left hand, and carefully felt the hilt in his hand as he examined the blade. For as many times as he had used it in his young life, it still did not possess any scratches or nicks in it; it looked as if it had just come out of the shoemaker's forge. It was a beautiful sabre, made by a master at the craft, and the superior workmanship showed. He tucked it into his vest.

He turned to walk out of his bedroom, and saw his mother standing in the doorway. "Mother, good morning."

Tarahnaha smiled and walked into his room. "Good morning. How is Merahlaha?"

He frowned. "That is a strange question, Mother. Ask her yourself."

"Forgive me, Zayo, but I was standing in the door for some time. I could not help myself. In three days, you have taught your sister more about being a queen than I was ever able to teach her."

"You taught her much more than you realize."

"How would you know such a thing?"

"From what I understand, there is only one thing you were unable to teach her, and that is respect for the crown she is to receive."

"I sincerely tried my best, but she tried my patience so much."

"You can tell her many stories and fables and ideas about the crown and what it means to our family, but for a young foal, endless words are meaningless. She needed to be shown. When she saw the eleven citizens have their tails clipped for the disrespect they showed Corbo, she learned respect for the crown once and for all. She has performed her share of scares to know better."

"But how? I do not understand."

"The morning I returned, before the caucus, she called Mehlanahr 'Mehl' once too many times, and he threatened to clip her tail off if she did it again. Just the idea of clipping off a tail scared her, but when she actually saw me clip eleven citizens, it hit home."

She smiled and touched his face. "Zayo, you are far more handsome than any other stallion on all of Equestra. Do not allow your success as our king to be blinded by your physical appearance."

He took his mother's hand in his right hand and said, "What do you mean by this?"

"Any mare alive would gladly be honored if you chose her to be your queen because everyone thinks very highly of you. But when the time is right, be sure that you choose a mare who fully understands your soul, and who comprehends your duty."

"Why?"

"Because your duty as our king is your life. If a mare cannot understand what it means to you, then she does not deserve to be your queen."

"Mother," he began, but he stopped himself.

"If I were your age, I would feel the same way, Zayo. You do not have to say anything to me. I can guess what happened when you awoke in Acaballia."

"I am not a criminal!" he whinnied.

She hugged him and said, "I know that very well, my beloved son. Your duty as our king means much more to you than that... you would not allow yourself to be destroyed by something so terrible. But a trained eye can detect spiritual indulgence. When you combine that with how you look at her and speak of her, I know it is true. And I know that you would die for such a thing to become a reality. I am so proud of you, and I am sure Kayloor would also be proud if he were still alive."

He loosened his nerves and said, "Many things are more important than Father's memory. My own life and duty is what means the difference in our future."

"Does she know?"

"She forced me to tell her."

Tarahnaha laughed. "I am sure she said some things, too, which were just as revealing on her part."

As they awoke and prepared for the final leg of their journey, the Acaballians were finally afraid. They were not afraid of the things they knew, like Zayo and Tahrmaha, but they were afraid of the unknown. They had never before come upon the land like this, not in millions of years since they fled the wars. Some of them wondered if they were traveling into a deathtrap by returning to their brethren in such agreement. But these thoughts were quickly dismissed as they remembered how Zayo had cornered Khasadro into feeling so small, yet had spent time enough with every one of them to get to know them. They believed that the young king's interest was genuine.

They did not have a governor, and Corbo was not with them, so it was difficult for them to face up to what was happening without any fear. But many of them felt that Corbo had prepared the way for them, and that their Caballian brethren in Caballia would be much more receptive because of Corbo's advance entry into Caballia.

Among the Acaballians, Jeha was the most fearful one of all. She was Corbo's wife as well as a sentinel, and was hoping and praying that the Caballians did not excommunicate her beloved husband for the crime of the sentinel who had murdered Hehlehf. She and her son, Mehro, were traveling at the front of the convoy; she wanted to be the first to greet her husband when they arrived at the council meeting. Fifteen thousand vehicles were quite a lot, though they did not think so.

All of the Caballians were going to have to become accustomed to a much larger population—it was now well over ninety thousand. And Zayo knew just about every one of them.

Once the crowd at the palace had eaten breakfast, Zayo went up onto his platform by himself. Merahlaha stayed with her mother, Mehlanahr, and Corbo at a spot on the side of the platform. Zayo raised his hands in the air to get their attention. "My beloved people, the time is drawing near when you shall see that there are much more than ninety thousand Caballians on all of Equestra. We shall not conduct any business until all are here."

"They are late for the caucus," someone called out.

"They are three days behind myself, so they shall be arriving at about the same time as I arrived three days ago."

"Then why did we rush to prepare ourselves?" someone else asked.

"If they arrived last night as many of you did, then there would have been no surprise in their arrival this morning. That is why we needed to collect and wait, to be ready for them. When they arrive, we shall greet them with festivity and gladness. They have traveled long and far. Do any of you doubt that they are coming?" Remembering what happened three days ago, they all shook their heads no. "Merahlaha, Mehlanahr, and

Corbo, the three of you shall walk with me as I go to greet them first because they know Corbo and myself. Everyone else shall ensure that there always remains a clear path to the platform." He held up his arm straight in front of him. "There is to remain a free path in front of the platform, as wide as the platform itself, so that there shall be no obstacles for anyone who wishes to approach. Why do I see so many transports among thee?" There were a vast number of transports mixed in with all of them; many of them were empty, though some were filled with food. A number of people went to their transports to move them behind the palace, near the Sea of Serenity. A few transports remained among them, so Zayo called out, "Why are these transports still here?"

"Your majesty," a spinner replied, "those transports contain the vests. If you wish, we shall put all of the vests upon the platform. If we do that, there will not be room for you to stand."

"Which color are we to start with?"

"The indigo vests," Zehnoraha called out.

"Put the indigo vests on the platform, and move that transport out of the way. The black vest will be given to my mother to hold until it is time to give it to Corbo. The other transports that are holding vests are to be lined up behind the platform. Think of all of the people who shall be here shortly, and remember that they must be able to get water!"

It took them nearly ten minutes to empty the transport of the indigo vests and move it behind the palace. Many people were eyeing the vests, because they were a beautiful color never before seen in a vest, but only in the moonsflowers. They were absolutely beautiful.

It was not long before the required path was cleared in front of the platform. Zayo, Merahlaha, Mehlanahr, and Corbo began their walk to meet the approaching convoy. Zayo proudly wore his crown.

The four of them walked a half-mile away from the caucus before they saw the approaching convoy loom on the horizon; it was massive. They all knew immediately that the rest of the Caballians were indeed drawing near. They continued to walk away from the caucus until the convoy stopped in front of them. A comely mare climbed out of the foremost vehicle with a colt, and walked up to them. When Corbo saw her, he ran to her, and clutched her for dear life, almost as if he thought he would never see her again; it was Jeha, his wife. "Jeha, my beloved," he said to her amidst tears, "how my soul felt ye three days wouldst never end!"

"My heart ist always with thee, dearest Corbo." She kissed him, and broke free from his clutches. "Ye Acaballians consider thee yon hero."

"My soul rejoiceth at thy presence. Mehro," he said, hugging his son, "thy vehicle ist full of food and supplies?"

"Aye, Father," he returned.

"Thou hast done well. My soul ist proud of thee. Pray thou must meet my friends." He brought them back to Zayo.

"Thy majesty," Jeha said, "good morn."

"Good morn," Mehro added.

"Jeha," Zayo replied, "good morn."

"Thy majesty," Jeha said to Merahlaha when she saw the filly's head, "good morn." Mehro said the same.

"Good morn," Merahlaha replied.

"Merahlaha ist my sister," Zayo said. He glanced at Mehlanahr and said, "My adjutant, Mehlanahr."

Jeha saw Mehlanahr's vest, and could not resist reaching out to touch it. "Tis ye vest which thou hast spoken of, ye black vest which thou shalt giveth to Corbo?"

"Aye, though with different trim. Corbo's color shalt be indigo, as wouldst thy whole vest."

"Tis beautiful." She looked at Mehlanahr's collar and said, "What canst we call thee?"

"Thou canst call him Sir," Corbo said quickly. "Tis respectful, as ist majesty."

"Aye, tis well. Sir, good morn."

"Good morn," Mehlanahr replied.

Zayo looked up, and saw that all of the Acaballians had left their vehicles and were walking up to them. "Thou shalt come with us, and drink thy fill. Art thou hungry?"

"Nay," Jeha replied, "ye breakfast wast good."

When they reached the caucus, the Caballians had striated themselves so as to enable a fair number of the brethren to hear Zayo equally well from the platform. They filled in all of the empty space and much more, although they were mindful enough to leave the central pathway clear; it was obvious what it was for as Zayo, Merahlaha, Mehlanahr, and Corbo walked up to the platform. Merahlaha, Mehlanahr, and Corbo walked around to the side of the platform; Zayo was the only person who climbed up onto it. It was only three feet about the ground, so he jumped up onto it moreso than he climbed it.

He turned to face the largest part of them, who were in front of the platform. Looking at the remarkable size of the council, he was awestruck by the immensity of what he had done. He had actually succeeded in doing what none of his ancestors had been able to do: he had reunified his people for the first time in more than fourteen million years. And he was proud of himself, because he knew virtually all of them. He raised his hands above his head, which was ever more effective at silencing them. In his loudest voice, he called out, "Canst thou heareth my voice?" There were many mumbles and murmurs, so Zayo immediately knew that not all of them could hear him.

As soon as he heard this, Mehlanahr nodded at Zayo and got moving. He picked two dozen citizens, brought them to where the transports were all parked behind the palace, and had each one of them move a transport to a specified position around the outside perimeter of their people, and turn on the speaker/receiver part of the visiphone. Mehlanahr brought the transport he was operating to the front of the platform, and turned on the transmitter and microphone so that it would pick up all voices from the platform. He jumped out of the transport and said to Zayo, "See what you can do now."

The crowd had become somewhat noisy again, so Zayo again put his hands over his head and silenced them. He took a long, thoughtful look at all of them before he said, "My soul dost thank thee. Thou art ye beautiful sight, one which my mind hast only dreamt of!" He dropped his hands, and a tremendous cheer erupted from them all. It was loud, and it was boisterous, but it was magnificent. Now he felt as if he had accomplished something in his reign, and he was not yet thirty-five years old. How much more could he possibly do? He knew that there was so much more work to be done, but most of it was for his people to do—they had to see to all of the details which the reunification brought about. He would be needed to oversee it, but not much else. He had done his fair share of it, and so had Tahrmaha.

He again raised his hands over his head, and attempted to lower them to see if the crowd remained quiet, but they did not, so he raised his hands again and said, "Tis not an easy task to talk with thee whilst my arms ache and sting! Whenst I put my arms down, I beg of thee to be quiet." He put his arms down. And this time, they stayed quiet.

"All of thee have abided for many eons apart from each other. All of thee from Acaballia have known all along that upon ye land existed yon brethren. But all of thee from Caballia knew nothing of thy brethren until thou saw Corbo three days ago. Now, everyone shalt know everything, and no one shalt live in fear of yon brethren. Tis not proper or becoming actions for true Caballians! Tis time for me to make my decrees for thee which shalt help thy lives.

"My first decree ist that thou art ye beautiful and magnificent people. Never again shalt war divide us, and never again shalt yon aliens harm us in any way! To preserve this decree, we requireth ye number of thee to protecteth Equestra and ye inhabitants from alien exploitation. Thou shalt be required to maintain that no one ever uses ye forbidden valley or ye cave of ye magical mists—ye twins—so as not to disturb ye unpredictable ancient powers. Thou shalt be required to maintain that every citizen works as long as he or she ist able to do so. Thou shalt never raise thy hands in anger or hatred; thou shalt preserve thy brethren and thy home Equestra; thou shalt uphold ye values of thy people. Thou shalt relocate and return all misplaced and broken transports and vehicles, thereby relieving ye engineers and shoemakers for yon craft. Thou shalt all carry imploders in thy transports, so as to remove ye corpses whence none other canst do such a thing. Thou shalt never raise thy imploders to thy brethren in anger, neither shalt thee punish thy brethren, unless thou hast witnessed that thy brethren have harmed me or my family. Thou shalt be responsible for transporting criminals to and from prison, after ye criminal hast committed ye crime ere I have punished ye criminal. If thou seest ye crime, thou canst imprison ye offending brethren until I am able to question ye criminal. Thou shalt be fair, and of good mind and character, and shalt do thy best to stop ye crimes before they escalate into yon war. Wherein thy people need to settle ye bitterness and anger, thou shalt do so wherein I cannot. Thy duty ist to help ye crown maintain peace. If any of thee shalt raise thy imploder in haste, and dost not take ye time to question thy actions and thy brethren, thou shalt be excommunicated for thy abused disrespect. Thou art being given ye grand purpose as sentinels; thou shalt never abuse thy vocation, as thou art required to assisteth thy king.

"Among ye Caballians of Caballia, erein exists yon number of guards. Thou shalt be my commissioned servants, and shalt no longer be called guards, but sentinels. Tis thy right to challenge ye master sentinel for ye black vest, if thou feelest that thou art more honorable and thorough in thy duty to me. All of ye guards shalt remove thy orange vests, and shalt be given vests of a new color." He saw them start to move, so he raised his hands. "Not yet, tis not ye time yet. Among ye Caballians of Acaballia, erein exists one hundred sentinels. Thou shalt also be my commissioned servants, equal to yon guards whom art also to be called sentinels. Among thee ist one whom I decree worthy to be called ye master sentinel. He shalt be ye first Acaballian to receive ye vest, for he hast abided with my sister and myself for three days. Tis Corbo. Corbo, come to me." Zayo looked towards his mother, and motioned for her to join him on the platform. Tarahnaha ran up to Zayo's side, and waited while Corbo was more deliberate about climbing the platform. Corbo had mind enough to kneel in front of his king at a distance of ten feet, and bowed his head.

Tarahnaha carefully unfolded the black vest with the indigo trim, and held it carefully in her hands. Zayo walked up to Corbo, touched his right shoulder, and said, "My friend, thou art worthy. Stand, and examine thy vest." Corbo arose, and as he did, Tarahnaha walked up to him.

Corbo smiled, and Tarahnaha slipped the vest over his head as he carefully slipped his arms through. "It shall be your duty to give vests to all of your sentinels," she told him.

"My heart thanks thee," Corbo said to Zayo and Tarahnaha.

Zayo then said to the crowd, "Ye sentinels shalt line up down ye central aisle double file, and Corbo shalt present thee with thy vests."

It was going to take them a while.

Once all of the sentinels had their new vests, Corbo went to leave the platform, but Zayo motioned for him to stay. He reclaimed the attention of the crowd. "Two weeks ago," he began, "Khasadro resigned ye governorship of Acaballia. And in accepting ye laws of Caballia, many Acaballians felt yon need to have Corbo be appointed ye governor. Yea, hearken, for only my family or my commissioned servant couldst assist in leading thee from Acaballia, for that ist ye Caballian way. Yea, Merahlaha ist too young to attendeth to thy needs. Henceforth, I must changeth ye law to hearken to thy needs.

"All of my ancestors have held ye privilege of one adjutant. Twas fine with forty thousand Caballians. Yea, behold ninety thousand hearts and souls, betwixt two different countries. One country, Caballia, has ye adjutant for to hearken to thy needs, and persuade my heart to hearken to thee. Acaballia, wherein art fifty thousand Caballians with ye different history and ye different culture, requireth ye Acaballian adjutant to hearken to thy needs, and persuade my heart to hearken to thee. Henceforth, I desireth Corbo to continue to serve me as my friend, and as one whom shalt always protecteth Acaballian needs through his service as ye master sentinel. His heart ist noble and honorable, and his wisdom educates me." Zayo then saw that many of them were talking among themselves.

Vehdoor walked up onto the platform, and knelt ten feet from Zayo. Zayo walked up to him, and accorded him to stand. "Master historian," he said, Awhat dost thou foresee for Corbo?"

Vehdoor slowly said, "You have stated your opinion and your feelings to our people. But who has questioned Corbo and yourself to see if this is a wise choice?"

"It was Mehlanahr. He and Corbo pushed me into making the decision." A number of laughs arose from the crowd. Zayo then called out, "Mehlanahr, come here." Mehlanahr went up on the platform and knelt, and Zayo had him stand. "Mehlanahr, tell Vehdoor and our people what you think."

"The Acaballians are a proud people who need to retain their identity and their history," the adjutant began. "And in watching Zayo speak with Corbo, I am convinced that Corbo is able to keep our king mindful of their needs. People always remind me of how I am able to command Zayo's respect. Corbo commands his respect in a different way—always so that it ensures respect for the Acaballian natives. He fires Zayo's eagerness to learn more about Acaballian culture, and in exchange, Corbo is showing he is able to teach them how better to unify our needs. To think that, for fourteen million years we have lived apart, yet now, mostly through Corbo, Zayo is realizing just how much we need each other, and how easy it should be for us to depend on each other. We are all kinfolk with a shared ancient history. If we cannot be friends, then what is the sense of living? Corbo feels the urgency of the reunification as much as Zayo does."

"How long have you known Corbo?" Vehdoor asked Mehlanahr.

"Three days," he replied. "Two of those days I worked, and much of my spare time was spent with my wife, as well as with Corbo."

"So you have learned so much about him in only three short days?"

"It is easy to learn about someone when we are all striving for the same goals. Corbo and Zayo have a shared vision to reunite our people. I was there for Zayo when his father was killed, but this is something I cannot do for him, for it is out of my realm."

"You are not a shaman."

"I know what I am capable of doing as the master engineer and as Zayo's adjutant. And I am the first one to admit when something is not within my knowledge, and for knowing whether or not I am capable of learning enough about it. For the knowledge required for the job at hand, Corbo is best qualified."

Zayo then said, "Now you understand why Mehlanahr and Corbo convinced me to make this decision. It is unorthodox, but it is obviously the right move for all. The Acaballian natives are working to adopt our laws and political way of life, and this will only help them succeed."

Corbo was shocked. "I am not ye politician!" he whinnied.

"No," Zayo said. "If that were so, I wouldst have endorsed ye Acaballians to electeth thee as ye governor. Ye political way of life ist ye diplomatic caucus, whenst ye Caballians canst expresseth yon desires without discord. Tis why we discuss this now, rather than my decree to appoint thee as my adjutant."

"Thou changest ye law unquestioned."

"Aye, hearken, I canst changeth ye law, and request ye second adjutant, but if yon people dost not agree with ye selection, then ye new law becomes null. Our people must understandeth why thou art my friend. Only ye friend wouldst question my statements and opinions concerning him and his people. Only ye friend wouldst keep me honorable. For as much help as thou hast given me whilst I was in Acaballia, I continue to requireth thy assistance. Wouldst thou alloweth ye Acaballians to be left without thy help in assimilating? Ye Caballians of Caballia art working just as hard to reunify. Ye honor ist thine."

"Thou hast directed thy people due to our discussion with Mehlanahr."

"Aye, tis what ye adjutant does. Assist me in directing our people."

"Aye, hearken."

Vehdoor smiled, for he finally saw what Zayo and Mehlanahr saw in Corbo. Everyone else saw it, too, and a loud cheer went up for him. When it quieted down, Zayo called out, "I requireth Jayexeeyo." Several minutes later, Jayexeeyo was up on the platform kneeling, the new collar and sabre in his hands. Zayo touched his shoulder and said, "Master shoemaker, I seeth that thou hast fulfilled my commission."

"It was an honor," he replied, standing up. He handed the collar to Zayo first.

Zayo eyed it carefully and said, "It is a beautiful collar, like Mehlanahr's collar, but somewhat different." It was mesh with twenty-seven inlaid crystals; whereas Mehlanahr's collar was pewter mesh, this new one was platinum mesh.

"Did you desire for it to be exactly the same?"

"No, that would not do." Jayexeeyo then handed him the sabre. Zayo carefully inspected it, and saw beautiful metal that had been perfectly formed and polished by the master at the craft; it was platinum in color, and had twenty-seven tiny crystals embedded in the hilt. "You have outdone yourself, shoemaker. My heart thanks thee, and all ninety thousand of our people thank thee." Jayexeeyo smiled, and left the platform.

Zayo walked back to Vehdoor, Mehlanahr, and Corbo. He handed the sabre to Mehlanahr for the moment. Vehdoor then said, "Corbo, you shall do as you are directed to."

"Aye," he replied, "directeth my soul."

Zayo felt the collar in his hands, and then suddenly started to worry that it would cover his gills and impede with his ability to breathe water. He brushed his worry aside, feeling that if there was a problem with the collar, then Jayexeeyo could correct it. He clipped it around Corbo's neck, but was amazed as it hung just below the lower edge of his gills. It sat lower than Mehlanahr's collar did, but Jayexeeyo had obviously taken the gills into account. Even so, it was strikingly beautiful on the Acaballian. Zayo pulled his sabre out of his vest, pierced his hand with it, and purposely put a drop of blood on Corbo's head. The king then said, "This ist ye reminder that I shalt always risketh my life for thee. Thou shalt taketh thy sabre from Mehlanahr, and put thy blood on my blaze, so as to show our people thou art willing to risk thy life to protecteth ye crown."

Corbo did so very deliberately, and when he had put his sabre in his vest, he hugged Zayo.

Zayo kept his company on the platform. Once the excitement died down, Zayo began to speak again. "Thou knowest Mehlanahr, Corbo, and Vehdoor. Now, thou shalt seeth all masters. Whenst I shalt summon thee, cometh to ye platform. Hohnoor, Zehnoraha, Pleeyedraha, Naijoolo, and Jayexeeyo, cometh to me." He watched as they slowly made their way to the platform. They all went up onto the end of the platform and knelt. Zayo touched each one's shoulder as he spoke to them. "Hohnoor, ye master chemist. Zehnoraha, ye master farmer. Pleeyedraha, ye master healer. Naijoolo, ye master artisan. Jayexeeyo, ye master shoemaker." A cheer went up from the crowd. "Tis ye rare moment whenst all masters art upon my platform at once. Acaballia, hearken, for tis ye opportunity for thee: thou art entitled to challenge for ye black vests if thou feelest upon thy merit that thou art ye master of all." There were a number of laughs among their cheers.

"Tis time for all remaining Acaballians to receiveth ye vests." It became hard for him to speak through the cheering, and he had to wait for them to quiet down. He then said to the masters, "It shalt be thy duties to giveth ye vests to all residents of Acaballia." Corbo had a confused looked upon his face, but said nothing. The rest of them grimaced at the thought of the task ahead of them, but Zayo continued, saying, "Whenst thou shalt giveth ye vests to thy vocational subjects, thou shalt be required to learneth all names. Then, throughout as many days as it takes, thou shalt learneth everything about thy new subjects. Erein art fifty thousand Caballians from Acaballia. Thou shalt be inclusive for all talents. If any of thee dost not honorably giveth thy vest to ye proven superior talent, thou shalt be clipped. If thou still refuses, then thou shalt be excommunicated. Behind my platform art seven transports. Zehnoraha, since there art more farmers by far, thou shalt station thy transport in front of my platform. Corbo shalt assisteth thee." She nodded, and left with Corbo following her.

The crowd remained silent as Zayo proceeded. He assigned the other six masters to station themselves at every fourth transport which was serving as a speaker. Some of their vocational subjects went to their masters to help with the vests. Zayo then said to the crowd, "All of yon Caballians from Acaballia shalt receiveth thy vest now. Each master ist at ye different location. Thou knowest which vest thou art to receive. There art just enough vests for all, so ensure that thou dost not obtaineth ye wrong vest. If thou dost such a thing, thou shalt be clipped."

All of the orange vests from the guards were recycled and given to other deserving citizens from Acaballia. The masters worked throughout the morning. Farmers occasionally brought them water. When lunchtime approached, and the farmers were spreading food for lunch, they gave food to each of the masters as they worked. All other people busied themselves with making new acquaintances.

The masters worked throughout the afternoon, finishing less than an hour before supper. Then, the remaining vests were brought in to the platform, and were given on the platform to the new citizens who had not yet been placed. There was one citizen from Caballia who celebrated his passage, and two from Acaballia. They finished just before supper, and every single adult Caballian now wore a vest, as well as every intern. Once supper was over, it was getting dark, so the caucus was postponed until the next morning.

ANCIENT TREASURE

At the first signs of twilight, a number of citizens went to their vehicles and brought out enough pickled coral for all for breakfast. Many of them ate pickled coral for the first time, but they all liked it very much. Once breakfast was over, Mehlanahr turned the speaker system back on; it had been turned off for the night. Zayo then went back up on the platform, and got everyone's attention. "'Tis time for Caballia to heareth ye fables from Acaballia," he said.

He saw some movement among the crowd, and slowly but surely, the storytellers all came up, one at a time. And it took all morning, but they told their hosts many of their fables, detailing much of their oral history for the eons that they were living in the cavern.

When the storytellers had told as many fables as the crowd could handle, the crowd quieted down to a dull murmuring. Soon afterwards, they were all shaken out of their conversations by the shaking of the ground; it was an earthquake, and it lasted several minutes. One of the sentinels ran to speak with Corbo, who was not too far from Zayo. Corbo said to him, "Hearken, Dolque."

Dolque, who was a very interesting stallion to look at because of the golden-colored fur on his body and his golden mane and tail, said to the new adjutant, "Ye final disaster hast occurred."

Without another word, Corbo brought his assistant to speak with the king. When Zayo saw the distressed expressions on the sentinels' faces, he said to them, "Corbo and Dolque, what troubles thee?"

294

Corbo was very upset, but he kept his voice controlled. "Thy majesty, tis urgent to addresseth ye council."

Zayo brought them up onto the platform, and did not have to do anything to get the attention of the crowd; everyone fell silent when they saw him. Zayo looked back at the sentinels, who seemed as if they were too afraid to speak. What had happened? Zayo thought to himself. "Corbo and Dolque, tell mine heart what ist troubling both of thee."

Corbo studied the young king for a moment, then began. "Thy majesty," he began, "upon ye day when I had directed Beltadro to removeth thee from ye cave and bringeth thee to ye Acaballian council, twas ye desperation. Ye crystal forest wast endangered. All of ye attempts to secure ye homes went for naught. For ye last resort, whenceupon I had been keen upon keeping ourselves secret from thee as we calleth ourselves ye spies of ye sea, ye Acaballians needed ye advice of ye king."

Dolque then added, "Ye Acaballians wert in ye great danger in ye cavern, yea, we needed ye new homes. Tis ye great task for all of ye Acaballians. Yea hearken, for ye crystal forest wast much more dangerous than ye miners foresaw; ye final collapse caused ye ground to shake."

Zayo was shocked. Corbo then added, "Tis ye miracle that thou hast brought us here in ye timely manner, and in ye peaceable fashion. Thou knowest that my needs for ye reunification to be successful wert genuine." Corbo was about to say something else, but Zayo stopped him.

"My friend," the young king replied, "thou allowed me to travel around Acaballia with thee and Tahrmaha, knowing that ye lives wert imperiled by ye crystal forest?"

Corbo let Zayo see that he was slightly insulted. "Thy majesty, ye Acaballians needed to be convinced that thou wast able to protecteth them and ye Acaballian way of life from ye ancient wars. Thy instinct wast correct."

"Thou hast saved ye Acaballians from ye death," Zayo told both of them.

"Tis ye sentinel's duty to protecteth ye people," Dolque answered.

Zayo thought about their words for a moment. "What personal belongings have ye Acaballian spies of ye sea brought with them?"

Corbo looked at Dolque, who replied, "Ye Acaballians wert directed to bringeth all personal belongings, supplies, and food."

Corbo then said to Dolque, "Didst thou removeth ye ancient treasure?"

Dolque let some tears fall, and he said, "Ye ancient treasure wast not touched for ye eons, yea, hearken, tis now in ye vehicle."

"Ye king hast rescued us, yea, his family shalt forevermore protecteth ye ancient treasure." He saw the sorrowful expression on Dolque's face, so he said, "Ye vehicle tis no place for ye ancient treasure. Fetch it for ye new home in ye palace."

When Dolque had left, Zayo asked Corbo, "Thou hast not told me of ye ancient treasure. What is it?"

Corbo deliberately waited a moment before answering. "Twas not proper before to frighten thee with knowledge of ye ancient treasure, for thou wouldst have thought twas ye weapon. Tis ye stone coffer which containeth ye ancient magic from ye emperor. In ye ancient times, thy people protected ye cave and ye valley, and ye Acaballians protected ye casket; twas what began ye wars."

Zayo was struck speechless for a few minutes. He then managed to say, "What kind of magic ist in ye casket?"

"Tis forbidden to open it and useth it, for ye magic changed ye Acaballians eons ago to be as we art—with gills and webbing, but no hair upon ye heads. Tis why ye sentinels protecteth it from being touched."

Moments later, one of the Acaballian vehicles was brought up to the platform. Corbo and Dolque carefully lifted an ancient-looking intricately carved stone box out of the vehicle, and placed it upon the platform. It was not very large, a cube about eighteen inches on all sides. "Sentinels are ye sworn protectors of Equestra," he told them. "Thou shouldst continueth to protecteth ye ancient treasure."

Corbo and Dolque were quite serious, and both of them had tears in their eyes. "Whereupon shouldst it be housed?"

"Where wast it kept in Acaballia?"

Dolque then replied, "Twas housed in ye vacant field, whereupon no one strayeth. Twas safe."

"And now thou shalt expecteth me to keepeth it in my residence? What ist thy reasoning for ye recommendation? Thou art greatly upset by ye loss of ye homes."

It was hard to tell whether Corbo or Dolque was the first person who began to cry. Zayo looked at them, but he did not know what to say or do. To the shock of the crowd, Tahrmaha walked up upon the platform with tears in her eyes and knelt. She knelt for about ten minutes without being noticed because their people were actually on the verge of beginning another war, so Tahrmaha finally stood up of her own accord and walked towards Zayo, Corbo, and Dolque. She got their attention and stated, "Our people art required to be healed. Corbo and Dolque, thou art thankful for thy lives, and thou hast performed thy duties nobly. And Zayo, thou art thankful for thy friends, but thou art too humble at this moment; thou must showeth courage right now to leadeth thy people." She smiled at all of them, and continued. "Tis time to taketh ye action, and maketh ye decision, Zayo. Since ye peoples art reunited, ye ancient treasure shouldst be retaineth at ye meeting grounds for ye council meetings. Every time we meeteth in ye council, all shalt know ye magic ist here in ye hallowed grounds. Thy sentinels knoweth ye spiritual import." She smiled at Corbo, and gave him a quick hug. As the young doctor did so, Zayo hung his head in shame. Tarahnaha saw how Zayo reacted to Tahrmaha, and she could not hold back the tears. Many people among the crowd saw what transpired between Zayo and Tahrmaha, and the crowd began to whisper among themselves.

Zayo snapped out of his obvious doldrum, and looked at his mother, only to notice her sobs; he was not the only person to notice. He then said to Corbo and Dolque, "I too wast upset by thy sudden events today. Tahrmaha, my heart thanks thee for thy astute observation, and thy keen recommendation. Corbo, if ye people shalt agreeth, then ye ancient treasure shalt be retaineth here, near ye platform."

It was music to their ears when the council agreed with Tahrmaha's recommendation. Tahrmaha shot a quick glance at Zayo, and he nodded at her, so she left the platform. When the cheering died down, there was still much whispering going on among the crowd, and one person near the platform, Bento, a stallion from Acaballia, called up to Zayo, "Claimest thy soul's desire."

There were a number of shocked expressions as they all knew what was intoned by this statement. Zayo saw this, but knew he could manipulate his temper through Acaballian diplomacy. "Perchance, at ye age of facial growth," he told Bento.

"Ye passion of thy soul ist incomplete."

The fire suddenly grew in Zayo's eyes. "Thou knoweth thy laws. Thou shalt not desecrateth such a thing."

"Tis in good humor, thy majesty."

"Ye eon shalt end whereupon ye age of facial growth. Dost thou remembereth?"

AThou art true."

Zayo shook his head. "Testeth myself, yea, hearken, thou wilt be crashed."

"Crashed, sire?"

Zayo put his left hand on the hilt of his sabre and replied, "Have thy tail clipped."

Bento was grief-stricken. "Perchance thou shalt forgiveth my tongue."

"Perchance ye infringement shalt occureth again, tis not my policy to forgiveth such disrespect of our laws."

Bento fell to his knees. "Thy majesty, please."

"Know thyself," Zayo replied. "Thou shalt come upon my platform, and have thy tail clipped."

Bento knew better than to argue with Zayo. "Aye," he remarked, and he climbed up onto to the platform. Bento was embarrassed, because enough Caballians knew enough about what Bento had said so as to start circulating many rumors about Zayo and Tahrmaha.

It took a while for the rumors to circulate and grow before Zayo caught wind of the things they were saying about him and Tahrmaha, despite the fact that he had clipped Bento's tail. Many people were surprised to see Zayo take to his platform later that day. Mehlanahr turned the speaker on, and they became silent very quickly. Zayo then said deliberately, "My beloved people, this morning was a turning point in our history with the ancient treasure of Acaballia and its relocation. However, my heart wonders if you are deserving of this honor, or is it a facade?" Some grumbling began, so he put his hands up in the air. "My ears have heard of the vicious rumors which many of you are conveying concerning my friend Tahrmaha." There were many shocked faces, people who were surprised that he found out what was being said.

He grew furious when he saw their expressions. "Do not look at me so! These rumors are food for wars! I hereby command that <u>all</u> of the offending parties will come up here right now, and I will disprove everything you suppose." None of them moved an inch, so he continued. "I see that no one wants to take the blame for starting a war. Suffice it to say, I will learn who is guilty from Karayo and Vehdoor, and you will be excommunicated tomorrow morning for treason—treason for not owning up to your disrespect of Tahrmaha." He watched as all of them began pressing towards the platform, and he was utterly shocked. "Back off!" he whinnied, and he withdrew his sabre from its holster. When they saw the sabre, they were quick to back away from him. "Perhaps I should excommunicate all of you for your conspiracy against me! You are a bunch of savages! All of you, to speak such things without asking me of your suppositions, whereby to prove or disprove! Need I clip fifty thousand tails, or more? Are you afraid to question my friendship and my duty? Can you be so disrespectful as to do such a thing to Tahrmaha and myself? Are you human? Do your souls desire what exists outside of our laws?

"Yes, it is true that Tahrmaha's passage will be in two weeks. However, it is true that I am only thirty-one; it is unlawful for me to claim any such honor until I am thirty-five! You will not press me into breaking our laws for your insatiable thirst! It is also true that the cave has wrought changes upon Tahrmaha and myself. You will not speak of such dishonorable things which you think, as Tahrmaha and I have abided by our laws. Perhaps my ears should be disturbed with your proddings again, and all offending parties will be excommunicated!"

A solemn silence hung over the crowd as they realized just how cruelly they had mistreated the mixed blessings of the return of Zayo and Tahrmaha. After a long silence, Zayo spoke again. "You will never again abuse my friendships, for every one of you knows that you are my friend. You know the laws. Respect the wisdom behind the laws, and abide by them, or else the wars will return. Hold your patience to your tongue. If you desire to know such things, then you must wait until I am thirty-five."

A number of people walked up to the platform. "Thy majesty," the first person said, "thou must clip my tail."

"Clip my tail," someone else called out. Many others began to call out the same words, because they truly felt bad about what they had done, and knew that they deserved to be punished for the disrespect that they had shown Zayo and Tahrmaha. Zayo was grateful enough that they had conscience enough to know when they deserved to be punished. He knew that it was his duty to clip them all for it. But there were so many of them—at least two hundred were already lined up in front of the platform. He did not like the duty ahead of him one bit, but he knew the only way to stop what had happened was to clip them all.

One by one, they walked past him on the platform and received their punishments. The stone box was tripped on once, and was quickly moved off of the platform and placed directly beneath it. By the time Zayo was finished, it was well past the supper hour, and was much darker than it had been. All in all he had clipped more than two thousand tails. The discarded tails, a pile of hair and webbing, were piled up a fair distance from the crowd and torched.

As soon as breakfast was finished the next morning, the crowd was split into nine groups. Eight of the groups consisted of all those who wore one particular color vest, their interns, and the appropriate master. The last group was not much of a group—it was Zayo and Merahlaha. They had fun spending time together, and observing what all of the groups were doing. These meetings all broke up in time for lunch. Once lunch was over, Zayo called all of the masters up onto the platform. Once they collected, he said to them, "How dost thou fareth?"

All of them looked to Vehdoor, so he began. "The historians are basically prepared. What I need to do is examine the Acaballian education system, so there can be positive input as to how the two countries are united. Karayo and the storytellers need to spend time together. All historians and administrators shall stay with the foals they are assigned to for the time being, though some changes may be pending. If an intern requires different instruction after their passage, they shall be properly assigned to continue their studies."

"That is mild," Hohnoor began. "A team of chemists are preparing to study the differences between our refining processes. We also need to see if their vehicles would profit from switching to philinium."

"Acaballian native do not use beds," Zehnoraha said. "Their diets have been limited to what grows in the waters—coral, seaweed, and some other less populous plants. They never ate or heard of bread before they came here. Also, we need to figure out a way to braid their webbing...otherwise, they cannot wear hair ribbons." There were some laughs when she said that, but she had a valid point.

"I am too old to undertake the job at hand; most of you know that I am four hundred and fifty-two." Pleeyedraha said. "My mind is as sharp as it ever was, but my body is beginning the final breakdown. I have lived a rich, full life, and have been wonderfully enriched just living through the past few days of this remarkable caucus. However, my successor has already begun the enormous task of fully evaluating their health care system and all of its intricate details."

"Fooraha?" Mehlanahr asked.

"No," she replied, "she is not a fully qualified healer."

"Only you are," Zehnoraha remarked.

"Right now I am the only one. But I am not the best. My student possesses far superior analytical skills. She has precise microsurgical skills, and a remarkable knowledge of physiology and organic alchemy. I have already instructed Fooraha that, if I am to die within the next two weeks and miss Tahrmaha's passage, then she will wear the black vest until that time. Tahrmaha is already familiar with all residents of Acaballia, and has a remarkable photographic memory. She is best for the job ahead."

"Their most advanced machines are the vehicles they brought with them," Mehlanahr said, a smile on his face. "They are extremely limited in their technological skills. They possess a communications system which does not have any visual display, and have never heard of computers."

"All ye sentinels shalt be dispatched around Equestra in yon strategic locations." Corbo said, "Sentinels shalt continue to protecteth ye citizens from injuries due to ye philinium accidents and distribute ye philinium. Sentinels shalt also be assigned in and around ye cities with ye transports and vehicles, and shalt maketh ye rounds so as to cover much ground. Wherewith all ye sentinels, we shalt be able to protecteth all of Equestra."

"I need to examine their forgecrafting techniques as they begin to work with us in our forges," Jayexeeyo said. "I need to see firsthand the quality of their work, and the safety practices they employ. There has been an extremely high incidence of founder among the Acaballians because of the rocks, so I need to instruct them how to cure it, as well as treat many people myself who are currently imperiled."

"Acaballians do not know much of anything about our types of artistry," Naijoolo said. "Most of their artisans are stonecutters."

"Miners?" Jayexeeyo asked.

"Much more specialized than that, Jayexeeyo. They work with stone as we work with wood. Perhaps they know some secrets as to how to build a better forge. In all likelihood, their building techniques are superior to ours. After we have worked with each other and have completed establishing new homes for them here, it will be easier to judge who is the best artisan, although I believe the next master artisan will be a stonecutter. I will be spending much time to attempt to learn their stonecutting techniques."

Zayo looked at all of them thoughtfully and said, "It is time for us to address the council." The speaker system was turned back on, and he said to the crowd, "Every one of us has very much work to do to create new homes for the Acaballian natives and enable them to be a valid part of our society; it will not be easy. But exactly where shall they live?"

Gahrahnoor walked up onto the platform and knelt. When Zayo had acknowledged him, he said, "For many years, I have lived and served in Wateloqua as the analyst. Part of my duties is to inspect the surface tectonics of Equestra, and to approve or disapprove both proposed and older mines. The mountain range south of Wateloqua runs in the Sea of Serenity, and forms a number of islands there, some of them very large. One of the islands is very sizeable; it is fifty miles long and sixty miles wide. Surrounding these islands are steep cliffs in the water, which plunge into some of the largest coral reefs on all of Equestra. We cannot expect any

Caballian to give up on such a delicacy as pickled coral is, so it would be wise for some farmers to grow and harvest pickled coral among the islands. The islands themselves are capable of growing a vast quantity of different crops, including oats. In all likelihood, the islands can be as self-supporting as are any of the three cities.

"Additionally, there is a vast swampy area southeast of the mountains, which is an ideal habitat for growing grains and certain fruits like orange cane. With the location of several mining possibilities, the natives of Acaballia will be able to mine there whereas we could not because they have gills. Houses can be built there in the everyellow forest, which sits on a dry bed. It is large enough to support at least a city.

"The seaspies can also fill in various other areas. There is room enough for us to build a new city southeast of Tokanar, which is far from any known dangers, yet is rich in wild fruits and vegetables. The peninsula and archipelago southeast of Laerion are also good to build another city." Gahrahnoor saw Zayo's entranced face and said, "Need I recommend any other location, your majesty?"

Suddenly, a loud roar of approval arose from the council. They all liked the idea of four new cities. "If we are to do that," Naijoolo said, "we really need to know what will be the chief emphasis in each proposed city."

"Since the islands are rich in coral, stone, and mineral deposits," Pleeyedraha said, "it would be wise to make that city the center for stonecutting artistry and pickled coral, with a secondary emphasis on mining. The swamplands are ideal for a vast mining center as well as farming, with perhaps a secondary emphasis on the shoecraft."

"Because of the central location of the peninsula," Jayexeeyo said, "it would be ideal for sentinels, bakers, and spinners."

"The other location southeast of Tokanar would be suitable for harboring the storytellers and a vast refinery," Zehnoraha said. "Also, it would be an ideal place for fruit and vegetable farming."

"How will we know who shall live where?" Zayo asked them.

"For much of it," Mehlanahr said, "we will have to play it by ear, and make changes once the cities are built up. But if the cities are to be built as they should be, they should be given names, like we would give to new foals."

They all fell silent. After a long moment, Vehdoor said, "Zayo, since these are cities and not foals, it is not the privilege of the masters to name them. The honor falls on you alone. You are the one who worked the hardest to make this all a reality, so it is only fair that you accept your fair share of the honor reaped."

Zayo was caught off guard, and was surprised by Vehdoor's request. All of the other masters looked at him when Vehdoor said what he did; however, Zayo knew what he had to do. "Whenceupon the three hundred and thirty-second day of the seventh year of my rule, I hereby make the following pronouncements: In the everyellow forest bordering the swamplands southeast of Wateloqua, a city shall be built, and it shall be called Patoron." Corbo's heart leaped in his chest when he heard this, for he knew Zayo was using the names of the cities from Acaballia. "On the largest island among the island group west of Wateloqua in the Sea of Serenity a city shall be built, and it shall be called Vayaar. On the peninsula southeast of Laerion which extends into the Sea of Serenity, a city shall be built, and it shall be called Rofae. On the plains southeast of Tokanar, a city shall be built, and it shall be called Belura." A loud cheer went up from the crowd as Corbo gave Zayo the biggest hug. The Acaballians natives were thrilled with his proclamations.

Once it quieted down, Zayo continued. "These cities will not be built overnight. In the meanwhile, it will be up to all of us to share housing and service facilities. Every individual must have a place to sleep and call home. No one shall leave this council meeting until every seaspy has a place to go."

After fourteen couples were married that afternoon, it was amazing to see how fast they were able to organize themselves and make sure that everyone had a home to go to. After a wonderful supper feast, Zayo made sure that there would be no one left behind, then he called an end to the caucus, and requested that they all be back on the three hundred and thirty-third day, which was the day of Tahrmaha's passage.

It took Tahrmaha but one week to prove to Pleeyedraha that not only had she retained all of her knowledge and skills, but that she was remarkably improved; she seemed as if she could handle the finest microsurgery with one eye closed. Her diagnostic skills were vastly improved, and she was much better prepared to take charge of a situation, especially one that required a fast mind.

Pleeyedraha was amazed at Tahrmaha's ability as a healer, because the younger doctor proved to have far superior talent to Ahrtoor, who had been better than Pleeyedraha. Tahrmaha was now so good that she was the final authority on many treatments. Once she took charge of a patient, her mind had already postulated effective treatments, and had selected which one would be the most beneficial. Pleeyedraha was never able to be so

303

selective in her treatments, so nearly everything she did was standardized. Tahrmaha was able to adapt to each different situation and case, and had such an open mind that she saw everything as it was happening. From one look at a pregnant mare, Tahrmaha could tell if the developing foal was healthy or not, and that was even before scanning any part of the mother. She would glance at a sick foal, and knew what was wrong with it and how far developed its immune system was. One glimpse at a new foal, and she knew if it had bonded to its mother. She could also correlate seemingly unrelated aches and pains.

Tahrmaha had mastered all skills, but her forte was holistic alchemy, which even Pleeyedraha had problems with. Tahrmaha was excited, and prepared for her passage.

MASTER HEALER

By the time breakfast came, Tahrmaha was prepared. Her golden hair was immaculately braided with like ribbons, and the rest of her was spotlessly groomed to perfection. She was by far the most beautiful mare alive, which did not faze her at all. Her mind was set on her work, and the fact that she was to be given the black vest.

But there were others who needed to be given their vests before Tahrmaha, five others who had turned thirty-five during the past twenty-one days. "My beloved people," Zayo began when he was on the platform, Awe must take the time to celebrate passages. There shalt be six passages now." Mehlanahr and Corbo held the vests, as Zayo called up five people before Tahrmaha; they had all turned thirty-five before her, within the past twenty-one days. As each one received their vest, they each requested where they would like to fulfill their duties. "Now tis time for Tahrmaha to request her placement, as today is her passage. Tahrmaha, where art thou? Come to my platform for thy recognition."

Tahrmaha gracefully climbed up onto the platform, and knelt ten feet before Zayo, elegantly bowing her head. A great cheer went up from the crowd, as they all admired what she had done to help Zayo, and most of them knew her. When they quieted down, Zayo touched her shoulder, and she stood up, and walked to the center with him. She fought the butterflies in her stomach and said to the crowd, "For my placement, I dearly request of all of you that I be allowed to serve you as the master healer."

305

EQUESTRA

A hush fell over the crowd as Zayo said to them, "A challenge has been made to Pleeyedraha. Pleeyedraha, as ye standing master healer, I requireth thy assistance." Pleeyedraha slowly came up onto the platform and knelt beside Tahrmaha. As Zayo went to touch her shoulder, he saw Tahrmaha look at Pleeyedraha; he heard the young doctor gasp, and saw her start to cry. He suddenly realized Pleeyedraha was dying, but he had to retain control and allow Tahrmaha's challenge to be fulfilled. He touched Pleeyedraha's shoulder and said, "Master healer, Tahrmaha was thy student, and she has challenged thee to take over thy position." Pleeyedraha struggled to stand, so Zayo and Tahrmaha helped her to stand up, then Zayo and Tahrmaha stepped back from her.

Pleeyedraha carried the black vest with green trim she had worn so many years; she wore a green vest with white tassels. "My life has been enriched by having a student such as Tahrmaha has been," she began. "In the course of her studies, when she reached the age when an intern would have progressed into his specialization, she proved to possess mastery of most specializations. She quickly proceeded to master the rest, and then wanted to pursue advanced professional studies. She proved an excellent student at holistic medicine. When the time came for her to try her hand at holistic alchemy, which only a healer can learn and not a doctor, she found her specialty. This took place just before—just before the accident which nearly claimed her life. She was in a coma for a month and a half when Zayo brought her to the cave of the magical mists.

"When she was in the cave, her mental capacity and healing abilities became so far advanced as to make my ability as the master healer seem vastly inferior. Never in my life have I seen a healer who can look at a new foal and know whether or not the foal has bonded to its mother just by looking at it. She can look at a pregnant mare, and know when the parting is within two weeks. She can look at a foal, and know how advanced its immune system is by the overall appearance of its health; these things she does without even a scanner to help her, and she is very accurate. An ailing patient can describe seemingly unrelated symptoms to her, and not only does she know what is wrong, but has chose the best course of action for that particular patient. She has a remarkable photographic memory, and has certainly proven herself to be a superior healer to myself. Because of these and many other things about her remarkable work, it is my honor to say that she is the only citizen worthy enough to be called the Master Healer. Her challenge is with merit, and I accept her superior ability."

Pleeyedraha walked up to Tahrmaha, and slipped the black vest over Tahrmaha's head, while Tahrmaha slipped her arms through the sides.

Tahrmaha hugged Pleeyedraha, and they both had tears in their eyes. "Pleeyedraha," Tahrmaha said, "no matter what, you will always hold a special place in my heart."

"As do you," the elder healer replied. "I would have your passage no other way. You have more than earned your place, and truly deserve all accorded respect. You are now my master, because you possess a far superior talent to mine. It is my duty to acknowledge that; otherwise, I would be treating you disrespectfully." Pleeyedraha turned to walk away, but soon collapsed upon the platform.

Tahrmaha set beside her, and scooped up her upper body so that she could cradle Pleeyedraha's head and shoulders in her arms. "Pleeyedraha, you have fulfilled your duty. I know your soul is satisfied. All of our people are also satisfied."

Pleeyedraha grasped her hand and whispered, "Always, Tahrmaha, remember your duty to our people is more important than anything else."

"I know this." She saw Pleeyedraha fading fast. "Maketh thy claim, and let thy soul embrace the support and love of the emperor. Thy duty here ist finished."

Pleeyedraha smiled, and died.

Once Corbo imploded Pleeyedraha's body, the Caballians finally began to breathe again. What had begun as an ordinary passage ended up as a breathtaking transferal of the vest of the master healer.

In his closing words for the council meeting, Zayo proposed to them that, instead of meeting every two or three days for a passage or a marriage, they meet once a week on ninthday for a weekly council, at which they would celebrate all passages and marriages. It was unanimously accepted by them all, for it would give them extra time to complete the cities, and it was in accordance with Acaballian tradition. Much work had already begun in planning the new cities, but with the enormity of the job ahead of them, they would be working on them for three years. It seemed like such an impossible task, even though everyone followed Zayo's desire to succeed.

Once the council was over, they all set out to begin the enormous job ahead of them.

Like all of the other masters, Tahrmaha set to work on the building of the new cities the day after her passage: this was no longer just to outline plans, but to begin enforcing what structuring needed to be done. A certain number of transports were assigned to each city, so that all of its inhabitants would have ready transportation to councils. Vehicles were also assigned to each city, and would be used until their fuel ran out; they were good for transporting building supplies. With the number of miners and stonecutters available, a number of buildings were begun immediately. Jayexeeyo oversaw the construction of the forgefire hearth within each new forge, so as to ensure that it was safe to use with the fuels that were commonly used by shoemakers. All artisans who did not know anything about stonecutting learned it by working with the stonecutters as they procured the rocks needed to build all buildings.

A number of engineers put together a number of visiphones with what materials they had. These visiphones were first installed in necessary locations, then in random houses. A number of shoemakers and refiners busied themselves with crafting parts for visiphones, transports, and all other machinery. By the end of the year, all major buildings were finished. Then, they began on houses for all. Each of the new cities was given its own personality as the miners and stonecutters saw fit. Vayaar proved to be the most interesting of all: on the island where they were building the city was a tremendous rock formation. The stonecutters procured nearly all of their building materials from there. In the places they took the stone from, level surfaces were left on the rocks. This was in such a place as it was overlooking the sea on a corner of the island, so a number of residents decided to build their houses there. There was one place on the formation which was left open, and that was the uppermost area of all. It was not inaccessible, but because it was the highest elevation on the entire island, none of them felt comfortable with putting themselves on such a pedestal.

Patoron was equally as interesting. Because it was built in the everyellow forest, the city had a much greater number of trees in it than any other city did. There were so many trees that it could be difficult to determine how many buildings were near your house. It had a rather secret feel to it, and you had to know the roads so as to know where you were going. A few houses were built outside of the actual city of Patoron, although they were also called Patoron. They were built on platforms by the swamp, and were inhabited by a number of Acaballian miners who found it an ideal location for them to live.

Rofae was modeled after Wateloqua, because it had the same type of circular roads, although the central building was not a forge, but a bakery which was not only used for baking but for a large spinning center. A number of sentinels set their houses around the outskirts of Rofae. Belura was rather different from all other cities. The highlight of the city was the foremost refinery on all of Equestra, which Hohnoor himself was to head.

Each person was entitled to select where they wanted their house built, how many rooms they needed, the size of the rooms, and how they wanted the house laid out. Because of the enormity of this job, it took them three years to complete all houses, install all visiphones, and ensure that everyone who needed a transport had one.

The new forges were all at least as good as the central forge in Wateloqua, because the stonecutters and Acaballian farriers knew the ancient techniques, which had been long forgotten in Caballia. The Acaballian farriers were all instructed in better methods, and several of them were able to learn some of what they needed to know to treat founder.

Filro, the foremost seaspy stonecutter, easily mastered all principles concerning carpentry, and became Naijoolo's successor as the master artisan. It was no surprise, for Naijoolo had predicted it would be such.

To ensure that Acaballia had successfully made the transition to Caballia, Zayo, Mehlanahr and Corbo spent the last two months of the tenth year of Zayo's rule visiting all seven cities, and viewing all that had been done. Mehlanahr and Corbo had seen a lot of the new cities, but Zayo had not seen as much, so these travels taught the king very much. Mehlanahr and Corbo also learned quite a bit, but in a different manner: Mehlanahr got to meet all of the Acaballian natives, and Corbo got to meet all of the natives of Caballia. Not long after their travels, everyone began to notice the beginnings of a beard on Zayo's chin. He was happier than everyone else was, though he would not admit it. And, he was thrilled that the cities were completed before his passage.

EVOLUTION

The Caballians felt that now that their king had successfully led them through the reunification, they needed to celebrate his passage like no other. And, they all knew in their hearts that he would be married that day. Zayo did not hear anyone say anything about this to him, although he could feel it when people looked at him.

By and far, he was the tallest stallion on all of Equestra: he stood a hand taller at the withers, and six inches taller at head height. He was also as handsome as his father had been: he had rugged muscles, and a face neatly chiseled though ruggedly beautiful. His olive skin managed to reflect a fiery brilliance in the glow of forgefires, and also when Omistu shone on him. His eyes possessed a foreboding mystique when not fired by anger, and his blaze was ruggedly defined upon his forehead. He also had large, sound feet.

He carried himself with such remarkable confidence, and no one dared to cross him and disturb this because they all knew of his temper. His tail stood proud and tall. He had very quick reactions, and his hands were very nimble; he could do anything he set his mind to doing. Now, his mind was set to fulfill his life.

His passage was to take place on the twenty-seventh day of the eleventh year of his rule. He was awake long before first light, and took considerable time bathing, grooming, and braiding his hair with purple ribbons. He carefully manicured his fingernails. On his hooves were new shoes, which he had procured just the day before from Jayexeeyo. He did not don his lavender intern vest which he had used to hold his sabre;

rather, he decided to carry his sabre in his hand, and place it on the platform when he was called up there. He made sure that his crown was perfectly positioned on his head, and proceeded outside.

There was a broken cloud cover but no rain, so it was growing lighter already, although it was not quite time for breakfast. He greeted as many of his people as he possibly could; he knew them all well, and cherished them as only a well-loved king could. He was as confident of them as he was of himself, and felt as if they were all a part of his nuclear family. In this respect, he was very much like his father was. He had earned the undying support of his people by serving their best interests time and again.

He set down among a mixed crowd for breakfast. Once breakfast was over, Merahlaha, Mehlanahr and Corbo took to the platform. Zayo eyed them, thinking to himself, I belong up there instead of them.

Mehlanahr had the speaker system turned on, and then he addressed the crowd. "Good morning," he said, and they all looked at him with extremely bemused expressions. He saw their response and added, "You have all become so accustomed to Zayo's greetings that you do not appreciate a 'good morning' from me, which was satisfactory when Zayo was in the cave!" There were some laughs, and he continued. "Citizens of Equestra, thou art called to ye noble cause today. He will be forced to make public his deepest feelings, which we can do now that he is of age, and no one will be clipped for it. Rather, all of you will attend to Zayo's public exhortation today, to prove that he is indeed worthy of the privileges given to a citizen. And from what I have heard, we will find out if Zayo is ready to claim a mare as his queen." A loud cheer arose from the crowd, and Zayo laughed.

"Our tradition is that we fully test a crown prince on his passage to make sure that he is ready to be crowned when his father dies, and to ensure that his education is complete. However, since Zayo was crowned our king more than ten years ago, this is a bit ridiculous. We need to test him, though, and make sure that he has earned the rewards which have been bestowed upon him for the work he has done, for he will be given the last black vest. To do this, I need the assistance of all other masters." He signaled Merahlaha to leave, and he and Corbo stood there and waited while the other masters climbed up onto the platform—Vehdoor, Hohnoor, Zehnoraha, Tahrmaha, Filro, and Jayexeeyo. Zehnoraha carried in her hands the vest she made which was to be given to Zayo—a black vest with purple trim.

EQUESTRA

Mehlanahr lined them up across the back of the platform, leaving a space for himself between Tahrmaha and Corbo. He walked to the front center of the platform and said, "Zayo, come to the platform." Zayo walked up onto the edge of the platform, and stood there. Mehlanahr walked up to him and said, "You will leave your sabre here, and take your customary place in the center. When you get there, you will kneel facing our people."

Zayo smiled, set his sabre down, and knelt in the center before the crowd, with the masters behind his back. He turned his head back to see what the masters were doing, and Corbo called out, "Fiend! Keep thine eyes upon thy people! Art thou afraid of them?!" His head whirled back aright, knowing that his place was before his people.

Vehdoor then said, "Whom art thou?"

"I am Zayo, the king of the Caballians," he replied.

"By what right are you a king? You do not wear the vest of a citizen."

"By my birthmark."

"I see nothing which makes you special. I will ask you one more time: whom art thou?"

Zayo suddenly realized what Vehdoor was doing. "I am the son of Kayloor and Tarahnaha."

Vehdoor remained very serious. "Kayloor and Tarahnaha, come to the platform."

There was a loud hush among the crowd, and they were all wide-eyed as Tarahnaha climbed up onto the platform alone. In her hands she carried the crown which her husband had worn when he was the reigning king. "Master," she said, but no more.

Vehdoor asked Zayo, "Are you a bastard?"

"No," he replied.

"Where is your father?"

"My father is dead."

"Your father was young. How could he be dead?"

"One citizen murdered my father."

"Where is the person who killed your father?"

"It was my duty to excommunicate his murderer the next day."

"Were you a witness to the crime?"

"No. I possessed the testimony of the master historian, telling me how and when my father was killed, and who killed him."

312

Vehdoor walked over to Tarahnaha and said, "Tarahnaha, you are known to be Kayloor's queen by the ribbons you wear in your hair. Can you testify that Zayo is your son?"

"I was married to Kayloor almost one hundred years ago, according to the jurisdiction of our people, who agreed it was a benevolent marriage for all. My duty as his queen was to consummate his rule. Zayo was born of me one year after Kayloor impregnated me."

"What do you carry in your hand?"

"This is the crown which Kayloor wore while he was alive. If he were alive today, he would be wearing it."

"Our people agreed more than ten years ago to give Zayo his own crown. Cherish that which was Kayloor." Tarahnaha clutched her husband's crown to her chest, as Vehdoor fell back in line with the other masters.

Hohnoor then said to Zayo, "Whom art thou?"

"I am the son of Kayloor and Tarahnaha," he replied.

"How do we know that you are Kayloor's heir?"

"Our people accepted me as such more than ten years ago, when I was crowned."

"What was your first duty as our king?"

"To seek out and arrest the citizen who murdered Father, and to arrest two other citizens who committed treason against him which led to his murder."

"That is only part of your duty. When you give criminals to a guard or sentinel to hold, you must relieve them of said criminals and carry out any and all punishments."

"I did that at a caucus the next morning, before breakfast."

Hohnoor walked up to Tarahnaha and said, "Is your soul satisfied with the actions Kayloor's heir has taken in punishing the criminals who took your husband's life?"

"Kayloor's heir took the only proper course of action befitting a true crown prince," she replied. "I would fear for my own life if I knew that the criminals were still at large, but because our laws specified that they be excommunicated, I no longer live in fear."

"Kayloor's heir has given you peace of mind. Cherish it always." He left Tarahnaha, and fell back in line.

Zehnoraha then said to Zayo, "Whom art thou?"

"I am Kayloor's heir," he replied.

"How can you be heir to a king who has been dead for over ten years?"

"I am part of the consummation of his rule."

"Then you still live in your father's shadow."

"That is not true."

"What did you do with your father's corpse?"

"I could not do anything, because his murderer imploded him while he still lived."

"Is it not barbaric to excommunicate a person?"

"It was barbaric for the criminal to implode a live person; therefore, he did not deserve to live in the emperor's realm."

"So you were unable to signify the end of your father's rule."

"I signified the end of my father's time here by torching a bonfire on his platform, the only accepted tradition of our people."

Zehnoraha walked up to Tarahnaha and said, "Are you satisfied with the importance placed on the bonfire described by your son?"

"Indeed," she replied, "it was proper for a crown prince to do."

"Rest easy. Your husband's reign was properly ended by the bonfire of his platform. Cherish the actions your son took."

Zehnoraha fell back in place, and Tahrmaha said to Zayo, "Whom art thou?"

"I am the son of Tarahnaha," he replied.

"Your mother lives in comfort because of your actions. What about the parents of those who saw to Kayloor's murder, and their widows? How do they feel?"

"It does not matter if their loved one was such a criminal."

"It does matter. Their lives have been dishonored. Can their widows marry again to try and find the proper honor from an honorable husband? Can their parents wish that their sons had never been born? Can you truly feel comfortable with the fact that their lives were irrevocably changed by what actions you say you were required to take?"

"Their lives were not the only ones which were disturbed. All lives of all of our people were drastically altered by the fact that their beloved king was criminally taken away from them."

"If the lives of all were harmed in such a way, how did you go about setting up your own reign as being a departure from what had happened to Kayloor?"

"The harsh memories of Father's murder will always be there, like scars from old wounds and injuries. I set out to create my own rule, to set up my own interaction with our people so as to lessen the harshness of Father's memories. I performed my duty in ensuring that the humans did not also harm us."

"How can you say such a thing? Fagan tried to kill me! He desecrated my life, and left me in a coma!"

"When our doctors could no longer help you, I risked my life and brought you to the cave of the magical mists, as recommended by the master historian."

"What about the psychological injuries of our people?"

"To heal those, I brought more than fifty thousand Caballians here from the cavern under the Unknown Sea, and reunited them with the forty thousand Caballians here."

Tahrmaha walked up to Tarahnaha and said, "Are you satisfied with the actions your son has taken to heal the psychological wounds inflicted by Kayloor's murder?"

"Indeed, my son has acted most nobly."

"Rest thy weary soul. The crown prince has taken proper steps to heal the wounds inflicted ten years ago."

Tahrmaha fell back in line, and Mehlanahr said to Zayo, "Whom art thou?"

"I am the crown prince," he replied.

"The crown prince of what?"

"The crown prince of the Caballians."

"What actions have you taken to reunite all Caballians?"

"In response to a plea made by those living in the cavern, those living here accepted them, and worked with them in building four new cities so that all will have a place to live."

"Why give them a place to live when they could live anywhere?"

"Their lives were endangered where they were living, and they needed a safe place to live. It is my duty to ensure that all of our people can live with the same high quality of life."

"You cannot do this alone."

"No. I must retain the favor of all, and make sure that they are all willing to work with me to fulfill my duty. If they do not understand why and how I do certain things, then I must explain it to them. For just as much as I expect to know of them, they deserve to know of me."

Mehlanahr walked up to Tarahnaha and said, "Are you satisfied with the actions the crown prince is taking to ensure unity among our people?"

"Indeed," she replied, "he always acts in the best interests of all, even if our people seem to disagree with him."

"Cherish the heir to the throne, who has built himself a kingdom." Mehlanahr fell back in line.

Corbo then said, "Whom art thou?"

"I am heir to the throne," Zayo replied.

"Heir for which throne?"

"Heir to the throne built by our people."

"What ist thy duty to thy people?"

"My duty is to prevent the wars from returning."

"What wars dost thou speak of?"

"The wars which will commence if I do not retain unity among all Caballians."

"Why wouldst thy people fight?"

"They are all strong of heart. Every one of them feels as if they belong on a throne or pedestal. This cannot be denied for the nobility and pride they carry in their hearts."

"How wouldst thou protecteth ye pride and prevent yon wars?"

"My duty is to enforce all of our laws, and to ensure that all citizens abide by them. The laws prevent the wars from returning. Pride is preserved by punishing all criminals in a public spectacle."

"Whenst thou art required to clip more than two thousand tails, art thy people correct? Thou art but one."

"When so many people mutiny to have me break one of our laws, I would rather be dead than serve as the instigating factor for breaking our laws which leads to wars. If they wanted their wars, they would have killed me then. But they are people of good conscience, and recognized what they were doing wrong; they submitted themselves for the appropriate punishment."

Corbo walked up to Tarahnaha and said, "Art thou satisfied with how ye heir to the throne has built ye kingdom on good conscience?"

"It is the only way our people can survive," she replied.

"Cherisheth always ye king of good conscience." He fell back in line.

Filro then said to Zayo, "Whom art thou?"

"I am a king of good conscience," he replied.

"What dost thou respect?"

Zayo thought for a moment, and then said, "I respect every single person, for without everyone, we would not have been able to unite our histories into such a magnificent culture. I must work every day of my life to ensure that our lives deserve the blessings of the emperor."

Filro walked up to Tarahnaha and said, "Ye king of good conscience worships all that ye Caballians hold dearest. Art thou satisfied?"

"Indeed," she replied, "a king who can celebrate what is most important to our people is a king to be admired."

"Thou shalt cherisheth ye king of Equestra." He fell back in line.

Jayexeeyo then said to Zayo, "Whom art thou?"

"I am the king of Equestra," he replied.

"How important are shoes?"

"Without shoes my hooves would fall apart, and be prone to many diseases, like founder."

"You are the king of Equestra. Equestra is but a planet. What about the people hereon?"

"In order for me to be able to walk about in freedom, I must ensure that I have decent shoes upon my hooves. In the same way, I cannot walk among our people unless I keep decent shoes on my hooves, for hearken; the Caballians have built me a throne. I cannot allow my shoes to wear down; I cannot restrict my duty to one select group of Caballians, for I serve all. I must change my shoes often, and keep atop of all my sacred duties. It is what ensures that our society thrives, and that the wars do not overtake us."

Jayexeeyo walked up to Tarahnaha and said, "The king of Equestra knows his sacred duty to our people. Cherish always the king of the Caballians." She left the platform. Jayexeeyo fell back in line.

"Stand up," Vehdoor told Zayo; he stood up slowly.

"Stretch your legs," Hohnoor said, and he did so.

Zehnoraha walked up alongside him and placed the black vest over his head as he slipped his arms through the openings. She stepped back, and Tahrmaha stepped forward. Just as Tahrmaha was about to say something to Zayo, she heard a few people summon her from the crowd. The master healer knew right away that it was a medical emergency. She then said to the king, "Forgive me for being abrupt, but I am needed elsewhere." She watched him nod, and suddenly saw a smolder in his eyes; she knew what he was thinking, but she had her duty to tend to, and she ran from the platform.

Zayo watched as Tahrmaha and a number of other doctors whisked a colt by the name of Khahro, who was about fourteen years old, into the palace for emergency treatment. Zayo could feel his heart sinking, but tried to maintain the thought that Tahrmaha would return to him soon. But after about two hours, she was still in the palace. The crowd soon started to clamor for her, because they wanted Zayo and Tahrmaha to be joined as husband and wife. Zayo took leave of them, and ran to the palace. He walked inside his home, and approached the closed door of the den, which he knocked upon. Pakoor opened it from inside the den, and let the king in. Zayo did not enter the den too far, but he said to Tahrmaha, "How is your patient?"

Tahrmaha saw a distant look on the king's face, so she said to Pakoor, "Keep watch over him; I shall be right outside." She led Zayo out of the den, and closed the door behind them.

Zayo looked into her piercing eyes and said, "How sick is Khahro?"

Tahrmaha let out a deep sigh. "He nearly died." She saw how the look in his eyes wanted to hear more, so she continued. "He had a kidney infection, which backed up into sepsis."

"What is sepsis?"

"A fast-moving blood infection that kills within 24 hours if it is not diagnosed. None of the other doctors were able to pick up on it because there has not been a case of sepsis among our people for over a thousand years."

"How soon shall he recover?"

"Perhaps a week, if everything goes well. I must get him to the hospital, and keep him under constant surveillance. His condition is still critical, but he is stabilizing enough for transportation to the hospital."

He thought about her words for a moment, then he said, "Would it be possible to allow Pakoor to watch over him for a short while, and you return with me? The council...our people are expecting you to join me."

Tahrmaha saw the pleading look in his eyes, but she felt committed to her duty and was not ready to relinquish her patient to Pakoor. "Zayo, Khahro is a very sick colt, and his life is dependent upon my attendance and dotage upon him today. No one else is capable of getting him through the next twenty-seven hours." She saw the tears in his eyes. "When I am ready and able to complete the union, I will let you know."

"Impertinent mare," he said softly, but allowing her to see the fire of burning desire melded with anger in his eyes, "it is I who am responsible for claiming you, but you say you will let me know when you are ready and able. You could not entrust your patient to Pakoor for fifteen minutes to come back with me to the demanding council, yet you told me that your patient was stabilizing. Are you the only healer alive who can save a life, or do you trust the talent of Pakoor, who saved your life? And do you want to fulfill the demands of our people, or is your duty more important?"

Tahrmaha could not hold back the tears in her eyes, realizing what she had done to him, and how wrong she was. "Forgive me," she whispered, choking back a sob.

"Have you forgotten how our people were disrespectful to you, but I stood up for your honor and clipped thousands of citizens? Nothing I tell our people, except for your own death, will stop the probability of a war." He turned and left her standing there, neither stopping nor turning to look when her sobs became audible.

Shortly after he walked out, she collected herself. Their people knew what was best, and Tahrmaha knew that she and Zayo could not hide their passion even though it was unspoken. Tahrmaha also knew deep down inside that Khahro would be quite fine with Pakoor, and she needed to hearken to Zayo's bold claim to heal the demanding and proud hearts of their people. Without a moment to lose, she took leave of Pakoor, and headed outside.

As Tahrmaha exited the palace, the bright rays of Omistu caused her to squint. She heard the crowd grumbling at Zayo, who stood on his platform alone; desperately, she took off in a full gallop, which garnered the attention of many people, and the grumbling slowly ceased. As Tahrmaha ran into the crowd to get to the platform, Zayo caught sight of her, but he said nothing. The master healer struggled in making her way through the crowd. A very young foal walked right in her path and she jumped to avoid hurting it; when she fell down, her right hind leg came down and caught the handle of a water pump, snapping her tibia like a twig, the bone breaking into many splinters. She let out an ungodly scream which was heard by just about everyone; several nearby sentinels cleared the area around her, and seven doctors were immediately with her.

Zayo attempted to see what was happening in the crowd where Tahrmaha fell when Corbo ran up to him and said, "Make haste, sire. Time is quick. Attend to Tahrmaha."

Zayo jumped off of the platform, and reached her as fast as he possibly could. When he saw her broken leg bent, deformed, swollen, bleeding, and traumatized, he set down beside her, and scooped up her head and shoulders in his arms. He caressed her face, and saw the look of impending death in her eyes. One of the doctors gave her an injection of an extremely powerful and fast-acting pain killer. Zayo held her to his bosom for about ten minutes before the stress in her body began to subside.

Merahlaha could not see where her brother had gone, so she boldly stepped up onto the center of the platform; Andrux climbed up there with her. No one noticed them standing there as they gazed out to see what was happening without being underfoot. Where they were standing on the platform was directly over where the ancient stone box from Acaballia rested under the platform.

Tahrmaha slowly moved her head, and saw Zayo's face; she could not hold back the tears. "Do not speak," he told her, "but trust your doctors to heal you."

She then whispered to him, "I am dying."

"Do not say such things."

"No one has ever survived…such an injury."

"You are wrong," he replied, choking back a sob.

"No…let go of me before…it is too late…to choose another."

"I cannot do that, and I will never leave you. Remember how much we did together!" His sobs could soon be heard by many around them, and everyone soon hung their heads in mourning.

All of the other doctors with them closely discussed her injury, and they knew it was grave. None of them knew what to do until Behntahro, a seaspy stallion who was the best doctor among those from Acaballia, came up with a long shot plan that would give her a slight chance. Four of the doctors ran off to get supplies from their transports and vehicles. When they returned with more doctors and their supplies a short while later, Zayo could not help but notice. Behntahro walked up to Zayo, and when he saw the looks on the faces of Zayo and Tahrmaha, he knew that somehow his plan must be successful. "Thy majesty," he said to Zayo, "thou must be of good courage and bold love." He looked at Tahrmaha and told her, "Most distinctive doctor, alloweth thy staff to dote upon thee and tend to thy injury."

Tahrmaha drifted her eyes in his direction, and was somehow able to summon up the strength to weakly speak to him. "Thou knoweth thy fables…my leg is broken."

Behntahro allowed Tahrmaha to see an insulted look upon his face, yet he knew that the shock of the injury was advancing, and she needed to be treated soon. Zayo then said to her, "Tahrmaha, if Jayexeeyo can treat founder, then these doctors can help you."

She looked into Zayo's eyes, and she sobbed in agreement. She knew that if she had listened to him immediately earlier in the palace instead of trying to come up with an excuse to avoid him, and had rejoined the council with him, then she would not have been injured. Zayo had asked her to allow Pakoor to tend to Khahro, because he was a capable doctor. And now, Behntahro was pleading with her for her to allow her staff the chance to show her just how capable they were. Zayo saw the content submission settle in her eyes, and felt her relax in his arms.

Tahrmaha looked back at Behntahro and softly said to him, "Tell us…what thou hast planned."

Behntahro looked at all of the other doctors with him, and then he returned to Zayo and Tahrmaha. "I am neither ye king nor ye adjutant, but thy hearts must leadeth the healing of thy leg. Thou art strong together when thy hearts are charged. Continue to show thy hearts to thy people, and do not allow ye shock and stress to overtake thee." Zayo and Tahrmaha looked at each other, a bit shocked to say the least. But before either one of them could say anything, Behntahro continued. "Tahrmaha, thou knowest that tis ye shock, stress, and long surgical sleep art what shalt kill thee. Thou canst useth thy charge to stave off ye shock and stress. Ye long surgical sleep shalt be avoided by effecting local numbness and removal of pain."

Zayo saw the entranced look on Tahrmaha's face as she thought about their plan. She then whispered to Behntahro, "The required dosage…of the painkillers…may be what will kill me."

As the other doctors began to work on her unnoticed, Behntahro shook his head at her. "I must be conservative, and useth ye medicine in extreme moderation. Thou mayest feeleth some discomfort, but thou must remember that thy love is greater than any discomfort thou shalt feeleth in thy leg."

Tahrmaha managed a slight smile and whispered, "Thy plan has merit."

Behntahro returned her smile, and immediately set to working with the other doctors.

Three long tedious hours later, the doctors were still working on Tahrmaha's injured leg. Merahlaha and Andrux were still watching from the platform. Tahrmaha was bravely but barely clinging onto life; the duration of the surgical repair was beginning to take its toll on her. Zayo kept talking to her, and noticed that her eyes were starting to drift more. She was beginning to tense up ever moreso in his arms; Zayo knew she was at her limits. Behntahro and the other doctors continued to work.

It finally got to the point where Tahrmaha closed her eyes in her exhaustion, and would not reopen them. Zayo felt her breathing become much shallower, and watched as her body lost more tone and lay flatter on the ground. He looked at Behntahro and said, "She cannot handle any more;" he saw that they were using a heptalaser on her leg to close the wound. Her leg no longer appeared broken, but looked straight and in a normal position.

Behntahro then gave Tahrmaha an injection of a stimulant which usually helped patients to wake up from surgery. The other doctors finished and stepped back from her. When Tahrmaha did not wake up right away, Behntahro allowed Zayo to see the frustration in his eyes. He scanned his patient, and shook his head. Shortly thereafter, Tahrmaha's breathing stopped.

Zayo hugged her to his chest and yelled, "Do not leave me like Father did! I need you!" Zayo was suddenly knocked over from where he was setting when the ground shook, causing him to let go of her. The sound of thunder filled their ears, and an extremely bright light that seemed to emanate from the platform temporarily blinded everyone.

As Zayo struggled with his returning vision about ten minutes later, he felt tremendous discomfort in his lower back, and started to think that his back had broken when he had fallen back. As his eyes became a bit less cloudy, his back no longer felt broken, but it felt as if it were on fire along either side of his lower spine. After what seemed like a long time, the hot sensation left, but the muscles in his back felt as if they were in knots. The knots disappeared after a few minutes, and his back felt free and loose, although in a rather strange way. His eyes then quickly cleared up, and he was able to see again.

He looked at Tahrmaha as she lay before him, and was shocked beyond belief as he saw that she now had the wings of a pegasus on her back just like Andrux did, although her wings were purple. She still did not seem to be breathing. As Zayo observed her, she suddenly took in a deep breath, and began to breathe in a rhythmic manner. He reached out to touch her when she suddenly started to set up with her back towards him. Zayo stood up and walked around her. He reached his hands out to her, and helped her to stand up; a loud cheer erupted from the crowd as they saw her alive. Tahrmaha noticed that Zayo also had the purple wings of a pegasus on his back. She stepped close to him and laid her head upon his chest, and the crowd cheered even louder. Zayo caressed her cheek, and kissed her to symbolize the completion of their union. Zayo took a peek at the crowd, and noticed that everyone began to kneel before them in acceptance of their union.

As Zayo proceeded to lead Tahrmaha through the crowd, they saw that everyone else had also been changed. Mehlanahr now had a golden horn shooting out of the front of his mane up and away from his face; it was about ten inches long, and seemed to have strange runes carved in it. Corbo was still a seaspy, but the gills on his neck were enhanced, and he now had fringes of webbing on his forearms and lower legs. The only other pegasus they saw who had purple wings was Tarahnaha.

Immediately after catching a glimpse of his mother, Zayo was aghast to find that his platform was no longer there, and that the ancient stone box stood by itself. He looked back at his mother, and realized that his sister was not with her as she usually was. Zayo walked up to his mother, and was shocked beyond words when he saw the rapt expression on her face. "Mother," he said softly to her, "what happened?"

She hugged him with tears in her eyes. "They were on the platform," she replied.

"Who? Merahlaha and Andrux?"

"Yes. They were watching you and Tahrmaha. But they were standing right over the box when the ground shook and the thunder came."

"The ground shook right after...right after I thought Tahrmaha had died in my arms. Do you know what caused the thunder?"

She became a bit serious with him. "That was when the box opened, and the light of the ancient magic was unleashed."

He was shocked. "They were swallowed up by the ancient magic of the emperor?"

"Not swallowed up. Before I went blind, I felt the light coming, and was touched by the most incredible love. Just before I was blinded by the light, I saw Merahlaha grab the hand of her father. She has found what she has been searching for her entire life."

Overall approximately ten thousand Caballians had evolved into pegasi, and approximately thirty thousand Caballians had evolved into unicorns; all of the seaspies were still seaspies.

THE END

www.ingramcontent.com/pod-product-compliance
Lightning Source LLC
Chambersburg PA
CBHW060423030726
47495CB00003B/709